DOCTOR WHO

THE YEAR OF INTELLIGENT TIGERS

KATE ORMAN

FROM A STORY BY JONATHAN BLUM AND KATE ORMAN

BBC

Published by BBC Worldwide Ltd,
Woodlands, 80 Wood Lane
London W12 0TT

First published 2001
Copyright © Kate Orman 2001
The moral right of the author has been asserted

Original series broadcast on the BBC

ISBN 0 563 53831 7
Imaging by Black Sheep, copyright © BBC 2001

Illustration by Carolyn Edwards
sadianna_uk@yahoo.co.uk

Printed and bound in Great Britain by Mackays of Chatham
Cover printed by Belmont Press Ltd, Northampton

The tygers of wrath are wiser than the horses of instruction.
– William Blake, *The Marriage of Heaven and Hell*

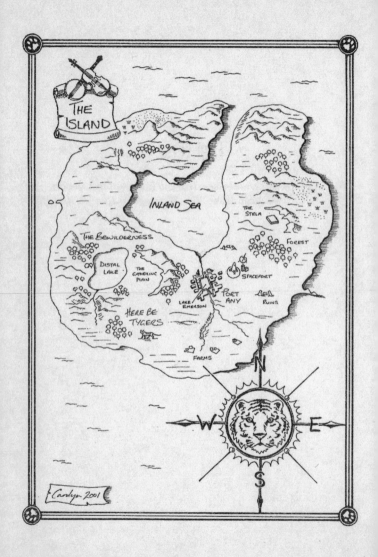

First Verse

Chapter One

Anji walked alone through the city of tigers. It was a fast walk, a bad walk, shouldering and dodging crowd. Sunlight splashing off concrete and glass, bright faces and clothes.

And on every corner, from every doorway, in every window, the music. Coming down from bedrooms, spilling out of cars and cafés, thumping and shrilling, twinkling and twanging. Opera and bossa nova, zydeco and disco, one tune crashing into another as Anji pushed and pulled her way down the street.

She panted in an alleyway for thirty seconds, seeking refuge from songs and symphonies. But shadows pursued her out of the corner of her eye, thrusting her back into the lunchtime crowd.

She had lost her sunglasses somewhere along the way, and the hot noon sky made her squint. The buildings of Port Any were scattered low and thin between avenues and malls planted with brilliant native trees, flaming reds and oranges. Anji's boots crushed fallen leaves as she let the crowd carry her along, sending up a smell of springtime and spice.

A tiger lay across the pavement, its lanky body stretched out in the sunlight.

Anji tried to stop, but the crowd jostled and bumped her, forcing her forward in tiny increments. The tiger's heavy body was an orange-gold mound, shining in the sunlight. Lying down, it was as tall as a young child. It panted in the warmth, yellow eyes watching the humans as they stepped awkwardly around it, trying not to tread on its restless tail.

The tiger eyed Anji as she stumbled past it. She caught the edge of its yellow gaze, and turned her head away as though that meant it couldn't see her any more.

When she was past, and safe, Anji looked back. A little girl was crouching down to scratch the tiger between its ears.

There was a merry-go-round in the plaza ahead. Nearby was a busker with a mandolin, face hidden by one of the wide-brimmed hats everyone seemed to wear; a woman selling chestnuts, shrilling a tune in a language Anji didn't recognise; a weary organ grinder with a dancing knee-high amoeba. The calliope at the carousel's heart overwhelmed them all with its jingling and piping.

She spotted one of the Waytes' red and gold uniforms, but was too embarrassed to approach the policewoman. A young man in an embroidered scarlet waistcoat and lime-coloured shoes was selling tickets for the carousel. She stepped up to him. 'Are you all right?' he said at once. 'You look like you've had a shock.'

There was no point in telling him. She'd told four people, and none of them had believed her. 'I need the Doctor,' said Anji.

'I'll call a medic for you.' The young man reached for the computer woven into his shirtsleeve.

'No,' said Anji. She knew what he was seeing: a lone lost tourist, unsettled and confused, trying to blend in by wearing local clothes: the loose hemp shirt and trousers, the sandals, a red and gold comb in her shoulder-length black hair. 'No, no. I mean I need to find the rehearsal hall. That's where the Doctor will be.'

'Which rehearsal hall? The Jerry Lynn Williams, the Albinoni, the Keiko Abe, or the Vermilion Rooms?'

'Albinoni. I think that's the one.' Anji massaged her left temple with a knuckle. The blasting of the calliope made it hard to think. The organ flashed inside the whirling animal circle, a mass of steaming pipes half hidden by mirrors and coloured glass.

'You're nearly there, then,' said the youth. 'Go back the way you came, then turn left down Akunastrasse. Look out for the statue of the angel.'

The swans and tigers on the merry-go-round had what looked like real feathers and fur. They chased one another, ridden by shrieking kids, glassy yellow eyes staring out.

'Are you sure you don't want to me to call a medic?' said the ticket collector. 'It's no trouble.'

'I can deal with it,' said Anji.

'Well, hey, enjoy your visit.'

She tried and failed to summon a smile of thanks. As she pushed her way through the crowd, the young man started singing along with 'The Merry-go-round Broke Down'. Across the plaza, the amoeba went wild.

The temperature plunged as she stepped into the gloom of the rehearsal hall. Spotlights were moving over the seated crowd and their instruments, switching on and off experimentally. It was as though the musicians were the audience, chatting and rustling, looking out at the empty amphitheatre. Waiting for her to perform.

She stumbled down the aisle, holding on to the backs of the chairs. Her legs started to tremble, as though they were made of some squishy substance, too soft to hold her up.

The conductor appeared from the side of the stage and went to the podium. She aimed for him, the one figure who wasn't facing her, the one familiar figure. He stood in a pool of pale light, examining the score. The instruments were tuning up, or playing chaotic phrases.

Sharply, the conductor raised his arms over his head.

Instantly, the orchestra snapped to attention, the muddle of sounds clattering to silence. The lights stopped their chasing game, changing into a soft illumination of the players, with a tight spot on the conductor. As he brought his arms down in a fierce gesture, the hall filled with a roaring buzz. Anji knew it was music, but she couldn't untangle the flooding jumble of sounds. Her brain had gone deaf. She couldn't hear a thing.

It. Was. Getting. *Louder*.

And suddenly it cut out. The hall was full of head-ringing echoes. A single, slender figure was standing, violin at the ready.

The Doctor's golden-brown hair shone in the theatre lighting, curling to his shoulders. He wore a loose white shirt over hemp trousers and a black waistcoat embroidered with brilliant orange designs.

His bow sawed sharply up and down in a complex arpeggio. The instrument's soprano voice curved and soared. The sound made Anji dizzy, breathless.

He seemed to see her, suddenly, his eyes locking on hers in the dark. He didn't stop playing, his surgical fingers flashing over the fingerboard, faster and faster beneath his teasing grin. The back of Anji's head was pounding. She closed her eyes tightly, but still he wouldn't stop.

Now the orchestra was joining in again, following the Doctor's frantic music, but the conductor was twisting in his pool of light to frown at her, and the sound of the violin was twisting as well, curling around and around the hall, and she couldn't follow it, her head turning and turning to try to catch the sound, her hands flying away from the seatback that was holding her up.

She was on the sloping carpet when the sound cut out.

Anji woke with her hands folded on her stomach. There were three people standing around the bed, three faces watching her, like mourners. She drew a violent breath and half sat up from the pillows.

The Doctor crouched down beside the bed. 'Are you feeling better?' he said softly.

Anji closed her eyes for a moment. He was a fake. He looked and sounded like a man, a human male with white skin, a long, strong-jawed face and large, pale eyes. But if you touched his skin, if you held his wrist, he was the wrong temperature, he had the wrong pulse. He didn't even have a name. She called the alien 'Doctor' because she didn't know what else to call it.

Anji opened her eyes again. It was her friend the Doctor, smiling at her, gently.

'I'll be all right,' she said. Her voice sounded cracked. He put a glass of water into her hands.

The others stood at the foot of the bed. They were the genuine article, two ordinary men: Fitz Kreiner, unshaven and scraggle-haired, fiddling with a cigarette, looking as always like someone you wouldn't want to share a taxi with; and Karl Sadeghi, composer and conductor, peering at her through his glasses.

'You're in one of the dressing rooms,' explained Karl, in his soft, hesitant voice. He had full lips and friendly grey eyes marked with

4

the beginnings of crow's feet. He spoke with the Port Any accent, a lilting melange of German and Middle Eastern sounds. 'We thought it best to, to pause the rehearsal until we were sure you were all right.'

'Heck of a symphony you've got there, Karl,' drawled Fitz.

'It wasn't that.' Anji sat up. 'It was the tiger in the library. Stop that!' Karl wiped the smile from his face.

The Doctor was still crouched by the bed. 'Tell us about the tiger,' he said.

That morning, Anji had dropped in to the Central Library. She'd been reading the papers each day, trying to get a feel for the Hitchemus economy. The colony didn't rely on tourism, despite the ebb and flow of spacecraft that used the gas giant next door as a refuelling point. It had been designed from the beginning to be small and self-sustaining, a single town in the middle of an island on a world that was seven-eighths ocean. Remarkably, if there was poverty here, she hadn't seen it.

The Doctor and Fitz had taken to Hitchemus like a couple of fish to water. Anji had bumped into Fitz and his guitar all over the city, busking on corners or performing in coffee houses with his impromptu band. The Doctor turned out to be able to play the violin, harpsichord, flute, transverse cello, harp, banjo, theremin and wobbleboard.

They had been here for more than a month. It was a long visit; the Doctor rarely had enough patience to stay put on one world, in one time. But all three of them badly needed a break, even him, and Hitchemus was spot on. No power-mad triplets, no killer wasps. The Doctor had rented a flat for each of them in the centre of Port Any, stocking his with recordings and instruments. He had tried to teach her the recorder, but Anji patiently explained that she preferred the swimming pool on the top floor of the building. She had spent some time looking for a beach before she realised that the Port was the spaceport, and they were miles from the coast.

Anji was from –

– did it make sense to say you were *from* the year 2001, as though it were a place? Wasn't she really from 1973, the year of her birth? Or from 'the twenty-first century' or something?

If anyone asked, Anji just said she was from Earth.

In the first week, she had gone on horseback tours of the ruins that dotted the countryside, taking binoculars and a sketch pad. The guides said almost nothing was known of the vanished people who had built them. There were even ruins in the centre of the city, barricaded off. Port Any had been built right over the site of an ancient town.

In the second week, she had joined groups hiking through the hills to the east. Many of the faces were familiar; she didn't think there were more than fifty visitors on the whole planet. It was just too far away from anywhere else, right on the edge of explored space.

The Doctor had a spare hour to come sailing on the artificial lake, past the hydroelectric plant that supplied the Port with its power. Anji didn't think that was too futuristic, launching the Doctor into a lecture on voluntary low-tech simplicity. Given the colony's limited resources, she wasn't sure how voluntary their simplicity happened to be. From the boat they watched flocks of flightless birds bending stiff-legged to drink from the water's edge.

The tourist guides all praised Hitchemus for its good weather, but her expeditions were constantly disrupted by squalls and gales. She'd spent the third week shopping and going to lectures. Port Any's buildings were long, low curves of concrete and glass, but inside you would find wooden furniture, pottery, tapestries. And music, always music, almost always played live.

She spent one of the short nights at an observatory. The neighbouring gas giant was a brilliant star that became a brightly coloured ball through the telescope. She watched the pale ring around the moon, and waited for Earth's sun to rise: just another dim star in the east.

Now she was running out of tourist attractions, and the constant round of concerts and recitals and talent quests was wearing a bit thin. The restaurants mostly served the same vaguely Middle Eastern cuisine. And, while the Doctor and Fitz practised their skills, hers were getting rusty. So it was time for a trip to the economics section of the Central Library.

But there was a tiger in the economics section of the Central Library.

The library was small and pleasant, lit by sunshine and smelling of carpet and wood. Pits in the floor were filled with people relaxing on cushions. Schoolchildren sat at desks, scribbling on computer slates or whispering to each other.

It must be the only silent place on the planet, thought Anji. Not one note of music.

The teenage boy at the information desk explained that Anji could take a book reader, a sort of hand-held screen, and load any title she wanted; or she could browse the library's modest collection of local works, shelved individually in electronic-book format.

Anji followed the call numbers along the shelves, running a finger along plastic spines, until she came to the aisle she wanted.

She started when she saw the tiger. It was lolling in the aisle, its oblong body filling up the narrow space. Most of them lived far away in a tangle of wilds the locals called the Bewilderness, but there were always plenty of them hanging around the city. She was used to seeing them on the streets, sometimes in the coffee shops, even in people's houses. But what was a tiger doing in the library?

The call numbers Anji wanted were somewhere behind it. She walked down the next aisle, turning back into the economics shelves. The tiger was sitting with its back to her, its short tail curled against its side. It glanced round at her, yawning pinkly. Its sleek fur shone.

Anji edged up to the shelf she wanted and slid a book out. It was a slender, light rectangle, opening out to two printed pages. The book worked the same way as the newspapers: text and graphs appeared and disappeared, softly, at a touch. It wasn't much different from hypertext, she thought – like the printed book, a basic technology that would last for hundreds of years without much real change.

When she looked up, the tiger was watching her.

It had slid closer without her even realising. She took an involuntary step backwards. The tiger didn't blink; a membrane swept across both eyeballs, like windscreen wipers, without breaking its yellow stare.

Anji frowned at the animal. What was she supposed to do? Talk to it sharply, as if it were a naughty puppy? Swat its nose with her plastic book? Or did it just want its ears scratched?

The tiger reached out and casually hooked a claw through the cloth of her trouser leg.

She pulled away hard, and the cloth tore. She almost overbalanced, dropping her book and grabbing for the shelf.

The tiger grinned at her as she backed out of the aisle.

A couple of students looked up from their desks as she bumped into a window. She opened her mouth to tell them: I think this tiger is following me. But she could feel the blush rising up her neck and into her ears. It sounded so stupid.

Maybe it was stupid. It hadn't tried to bite her or scratch her, had it? It was just being playful. She had seen the Doctor tickle one under the chin, absently, as though it were an oversized pussycat.

How could she know? How can you tell what a tiger is thinking?

Before it could catch her up, she chose an aisle at random and walked down it, fast, watching through the books for a flash of black and orange. She turned at random, turned again, finding herself in the children's fiction: brightly coloured spines under a hot square of skylight. There were human beings nearby, someone coughing, a couple of schoolgirls giggling, out of reach behind the shelves. Where was it?

She almost tripped over the tiger as she emerged into the central area. Anji back-pedalled as the animal stretched out a lazy paw towards her. She slipped past and walked, fast, to the information desk.

The teenager looked up from the desk, where he was drumming his fingers. 'There's a tiger in here,' whispered Anji.

'Oh, yeah,' said the boy. 'They come in sometimes. Curious, I guess.'

'It's following me,' she said. 'I think.'

'I'm sure it's just trying to be friendly.'

'I don't think so. It clawed my leg. I mean, it clawed my trouser leg.'

The boy sat up, trying to see the damage. Anji followed his gaze. The tear was barely visible.

'Well, look,' he said. 'If you just ignore it, I'm sure it'll take the hint and leave you alone.'

Anji's mouth pulled up at the corner in irritation. She looked around. There was no sign of the tiger.

She went back to the economics aisle. Her book was lying where she'd dropped it. She took it to one of the partitioned study desks under the window – lots of other people around.

She settled into the privacy of the partitioned desk. The window must have been soundproofed: in the plaza below, it looked as though war had broken out. She counted at least four buskers, all playing full tilt, each trying to monopolise the morning crowd's attention.

There was a flash of yellow in the glass. Anji turned. She was alone.

No. She wasn't imagining it. She could see those yellow eyes watching her from behind a row of dark-spined books.

Anji stood up sharply, knocking her chair over. Behind her, a voice said, 'Are you OK?'

A greying woman was looking over the top of the wooden partition. 'There's a tiger. It keeps following me,' whispered Anji, fumbling with the chair. 'They don't normally do that, do they?'

'Oh, don't be frightened! They're harmless.'

'I'm not a tourist,' whispered Anji fiercely. 'I've been here for weeks.'

The tiger slouched up to the desk. It sat down next to the greying woman. 'Here it is. Look at you.' The woman rubbed the tiger's head. 'Cheeky thing.'

The tiger gave Anji a sarcastic look, rolling its head under the woman's hands.

The blush was back, reddening Anji's earlobes. 'Sorry if I disturbed you.'

'Don't worry about it,' said the woman.'Cheeky cheeky cheeks,' she told the tiger.

Anji found somewhere else to sit and read. She was finding it hard to focus, constantly stopping to glance around. But the friendly tiger had apparently decided to pester someone else.

What should she have done? Shouted at it to piss off? It might have worked on a man, but how would a tiger react? What if everyone told her to shut up, they were trying to read, it didn't mean any harm for God's sake, why was she overreacting?

She replaced her economics text, chose another. Her notebook was already half full of jottings, including several intriguing citations. By now she was convinced that Hitchemus's odd economy could work, but she was sceptical of its long-term prospects. She'd done some general reading on the screen back at the apartment, but the local publications took a while to make it into libraryspace; sometimes they never made it, and you had to use these individual books. The surface of the desk contained a catalogue. She spent a few minutes hunting down call numbers.

Anji got up, stretched, looked around. She'd browse through a few more local texts, then break for lunch. She slipped into an aisle of shelves, consulting her notes.

She didn't realise she was in a dead-end until it was too late.

The tiger's body filled the aisle. It walked like a monkey on a tightrope, all limber grace, the balancing tail sticking out behind it like an extra leg.

It stalked towards her, grinning. She had no idea what to do. She had no idea how to make it stop. She had no idea how to make it go away.

The tiger darted forward, silently, and knocked her to the floor with a pat of its paw.

Anji fell backwards, banging her head against the wall. She was sitting in the aisle, trapped between the shelves. The tiger loomed over her. Its damp breath rolled over her face.

It reached out with a long arm and, casually, it hooked one of the books from the shelf.

Anji stared. The tiger examined the book for a moment, its head low to the ground. Then it picked it up in its mouth, turned in a lithe, narrow movement, and was gone.

Anji stared after it. Her stomach was churning. She leaned hard against the brick wall.

When she plucked up enough courage to walk out of the aisle on shaking legs, the tiger was gone.

Chapter Two

That afternoon, the Doctor announced they were going on a picnic, so Karl rented one of the electric cars and drove them into the countryside, flying part of the way over a terrain of bumpy hills. The Doctor sat in the front, fiddling with the map in the dashboard, while Anji and Fitz crammed into the back with the picnic baskets.

It was one of those increasingly rare days when the weather behaved itself. The days were stretching out to twenty-two long, hot hours, with barely six hours of darkness in between. The Doctor and Fitz sang loudly that they were all going on a summer holiday, in an erratic two-part harmony. In the back, a still agitated Anji looked very much not amused.

They landed in a bald patch of ground a mile from the creek. Karl put on his wide-brimmed hat. The Doctor was already striding off across the field, picnic basket cradled in his arms, while Fitz followed with basket number two.

Anji was looking around nervously through her new sunglasses. 'Don't worry,' said Karl. 'We might see a tiger or two, but they give people a, a wide berth.' She gave him a difficult smile, and let him lead her across the grass towards the sound of water.

There had once been a small dam across the creek here. All that was left of it were two grassy banks on either side. A pile of stony rubble between them formed a rough bridge over the water. There were a handful of families already spread out on the grass. Children were giggling, trying to ford the creek on the submerged stones, losing their footing and splashing into the water.

There were similar ruins all over the landscape. The fallen bridge, the Stela, the artificial lake in the centre of Port Any. Whoever had once lived on Hitchemus, they had left little behind but these piles of stone.

The foursome spread their blankets and cushions in the wide shade of a bowl tree. The grass was covered in fallen orange petals. The Doctor had been busy in his kitchen: once they had unpacked, a whole blanket was covered by cheese, crackers, dips, home-made bread, cold pasta salads and bottles of wine. After the long walk, they were ravenous.

The Doctor always seemed to be trying to feed his friends, thought Karl. He'd held a dozen dinner parties since his arrival, and there always seemed to be something edible in his pockets, a toffee or an apple or a grape-flavoured lollipop. It was like an impulse he didn't know what to do with, on a world of peace and plenty – a need to be kind, to take care of people. Almost a maternal impulse.

Afterwards, they lay around on the grass, watching tiny creatures meandering between the individual flat leaves. 'Ants,' said Fitz.

'Space ants,' said Anji drowsily, lying half on and half off the blanket. 'From outer space.'

'Them,' said Fitz.

'Don't let them eat the cheese,' murmured the Doctor. 'They may not be able to metabolise it properly.'

Karl watched the Doctor doze. He had flopped back on to the soft grass, his golden-brown hair spreading around his face. The bright sunshine highlighted the exotic whiteness of his skin. His arms were spread out, fingers entwined with the green strands. He seemed to have only two speeds, thought Karl – *presto* and stop.

He had been worried that the Doctor's friends might resent him a little. They had been travelling together for a long time; it must seem strange that the Doctor was suddenly so centred on Karl and his concerto. But they seemed able – if sometimes not exactly willing – to accept almost anything, as though travel had broadened their minds to an extraordinary width.

Fitz was sitting cross-legged, tuning his guitar. After a few minutes of twanging, he began to strum. In a rough-edged voice, he sang:

> *Now in this age of quiet desperation*
> *Where thoughtful men are often moved to tears*

13

> *I raise a glass to wanton dissipation*
> *And all the grief it's spared me through the years*
> *'Cause I'd rather by far*
> *Be left standing at the bar*
> *Than at the altar…*

When he had finished, Anji clapped her hands and laughed. 'Who did that?'

'I did,' said Fitz, grinning modestly. 'A Kreiner original.'

He played a few more tunes, then lay back on the grass, using the guitar as a pillow. Clouds sailed lazy and low, striping the landscape. The trees filled the air with a soft, planty scent, a cross between citrus and nutmeg. A harmless creature a little like a wading bird stalked between the picnickers, with a cheeky eye out for scraps.

'Look,' said Fitz. A tiger had meandered out of the long grass. Anji was frowning at it, but she still seemed relaxed. The tiger sat up, in that perfect bottle shape that cats assumed, watching the swimming children.

Karl missed cats. And dogs, and bees, and songbirds. Only a handful of Earthly animals were allowed on Hitchemus, mostly left over from settlement, like the horses.

The Doctor opened an eye. 'That tiger wants a drink,' he said.

'It probably wants a swim,' said Karl. A moment later, the animal slid into the creek, stretching its sleek body.

Someone shouted, 'There's a tiger in the water! Get out, get out!'

A couple were running to the creek, grabbing their children out of the water. No one else moved, watching the panic with amusement.

'Tourists,' said someone, prompting scattered laughter.

The tiger swam down the river to a pile of rocks and pulled itself up on to them, blinking sleepily at the frightened family. A tall woman was taking photos of it, balanced precariously on a rock at the river's edge. 'There's one tourist who doesn't seem to be particularly worried,' said Fitz.

'That's Besma Grieve,' said Anji, propping herself up on an

elbow. 'I met her once. She's here studying the tigers. Maybe I should talk to her about the library.'

'I'm sure I have her business card somewhere,' said Karl.

'Tomorrow,' said Anji, sleepily.

'Argh!' said Fitz. 'What's this?' He plucked a tiny glittering object from his hair.

'That's a hailstone,' said Anji, as two more of them landed in her drink. A moment later, the tiny rocks were showering down all over them. The Doctor and Karl unfolded an enormous umbrella from one of the baskets and erected it over their spot while Fitz and Anji plucked bits of ice from the blanket.

They sat there looking at one another while the hail drummed on the umbrella. 'Couldn't anything on this planet be consistent for five minutes?' quavered Anji.

'There's pumpkin pie, if anyone has room,' said the Doctor.

Fitz Kreiner slouched down Ruddstrasse, guitar strapped to his back. He whistled as he walked, hands shoved into the pockets of his new hemp jeans. Last night's snow was rapidly melting to nothing in the morning's heatwave. A hot breeze ruffled his squiggly hair.

He loved this planet. Grokked it. Dug it to the tips of his toes. Jam Tomorrow were getting quite a few gigs, and, in between, he got to play every kind of thing. One night he'd sit in with the snake-hipped rhythm section in a tango bar, mainly as an excuse to wear leather trousers; another he'd try his hand at playing third shimba in the zockestra in a Daheelian restaurant, producing whining chordal wails which sounded like an Arabian Jimi Hendrix; another he'd borrow a star-shaped bass and spout gibberish about Sir Nose D'voidoffunk in a pickup street jam.

There weren't many places where you got respect just for being able to carry a tune. Not just respect. The Doctor was paying their living expenses, as usual, but Fitz could have lived comfortably on the musician's dole. Anyone who could play or sing was paid a basic stipend to live on while they pursued their art. And so everyone played, or sang, or both. If you wanted more than that –

and most people did – you worked for the city council or for another citizen.

The Doctor said the colony was designed for self-sufficiency and a guaranteed minimum standard of living. Fitz liked their idea of a minimum – nobody starving, nobody freezing. That was one reason there was just one small town, so they didn't overstretch their resources. Of course, most of the planet was covered in water, so they had only one temperate continent to choose from, not much more than a large island. And a lot of that continent was off limits because of the ruins and stuff.

Anji said the colony was designed to let kids sit in their bedrooms playing the guitar badly. But Anji also reckoned a tiger had chased her around the library.

The tigers were harmless, anyone could see that. The colonists let them wander wherever they wanted, like sacred cows. On the other hand, Anji was a pretty level-headed bird. She wouldn't imagine something like that. Would she?

He was going to meet up with her for lunch, and then they were off to see the tigerologist. It was funny the Doctor hadn't come along with them – usually he'd jump at the chance of talking up a tornado with a fellow boffin. But he never missed a rehearsal. He and Karl Sadeghi were like old friends, after just a few weeks working together on Karl's big symphony. Well, that suited Fitz just fine: while the Doctor was fiddling around, he wasn't looking for monsters to fight.

It was a hell of a life they lived. You didn't really have time to think about it when you were running around trying not to get shot or turned into slime. It was only now, when you hadn't been hungry or filthy or scared for a couple of months, that you looked back and marvelled at how brave you were. Or how stupid. But the Doctor just couldn't help himself. Wherever people were in trouble, he just had to stick his oar in.

A fat raindrop landed right on his nose. Fitz struggled with his flimsy umbrella as he crossed the street.

Anji had first met Besma Grieve at the same party where Karl met the Doctor, a few days after they had arrived on the planet. Both women had been hovering around the buffet, holding drinks or bits of cheese while watching the proceedings with the same polite, puzzled smile. Grieve was a Black woman in her early forties, with the wiry figure of someone who spends a lot of time outdoors. She wore a flowing embroidered robe. Anji thought she looked like a model.

They both reached for the kebabs at the same moment, making eye contact. 'Feeling a little left out?' Grieve had murmured.

'It's not really my cup of tea,' Anji said. 'Most of the discussions are going right over my head. Everyone's so enthusiastic…'

'I think I was only invited out of politeness,' said Grieve. She had a warm, rich voice full of humour. 'They *love* to get the foreigners along. Although I *must* be a bit stale after two years here.'

They wandered towards a flock of empty deckchairs in a corner of the gardens. 'My friends are having a marvellous time. This is no place to be if you're not a music lover,' Anji sighed.

'I *like* music,' said Grieve. She nibbled on the cold kebab. 'But I don't think music is as important as other art forms. It can only convey *emotions*, you know? Never thoughts. I'm not here for the music – I'm here for the wildlife.'

The whirl of discussion went on around them while they chatted. Besma was originally from Gidi – Beta Coma Berenices – and she had spent years observing life forms on three different planets. 'It's about time the university handed me a cushy job,' she said. 'I've been up to my navel in more kinds of alien *mud* than I care to remember. Here I've got a house, with all the facilities I need. Better still, the wildlife here will come to you, instead of the other way around.'

'Oh, the tigers?' said Anji. 'You study them?'

'I live with a few of them,' said Besma. 'My little pets.'

After enough drinks, they ended up talking about their exes. 'I lost my husband to the Annihilists,' said Besma lightly, but she didn't say more. Anji wondered if he'd been sacrificed by some outer-space cult. She'd have to ask the Doctor about it later. 'How about yourself?'

'I was with someone. Until just recently.' Anji thought about how to put it. 'He died after a short illness.'

Besma nodded sagely. 'More drinks.' She hauled herself out of the chair and went in search of a waiter.

Anji sighed, leaning back in the chair. Fitz alighted on the edge of Besma's empty chair. 'Watch out,' he said, grinning, 'I hear that everybody's bi in this time period.'

'You're just saying that to be coarse,' said Anji.

'Of course.' Fitz's chin lifted. Anji could almost see the dotted line from his eyes to the redhead who was walking past. 'Hey, Ann!'

The woman turned. She was fashionably short and plump, her dark eyes mismatching the vivid orange of her hair. 'Hello, Fitzie.'

'This is Anji,' said Fitz. Anji waved, but Ann was standing on tiptoes, trying to see through the crowd. Anji heard the sound of furious violining. She stood up on the chair with a bit of difficulty, leaning on Fitz's shoulder.

It was the Doctor. He had got a violin from somewhere, and was playing it madly, watched by a little crowd of partygoers. He seemed to be pretty good at it, thought Anji.

'Isn't he something?' burbled Ann.

Fitz looked at Anji and mimed a flinch. Anji grinned, enormously amused. The Doctor could have outpulled Fitz by a factor of a thousand – if he'd shown any interest at all. To Fitz, who was full of interest, it must all seem appallingly unfair.

Ann said, 'They say he's related to royalty – you know, unofficially.' It took Anji a moment to decipher that. 'He won't give any concerts or tell anyone his name. A genius in disguise.'

'Would you like to meet him?' said Fitz, bouncing to his feet.

Ann mugged delightedly. 'I'd love to.'

'He just happens to be an old friend of mine...' He took Ann's arm and steered her away into the crowd, throwing Anji a wink. She picked up her champagne and followed them.

That had been weeks ago. Now Anji was sheltering in a shop doorway, peering up at the clouds. The rain started to pound as

Fitz walked up to her. 'It came out of nowhere,' she said angrily.

'You know what they say about the weather in Port Any,' said Fitz, trying to be reassuring. 'If you don't like it, wait five minutes.'

The rain was pelting down now. The street emptied as everyone dodged into shelter. 'These sudden storms are happening all the time. You just don't know what's going to happen next,' she said.

'Are you doing all right?'

Anji glanced around. They were surrounded by people. Fitz followed her into the bookshop.

They found an empty aisle in the section for handcrafted paper books. Anji murmured, 'Do you believe me? About what happened the day before yesterday?'

'Course I do,' mumbled Fitz. 'Something happened, anyway.'

'That's what I mean,' said Anji. 'I get the same reaction every time I try to talk to someone about it. The tigers are harmless and fluffy. I don't think even the Doctor believes me.'

'Come on...'

'He's too wrapped up in his new hobby and his new friend to take much notice of anything,' said Anji glumly.

Fitz put a hand on her arm. 'Let's grab some lunch. Then we'll go and see the tiger lady.'

'I'm not hungry,' she said.

Five minutes later, in bright sunshine, they were standing outside Besma's town house. Anji rang the doorbell. Inevitably, it played a short musical phrase. They glanced at each other, rolling their eyes.

Something large and orange and stripy opened the door.

Karl lived in a small flat above the Albinoni Rehearsal Hall, surviving on his stipend and his teaching salary. The study and kitchen were cramped, the embroidered furniture and the Persian rugs were fraying, and the living room was interrupted by a concrete pillar. It would all change when his new concerto was performed.

Karl wandered out into the living room in his dressing gown. They were having a rare day off from rehearsals. The Doctor was still thumping away at the harpsichord. Half an hour ago Karl had set him a theme. He had been grinding away at it ever since, zooming and twiddling up and down the keyboard.

The sun had come up. Karl sat down in its hot slanting beams on the battered chaise longue. He thought his yawn was invisible, but the Doctor crashed to a halt at once. 'What a lot of nonsense,' he said, sitting back from the harpsichord. He was in his shirtsleeves, his hair all over the place. 'What a lot of *noise*. I can't do this, Karl. I don't have an ounce of talent for improvisation, not this kind. Let alone composition.'

'Perhaps it's not your instrument,' said Karl. 'Let's try again on the violin.'

'Oh, it's just the same. I'm an idiot savant,' said the Doctor glumly. 'I can play the violin like a genius, so long as some other genius writes the notes for me to play.'

A month ago, the Doctor had appeared from nowhere at a party at Palmer Gardens. Musicians who were between jobs often played at these big evening do's. A little circle had formed around him, among great bunches of roses and trays of bubbly. Karl had manoeuvred his way through the crowd towards the 'Sabre Dance'.

The Doctor was standing with his eyes closed, absolutely absorbed in his playing. He looked every inch the devil's fiddler, thought Karl – his slender body carelessly slouching, long fingers flashing, aristocratic face taut with concentration, long copper-gold hair flying. His audience's appreciation was more than musical.

But Karl was seeing something different.

When Karl Sadeghi listened to music, he could feel the notes moving around his body. A dancing bass line would crawl up and down his spine. Percussion flashed in the back of his skull. High string sounds burst from the top of his head like fireworks.

He was certain that the same thing was happening to the Doctor. Khachaturian was all over him, in his toes and elbows, tingling in his chest, running over his back. He grinned with furious delight as the notes tickled him.

The 'Sabre Dance' ended with a flourish. The Doctor opened his eyes again, and was startled to be met with a soft wave of applause. He gave a sheepish grin, sawed out the beginning of a square-dance tune-up, and handed the violin back to whoever it belonged to.

An unshaven young man was perched on the edge of a huge pot plant, watching him. 'You see, Fitz?' the violinist said. 'It's not as difficult as it looks. No need to fret.'

It was obviously a running joke between them. Fitz smiled and said, 'I'll stick to my Fender.'

The little crowd was dispersing, but a young woman had stayed behind, a glass of champagne in her hand. Karl caught her eye and murmured, 'Who is that?'

'That's the Doctor,' said the woman.

'Is he free?'

'Oh yes,' said the woman, taking a long drink. 'Absolutely.'

It hadn't been hard to persuade the Doctor to audition for the new concerto. Since then, they had been in constant rehearsals. When they weren't rehearsing, they were stoking up on sweet, hot coffee, and talking. By now, the Doctor knew all about Karl's surviving family, his erratic career, his efforts to promote Octagonal Serialism. But Karl's picture of his first violinist was still maddeningly vague. Whenever his questions got close, the Doctor would plead amnesia, some unknown trauma that had slammed the door on his earlier life. After a month, Karl didn't even know the Doctor's real name.

Karl remembered hearing the Doctor's heartsbeat for the first time. He'd had the mad idea to write a rondo based on the violinist's pulse, pressing a miniature microphone inside the Doctor's shirt. The sound made them both sit and listen, wondering.

'Where have you come from?' Karl whispered.

The Doctor shook his head, slowly. 'I dropped from the sky one morning.'

The colony worlds were always full of rumours about aliens who looked like humans, or disguised themselves as humans, and

21

walked quietly among the human pioneers, watching. It pleased Karl that he knew something about the Doctor that none of the gossipmongers knew.

The Doctor was still sitting at the harpsichord, looking grumpy. Karl said, 'When did you learn to play? Do, do you remember learning?'

The Doctor folded his arms and squeezed his eyes shut. 'I remember...' he said. 'Playing music with... my family? I remember terrible piano lessons with a ferocious old German who could only hear about half of what I was playing. Someone with four arms, playing the viola and the cello at the same time... Wait!' he exclaimed. 'Something is coming back to me...' He pinched the bridge of his nose, contorting his face with concentration. 'Yes... I can picture it...'

Karl got to his feet, leaning over the harpsichord. 'What is it?' he breathed.

The Doctor's face broke into a slow grin. 'The recipe for chocolate martinis.'

Karl laughed again. 'I absolutely believe that you dropped out of the sky,' he said.

'On to my head,' moped the Doctor. 'Do you have any vodka?'

Anji backed down the steps so quickly she nearly squashed Fitz. He caught her efficiently on the bottom step.

The tiger was peering at them around the door. You didn't realise how big the buggers were until you got this close: nine or ten feet long, slender, but packed with muscle, rippling under its skin as it sat down in the doorway.

It opened its mouth and barked, 'Hullow.'

They stared. 'Hullow, hullow,' coughed the tiger. Its eyes were surrounded by short black stripes which gave it a scowling expression.

Anji pulled free of Fitz, fighting the urge to bolt. But then a voice from somewhere behind the orange wall said, 'Tiddles! Get back *inside*!'

The tiger snorted and slunk back into the house, squeezing past

Dr Grieve. She wore a red jump suit. 'Come on in.' She beamed down at them. 'I've just brewed up some coffee.'

Tiddles was settling itself on the floor of the lounge, next to the second tiger, as Besma led them in. The animals filled half the sparsely furnished room. 'You live with these guys?' said Fitz.

'Sit, sit,' said Besma, indicating the narrow sofa. 'Help yourself to bikkies and things. Yes, I've got four of them living here. I've made a pretty *thorough* study of these beasties.'

She ruffled Tiddles's fur. 'Listen, Anji, I read through the message you sent. I've got to tell you, I've never observed behaviour like your library encounter. These two are pretty typical. Aren't you, Roo?' Tiddles's companion yawned voluminously. 'When they're not sleeping, they're soaking in the pools out the back. They rarely show aggression, and when they do it's usually at one another. The only exception is a male guarding the nest – they'll attack anything in sight.' She leaned against a glass-fronted cabinet filled with suspicious-looking biological knick-knacks. 'They do engage in a fair bit of rough-and-tumble play. Maybe the one who swatted you was inviting you to have a game with it.'

'It wasn't a game,' said Anji. 'I wish you could have been there.' The tigers were listening from the rug, she was sure of it. 'Just how intelligent are they?'

'About as smart as a gorilla. Which is pretty smart. Their parents, though, were no more intelligent than a real tiger.'

Fitz said, 'So, how come they're smarter? Are they sort of evolving?' He was staring at the biologist. Anji nudged him.

Besma said, 'Your tiger was dark orange, right?' Anji nodded. 'If the colony records are right, there's a sort of alternation of generations – smart tigers have stupid kids, stupid tigers have smart kids.'

'Why?' said Anji.

'We don't know. No one's done the work. There was a burst of interest in Hitchemus last century, when it was first colonised. A couple of university teams did some work on the tigers. But then, nothing, for decades. If the university keeps up my funding, we might just find out how their brains work.'

'When you say they did some work on the tigers…'

'Mostly taking specimens offworld. Some of them ended up in zoos. They wouldn't breed in captivity.' Besma saw Anji's frown. 'Things were better for the tigers once the scientists arrived. Before that, some of the first colonists had been shooting them.'

'What for?' said Fitz. 'Were the tigers attacking them?'

'For fun,' said Besma sourly. 'There are tiger skins in the museum, you know.' She changed the subject back. 'It's easy to tell the stupid parents – their fur turns yellow with age. They rarely come into the city, though.' She nudged one of the sleeping tigers with her foot. 'These guys are smart enough to understand some human words. I've even taught them to say a few things.'

'Yeah, the one that answered the door was pretty chatty,' said Fitz.

'They can't speak human languages, of course. Even gorillas can't do that – the anatomy is wrong. They can approximate a few sounds.'

'Can they read?' Besma shook her head. 'Then why would a tiger want a book?'

Besma said, 'My best guess would be imitative behaviour.'

'It was playing at being human?' said Anji.

'Could be. Sometimes they think they are human. Don't you, my girls?'

'So they're harmless?' said Fitz.

'Harmless,' sighed Anji.

The quest for vodka took the Doctor and Karl through the city, in and out of the tiny import shops, to two garden concerts and a drumming demonstration, lunch at the Conservatory, another concert, and finally down to the lake for a long meander out of the city and into the twilight.

They followed the river north. The silence of the countryside rang in their ears. Eventually they staggered to a halt in a meadow by the twisting water. The Doctor stuck a lightstick in the ground, opened up the cold pack he had been carrying all day, and set the mostly empty bottles out on the grass. Vodka and white crème de cacao, both imported from Earth.

Karl went down to the riverbank and rinsed out the martini glasses in the chilling Emerson. The Doctor never seemed to worry about money, even think about money, just throwing it about on a whim. It lent credence to the rumours that he was related to the aristocracy of some planet or other, but Karl didn't believe a word of it. The Doctor was something far more special and strange than a mere lost princeling.

A mighty squawk behind him almost made Karl drop the glasses in the river. He turned around, a little too quickly, and nearly propelled himself into the water. He sank to his knees, staring up the bank at the Doctor, who had taken out his violin and was scratching an appalling noise out of it.

'What the hell's that?' Karl shouted.

'It's a donkey,' said the Doctor, letting forth another dreadful bray. 'You've never heard a donkey?'

'What the hell's a donkey?' Karl pulled himself to his feet with as much dignity as he could muster. 'Play something.'

The Doctor lay on his back and launched violently into something it took Karl half a minute to recognise as 'Winter' from Verdi's *The Four Seasons*. 'But you're playing all four parts,' he said, sinking breathlessly on to the grass.

'Why not?' said the Doctor, without stopping.

'Because it's ridiculous.' Karl stared at him from where he knelt. The Doctor played on, casually, frantically, bouncing his foot to the rhythms of the *allegro non molto*. The notes flew off like sparks, hurtling over Karl's shoulders. 'Impossible. It doesn't have the range, for one thing.'

The Doctor screeched off in the middle of a phrase. He carefully put down the violin Karl had given him, and mixed the last of the chocolate martinis. 'You know this thing in the stem,' said Karl. 'Of the glasses, I mean. The thingamajig which lets you chill the drink. I mean, does the glass let you heat the drink up? Hot chocolate martinis? I'm drunk.'

The Doctor laughed. 'Of course you are.'

'You too!'

The Doctor shook his head. 'Only if I want to be.' He laughed, pushing the back of his hand against his mouth. 'Which I do.'

'You're a fake!'

'Well, if I'm going to fit in with you mere mortals…'

Karl didn't laugh at the joke. He was thinking about the Doctor's double heartbeat. What else was wired differently inside that lazing body?

Karl let his forehead drop to the cool grass. The air was thick with a scent like lemons and baking. All that alien pollen they were breathing in. Imagine an alien whose nervous system was a hundred or a thousand times as complex as a human being's, whose hands were interchangeably ambidextrous, whose fingers were all equally agile. An idiot savant, or a technical trickster, just the imitation of a real virtuoso with feeling and understanding.

'Why are you here?' he whispered into the gathering darkness. The lightstick threw half the Doctor's face into sharp relief. 'What is it you want?'

The Doctor shrugged. 'What does anyone want?' he murmured. 'Happiness, I suppose.' He sank a little more into the grass. 'I think there's some of it about the place.'

'Is that why you travel?' said Karl.

'All through space,' said the Doctor, 'and all through time. We can go anywhere, Karl,' he said in a low voice. 'We can drop down into any point in history. But we are not mere tourists. We are adventurers. That old-fashioned word.'

The Doctor sat up suddenly, as though the ground were becoming too cold for him. They should have brought blankets. Karl sat cross-legged, listening. 'We seek trouble. Or it seeks us. We save worlds possessed by terrible creatures. Terrible. We battle Promethean scientists whose minds and machines have gone haywire.'

He reached out and grabbed Karl's arm. 'It sounds ridiculous,' he said intensely. 'Travelling through space and time and having adventures. It all sounds so pointless and – and silly. Tell me it's not all pointless. Tell me it's not ridiculous.'

'It sounds wonderful,' breathed Karl. 'Wonderful.'

'Then why isn't it enough?' said the Doctor. He was gripping Karl's arm. 'I tried living in a straight line for a hundred years and that wasn't enough, either. Why am I looking to be something else? Something in one place, one time?'

Karl didn't know. He said, 'Perhaps you were once a famous violinist,' he said. 'Perhaps that's what you can't remember. You've just naturally come home to your calling.'

'Is this it?' The Doctor let go of Karl. His gaze swept around – the cool river, the sweet meadow, the silent trees. In the east the ringed moon was rising, silvering the deep blue of the sky. His eyes came back to the composer. 'Is this home?'

Karl hoped so. But he didn't say anything.

For the evening rehearsal, Karl changed into his formal work clothes, a dark cotton suit. No matter the weather, the rehearsal hall was always arctic. He was wearing the long russet coat the Doctor had given him. There was a clock face on the left breast, white hands silently changing on the minute.

Karl had given the Doctor the violin he would use for the performance. He had brought the instrument from Earth, all those years ago, packed into the tiny cargo container. He'd spent the trip to Hitchemus playing cards with composers whose careers were going nowhere, all of them hoping the colony would give them the breakthrough they needed.

On Earth he had been a composer and a prep chef, a composer and a library assistant, a composer and a fruit picker. He had busked and tutored. His work had been performed just often enough to give him a name, but no real money to go with it. Hitchemus was a badly needed Mecca for people like him.

Bits of furniture and half painted scenery were set up on the stage. They shared the rehearsal hall's schedule with another orchestra, two operas, and whatever visiting musicians could be fitted in in between.

Karl's orchestra spent an hour working on the bridge in the *allegro*. After a ten-minute break, he decided they'd run through the whole movement from the top.

27

It started with an explosion of sound, the whole orchestra playing a single note, then slowly splitting up into the harmonies that would become the theme of the first section. Karl's feet and shoulders tingled with the roar and the flutter. He found himself grinning wildly, hands balling into fists as he drew that sound from the players, wishing he could add more and more instruments until their collective volume blew the roof from the hall.

The Doctor's solo came in the second section, just after the dialogue between the strings and the percussion. They had worked on it in Karl's apartment, marking up the score. He would state the theme, then improvise around it for twenty-four bars, restating it an octave higher to bring the whole orchestra back on board.

The Doctor stood, took a deep breath, and began to play.

Karl was arrested by the sheer force of the music he'd written, the intensity of the Doctor's playing. The notes crawled across his scalp and burst in waves over his shoulders.

He snapped out of it when he realised the Doctor was up to thirty-six bars. This wasn't the first time he'd got carried away, played for an extra dozen bars or more. But there was always the high theme, at last, to cue the other players.

Forty-eight bars. Still the Doctor went on playing, racing ahead, the violin climbing the peaks of hills and racing into valleys, swooping and soaring, his fingers moving impossibly fast. Faster than humanly possible, thought Karl. So that's how it's done.

He lowered his baton, but the Doctor didn't notice. There was an uncomfortable shuffling in the orchestra. Please, he thought, please snap out of it. He tapped his baton on the stand, feebly. It was no use. The Doctor was gripped, transported, possessed. Sixty bars. A hundred. The other players were staring, or whispering among themselves.

At last one of the violin's strings snapped, curling with a damp plunk, narrowly missing the Doctor's face. His frantic playing slowed as he realised some of the notes simply weren't there any more.

The Doctor opened his eyes. He put down the violin, carefully, and pushed his damp hair out of his face. Then he started, suddenly realising he was the centre of attention. One of the lighting technicians shone a sarcastic spot on him.

The timpanists were fanning the swooning harpist with the pages of their score. The first violist got up and huffed out of the rehearsal hall.

Karl crooked a finger at the Doctor. 'Fifteen minutes, everyone,' he said softly, his voice ringing in the silence.

Karl made the Doctor wait in his flat. When the composer returned, his concertmaster was sitting on the chaise longue, his hands folded in his lap, looking for all the world like a schoolboy about to be disciplined by the headmaster. 'How's Kareem?' he asked meekly.

'I've managed to persuade him not to take his viola and go home,' said Karl. He sank into a chair and pressed his fingertips to his forehead. 'You simply cannot deliver the solo in that – that manner. Your performance has been becoming more and more overblown and dramatic with every rehearsal.' Karl got up, finding himself pacing. 'Doctor, I know you haven't had much experience at performing with an orchestra, but you have to play *with* us, not *against* us.'

'It's good, though,' said the Doctor. 'Isn't it?' Karl caught his eyes for a moment, finding the steady blue gaze unnerving.

'That's not the point,' said Karl. 'This isn't the first time we've had to talk about that solo. And it's not the first time one of the other musicians has complained.'

The Doctor stood up. 'They've been talking about me?'

'Oh yes.' Karl nodded. 'Kareem informed me that the viola and the violin are actually the same size. The violin just looks smaller because the player's head is so large.'

The Doctor smiled slightly. 'That is a very old joke.'

'Nonetheless, he has a point. If you can't make your playing fit in, we're not going to be able to continue with you.'

The Doctor's serene expression turned into shock. He grabbed

Karl by the forearms. 'Don't. Don't do this to me. Don't cut me off like this.'

'Listen to yourself,' said Karl. 'I can't let you go on acting like a prima donna.'

'That's not what's happening,' urged the Doctor. 'It's your music that's doing this. It's going to do the same thing to the audience. All I'm doing is giving in to it.'

Karl broke away with a snort. The Doctor said, 'No, no, no, listen.' He snatched up the violin, took a deep breath, and started from the top of the solo.

Karl watched as the Doctor's body tensed, his eyes screwed up with concentration, his hands moved faster and faster as he screamed out the middle bars of the solo. He was quivering with effort. To Karl it was as though he were flashing with light, each phrase glowing and leaping up from the instrument, matched by the same colours in his own body.

At last he opened his eyes and looked at Karl, expectantly. The composer wiped his damp palms on his jeans.

'No,' he breathed. 'That's not it.' He tapped at his skull. 'That's not the way I hear it.'

'Then you're not listening!' said the Doctor.

'*I'm* not listening!' cried Karl. 'I *wrote* that!'

'Oh, that's so typical of your species,' snapped the Doctor. A chill went down the composer's spine. 'You've got to control everything, you've got to have everything your way, or it doesn't count.' The Doctor's voice was low, vibrating. 'Maybe there's something more in the music, something you can't control.'

'Your playing is just a parlour trick, isn't it?' said Karl. The Doctor started as though he'd been struck. 'You didn't have to spend a lifetime sweating blood to become a virtuoso. The way your superior brain is wired, you could probably play the concerto with your feet. You're just amusing yourself with us.'

'How dare you?' thundered the Doctor. 'How can you say that?'

'You're a cuckoo chick. A pretender. You're just doing your impression of a first violinist.'

The Doctor gave a bitter laugh. 'And you're jealous. Of me.

Because I'm something more than human. Jealous.'

'Oh yes?' snapped Karl. 'Written any symphonies lately?'

The Doctor spun, suddenly, his arm arcing out.

The violin shattered against the concrete pillar. It tore in half, the back bursting into chunks and splinters, the strings tearing out of their pegs or snapping in two. In an instant, the Doctor was holding a useless stick tangled in strings and hanging fragments.

He let it fall from his hand. It made an ugly twanging thump as it hit the floor. Karl didn't look at the Doctor's face. They both stared at the ruins of the violin.

Karl walked across the room. His steps were even and measured. When he reached the door, he opened it.

They stood there like that for several seconds.

The Doctor grabbed the pages of the score in his fists and hurled them into the air with a roar. They exploded like a snowstorm, filling the room. Karl snatched at the handwritten sheets as they wheeled and fluttered.

As they settled, randomised, to the wooden floor, Karl realised that the Doctor was gone.

Out in the savannah, where the glass and water of Port Any are a distant glitter, a tiger sits crouched on a dirt mound. Waves of heat rise from the grassy plain all around, shimmering. The tiger sits upright, its stumpy tail turned to one side. Its long chin rests on one paw.

It holds the book it stole from the Central Library in one of its feet, lazily, stretching its flexible toes to turn the pages.

After a while, the tiger reaches down and picks up its violin. The instrument is lying, carefully positioned, on a tussock of grass. The tiger grasps it firmly in its six digits, sliding it up under its jaw, allowing it to rest on its shoulder.

The tiger squints at the book again. Its eyes have evolved to detect movement, not fine detail. It must switch to its less reliable, focused vision to read the score.

Balanced on the dirt hill, its clawed fingers sliding over the strings, bow clutched in a furry paw, the tiger begins to play.

Chapter Three

Fitz emerged from his flat, guitar slung on his back. The voice of a mournful violin was drifting down the hallway, past the dark wood panelling and the soft glass lamps. Fitz went to the last door in the hall and knocked.

'Doctor? I'm just going out for a coffee. D'you want to come along?'

No answer. Fitz pressed his ear to the door, listening to the tragic music. I know you're in there, he wanted to shout; stop mucking about. 'Go on – come and have a chat.'

The Doctor stopped playing. Fitz heard a series of noises not entirely unlike the tuning of a violin.

'Anji's worried about you,' lied Fitz. 'She's still pretty shaken up, you know.'

'Keep an eye on her for me,' said the Doctor. Fitz could barely hear him.

'Course,' said Fitz. 'But I think she'd feel safer if you were, you know, around.'

'Hmm,' said the Doctor. Or maybe Fitz imagined it. The violin started up again, scratching away at some classical piece in a dripping minor key.

News of the fight had reached Fitz after only a few hours. Kareem the violist played in a string quartet, and the quartet's cellist played sitar in a classical Indian/jazz fusion group, and the group's pianist was part of Jam Tomorrow along with Fitz and the twin flautists. The morning's rehearsal had been cancelled, said the pianist, and Kareem was gleefully awaiting auditions for a new concertmaster.

After lunch, Fitz had gone to see the composer. 'I hope you're not a messenger,' Karl said.

'Nah, the Doctor didn't send me or anything. I just wanted to find out what happened.'

Karl showed him the shattered violin, his gift to the Doctor. He cradled it in his lap like the body of a pet. Fitz stared at it. 'You can't fix that,' he said.

'No.'

'Are you really going to get someone else?'

'If necessary,' said Karl stiffly.

'He just goes a bit over the top sometimes,' said Fitz. 'You know.'

'Yes,' said Karl, 'I had noticed.'

That was yesterday afternoon. Karl didn't want to talk, so Fitz went to visit the Doctor to find out what the fight had been about. But the Doctor wouldn't answer his door, and as far as they could tell he'd switched off all the computers in the flat so no one could contact him. He'd got another violin from somewhere. All he did was sit in there, sawing away at it, playing one teary tune after another. Anji said he was wallowing in pathos. 'Best leave him alone,' she said. 'He'll come out of there when he's ready.'

Fitz took off his guitar and sat down in the hallway, his back to the Doctor's door. 'They're performing *Smile* tonight,' he called.

The violin stopped on a single note, holding it, like a stuck record. The Doctor said, 'Whose reconstruction?'

'Hunt and Lane, I think.'

'Hmmm.' The violin held the note.

'You've got to come out of there sooner or later, you know,' called Fitz. 'I mean, if nothing else, eventually civilisation will crumble. And so will the building. And then where will you be?'

The violin wavered. Then it crashed back into the music, a furious vibrating slide up and down the neck. A scorching glissando, flames and sirens in one.

Maybe Anji was right. Fitz frowned and got up, slinging his guitar into its home on his back. 'See you later, then,' he called. The Doctor was too busy with an arpeggio to answer.

Fat clouds rode a sluggish breeze. Fitz strolled down Port Any streets with his hands in his pockets, whistling. Anji was waiting for him at the Central Library. She was sitting out in the open, in one of the reading pits, a book reader in her lap and a notebook – a real one – by her side. It was so quiet in here it made Fitz's ears ring.

She smiled when she saw him. 'No trouble?' he whispered.

'None at all,' said Anji. He gave her a hand up out of the pit. 'I think I've got everything I need.'

When they were out on the street, Fitz said, 'He's still in there.'

'Did you talk to him?'

'I mostly talked to G flat minor. I just wish I knew what they'd fought about.'

'Artistic differences.' Anji shrugged.

'I dunno. It doesn't sound like him. Anyway, so you got everything from the library you wanted?'

'What I *want* is a rational explanation for what happened to me. I don't have to like it, I just want to understand it. And I want to know what to do if it ever happens again.'

'Yeah, well, there's not a rational explanation for everything.'

'Like locking yourself in a room and playing the violin all night?' The corner of Anji's mouth twitched. 'He's like a teenager who's had a tiff with his best mate. He'll be all right.'

'I can't believe he broke that violin,' said Fitz. 'I feel like something's really wrong.'

Anji patted her bag. 'Well,' she said, 'once we've spoken to Dr Grieve, we might have something interesting enough to tempt him out. I've got a theory about the tigers.'

Besma said, 'I'm afraid that's the same theory everyone has about the tigers.'

'You what?' said Fitz.

Anji stared down at her notes, dejectedly. 'I didn't come across it in my reading.'

They were in the back yard of Besma's town house, sitting on wicker chairs. It was a huge, grassy area, dotted with glass sheds and above-ground swimming pools like huge canvas drums. Today the xenobiologist was wearing a red dress that fell to her calves and a pair of gold-coloured sandals. She was holding a large rubber duck. 'If you check the newspaper archives, you'll find some references. People have been coming up with the same idea for years.'

'So am I right?' said Anji. 'The tigers are the remains of an intelligent culture – the people who left the ruins?'

'It's possible.' Besma got up and threw the rubber duck into the nearest pool. Anji started at the loud splashing sounds coming from inside the tall canvas cylinder. 'I think they have the potential for intelligence, but once they lost their civilisation, that potential couldn't be realised. But I prefer the theory that the ruins were left by a previous colony that died out. Someone else was here before the human race.'

'Perhaps the tigers ate them,' Anji said. Fitz wasn't sure if she was joking.

Fitz said, 'So that kind of brings us back to where we started from. Maybe Anji's tiger was just trying to imitate humans.'

Tiddles stuck her wet head up over the edge of the pool. 'Hullow,' she said.

'Hello to you, too,' said Anji. The tiger disappeared back into the water with a splash.

Karl blinked into wakefulness on the narrow chaise longue. He was covered with manuscript paper. The electronic stylus had rolled away across the floor.

The balcony window let in a pattern of light against the empty white wall. Karl watched the late-morning sunlight and the clouds chase one another across the plaster.

From the beginning, Karl had known that the Doctor would not stay. He would be here for the rehearsals, he would be here for the performances, he'd promised. But, after that, there were no guarantees.

And now... and now, there was nothing tying the Doctor to Hitchemus, to Karl, at all. He could leave whenever the whim took him.

Once, a group of tourists had wandered into the rehearsal hall, chatting and rustling and spreading crumbs. They had been trying to work out a few kinks in the woodwind part of the second theme of the third movement. Karl gave the tourists a meaningful stare, but they just cheerfully waved and went on chattering and crunching. Officially, the rehearsal hall was open to anyone; he couldn't just throw them out.

After a while, the Doctor – who had been sitting quietly with the other violinists, reading an old-fashioned book – slipped up to the stand and said, 'Why don't you rehearse the contrabassoons?'

'What do you think we've been doing for the last ten intolerable minutes?' whispered Karl.

'I mean,' said the Doctor, '*just* the contrabassoons.'

A slow grin spread across Karl's face. 'What an interesting suggestion.'

In the second theme, the deep and threatening voices of the contrabassoons were used three times, each time to lend emphasis to the bassoons. Karl stood there counting out the bars with his baton in silence broken only by the tourists. Thirty-two bars of nothing. Three heavy tones from the contrabassoons. Thirty-two more bars of nothing. Two honks. Sixty-four bars of nothing. It took the tourists two hundred and seven bars to get bored enough to leave.

That night, every time they thought about it, it set them off. As soon as they'd stop giggling, the Doctor would say 'Honk honk', and off they'd go again. Thinking about it made Karl smile, even now.

Every time he went over the fight in his mind, he couldn't work out how it had become so bitter, so terrible, so quickly. Had he been so wrapped up in his work that he hadn't seen it coming?

Was any of what he'd said true?

If it was, the Doctor would simply get back in his flying saucer or what have you and move on to his next bit of fun with the human race. Perhaps he would never stop hopping from one thing to another, trying to find something he could be bothered with.

Karl sat up, slowly, gathering pages of the score. His face was rough with an embryonic beard, and his neck and shoulder complained. He would need to shower, and eat something, and then start looking for a new first violinist.

Perhaps, in a little while.

* * *

36

Fitz tried playing along with the Doctor – sitting on the floor, nestled against the doorjamb, filling in chords and fragments of countermelody around the Doctor's meanderings. Backing them up, keeping them company. They meshed well, for a while; for a few dizzying moments he got the sense they were actually playing together, even that the Doctor was letting him lead. But gradually the Doctor's zigzagging leaps spiralled faster and faster, the notes merged into a single high keening wail, and in the end Fitz put down his guitar and slunk away, feeling like a spy.

It wasn't just that he couldn't physically keep up – like that first time he'd seen Danny Gatton play, and had found himself squinting to check that the bloke didn't actually have extra fingers on his left hand. It was more like that time in sixty-seven, when he and Maddy listened to the B-side of the new Beatles single over and over again all night. Hazily watching the little bit of vinyl and its 'I Am The Walrus' label go round and round, endlessly wondering where in hell did *that* come from? The music was expressing something so far outside anything he could imagine for himself that it gave him the shakes.

When he finally came back, fortified by a pint, if anything the playing sounded even more tragic than before. 'That had better be you and not a recording,' Fitz called through the door.

He sat down outside the hallway, pulling his guitar off his back. 'I've got a mystery for you. It's just this idea that the tigers used to run the planet. It doesn't make any sense. I mean, a fallen civilisation is one thing, but how can people stop being intelligent?' No reply, yet again. Fitz said, 'Did they watch too much telly, or what?'

No answer. Fitz plucked out the funeral march on his guitar. Still no answer.

'I'm going to go talk to Karl again,' said Fitz. Nothing. 'If you don't want to me to go, you'd better come out here and stop me.'

The violin playing stopped. Fitz scrambled to his feet, swallowing. A moment ago he'd been sure that an angry Doctor was better than no Doctor.

But nothing happened. The door stayed obstinately shut.

'Right, then,' murmured Fitz.

'No rehearsals today?'

'No.'

'Found any new violinists?'

'Not yet.'

'Have you actually been looking?'

Karl sat back from his coffee. The café was half full of people taking a late breakfast, the smell of toast and the soft clatter of cutlery. The jukebox played a soothing mixture of scratchy old jazz records and Youkalian ambient. He had grabbed a small, round table in a corner, by himself, trying to hide behind a newspaper.

He sighed and put down the paper. 'I don't mean to be rude, Fitz,' he said, 'but I'd really rather you left me alone.'

'It's not good for people, though, is it? Being alone.' Fitz touched an icon on the newspaper, and the text on the single sheet of paper changed. He flipped forward and back, looking for cartoons.

'You have to understand the role of the concertmaster,' Karl said patiently. 'The Doctor isn't just a fiddler: he's my right hand. He keeps the players together, he organises some of the rehearsals. Were I run over by a bus, he would take over as conductor.'

'Right. So it's important to get this sorted quickly.'

Karl shook his head. 'A temperamental concertmaster simply cannot do his job. We have to work together hand in glove.'

Fitz slouched in his chair. 'You know, he doesn't usually like to stay in one place for so long. We're the only friends he's got, 'cause he carries us with him. But now there's you.'

'It's not me.' Karl looked Fitz in the eyes. 'It was never me.'

Fitz looked away. He started doodling on the napkin. 'Come over,' he said earnestly. 'I'll bet he'll open that door for you. I know you groove on, whatsit, atomic-age rock – the Doctor played me a recording of your concerto for fuzz bass and Hammond organ. Did you know I studied under Hendrix?' Karl raised a sceptical eyebrow. Well, all right, Fitz had seen Hendrix only a few times in sixty-seven, but they were *great* seats. 'I could give you an exclusive – all those lost secrets and tricks…'

Karl leaned his forehead on his fingertips. 'I haven't decided what to do yet,' he said. 'It doesn't matter whether the Doctor comes out of his huff or not. I'm going to have to decide.'

They both looked up. Anji was standing by the table. She smiled hello.

'I was just leaving,' said Karl. He picked up his newspaper, then thought better of it. 'You read that if you like.'

Anji took Karl's seat, watching the composer as he left. 'It's getting a bit silly, isn't it?' she said.

'Playing in that concerto means a lot to the Doctor. I haven't seen him this wrapped up in something this way since…' Fitz sat back. 'Actually, I don't think I've ever seen him this wrapped up in anything. Except saving the world and stuff. This is different, Anji. I don't want him to screw it up. Besides, if –'

Fitz's jaw hung open. Anji's menu dropped from her hand. They sat, paralysed, for several seconds.

The café's conversations fell as one into silence. The only sound was the jukebox burbling, and Anji's footsteps as she crossed to the front window. She pressed her face to the glass, staring out.

'What the hell…?' said Fitz.

Tigers were marching down the street. Sauntering, really, out of step, but in such a crowd. They filled the road, pushing pedestrians to the side. Dozens of them. Hundreds of them. Muscular shoulders pumped easily, tails were held high, golden glances shot around. They were like a parade for a circus with only one act.

'Where are they all coming from?' said Fitz.

'The Bewilderness,' said Anji. 'They must be. All the tigers are coming to town.'

Besma sat at her desk in the lounge, absorbed in her notes. Only her thumb moved, pressing the CHANGE PAGE icon.

Tiddles was stretched out on the rug. The lanky tigress rolled over, yawning. Besma slid off her shoe and caressed the animal's stomach with her bare foot. '*Look* at you, you beastie,' she murmured absently. 'You tickle machine. You furball gerbil.'

The doorbell rang, once. Besma was getting up from her seat when it rang again, insistently. 'All right,' she called, hauling on her shoe. It was probably that young couple again.

It wasn't. Her front steps were covered in tigers.

The one in front, a big male, grinned. Besma jerked back from the door, involuntarily, and he took the opportunity to come in. His big shoulders pushed her back as he slid inside.

Besma backed up and found herself on the stairwell. She went up the stairs, backwards, one step at a time, watching in astonishment as half a dozen tigers oozed into her house. They weren't paying her much attention. If she didn't make any sound, if she kept moving slowly, she could make it to the relative safety of her room.

Tiddles lifted her head as the other tigers crowded into the living room. Two of them sat down on the sofa, while another hauled itself up on to Besma's desk, paws dangling off the edge. The wood strained under the weight.

'Hurrah,' said Tiddles.

Anji turned from the café window. 'Let's get out,' she said. 'Out the back way.'

Fitz followed her as she banged through the kitchen door. They pushed past a startled cook and into the alleyway behind the building.

'Look.' Anji ducked down behind a crate of vegetables. Fitz looked. They could see marching tigers at both ends of the alley.

'We're stuck,' said Anji.

Fitz took Anji's hand. 'Let's leg it – all they'll see are a couple of blurs.'

'We've got to tell the Doctor,' said Anji. 'God. They're everywhere. They're everywhere.'

They dashed into another alley. Fitz followed the maze between buildings, familiar after weeks of haunting coffee clubs and jazz cellars. Every time they turned a corner he thought they were going to run smack into one of the big cats, but the tigers seemed to be sticking to the main streets. They caught glimpses of them between buildings, a parade of gold and black. Sirens sounded, in the distance, whooping, then dying. Fitz doubted the Waytes could get through. The streets were choked with tigers.

'Where are they all heading?' he said.

'They obviously know what they're doing,' said Anji. 'It's like they're following a map. Can you get us back to the block of flats?'

Fitz looked around. 'Yeah,' he said. 'Yessiree. Come on.'

He pulled Anji through a doorway. They were in a concrete stairwell. Up one floor, two, three – Fitz pushed open another door, and they burst out into a shopping centre.

They looked around in confusion for a moment. Crowds, stalls, shopfronts – everything looked so normal. 'The bridge,' said Fitz.

Anji followed him at a jog to a covered walkway high above the street. The bridge connected the shops with the swimming pool above their block of flats. The windows on either side were hidden behind a wall of people, all of them watching the animal procession below. Fitz and Anji dashed through the clear space in the centre of the crowd and into the hot chlorinated air of the pool area. Anji led the way down the stairs. They were back in the hallway outside their rooms.

They could hear the Doctor playing away, oblivious. Fitz hammered on the door. 'Doctor! The city's being invaded. Will you please stop fiddling about and come out?'

Nothing. Anji and Fitz looked at each other.

'Oh, all right,' said the Doctor.

Break: 1935

Morning, and the man stands facing the ocean ahead, rolling with the foredeck each time it dives into the waves. The cloud of black smoke from the *Sarah Gail*'s twin stacks disappears aftwards. There's nothing in front of him but a hundred and eighty degrees of sunrise.

Hold on him there: compact man in dark pullover to hide the grime, short cropped hair bringing out the angles of his face. Slight but solidly muscled, energy carefully guarded on an inner flywheel. He's just brought his shift to a close, oiling and adjusting the winch motor on the forward derrick, and has turned to study the sun. His spiky-blue eyes give you the impression he's watching you from a safe distance.

They tighten against the sunlight, studying the range of colour spread across the water and smearing up the dome of the sky. The shading and backlight brings out the height of the clouds - a sky big and high enough to finally swallow you up.

Smitty rises from belowdecks on the ladder, gives the man a cheery thump on his back. He's a stocky lifter with a browned hand-carved face, his hair bristly as his beard.

—Looking for somethin'? Smitty asks.

—Of course.

—What?

—Anything different. (The man turns to Smitty, gives a fleeting, deflecting grin.) —The day they start all looking the same, that's the day I go over the side.

Smitty grins back, face crinkling like leather, and grabs the man round the waist to mime pitching him over. —Lemme know when you want it, I'll see how far I can hurl you.

—Should've been here Thursday.

With a slippery smile and a backhanded wave, the man picks up his newspaper and disappears below.

* * *

42

It's the comfortable routine of months now, ever since he'd signed on in Sydney – affecting a vague doctorate, deflecting any personal enquiries with a few words about lost memory, shell shock from the last war. He's never provided any details of his prior work on the seas, but after his first day the crew were ready to swear that he'd been born with a belaying pin in his hand.

And a belaying pin at that, not a coal shovel – the man moves as if he belonged in the rigging in the days of sail, following the caprice of the wind instead of setting a course and steaming straight through. The days of instinct and struggle that the old-timers still go on about, when the challenge and joy was in the doing, not just in what's seen and where's been.

But the *Sarah Gail* has a better lot than most, in this coal-fuelled age – she still wanders wherever the cargo takes her. Two months back they circled the New Hebrides delivering kero and cement, then brought sweet potatoes and kava root to the Ellice Islands. At Bougainville the captain had missed out on a booking, which meant several nights misspent – the man had drunk everyone else under the table, seemingly baffled by his inability to lose himself to the booze.

This week is Dairen, in occupied Manchoukuo, where he's found his latest lead.

The crew cabins fill the fore end of the deck. He heads aft, to the lone cabin shoehorned in over the engines. He's bunking with Smitty now, the other hard case of the crew – a gap-toothed bruiser whose willingness to swing first is matched only by his relentless sledgehammer enthusiasm for whatever strikes his fancy. Still, they've struck up a comfortable co-existence, aided by working opposing shifts, alternately companionable and aloof.

The noise of the screws leaps up as he opens the door to their cabin. It's a closet, twin bunks opposite the porthole, the air still and thick and the deck steadily shuddering. He unfastens the porthole, the precious breeze rustling the pin-ups and Virgin Mary pinned over Smitty's bunk, and settles cross-legged on to the deck.

The walls by his bottom bunk give nothing away: they're as bare as the day he arrived. (Save for a meticulous pencil sketch of a

43

Polynesian woman, soft hair and wary eyes, holding her two-year-old boy.) But from under the bedding he slides a slim leather-bound scrapbook. He opens it, then with precise movements he unfolds the newspaper he picked up in Bouganville.

The fact that it's in Chinese doesn't give him a second's pause. With ease he turns to the story he wants, on the inside page: a dragon, sighted by peasants near Fushun.

Manchuria smells of coal smoke and war. He'd claimed one night over rice wine ashore that he could feel it coming: something bigger than the latest squabble between Japan and China over the province, something that sometimes makes him look at the black smoking funnels of the *Sarah Gail* and shudder, for reasons he can't explain. But he keeps his head low, doesn't fight the tide, skirts round the edges of the conflict in a rattling tramp steamer. If he's going to hunt for dragons, he'll have to leave the fight to the experts.

He folds the newspaper, carefully tears out the dragon story, and pastes it into the scrapbook, next to a ragged clipping about a cloud of wasps attacking a train outside Arandale. The book is full of mysteries the world over, puzzles to follow up on, reasons not to go over the side.

Finished, he tucks the scrapbook back into its hiding place, then settles on to the bunk for another morning of nonsleep. Changes his mind. Tries to pace, finds the floor too small. Casts about for something to fill the next minute, and the next, till he sees –

Smitty's battered old fiddle, discarded on his bunk, a chip out of the belly and the bow shedding hairs.

Might be interesting to try.

Absently he picks it up, plucks a few open strings, hesitantly twists a tuning peg. Raises it to his chin, lifts the bow. A curious look on his face, he draws it across the strings –

– and teases out a first perfect note.

Smoothly he reverses direction, shifts angle. The tone eases up a fifth, without a hint of hesitation. He picks out a scattering of notes, his hands moving instinctively from one to the next. Then a scale, note-perfect. A swooping legato phrase. His face remains carefully set, masklike; only the one eye nearer to the fretboard creeps wider with amazement.

The notes tumble over one another, falling into a rhythm. Swaying triplets, matching the thrum of the deck, skipping about in search of a direction.

Smitty pokes his head in, back for his smokes. He takes in the man, all elbows and cheekbones in his grimy pullover, suddenly a presence filling the room.

—Didn't know you played, mate.

A smile over the strings, just a hint of fear. —Neither did I.

Smitty settles on the bottom bunk, his face saying, Don't that beat all?

Out of the meandering notes forms a haunting six-note melody, calling to them. Rising and falling and bending upwards again. He lingers on it, adding slides and grace notes, toying with the phrase like a child rolling a sweet round in his mouth. He meanders away from it, embroidering on the rhythm, turning the notes on their head, then always looping back to the same six-note thought. A questioning phrase, unresolved.

—Woss that, then?

—Don't think it's been written yet. I'll let you know when someone does…

He goes on, on, as Smitty makes his excuses and heads topside. His feet stay fixed, his body swaying, as the music spills out of him. On, on, much of it gibberish, notes without melody, notes out of time – a child who's just discovered his own voice. Faster, then higher, then lower, trying to find the limits of the gift he's been given. Never the same from moment to moment, hour to hour. He stands there, plays there, his face opening with awe as he dives deeper into this ocean of sound. Sinks to his knees, wraps himself round the violin, clutching it to him as he plays on and on. Scared to stop in case he can't ever start again.

—I never knew, he cries. —God in heaven, I never knew.

When Smitty comes back nine hours later, he snatches the fiddle out of the man's hands, shakily crosses himself, and tells him never to touch it again.

* * *

Besma Grieve, xenobiologist, insists:

The 'tigers' are not tigers at all. Not even mammals, not even mammal-like. Observe: at first glance, you have a four-limbed, tailed creature, covered in orange and black fur. Now, bring your eyes closer. Do you see? The 'fur' is soft, raised spines on hardened, flexible skin plates – three to a plate. Something like scales, although not so effectively water-resistant: the tigers are prone to losing moisture through their skin. They drink prodigiously, and love a good swim.

When a tiger is lolling on its back, examine its chest and belly. (This position indicates a friendly, relaxed mood. The tiger may even let you touch its vulnerable underside.) You will find no nipples, not even ducts. These 'tigers' make no milk for their young.

There are other differences, large and small. Vertebrates are pentadigital; but the tigers' paws combine two symmetrical tridigital plans, giving them remarkable dexterity – two thumbs on each paw. The shoulder and hip joints are unlike anything seen in Earthly vertebrates.

But the final proof comes at the molecular level. Although many of the proteins are similar to those found in Terran animals, even in humans – naturally, since those proteins must do similar jobs – the tigers' DNA uses an entirely different code to indicate the sequence of amino acids. That code is unique to each planet's life, the ultimate fingerprint. Every world a separate creation.

Despite the remarkable products of parallel evolution, it is impossible for any planet to duplicate the biome of any other. Evolution has no goals: one successful life form, at any given time, will do as well as another. While the early stages of life do tend to be similar, with each step a planet traces out the course of its own biological uniqueness. No world but Earth could ever develop true tigers – no matter how fearful the symmetry of creatures on other worlds, they are not members of the species *Panthera tigris*, not members of the order Carnivora or the phylum Chordata, relatives of all other life on Earth.

Do not be fooled by the final product, by the wrapping. Nature has only made them in the image of tigers.

First Chorus

Chapter Four

The city was silent.

Besma walked the empty streets between a pair of tigers. The only signs of life were the news cameras she saw now and then, fist-sized globes hovering in alleyways or behind signs. Was she on the broadcast now? Was the net still working? Or were tiger eyes watching through the lenses?

The animals that flanked her were not any of 'her' tigers, the quartet that had shared her home in Bundastrasse for the last two years. They trotted right down the centre of the road, paws padding on the asphalt. It was drizzling. They had let her bring her coat, but not an umbrella.

They had waited for over an hour before herding her out of the house. More and more tigers arrived, filling up the entire bottom floor. She had hovered at the top of the stairs. In her study, there was a locked cabinet, with a stunwand inside. But the keys were in her desk drawer. And her desk was an island in an ocean of orange fur.

It was probably for the best. In her initial panic, she could easily have got herself killed trying to fight them. A casual blow from a paw would be enough to do it.

Here and there, Besma saw tigers leading – or dragging – people from their houses. Not every house: most doors stayed safely locked. Occasionally she glimpsed someone peeping out from behind their blinds. But, while Besma was heading for the eastern side of the city, the tigers' new captives were heading west. Where were they being taken? Where was she being taken?

The tigers stalked on, silently, slow enough for her to keep pace. They were both adults – she had seen no young, no sub-adults, no older tigers in the flood of creatures that had poured into the city. Just bulky, healthy males and females in their prime.

Besma racked her brain for any memory, any hint that the tigers had begun to display signs of organised intelligence. Did their

50

brainpower increase through the life cycle? Or had some event, some biological change, suddenly switched their thought processes into a new state? Could it even have been her experiments, her efforts to teach them language, that had somehow caused the change?

Or was this simply some complex instinctive behaviour – something stirred up by the changing weather? Besma knew how easy it was to read sentience into the actions of animals. But how could such behaviour ever have evolved here?

Nothing but questions, nothing but questions. Who were the people they were rounding up? Why? What did they think of her? Had she treated them well, better than other humans? Or did they count her as one of their enemies, as patronising, as exploitative? Did they have any memories of the first human beings to come to their world, the big-game hunters, the specimen collectors?

She *mustn't* anthropomorphise them. The human mind wants to see itself in everything – but a dolphin smiles because its mouth is shaped that way, not because it's happy. She had spent two years of research on the tigers, carefully filtering her observations, looking for real intelligence, not trial-and-error success or mindless imitation.

Perhaps she had been trying so hard not to see minds that weren't there that she hadn't seen minds that *were* there. She had the sudden wish that her husband was with her, so she could make him stick that in his pipe and smoke it. Confronted by tests that would give them away, were the tigers smart enough to play dumb?

There was one fact to hold on to. They were not aggressive. Only a male guarding the nest showed aggression. But she had seen them kill. She had captured the moment with her hologram camera, as they streaked after their prey, bringing down the giant birds in a tangle of limbs or wings. Like the predators of Earth, they did not need to kill their meal at once: just keep it still enough to eat. More than once she had seen them begin to devour the legs of a bird while the head still struggled for life.

Besma found herself stumbling, her legs shaking with the effort

51

to hold herself up. One of the tigers reached out and caught her, six fingers clamping down on to her shoulder. It lifted her, easily, until she was back on her feet. And they marched on.

Karl was slumped on a tiled sculpture of a sofa, huddling inside his coat. On the lapel, the clock hands moved slowly forward. He hunched forward, elbows on his knees, forehead on his hands, trying to make himself as small as possible.

The plaza had been efficiently turned into a cage. It was ringed with crowd-control barriers and tigers. From time to time, one of the animals would usher another human being past the barricades and into the slowly growing group. They stood in small knots, murmuring, or stood alone, paralysed with fright. The animals of the silent merry-go-round watched them, yellow eyes behind wire mesh.

He recognised a lot of the faces, although he couldn't put names to all of them. There were several teachers from the Academy, colleagues he saw every week. The aristocratic Black woman had been in the newspaper this morning – a visiting conductor. The tigers must be rounding people up from all over the city and bringing them here. But there were only a few dozen people crowded into the plaza. Where was everyone else?

Karl stole a glance at their guards. They were talking to one another, in their own language, a mix of hisses and growls. They weren't animals, he thought. Not any more. Something had happened to the tigers, something that had changed them from lazy beasts, background detail, to an invading army.

The news of the invasion would take some days to reach Earth, and Karl's sister and cousins.

When would the news get out? If the tigers had cut off communications, it might not be until a ship tried to land. Karl had no real idea what the ships' schedule was. Or did they even have a schedule? Space exploration probably wasn't run like the buses. It might be months before the next lot of visitors noticed anything amiss.

For the first time since the day he had arrived on Hitchemus,

Karl felt the stomach-dropping knowledge of just how distant and alone they were. A tiny, unimportant dot, near the edge of human space.

Doctor, he thought.

The thing he wanted most was for the Doctor to be sitting next to him on this cold concrete seat. He wanted it so much, for that one moment, that it was almost hallucinatory, as though the violinist were right beside him.

Where are you, Doctor? Are you caught up in this terror, or have you already hitched your ride to the next planet? Are you laughing at us? Will I ever see you again?

No. Make it a statement. Kill hope, now, forget the future, get through this moment, then the next. I will never see you again.

Karl tried to relax his body, clenched like a fist. One of the tigers was striding across the plaza. His eyes locked on the movement. He had never really looked at them before, he thought; never noticed their easy slouch, the way their muscular shoulders pumped. Its stripes seemed to ripple across its skin as it moved, like text flickering across a page.

The tiger was looking at him. Not near him – right at him, meeting his stare with its big yellow eyes. Karl looked away, sharply. But it was coming closer, crossing the paved area, zeroing in on him.

He started to get off of the bench, then forced down his panic, forced himself to stay sitting. If you look frightened, he told himself, you'll look like *prey*.

The tiger sat down in front of him. Its head was almost as high as his. He kept his gaze down, submissive, but glancing up at it so that it knew he wasn't ignoring it. Could they understand his body language? What was going on behind those yolk-coloured eyes?

'Hullow,' barked the tiger.

'Hello,' Karl gasped.

'Eye yem Geff Ree!' growled the tiger. Karl stared at it in confusion. 'Geff Ree, Geff Ree.'

'Jeoffry?' said the composer, at last. 'That's your name?'

The tiger bobbed its head up and down in imitation of a nod. Karl knew that some people gave the tigers nicknames. He grinned, then decided it was better not to show his teeth, and turned it into what he hoped looked like a friendly smile.

Then, suddenly, Jeoffry was rearing up, its paws coming down on the bench on either side of Karl. Its mighty arms pinned him on either side as it brought its face up to his. Its mouth was full of tiny shark teeth, pointing inwards.

'Each violence,' said Jeoffry.

Karl heard frightened people, somewhere behind the animal. All he could see was that immense mouth. Its breath was fogging up his glasses. 'Each,' enunciated Jeoffry patiently. 'Violence.'

'I'm sorry,' stammered Karl. 'So sorry. I can't understand what you're saying.'

The tiger let him go, flowing backwards until it was sitting on the ground at his feet. Karl could not control the shudder that racked his body. He grabbed his own arms, holding himself in, trying to keep his teeth from chattering.

Jeoffry turned and hissed at one of the other tigers. It strode towards them. Keep calm, keep still. They're not going to kill you, they want something from you. Unless you can't give it to them. What do they want? Can they even tell us apart? Have they perhaps mistaken me for someone important?

The other tiger was carrying something in its mouth. As it got closer, Karl was shocked to recognise a violin and a bow in the monster's jaws.

The tiger laid its head in Karl's lap and opened its mouth. The instrument landed on his knees, undamaged.

'Dear God,' said Karl. 'You want me to teach you, don't you? Of all the things – you want me to teach you how to play the violin.'

Jeoffry rolled its immense eyes. 'Each violence, *stupid*.'

The other tiger reached up and ran a rough paw over Karl's head, stroking his hair. 'Kitty kitty,' it said.

Besma sat on damp stone between two tigers. The open-air amphitheatre was half filled by a frightened crowd, maybe a hundred people. A loose scattering of tigers was enough to keep everyone still and quiet.

Many of the humans were clutching hemp shopping bags. Some had kids, generally held in a fierce grip while the children stared goggle-eyed at the animals. Couples held hands, fiercely. A few couldn't stop trying the phones sewn into their sleeves or collars, unable to believe they wouldn't suddenly start working. The net was down, then.

Besma guessed that anyone who hadn't locked themselves away had been brought here, anybody the tigers found on the street. An entire marching band had become a frightened cluster near the stage.

None of the tigers had weapons. That had to mean something. Were they smart enough to work out how to use them? Could tiger paws manipulate a device built for human hands? Besma kneaded her own hands together, agitated. She had never been able to teach them to use simple tools; they would not even push a ball along with a broom. But their hands were *more* flexible than human hands. With their new intelligence, anything was possible.

She had been sitting there for about half an hour when someone came out on to the stage. The whispering and weeping fell into silence.

It was a huge male, almost four metres long. His face was oval, with a pointed snout. His short neck and wide shoulders made him look like an orange wall. The wooden stage thudded as he strode across it to the podium. Besma saw that he had a device slung around his neck on a plastic strap, a broad purple disc. It was a vocoder – she had considered using them in her research, to clarify the tigers' rough speech.

The bulky male picked up the music stand in a huge paw and dropped it into the orchestra pit with a clatter that made everyone gasp and jump.

'CALL ME BIG,' bellowed the tiger.

A ripple went through the audience. A man half stifled a groan of fear, burying his face in his hands. The woman sitting next to him put an arm around his shoulders.

Big adjusted the volume on his vocoder. 'Better?' he said, voice booming around the amphitheatre from a dozen miniature speakers. 'Better. Call me Big. I speak for the tigers.'

The audience was stony silent, gaping at the talking animal. He turned his head as he spoke, making eye contact.

'We have control of the entire colony. That includes power, water and the spaceport. You have no way of contacting other humans on other planets. Your government and laws are suspended.

'We want your culture. We want to add everything you know about music to everything we know.

'We're not interested in your machines, or your art or literature, not for now.' The other group, thought Besma. The ones the tigers had taken from their houses. Musicians? Teachers? 'You can continue going about your ordinary business, under guard – except for the spaceport and the net, which are off limits to humans as of now. And except for certain people, including your Waytes, who will be kept under house arrest. We have killed as few humans as possible, and we'd like to keep it that way.'

There were little gasps and sobs. Who had been killed? Most probably some of the Waytes, thought Besma, hopelessly trying to defend the city.

Big went on, 'We know some of you are going to try to fight us. We'll kill the ones that do. That will be a waste, because you can't win. We've been planning this for a long time, and everything is going right.'

Big coughed and squinted, as though trying to think of anything else he needed to say. 'There will be a meeting like this every day, but not always at the same time. If you have any questions, you can ask them then.'

'Oh, God.' Besma said it out loud. She couldn't help herself. 'Oh, God. They haven't become intelligent. Nothing has changed. They were like this all along. Nothing has changed.' Her voice had turned into a hollow moan. She stuffed her face into her hands, trying to muffle it. 'They were like this all along.'

A man was on his feet, swaying. 'Too bloody right we'll fight you!' he screamed. The people around him inched away, their eyes locked on the grinning tigers nearby. 'We'll kill you all! The lot of you!'

Big turned his heavy head, and hissed and growled a stream of syllables at a tiger standing at the side of the audience. It bounded up into the stone seats, padding towards the shouting man. He sat down, hard.

'God, please!' someone cried. 'Don't kill him!'

The tiger caught the drunk man's lapels in its six-fingered hands and shoved its shaggy face into his. 'Shut up,' it told him.

Incredibly, the man grabbed hold of the tiger, as though he were trying to wrestle with it. Besma buried her face again. She didn't want to see what happened next.

There was a mighty trumpet blast, like a fanfare. It tripped up and down several notes and ended in a raspberry.

Something heavy flew up on to the stage, rolling across the wood. There was a soft whoomph, and multicoloured smoke began to pour from it.

Besma leapt to her feet. But one of the tigers sitting beside her caught her arm, pulling her back into her seat.

The speakers squealed, and suddenly began to gush Mozart, painfully loud:

> *Se vuol ballare,*
> *Signor Contino,*
> *Il chitarrino*
> *Le suonerò...*

Big roared orders from the stage. The tigers ran back and forth in the rainbow smoke, coughing and sneezing, looking for the source of the noise, grimacing with anger. A tiger poked its head out from behind the curtains and growled something at Big. Another ran out, lost its footing on the smooth wood of the stage, and slid several metres, spinning slowly. Besma laughed, a strangled hiccup, biting her fingers to stifle the sound. Around her, other people were hiding smiles.

'*Saprò!*' sang the tenor. '*Saprò! Saprò! Saprò! Saprò, ma piano…*' The music faded to nothing.

'Ladies and gentlemen,' said a man clearly. 'This is the voice of the Movement. Things are not quite so under control as our furry friends would like to think. If they want to dance, we'll teach them how.'

There was another squawk. A tiger appeared from the wings, dragging wires and circuits in its jaws. Besma covered her mouth with her hand so her guards couldn't see her smile. For just a moment, she hadn't been afraid.

The Doctor stood in the centre of the recording studio with everyone's attention and a hair-raising grin. He had changed into work clothes, dark slacks and pullover, with his hair tied back in a businesslike ponytail.

The studio was three floors below ground level, large enough to hold a marching band. Now it held Anji, and Fitz and the Doctor, and two dozen Hitchemians. Chairs and music stands had been pushed to the walls to make room for the newly formed Movement.

They were ordinary citizens: shopkeepers and buskers. The tigers had surrounded the Waytes station and locked all the colony's police in, and were keeping the town council in its chambers. The twin flautists from Fitz's band were there, Ann (with the electric-orange hair) and Maria (without it), sitting on a crate of canned food. Kareem the violist had taken one look at the Doctor and shaken his head, half smiling, as if to say, 'Never mind all that now.' They were frightened but determined, grateful for these odd foreigners who seemed used to this sort of situation.

While Fitz hurried around carrying chairs, still pumped from the raid, Anji picked up her blipboard and worked her way through the new arrivals, blipping in details: names, contact info, who could contribute what. She could feel briskness in her steps again, she thought – the old hurrying-across-the-office rhythm, the excitement of keeping pace with a crisis you knew you could manage. Being able to pull something useful out of a pile of scattered facts.

A single sharp handclap. Everyone stopped and turned.

'*Now* then,' said the Doctor, rubbing his hands together. 'Let's take stock. What have we accomplished? We've got the word out now. Shown that the tigers aren't in complete control of the colony – good job on the smoke effects, Fitz.' She saw a grin peek out of Fitz's face. 'Now, next move. How many people found us through the message hidden in our broadcast?' About two-thirds of those present raised their hands. 'Good. We'll need to reinforce it. Rebroadcast. Arrange more performances, clue more people in. Other resources?'

Fitz reported, 'We've kept a bunch of vehicles out of the tigers' hands. Paws. Whatever. Six hovercars and twelve trucks are locked up in the underground garage. And you'll like this – the tigers are too big to use them. They can't fit in the seats.'

The Doctor paced. 'What about the hostages?'

Anji said, 'We've sent two hovercars out to look for them.' The Doctor nodded, agitated. 'The net is still down, and I think the tigers are going to keep it that way. They don't seem to be interested in communicating over a distance.'

Ann piped up. 'If it's down, can we talk to the hovercars?'

Anji nodded. 'Yes – by old-fashioned radio.' A sort of ripple went through the little group: of-course-why-didn't-we-think-of-that? 'We dug up a few transmitters from the museum. We're using coded broadcasts, just in case the tigers find a way to listen in.'

'Broadcasts,' the Doctor blurted. He pressed his hands to his forehead, moulding the thought into shape. 'Got to get a message out. Off planet.'

Kareem pulled a face. 'We need all the help we can get.'

The Doctor turned sharply to look at him. 'There's plenty of help we *don't* need.'

'Even so,' said Anji carefully, 'contacting the outside world has got to be a priority.' With a faintly irritated twitch at the corner of her mouth, she set about rearranging her notes on the blipboard; if the Doctor wasn't going to work through things in a sensible order, she'd have to be sure to bodily drag the conversation back there later. 'Where's the nearest source of help?'

'Chi Bootis,' said Ajamu Quick. He was a well-dressed Black man with greying hair, the manager of a coffee house in the Bundastrasse. 'There's a military base there. I guess it's about four days away.'

'That's close,' said the Doctor. 'We're lucky. But we're still going to have to rely on ourselves.' He set off on another sharp angle, his fingers drumming a tattoo in the air. 'Planetary defences, planetary defences...'

'They're useless, mate,' said Kareem. 'Even if we could contact the satellites, they're designed to prevent attacks from outside, not inside.'

'Send a *signal* through them,' the Doctor insisted, hopping from foot to foot with impatience.

'With the net down, we can't even talk to them,' said Quick, 'or any of the other satellites. We're completely cut off.'

Fitz said, 'So when is the next ship due to arrive?'

'With the net down, again, there's no way to find out,' said Quick.

'Wait,' said Ann. 'Aren't there separate systems for the spaceport? Could we find out there?'

The Doctor clapped his hands. 'And perhaps get a message out as well,' he said. 'All right. So there are two jobs to do, for a start: find and rescue the hostages, and get into the spaceport.'

'The tigers weren't just rounding people up at random, were they?' said Ann. 'From what people are saying, it's just the music teachers that are gone.'

'What about Dr Grieve?' said Anji.

'I think she's being kept under house arrest,' said Kareem. 'I saw a couple of tigers escorting her to the meeting in the theatre.'

Fitz said, 'That's good – at least we know where she is.'

'We'll need her help,' said the Doctor. 'Especially for our third job: negotiate with the tigers.' Another ripple of surprise.

'They've got the upper hand,' said Anji quickly. 'So we talk to them. Do they really just want music lessons? If so, can we offer them a trade? Will they try co-operation instead of conquest?'

'We have to do more than just talk. We can wear them down slowly,' said Quick, 'make it not worth their while to guard the whole city. Or we can persuade them to negotiate by a show of strength.'

The Doctor rubbed his chin thoughtfully. 'Or by convincing them that one is on the way – from Chi Bootis, perhaps. If they know we've got a message out, they'll be more open to a peaceful solution.'

'Do we want a peaceful solution?' Quick asked seriously. 'They've torn people apart in the streets! For all we know, those hostages are dead.'

The Doctor raised his arms, as if to ward off Quick's points. 'The last thing we're going to do is escalate the situation,' he insisted. 'That will only get more people killed. Patience, Mr Quick. Patience.'

Anji said, 'As far as we know, they've killed six Waytes and two civilians – out of a population of tens of thousands. Their coup relied on speed, surprise and weight of numbers. They're not random murderers, they're strategists.'

Kareem admitted, 'It doesn't make sense for them to kill the hostages. What good is a dead teacher?'

'We don't know what they've got planned,' said Quick. 'We can't let them keep control of the city. A series of short, intense strikes will loosen their grip.'

'Do you have military experience, Mr Quick?' said Anji.

'Training,' admitted Quick. 'I was a quartermaster sergeant in the marines.'

Before the Doctor could say anything, Anji said, 'That could be useful. But isn't our best course of action to persuade the tigers to talk? Any fighting means putting more human lives at risk. We don't even have any weapons, not yet.'

'No,' muttered Kareem. 'The tigers have taken all the guns.'

'What if they see us as an inferior species?' said Quick. 'Not worth talking to?'

'They're not stupid,' said the Doctor. A couple of people

laughed, ruefully. 'They'll know what's in their best interest. Besides, it's their planet.'

His audience was shocked. Anji stepped in again. 'There's every chance they see us as the invaders. Offer them genuine co-operation, and the whole picture changes.'

'Chi Bootis might have different ideas,' said Kareem.

A computer screen opened up in the air. It hung there, a crackling green and black rectangle, marking an incoming radio transmission. 'Superfly four here. The band on the run has been located. Repeat, the band on the run has been located. I estimate fifty, er, band members, and ten Felix, repeat, estimate ten Felix. Co-ordinates follow.'

The Doctor's shoulders lost about a third of their tension. 'My gods,' said Maria. 'They're alive. They're still alive.'

Fitz grinned. 'There's method to their madness after all.'

The Doctor opened another screen, bringing up a map of the area, and marked the co-ordinates with a red dot. Quick said, 'They're heading for the Bewilderness. How fast can tigers go?'

'Well, not any faster than their hostages can walk,' said Fitz.

'Of course!' said the Doctor. 'Excellent, Fitz. They've only been travelling for an hour or so. We can catch them up.'

'In that open terrain, they'll see the hovercars coming,' said Ann.

Anji suddenly grinned, looking at one of the notes on her blipboard. 'I've got an idea,' she said.

'I want those hostages back,' growled the Doctor. 'Let's go and get them.'

The rain trickled, unending, blowing around in the bad-tempered wind. Not all of the captives were adequately dressed for the weather. They huddled together, sometimes walking hand in hand, sometimes leaning on one another.

Karl glanced back over his shoulder. They were marching across the wide olive-drab plain to the west of the city. The buildings were distant and vague, like a mirage. They were at the edge of the area the colonists called the Bewilderness, for the number of people who had got lost here.

He estimated there were sixty human beings in the group. Twelve tigers formed a loose circle around them. The tigers didn't seem to mind when they whispered among themselves, compared notes. They were all music teachers, mostly from the Academy, enough of them to form a small orchestra. There were no singing teachers. Karl tried to imagine an opera of tigers, and failed.

Each of them had been singled out, brought from home or class to the plaza. The tigers' efficiency was terrifying. They had known exactly who they wanted. It took them only a few hours to finish rounding up the teachers. In that time, Karl had seen no real signs of human resistance. Distant sirens and shouting, some shots, a lot of growling. There was no reason to believe that the tigers were not now in control of the entire colony.

Except perhaps one. An hour ago, Karl was certain he'd heard a hovercar somewhere above them, hidden by the clouds. The other musicians had turned their faces to the sky, squinting into the rain. He'd wanted to shout, don't give them away, you fools. He trudged on, pretending he hadn't heard a thing.

The ground began to ripple in a series of gentle downs. Karl glanced around at the creatures striding beside their human herd. Surely these animals were in the employ of some other creature. Invaders programming the local wildlife as shock troops? Shock troops who wanted to learn how to play the violin? However the tigers had suddenly become intelligent, it would be a mistake to underestimate them.

Why were they being moved to the Bewilderness? If they had taken the city, why not stay there? My God, thought Karl, how many of them are there out here? Do they have a city of their own? An invisible city of tigers?

Without warning, a voice boomed out across the plain. 'Let's teach them to dance!'

The march stopped on the spot. Musicians and tigers alike whirled in confusion, looking for the source of the shout. There was a pounding, distant kettledrums echoing around them.

The riders swarmed over a rise in the ground, seeming to come out of nowhere, horses breaking the surface of the grass like sea creatures coming up for air. There were a dozen of them, all carrying long rifles.

Two of the tigers broke their paralysis and charged the riders. Horses reared and wheeled, leaping over the big cats, and still the riders came on.

A tiger near Karl snarled explosively. There was a great dart in its shoulder, a metallic length tipped by a puff of red fibres.

Karl froze, staring at the leader of the riders. The Doctor – that was the Doctor, all in black, astride a tremendous black horse. Karl's heart thudded. The Doctor's hair streamed out behind him as he thundered across the wet plain, seemingly merged with the horse, a dark centaur roaring down to save them.

As Karl watched, the Doctor charged a cluster of tigers, scattering them. Musicians fled through the gap to the safety of the other horses. One of the Doctor's riders threw something into the grass. Instantly, a great river of smoke began to stream across the grass, obscuring half the travellers.

The horses were everywhere. Riders were grabbing musicians and hauling them up on to the steeds the best they could. Darts were whizzing through the air, landing in flanks and limbs. Tigers roared in distress as they lost the ability even to stand. They lay, eyes open, panting on the grass.

Musicians darted back and forth, trying to get past their guards. Karl turned from side to side, peering through the smoke, watching for his chance to make a break for it. The Doctor was a shadow in the centre of the smoke, the heart of it all. Karl caught a glimpse of Anji, reins gripped in her hands, dodging tigers.

A snarling tiger leapt up on to one of the horses as it pounded past, bringing horse and rider down in a shrieking mass of limbs. The tiger raked the horse's belly, tearing it open as the human tried to get free of the flailing, screaming mount. Karl shouted as the tiger sprang on to the human, catching her neck in its mouth. Her arms and legs thrashed in panic, and then she was hanging limp. The tiger dragged her body into the smoke like a bloody side of meat.

'Karl!'

The Doctor was riding right for him, hand outstretched, ready to drag him up on to the horse and away. A tiger bounded in front of him, but the Doctor tugged on the reins and his horse leapt the startled creature as it ducked, covering its head with its arms. Karl laughed and reached out his hands.

An immense weight slammed into Karl's back, hard and hefty as a battering ram, crushing him to the ground. He couldn't help crying out, flinching helplessly down with his face in the grass and the mud, scrabbling uselessly to get away from the killing bite.

It didn't come. He tried to push up from the ground, to get his mouth and eyes out of the water, gulping breath. He was completely covered by the furry mass.

It held him there for what must have been ten endless seconds. Then it gripped him in its powerful six-fingered hands and dragged him up to his knees, one orange arm closing across his chest like a seatbelt.

Karl wiped at his face, scraping mud and hair out of his eyes until he could see.

The riders were standing well back, away from the tight circle of tigers, a muscular fence ringing in their captives. Karl and the tiger on his back were at the centre of the circle. He could see a handful of escaped humans, protected behind the riders.

The Doctor's eyes were fixed on Karl. The composer realised, suddenly, that he was the reason the rescue attempt had halted. He was their hostage. While his life was threatened, the Doctor wouldn't risk another charge.

Karl rubbed at his eyes. The bitter smoke and the filth had got into them, but he knew he was also weeping with relief and gratitude.

The Doctor said something to the other riders, and they began to back away, pulling the rescued teachers up on to their horses.

'Let your hostages go,' called the Doctor. 'Sit down and talk with us.'

One of the tigers reared up and spat out a string of sounds, words in the coarse tiger language.

'We want to hear your demands,' replied the Doctor. 'But not while you have prisoners.' My God, thought Karl, he can understand what they're saying!

More growls. The tiger put a heavy paw on the body of its companion, two of the metal darts protruding from its side. 'They're unharmed,' the Doctor promised. 'They'll wake up in a few minutes.'

The Doctor listened to the tiger's reply. His eyes met Karl's. The composer felt the tiger's grip on his chest tighten.

'I'll be back for you,' shouted the Doctor. 'We'll be back. For all of you!'

The horses wheeled, suddenly, and vanished over the low hill.

Karl dropped to his hands and knees as the tiger released him. Two of the other captives helped him up.

The tigers looked at one another, exchanging a few words in their secret language. Then they fell on the corpses of the horse and the slaughtered woman. The musicians moaned and screamed and threw up. But none of them ran.

Chapter Five

The empty theatre was deadly quiet. Fitz was alone in a workroom, making his armour.

He had opened up four screens on the wall. Each showed a different area of the theatre – the stage, the stage door, the front of house and a high view behind the scenes. He looked up constantly from the suit of armour, glancing from one screen to the next. The flying cameras were one of the first things they'd grabbed, pinching a whole vanful of them. There was probably some way to set them to detect motion, setting off an alarm or something, but he had no idea how. It was enough that he could see there were no tigers sneaking around the place.

He had cut out long rectangles of foam, one for each arm, one for each leg, and a big one for his body with a hole in the middle for his head. For the helmet he was going to use an actual helmet he had found in the props department, made out of plastic or something, light but hard. It had a visor like a cage door which you could pull down and lock. It also had little wings on it. Fitz suspected it was meant for a Valkyrie. Oh, well.

A bit of a rummage had turned up sheets of the plastic and a propmaster's toolkit. After some fumbling around, he had worked out how to glue the tough plastic to the foam, and then glue the foam to the arms and legs of a jacket and trousers he pinched from the costume department. They were a bit small for him, but the armour needed to be snug.

Hell, he'd been stuck here four hours, and there wasn't anything else to do. He'd already run out of smokes.

Only a few people had turned up in that time. He'd seen them on the monitors first, as they looked around the theatre, nervously, wondering if they'd understood right. He let them get into the rehearsal hall itself, making sure no furry friends were following them, before he came out of the workshop and said hello, yes, you've found the Movement.

A banner outside the hall advertised just what was being rehearsed in there. The Doctor had hoped people would recognise the music played at the tigers' public meeting. It was Mozart, the Doctor explained, an opera. Sung by a servant who's going to get his own back on his scheming master. Right, mate, said the song, if you want to dance, I can give you some lessons. Even if they didn't pick up on the lyrics, they'd be looking for a production of *The Marriage of Figaro*. A member of the Movement would be present at the theatre, waiting to welcome them. And it was working – a joke the tigers hadn't understood, but that a slow trickle of humans had got.

A digital clock in one of the screens showed the time. Fitz was about due to be relieved, but he wanted to get the armour finished first.

He slid on the trousers. The plastic clanked, flapping where he hadn't used enough glue. The top part was more difficult, the stiff rolls of foam around his midriff and arms refusing to give as he pushed and pulled and grunted. In the end he pulled the damn thing off again and sawed it right down the front, adding a series of belts to the mess. That way he could put it on like a shirt, and then fasten the half-dozen buckles on the right side.

He stood in front of the mirror. The suit looked as bulky and awkward as it felt, but he was pretty much covered all over in tough foam and tougher plastic. He eased the helmet on, trying not to let it pull his squiggly hair.

'Oh my God!' said a voice from the doorway. 'What's that?'

Fitz spun from the mirror, staring. It was Anji, a cheeky grin on her face, one fine eyebrow raised. She had a soprano with her, one of those tall and skinny girls from Lvan with the white hair.

Fitz waved his arms, awkwardly. 'Do I look tigerproof?'

'You look like a demented Asterix.'

'Thanks.'

'I suppose this means you're ready for our big rescue operation.'

'I suppose so,' said Fitz. 'The twins got that car ready?' She nodded.

The soprano grinned at Fitz as he sat down in front of the

screens. Fitz shook the girl's hand. 'Well, good luck,' he said.

'You, too,' she fluted. 'You might want to wear gloves with that lot, mate.'

'Shaggity shag.' He peered at Anji through the visor. 'Gimme a minute to look for some.'

The Doctor moved soundlessly through the forest. Small creatures skittered away underfoot, startled by his approach. The wind made a harsh noise as it waved the feather-duster trees, like someone playing a distant washboard.

He was completely alone. The tigers were in the city, or in the spaceport, or in their homes in the Bewilderness to the west. They had left no guards in case a lone spy walked south through the trees to the rim of the spaceport.

The circular shape of the port was becoming visible through the trees, a gap in the landscape. The forest sloped gently down and ended, suddenly, about a quarter of a kilometre from the edge of the circular tarmac. Among the last of the trees, the Doctor lay down in the leaf litter and took out his binoculars.

Every world's soil had its own scent. You could tell you were on Earth just by that characteristic tang of actinomycetes. Here the loam had more of a woody, vaguely smoky scent. After he had been trapped so long on Earth, the universe was like a spice shop with laden shelves.

The port that gave Port Any its name was a great black circle, two kilometres across. The big ships had to land, he realised, rather than send down shuttles or use T-mat – it was a primitive design, even for its time. Two great curved buildings faced each other across the landing site: on the east side, maintenance sheds; on the west side, closest to the city, the terminal building. He had emerged from the forest on its western side, not far from Aerospace Traffic Control, an open-plan office in the southern end of the terminal.

The binocs had been volunteered by one of the Movement. The Doctor had made one or two adjustments of his own to make them more useful. He slid the spectacles with their green lenses on to his nose, and instantly his view of the spaceport changed. A heads-up menu let him shift wavelengths and magnifications at the flick of an eyelid.

It took a few tries to find what he was looking for, superimposing different views as he built up a picture of the terminal's insides. He zoomed in on a collection of moving shapes, towards the near end of the big building. The tigers hadn't kept hostages at the terminal, but they'd obviously left guards.

The Doctor took off the binocs and rubbed the bridge of his nose. With the net down, the Movement couldn't break into the spaceport computers at a distance, and they couldn't communicate except by fleeting, coded radio messages. More ominously, he thought, they couldn't collect data from the weather-watch satellites. A storm was brewing, a big one: there was a hint of salt in the air, the taste of huge waves crashing against the shores of the inland sea, hundreds of kilometres away.

He took the miniature radio from his coat pocket and murmured into it. 'The target is free. Repeat, the target is free. Estimate a dozen Felix, all indoors and south.'

The Doctor waited.

The hovercars seemed to come out of nowhere, shooting over the landscape, pushed to their top speeds. They began to descend in front of the terminal building, outside the sheds where hovercars-for-hire were kept.

The Doctor saw flashes of orange against the black of the tarmac. He slid the binocs back on. Tigers were leaping from the building to meet the hovercars, some of them armed with stunwands and shockguns from the Waytes' armoury. But the hovercars didn't land, dodging and twirling above the creatures' heads. One or two of the tigers took pot shots at them. Safari in reverse, thought the Doctor. They weren't practised enough with the weapons to do any damage.

Under cover of the distraction, a group of Movement members were running from the trees behind the ATC building. He had given them lists of instructions in case he wasn't there for some crucial operation.

He pushed himself up, brushing dirt and leaves from his coat. Time to join them.

The Doctor froze. There was something nearby.

There – footfalls in the undergrowth. It was most likely one of the flightless birdlike creatures that the tigers fed on, rummaging for edible fungus among the tree roots. A shape emerged from the trunks.

His eyes widened. It was one of the older tigers, the previous generation, its coat faded to a yellowish orange. Even so it was a flash of fire in the dim green forest. Despite its age it was huge, as big and bulky as a good-sized pony. It had probably been padding after him all this time, following his scent through the trees.

Lime eyes locked on him.

'Can you help me?' the Doctor called. He raised his hands, hoping it would recognise the gesture as surrender and not as a threat. 'I ran away from the city, and now I'm lost. I don't mean any harm.'

The tiger stared at him blankly, as though the telepathic trick of language translation had failed. 'Can you understand me?' said the Doctor. The tiger didn't respond.

The Doctor took a deep breath. Whatever had affected the young tigers, it hadn't touched the minds of their parents. He was facing a beast.

The tiger opened its mouth, flashing its shark teeth in a silent roar. Then it charged him.

The Doctor stood his ground as the creature pounded down the slope, sending a cloud of tiny flying creatures exploding up from the leaf litter, their bodies glittering around the golden shape of the monster.

He waited until it was about five metres away. Then he raised his arms over his head and shouted at the top of his lungs, 'Back off! Back right off!'

The tiger's charge faltered, slowed. It was close enough to spring. Instead it looked at him, puzzled.

The Doctor began to back away, in slow, measured, confident steps. If he bolted, the tiger would know at once what to do with

71

him. His chances of outrunning even an aged predator were slim.

He emerged from the trees, turning slowly to face away from the tiger. He hoped it would prefer to stay under cover, but it followed him right out into the grassy area between forest and tarmac. It stayed close, ambling, well aware he had nowhere to go. He knew it wouldn't let him get to the asphalt, with its unnatural smell and texture.

The Doctor started to run.

He heard the tiger break into a surprised charge somewhere behind him.

They raced across the grass. The Doctor prayed that the people in the ATC building had spotted him. He prayed his instructions had been clear enough. And suddenly he found himself laughing as he ran, the wind whipping the sound out of his mouth, springing through the grass like a young animal moving for the sheer pleasure of it.

The grass ended. The Doctor dived for the tarmac, into the shadow of the ATC building, rolling over and over on the hot, hard stuff. He came to his knees, panting, facing the tiger.

It leapt for him, claws outstretched.

The air shimmered between them where grass and asphalt met.

The tiger bounced off the force shield with a yelp. It landed and ran at the shield again, ricocheting a second time to roll across the grass in a tangle of limbs. It raised its head, staring at him. The Doctor grinned and waggled his fingers at it.

'Doctor!' called Quick, from a second-storey window.

'Marvellous timing,' called the Doctor.

'Come on up.'

Ann the flautist drove and Maria the flautist navigated. Fitz, wearing his armour, rode in the back with a somewhat squashed Anji. His gloves looked suspiciously like gardening gloves, but they were probably enough to stop a glancing bite or scratch. Well, he thought, we live in hope. He took off his helmet, looking around for somewhere to put it. In the end, Anji had to take it off him and hold it in her lap.

Their plan was dead simple: distract the tigers, grab Besma, and away. First they'd need to suss out the situation, and alert the tigerologist if they could.

Anji poked Fitz's foam-covered arm. 'Do you often do this?' she asked. 'Does it work?'

'What do you expect me to do if one of those buggers comes at me? Whistle famous Beethoven's famous Ninth Symphony?'

'I wish we had weapons,' said Anji. Her fingers drummed on the helmet.

'You know what the Doctor would say. We don't want to make things worse.'

'And getting ourselves or Besma killed isn't making things worse?' Anji's drumming became more agitated. 'We shouldn't be doing this. We're not qualified.'

'Yeah, well if you know any qualified tiger wranglers, bring 'em on. Sometimes you just can't dial 999. You just have to cope by yourself, as best you can.'

'Kreiner and Kapoor,' sighed Anji. 'First aid to the universe.'

Fitz grinned and gave her a thumbs up.

The news camera looked like an eyeball. The metal sphere was opaque on one side, transparent on the other, a yellow-orange disc staring out at the world. It even had a metal eyelid which closed to protect the lens when the camera wasn't in use.

The camera drifted softly down Bundastrasse, keeping low to the ground, until it came to the simple wooden fence that ran along beside Besma's house. Behind the fence was the yard, with its greenhouses and pools. The metal eyeball rolled, taking in its surroundings, looking for an opportunity.

There was a tree in the yard, close to the fence. Like many of the trees around Port Any, it looked less like an oak and more like a feather duster, a thick trunk ending in a burst of immense, fleshy orange leaves.

The camera inched up the fence and then followed the trunk, staying close to the wood, getting a close-up view of rings of yellow spores emerging from their scaly covers. Then it was nestled among the rust-gold leaves. The camera stopped, turning slowly, until it had a clear view of the yard.

A few streets away, Fitz and Anji and the flautists were sitting in their hot-wired hovercar. Port Any was small enough to allow you to walk comfortably from one side to the other in an hour, or cycle if you were in a hurry; the cars were mostly used for cargo, or for expeditions into the wilds. Or when you might need to make a quick getaway.

They'd sent the camera around the neighbourhood first: it was still and empty. A moment's twiddling with the controls turned the windscreen of the car into a transparent screen, displaying the camera's point of view and a row of control icons. They spoke in whispers. 'There's Dr Grieve,' said Anji, as the camera slowly zoomed on a human figure sitting on a chair. 'Good – she's out in the open.'

'She looks all right,' said Ann.

'She doesn't look too happy,' said Fitz. His armour was already itchy and sweaty. 'There must be tigers about.'

'Where *are* the tigers?' said Maria.

Ann touched a control, and the camera slowly panned left and right. The tigers were in the pool, swimming round and round, splashing each other. Another tiger was walking past. The ones in the pool launched themselves across the water, making a wave that shot over the side and drenched the one on the grass.

'They're playing,' whispered Anji.

'Two yellow ones, two orange ones,' counted Fitz.

'They've brought in some of the older tigers,' realised Anji. 'Look at them – the way the orange ones are pushing the yellow ones around.' She was right. The orange ones weren't talking to the older tigers, just butting them with their heads or giving them a gentle shove with hands or feet. 'Maybe whatever has upped the IQs of the orange ones didn't affect their parents.'

'I hope you're right,' said Maria. 'The fewer geniuses we have to deal with, the better.'

'The dumbest tiger can still bite your head off,' said Fitz.

'Hmm. Is there some way we can let Besma know what we're about to do?' said Anji.

'Watch this,' said Ann. She zoomed back in on Grieve's face, then touched the controls. There was a series of dull flashes. Grieve blinked, looking around. She saw the camera hovering in the leaves, and froze.

Fitz had a sudden thought. What if Grieve had gone over to the tigers' side? What if she was behind all this?

But Grieve looked away again, glancing back to the pool. Two of the smart ones were sitting, out of splashing distance, chatting about something.

The exobiologist got out of her folding chair, stretching and yawning. The tigers glanced at her, and went back to their conversation. Grieve slowly strolled over to the tree, leaning on the trunk, as if watching the tigers in the pool.

Ann worked the controls, and the camera drifted down to Grieve's shoulder level, hidden by the trunk.

'I'm OK,' Grieve murmured, barely moving her mouth. Ann turned up the volume. 'There are five tigers here. Three young and two old. Only one is in the house right now.' She coughed, putting a hand over her mouth. 'There's a stunwand. Cabinet in the front room. Key's in the top desk drawer.'

'Handy,' said Maria.

Anji shook her head. 'Never mind that. We need to get her out of there and run for it, as quickly and simply as we can.'

'Why don't we just knock on the front door?' said Fitz.

ATC was a single, long, curved room, with huge windows looking down on to the tarmac. The Doctor could see half a dozen tigers crowded at the edge of the force shield, sitting uncomfortably on the asphalt, looking up at them.

He turned from the window and paced the length of the room. Jaytea and Shellshear were already at work on a pair of terminals, the air around them filled with floating screens. Quick and Kareem were out of the room, scouting the building for weapons, food, anything useful.

The Doctor hovered beside the programmers. 'What do you think?'

Shellshear said, 'The tigers were smart enough to shut everything down. We're going to have to cold-start the systems before we can get the comms working.'

The Doctor drummed his fingers on a console. 'How long?'

'I normally just do programming for the tax office,' sighed Shellshear. 'Give us a couple of hours.'

Quick and Kareem had come back in, carrying a box of stuff. 'In the meantime,' said Quick, 'we're stuck in a cage with the animals on the outside.'

The Doctor went back to the window, looking down at the streak of tigers outside the force shield.

The shield was designed to protect the terminal building in an emergency. Its power source and systems were buried deep below the ground – there was no way the tigers could get to it. On the Doctor's instructions, Jaytea and Shellshear had modified the shape of the field to cut off most of the terminal building.

'You know, Doctor,' said Quick, 'I've been thinking. Would it make more sense to call for help, and then hold out here until the marines arrive?'

The Doctor didn't turn, but he was aware that the seemingly casual remark had got everyone's attention. 'I don't think so, Mr Quick,' he said. 'I mean, you can't keep tranquillising the tigers for ever.'

The café owner hefted one of the rifles. 'We've tripled the strength of the darts,' he said. 'It wasn't hard, a bit of home-made chemistry.'

'What!' said the Doctor. 'At that concentration, a single shot could be lethal.'

'That's the idea,' said Quick. 'We should have done it before the rescue attempt. Face it – this isn't a wildlife documentary. We're fighting for our lives.'

The Doctor breathed out a hard sigh. He said, 'The longer we delay here, the more likely it is that the tigers will find some way to make us lower the shield.'

'I thought you said there was no way they could shut it down,' said Kareem.

'There isn't,' said the Doctor. 'But what if they threaten hostages? Or find more ways of interfering with the computers?'

'That's just what I'm saying,' said Quick. 'We have to make them let the colonists go, now.' He stood next to the Doctor, looking down at their orange audience. 'It's not fair we should suffer. None of us were even here when the colony was settled. It's not our fault if the tigers suddenly became smart.'

'Maybe they haven't.' The Doctor loomed in Quick's face. 'Maybe they always were this smart. Maybe they've been playing possum ever since the colony started. Hiding their strength from the people who came after their parents with guns and darts and dissection kits.'

'You can't blame us for that, either. Not one colonist alive today was born when the first colonists encountered the tigers!'

'You're always talking about blame. Why don't you start talking about solutions instead?'

'Um,' said Shellshear. 'We have a problem.'

Quick turned around. The programmer said, 'The system software is gone.'

'Gone?' said Quick. 'How could they know enough about computers to do that?'

'It looks like they pulled out the physical module,' said Shellshear. 'It's not going to take a couple of hours to signal Chi Bootis. More like a couple of weeks.'

'Can we hold out that long?'

'We've got to,' said Quick. 'Without military backup, we've got nothing. Nothing.'

Jaytea was looking around, puzzled. 'Where did the Doctor go?' he said.

The decoy was simple enough, an old trick of the Doctor's. Ann crept up to the house, while Maria kept an eye on things through the camera. Ann glanced at her watch, said a silent prayer, and hurled an armful of primed fireworks over the fence.

There was an impressive flash and crash and sparkle in the back yard, followed by a lot of yowling and hissing.

A second later, Fitz stuck a crowbar between door and doorjamb and, with a groan of effort, cracked the house open. Anji ran inside brandishing a dart gun, with Fitz lumbering behind in his armour. In the past hour they'd watched as one of the young tigers and one of the old had departed together. That left two young, one old, all of them in the house. The decoy was working: two of the remaining tigers had run to the back yard to see what was going on.

Grieve was there, in the living room. 'Besma! Quick! This way!' shouted Anji.

Something came up over the sofa. The instant she saw orange, Anji lifted her dart gun and let fly. Tiddles ducked, and the first dart went over her shoulder.

Besma bolted from the room. 'Wait!' shouted Fitz.

Anji fired again, wildly, the dart clattering down the wall. Tiddles bounded over the sofa, knocked over the coffee table, and removed the gun from Anji's hand with a single bruising swat. Anji stumbled back, getting an armchair between herself and the angry animal. Fitz leapt for the gun, stumbling in his armour. This was *not* supposed to be happening.

'Besma!' screamed Anji. 'Out the front door, *now*!'

Tiddles leapt up on the chair, back arching, and aimed another swipe at Anji's head. She felt the air move as the fierce hand missed her face by inches. The wall was behind her; there was nowhere to go.

Fitz thumped Tiddles's arse with the butt of the rifle. Anji dived, landing hard behind the sofa, knocking the breath out of herself. She popped up, wanting absolutely nothing except to get back out through the front door. Fitz was turning the gun, trying to point the business end at the big cat, but Tiddles kicked backwards like a mule and sent him rolling across the floor, colliding with the fallen coffee table.

Tiddles came at Anji again, but Besma was suddenly in between them. She held a long, clear rod with a black grip and what looked like blue wires around the tip.

Besma waved her magic wand and brushed it against Tiddles's

78

chest as she came at her. Sparks flew, and there was a puff of the smell of burning fur. The tigress yowled and backed up. The door to the yard was still open. Before she knew what she was doing, Anji was running for it.

Roo had pinned Fitz to the carpet. He struggled uselessly underneath the tiger's bulk. It wasn't even *trying* to hold him down: its sheer weight was enough to keep him there while it bit and scratched at his improvised armour, looking for a way in.

'Shit!' yelled Fitz, and 'Argh!' and 'I could use some help in here!' But no one came.

Roo was sitting up, looking around. Nice kitty, though Fitz, maybe it'll get bored and go and pick on someone else. Or maybe it's looking for a can opener.

The Doctor said they should negotiate. Staring up at the tiger's jaws, Fitz didn't like his chances. 'Er,' he said. 'Do you want to talk about this?'

Roo glanced down at him. Fitz went on, 'I know you're probably pretty pissed off about your planet being taken over, and everything. But I don't think the folks here realised you were, you know, people. I'm just a tourist, myself,' he added hastily, 'just passing through. Anyway, why fight over a silly mistake?' He grinned weakly inside the helmet. 'Let's be friends.'

Roo snorted and started undoing the buckles on his armour.

It was cool inside the force shield. The dark tarmac was warm underfoot with the stored heat of the sun, but the shield blocked a good chunk of solar radiation. Luckily, it also kept the wind out.

The tigers were sitting a little distance from the edge of the force shield. As he walked closer to the wall of energy, the Doctor's hair and skin began to prickle. The shield was invisible to human eyes, but to him it was a swimming shimmer of hot violet motes.

He put his hands in his pockets. 'I'm going talk to you,' he said. The tigers looked at one another, puzzled. It was such a human gesture that the Doctor almost wanted to laugh. 'I'm coming out now.'

The Doctor took out his sonic screwdriver and aimed it at the force shield. The tigers winced, flattening their ears, as he traced out a doorway. He stepped through, his clothes crackling with static electricity. The rectangular hole sealed up behind him.

He hadn't been sure they wouldn't simply fall on him the moment he was in reach. But the tigers seemed to be taking him seriously. 'Call me Sprint,' said a sleek young male with a wide black stripe on his forehead. 'How come you can speak our language?'

'I'm the Doctor. And I'm extraordinarily clever.'

Sprint said, 'We know what you're up to in there. It's not going to be as easy as you think.'

The Doctor jabbed a finger at him. 'Face it: you can't keep control of this world for ever. Sooner or later, the humans are going to signal their army.'

'Are you threatening us?' said Sprint, and all the tigers smiled.

'You need a permanent solution,' insisted the Doctor. 'A way of getting what you want, and getting the humans to help you.' He had their interest. 'Sit down with the humans. Tell them what you want. See if you have things they want.'

The tigers murmured to one another. The Doctor pressed on: 'Both you and the humans are thinking the same way – that you've got to be in control to get what you want. But you must have ways of working out agreements among yourselves. The humans do. Use those methods now.'

Sprint raised a paw and pointed behind the Doctor.

He spun around. Quick and Shellshear were sprinting across the tarmac. Both of them were armed with the lethal rifles. 'Hold on, Doctor!' shouted Shellshear. He was holding a little device. The Doctor suddenly realised it was a field control for the emergency force shield.

'I don't need rescuing!' he snapped.

'What do you think you're *doing*?' Quick raised his gun.

In a movement that was almost casual, Sprint twisted out of his sitting position and grabbed the Doctor. Claws dug into his skin.

The Doctor turned inside the bear hug. The tiger tried to grab him more tightly, but he wriggled and turned until he slid out of its grip.

The Doctor pulled off his coat and threw it over the head of a tiger who was advancing on him. He had plucked the sonic screwdriver from the pocket. Now he raised it and gave the tigers' ears a good blasting. They growled in complaint.

A wide gap appeared in the force shield. Quick and Shellshear came through it, brandishing their guns.

'Stop! This doesn't have to happen!' the Doctor roared. 'It never has to be like this!'

Anji stood by the garden shed, peering around the wall. Besma was standing between two tigers, whirling the stunwand back and forth. Even the dumb tiger knew better than to get too close to the electric stick.

It was all going to pieces. Where the hell was Fitz? Where the hell was their transport?

A flash of orange movement caught Anji's eye. She turned to see a tiger loping towards her, its mouth open in a shark grin.

Anji dodged around the back of the shed. She knew it was useless: the tiger would simply stalk behind the miniature building and take her in its jaws. But her body kept her moving, panic jerking her away like a puppet on a string.

The shed's sliding door was partly open. She slipped in through the gap even as the tiger's shaggy head appeared around the corner.

The shed was cluttered with gardening tools. Anji grabbed the nearest one. If she could block the door with something, stop it from opening, she might be able to fend the monster off.

The doorway was suddenly full of stripes and teeth.

Anji screamed and struck out blindly with the pitchfork, putting her entire weight behind the blow. She felt the fork slam up against something, jarring her entire body, the end of the handle jabbing backwards into her ribs and knocking the breath out of her. It felt as if she'd run into a brick wall.

In the next moment, the fork was wrenched out of her hands,

splinters scraping across her palms. She flung herself backwards, slamming up against the rakes and hoes hanging from the wall, expecting the tool to be spun around and jabbed at her.

Behind her raised arms, she unscrewed her eyes.

The slim tiger was dragging itself away, the fork hanging from its side. Anji almost screamed again. The tines were buried in its chest up to half their length. The tiger reached back, twisting, trying to grab the fork. It murmured and growled with pain. After a moment, it reached forward with a foot, wrapped its toes around the shaft of the tool, and drew it out of the wound with an ear-popping snarl. Blood gushed from three neat holes, it actually gushed.

The tiger turned its head to look at her over its shoulder, eyes huge and round. It let out an almighty roar. Anji cowered inside the shed, but the tiger sank down on to the grass, panting, ignoring her.

'*Heeeeeellllllllp!*' bellowed Fitz, as Roo undid the second buckle. 'I need some *heeeeellllllppppppp*!' His armour was loosening around him, the padding sliding out of place to reveal his skinny, vulnerable body. As Roo's weight pushed down on his chest, spots and sparkles started to dance in front of his eyes.

Suddenly, Roo's mighty grin vanished. 'Yowp!' said the big cat, jumping up. It whirled, snarling, knocking over a chair. It was cornered.

Fitz took a deep breath. His vision cleared to reveal a six-foot stunner in a red jump suit standing over him, holding an electric cattle prod.

'Marry me,' he gasped.

'Get out of the way,' said Grieve, stepping aside. Fitz rolled, awkwardly, banging and crashing, opening up an escape route for the tiger. Roo took the hint and bounded out of the front door.

Anji was still frozen inside the shed when Fitz and Besma came to get her. 'Come on,' said Fitz, reaching in a hand. 'We're getting out of here.'

Anji took his hand. Her legs wouldn't move properly, and Fitz half dragged her out of the shed. Something banged against the doorway as she came out. She realised she was holding a rake in a death grip.

'They've gone,' said Besma. She was holding a plastic case in one hand and the stunwand in the other. 'We're clear. Let's go.'

A shadow fell over them. Anji looked up and started. The hovercar was lowering itself into the garden, ready to carry them away. It was one thing to know Hitchemus's cars were also helicopters, but another thing to see one parking from above.

'We did it,' she said.

'Yeah, we did,' said Fitz. 'Don't step in the blood.'

Jaytea's hand leading him away, suddenly clutching, then letting go – the man's eyes wide as a tiger tears strips from his back.

The torn-eared male, his flanks heaving one final time, sprawling on the pavement, his jaws still buried in the belly of Shellshear's corpse.

A tiger with a dart plunged deep in its eye, long red threads trailing down its face, lunging at the hovercar's door as it closes. Three tiger fingers lying on the floor of the hovercar, curling like headless snakes.

The Doctor staring down at the sudden pattern they form, huge splashes of red and orange on the black tarmac.

The Doctor, staring down.

What was left of the Movement met in the basement studio, sitting or standing in frozen positions, shocked into silence.

The Doctor sat in the corner. He looked like a wreck, thought Anji, his hair tangled and his face drawn. She stood beside him, Fitz sitting on the floor next to his chair. Besma Grieve was sitting on a crate, still clutching her stunwand.

At last, Quick broke the silence. 'How could you provoke a bloodbath like that?'

The Doctor looked him right in the face. Quick took a step back. 'Oh, of course. Nothing to do with you.'

Quick said, 'You just turned your back without a word and blundered straight into danger. Why?'

'Because I know what I'm doing. I thought you would have the simple common sense to stay put.'

Quick's mouth pulled into a mirthless smile. 'Oh, we're supposed to just fall into line behind the prima donna, are we?'

The Doctor visibly flinched. In a low voice he said, 'You don't understand. It had to be done, right then, or the moment would be gone.'

'Who are *you* to negotiate on our behalf?' steamed Quick. 'You've been visiting our world for a month. Do you expect us, our mayor, the city council, to be bound by what you agree to? Do you expect those of us who have lived here all our lives to live with it, years after you *tourists* are gone?'

'I made the Movement happen! You've been following my lead all along. I have been doing this for *centuries* –'

That was a mistake, thought Anji. Quick was addressing the room. 'I don't think people here think too fondly of you giving concessions to the *things* that have kidnapped and killed us. Turned our city upside down. It's time Hitchemians were in charge.'

'Meaning you, in particular,' muttered the Doctor.

Fitz had had enough. 'So what's your next brilliant move?' he asked Quick.

Quick was still addressing his audience. 'We need a proactive strategy. We've got to find another way of contacting the marines. In the meantime, we'll make life difficult for the tigers in any way possible.' The Doctor picked up a violin and began idly plucking at the strings. 'A campaign of constant harassment to wear them down. Retaliation for the killings.'

The violin gave an ugly screech. 'They retaliate. You retaliate. They retaliate. It's as predictable as – as the stinger at the end of a Sousa march. I've been there a thousand times before, I'm *sure* I've been there. But I can take you somewhere new. If you trust me.'

'I think we've danced to your tune for long enough.' Quick

turned his back on them. 'We're fighting to save our world. *Our world*. Not yours.' He went to the door. 'Come on. We've got work to do.'

The others filed out after him.

'Amateurs,' muttered the Doctor.

As the Movement members left, he started to play, scraping away at Saint-Saëns's *Danse Macabre*. Death's merry waltz with everyone. A few of them glanced at him as they went, but mostly they kept their eyes down. Still playing follow my leader.

Fitz and Anji got to their feet. 'What now?' said Anji.

'I'm going into the Bewilderness,' announced the Doctor.

'You'll die,' said Quick, from the doorway.

'Oh no he won't,' said Fitz. 'Come on, Anji, let's get our things together.'

The Doctor pointed his bow at the two of them. 'You stay here,' he murmured. 'Make sure these idiots don't do too much damage.'

'Doctor –' said Fitz.

'Doctor!' said Anji. This couldn't be happening; he couldn't just walk out on them! 'Look, give them a chance, they're frightened, they're only –'

'Human?' He took a deep breath, as though to stop himself from saying anything more. 'Now, *stay*!'

He tucked the violin under his arm and went out.

Solo

Chapter Six

Bounce could taste hurricane.

The strong winds had been swelling all morning, racing through the rolling hills of the Bewilderness. Bounce was one of six tigers standing guard over a nest hidden in one of the secluded canyons that pockmarked the landscape. The creek flared into a pond, just right for raising a clutch.

The father, Black and White, was one of the previous generation. He didn't understand why it was necessary to have so many tigers wandering about near his pond. At first he had grumbled and cuffed the younger animals, but after a couple of days he'd got used to their presence. They stayed at the far end of the pond, well away from the egg case in its submerged cylinder of twigs and mud.

Bounce sat at the edge of the water, in the shade of the feather-duster trees, tasting the wind. She was big for her age, with a square face and a heavy frame. She dangled a paw in the water. When the storm hit, she thought, and the creek burst like a rotten fruit, old Black and White might not have a nest to worry about.

The head and shoulders of another tiger emerged from the pond. It was Sneaker, plucking a bit of water weed from his ear.

'Taste that?' said Bounce.

'All morning,' said Sneaker. He pulled himself up on to the bank. 'Even Black and White is fretting.'

'Maybe we should move the nest,' said Bounce.

'Oh, Daddy's going to love that. Some of us will get our ears chewed good and proper.'

'Got to save those cubs. There's a groundwater pond higher up. We could drag it there.'

Sneaker twisted his neck, looking up. The sky was a slash of blue at the top of the canyon, a hundred and fifty metres up. 'How are we going to get it up the wall?'

'We'll manage. It's a good tough nest, the eggs should be all right.'

'They're almost ripe, you know,' said Sneaker. 'Six fat cubs. They're not going to be light.'

Bounce sat back, suddenly. There was a different taste on the wind, one she didn't recognise at first. She opened her mouth, taking in great draughts of the breeze, her tongue struggling to identify the new flavour.

'Human,' said Sneaker, bristling.

'I think so,' said Bounce. She shook her head, puzzled. 'That's all we need.'

'It's not close,' said Sneaker. 'The canyons are nearly invisible to them. It won't even know we're here.'

'I'd better go and take a look at it. Just in case.'

'All right. I'll tell the others.' Sneaker slid back into the water. He bobbed to the surface and gave her a cheeky look. 'You're only going so you don't have to try to explain things to Black and White.'

'This is important,' said Bounce. 'With everything that's going on, the humans are more of a threat than the hurricane.'

'You won't be saying that when your ears are full of mud,' said Sneaker. He dived under and raced away.

Bounce watched him go for a moment. Then she started climbing, hands and feet on the rocks and trees of the cliff face, her mouth open as she followed the nagging alien flavour.

The canyon was surrounded by the high smooth curves of hills. The intruder was in the next little valley. Bounce crouched among the raging trees, watching him, invisible among the bushes and the flying leaves.

He was light-coloured, with a long mane, and dark-coloured clothes. She had only been to the city once, and hadn't been much good at telling one of them from another. Sneaker had shown her how to get a pat on the head and something to eat. Then, the humans had seemed boring. Now this one had Bounce's undivided attention.

The human was walking fast. He wore a long coat that flapped in the wind, and was carrying a case for a musical instrument.

Unusually for a human outside the city, that was all he was carrying – no box in his hand or bag on his back. Bounce couldn't see any weapons, but there might be things hidden in his clothing. He must have run away from the city. Then where was he going?

Bounce had been one of the thousands of younger tigers who stayed in the Bewilderness while the adults took the city. The discussions had gone on for the better part of a year, but the current generation had been talking about it long before that. For as long as Bounce could remember, even when she was a cub, there had been vague plans about the humans. Take them all prisoner. Go to their schools. Eat them all up.

Only one thing had been agreed on by everyone: the humans mustn't learn how intelligent they were until it was too late. It would be too hard to act convincingly as completely stupid as their parents. But their grandparents, bright enough to understand and even speak a word or two – they were easier to imitate.

This close to the canyon, the air was cold with drifting spray. If the human was observant or curious, it might be enough to give their bolthole away. If he found it he could tell the other humans in an instant – maybe faster even than she could kill him.

The man slowed and stopped. Slowly, he turned his head.

He was looking right at her. It wasn't the look of a prey animal unsure of whether it had tasted something in the air, or spotted a tiny movement among the vegetation. He was staring right at her, his pale-blue eyes seeing her as clearly as she could taste him.

He called out, 'If the Pied Piper has no one to follow him, does he make a sound?'

In that moment, he almost died. Bounce's panicked heart beat fast, driving her paws to the charge. One leap, one run, one spring, and the whole matter would be settled.

But he didn't seem afraid. Instead, he sat down on a rounded, mossy rock, and took the violin out of its case. Giving her a cheeky glance, he started to play the thing.

Bounce stayed frozen, listening to the sound. So this was what all the fuss was about, she thought. In the city, all the different music had overlapped, forming a jumble that meant nothing to her. But this! A single line of melody from the thing he was holding, curling and rocking back and forth. And now he was singing!

> There were three men came out of the west, their
> fortunes for to try.
> And these three men made a solemn oath: 'John
> Barleycorn must die!'
> There's beer within the barrel, there's brandy in the
> glass,
> And little Sir John in his nut-brown bowl
> Proved the strongest man at last!

His high voice rang out, echoing from the hills, half carried away by the building wind. Bounce didn't understand all the words, but she didn't care. It was as though he were performing for her, trying to please her. Or was he making fun of her? She didn't care. Yes, yes, she thought greedily, this is what all the fuss has been about. We must make them give us this.

The man put away his violin. He got up and started walking, glancing back over his shoulder. Bounce froze in the bushes, uncertain of whether he knew she was following him. He must guess that she was, even if he couldn't spot her.

The man walked on until dusk. Bounce followed him the whole distance, keeping well behind. The land rolled slowly upwards. The wind's speed was gradually increasing, until they were both bent over in it. Branches and leaves whirled wildly in the gusts.

Bounce crouched in some bushes. They gave little protection from the gale's bite. The weather had been going wrong for a long time, she thought, the taste of it changing every day. The man had stopped a little distance ahead, and was stepping back and forth, as though examining something on the ground. There were canyons everywhere here, not much more than slippery cracks in the ground, too narrow even for the tigers to get into.

They had been heading roughly west the entire time, further and further from the city. Bounce thought she knew what the man was looking for. But she would wait and see, wait and see.

It was too late to go back and help with the nest. Bounce had let the man lure her too far, into the jaws of the hurricane. She wondered if Sneaker and the others were trying to shift the heavy egg case, even now, or if they were just hoping the flood wouldn't tear it free from its anchoring.

There was a shallow canyon ahead, which might provide shelter from the windstorm – the man was probably looking for a way down. In fact, according to Bounce's mental map, there was a way in via the creek at the southern end. If he went down there, she could use it to follow him in while staying under cover.

In the end he found a fallen log that let him clamber down into the crevice. The canyon was an old one, worn and crumbled. The creek had cut a deep gash in the ground here, but the walls had slowly eroded away, widening and shortening it.

Bounce followed the stream around, just as she had planned. She stayed downwind of him, keeping low. He didn't look her way, although she still had the tingling feeling that he knew just where she was.

They were well protected here. The sloping walls of the canyon kept out the worst of the wind. The creek was just a trickle, an infant daughter of the main flow; even when the waters rose it wouldn't breach its banks. Shelves of rock jutted from the eroding slope on either side, sheltering the ground from the worst of the rain.

The man sank down by the creek. The water rushed around stones and fallen tree limbs, breaking into miniature rivers and joining up again, sending up a soft cool spray. He sat there, absolutely still, for several minutes. Then, suddenly, he struggled with his feet. 'These shoes fit appallingly!' he cried, and hurled them into the bushes.

Bounce crept carefully through the bushes, aiming to get as close as possible without making herself obvious. Now he was bringing together twigs and bits of dried undergrowth to a bald, sandy patch of ground by the creek. He dragged fallen tree limbs across the ground to the little pile, stamping on them to snap them. Fascinating! She had never seen one of the humans light a fire. Would he make a hand drill? Or did he have some machine that would do it for him?

The man took a small box from his pocket and extracted something from it. He did something with his hands. Instantly, he was holding a tiny flame.

Bounce started.

The man must have seen or heard her. He looked right at her again, holding up the flame, cupped protectively between his hands. 'Clever things, aren't they?' he said. 'You could start a wildfire with a single one of them. Or light up a cigarette, and press its glowing tip to your prisoner's face. Or you could light the campfire that saves a near-frozen life. So much potential for harm or for good. Don't you think? Ouch!' The flame had bitten his fingers. He shook his hand, vigorously, until the tiny flicker went out.

He did the trick with the box again, lighting another of the tiny flames. This time he bent to the kindling. He had arranged a lot of stones under and around the campfire. It was a neat job, Bounce had to admit. She had never imagined a human making something with its own paws.

In the darkest part of the night, the man slept in the shelter of an overhanging rock. Bounce stayed awake, watching and waiting. She expected him to talk to the other humans, but she was starting to believe that he really was alone, with no way to contact them.

That made him less of a threat – whether she decided to let him live or not. All she really wanted, thought Bounce, was to hear him play the violin again.

Eventually Bounce put her head on her paws and let the distant sound of the wind lull her to sleep.

Lightning coiled across the sky like a map of hot blue rivers.

Bounce panted, watching the display.

A flash illuminated the man, standing at the top of the canyon. Bounce leapt up and bounded towards him. He was playing the violin, a furious sound to match the storm, nothing like the bouncing sound of the song he'd played when she'd first seen him.

'I hope I *never* remember!' he shouted into the teeth of the storm. 'That'll show them all!'

Bounce crept closer. The man pointed his bow at her, like a weapon. She should have known by now that she couldn't hide from him. 'Hidden things are coming to the surface,' he boomed, in a voice as stern as his music. 'Burrowing into the light.'

'What things?' panted Bounce.

'The gene hides in the blood for generations, passed on in invisibility, camouflaged among the pearly strings of the chromosomes.' Bounce shook her head, not understanding, but his voice rolled on unheeding. 'Until yes! The right moment! And it expresses itself. Thousands of genes, forgotten and dusty, expressing themselves at last. That's such a beautiful… expression. As though they're speaking. Recounting memories. Making art.

'How can we ever know what's under the ground?' His voice became softer. He put his bow and violin aside, and sat beside her, ruffling the fur at the base of her neck. 'Ground yourself,' he told her. 'Imagine the line of energy dropping from the tip of your skull, a white line describing your spine, falling into the ground. Imagine its journey: through dust and topsoil, through stone, perhaps through a cave, a river, through a layer of coal or oil, deeper and deeper until it strikes the magma, the hot blood in the heart of the world. But you can only guess. Guess at the journey.

'You don't know what's buried. What someone has come and hidden.'

Something had been revealed, like a shoot coming out of the soil: she knew his name was Doctor. A do-name like hers or Sneaker's, not a like-name like her brother Tailbend or old Black and White. He was for fixing things or people that were broken.

He sat beside her, stroking her fur like a father comforting a kitten. 'Go back to sleep, Bounce. Go back to sleep...'

In the morning, with the storm driving the black clouds across the sky like stampeding prey, Bounce pulled her head from her paws and watched the man making fire with his hands.

Water was running in rivulets down the sides of the crumbling canyon, its path broken by the jutting slices of rock. The creek had swollen to a river during the night. Bounce went down to the water and lapped at it. She could taste the distant ocean, taste mud and fallen trees, the destruction all around. And still the winds were rising.

Halfway through her drink, she realised the Doctor was watching her, silently. She had broken cover without even thinking about it. He sat cross-legged in front of the fire, scowling, trying to dry out his shoes. He gave her a little grin and wave, putting one of the shoes on the end of a stick so he could put it close to the flame without singeing his fingers.

Bounce sat up, mouth opening wide.

The Doctor frowned. He turned from the fire and arched his back and neck, trying to see around his rocky shelter.

The wall of the canyon above them tore across and burst in a single gushing movement. A great gout of mud and twigs and water roared down the side of the canyon like blood from a wound.

They both sprang to their feet, but the flood outran them both. Bounce's paws left the ground in an instant as the muddy deluge lifted her, hurtling her into the creek.

Bounce tumbled under the water. For several long moments she had no idea which way was up. Her side struck against something hard, rocks or wood under the water. Then she was moving more slowly, striking out intuitively for the surface.

Bounce's head broke from the flood. She sneezed angrily, combing mud from her face, but immediately had to start paddling again to keep herself afloat as the waters ripped and swirled.

She was racing down the canyon with all the other flotsam. Tree limbs sailed the surface, rocks danced underneath. She had already shot out of the canyon through the southern entrance, and was twisting through the countryside. Heavy rain fell into the water all around her.

There was no sign of the Doctor. There was nothing to do but paddle, and wait for the flood's anger to exhaust itself.

The sunshine was brilliant, almost blinding. The grass was drenched and puddled. Even the trunks of the trees were damp. The creek was still swollen, rushing on at the bottom of the valley.

The miniature flood had carried Bounce about a kilometre south. It had soon exhausted itself, leaving her stuck to a muddy hillside. The creek gurgled and raged, clotted with mud. Everything was brown-grey and stinking. Bounce had slept in the ooze for hours, not giving a damn about anything.

The Doctor was an angular tangle of limbs on the other side of the creek, decorated with water plants and twigs.

Bounce watched, panting, waiting to see if the Doctor was going to get up. The winds had begun to subside. If he didn't move soon, she would leave him and go back to whatever was left of the nest.

But, after a while, he began to stir, rolling on to his back. He looked like a kitten that had been playing in the muck, covered in mud and bits and pieces. For a while he just lay there, soaking up the sunshine, until he came back to life.

He found a rock whose heart had been warmed by the sun, and sat down on it, spreading out his sodden clothes to dry. He spent several minutes trying to comb the mud and twigs out of his hair, cupping water in his hands to try to loosen the mess.

He put down the comb, and took a folding knife out of his pocket. He grabbed hold of his hair, and began to saw through it with the blade. Bounce watched, fascinated. The movements looked rough, angry, but they were precise as well. He left the muddy hair lying on the ground where it had fallen.

The flood had carried away his shoes and his violin. He was

unarmed, except for that tiny knife.

When he had finished, Bounce came down the hillside. The Doctor looked up. 'Small waifs in the woodland wet,' he said, incomprehensibly, and slid the knife into the pocket of his drying trousers. His hair looked neat and soft as clean fur.

'Why are you here?' said Bounce.

'The same as you,' said the Doctor. 'The mudslide brought me.'

Bounce coughed a laugh. It seemed to please him, opening up a grin of recognition in his face. She said, 'No human has ever come this far into the Bewilderness before.'

'Oh, I'm not one of them,' he said lightly. 'I'm here because I can talk to your people. And someone's got to.'

'You mean the ones who took over the city,' said Bounce. 'All right, I can take you to see some of them.'

So, when they were both sufficiently dry, Bounce put him on her back and carried him away into the wet and shining Bewilderness.

Second Verse

Chapter Seven

Anji walked alone through the city of tigers. The only sounds were her boots crunching over broken glass and splinters of wood, and the wind that moaned endlessly between the buildings.

It had been two days since the hurricane. The coast was hundreds of kilometres away; Port Any had caught only the edge of the dying storm, the violent winds robbed of their force as they left the ocean and crossed the land. Roofs had been torn loose, windows smashed, wooden sheds and greenhouses stomped flat, homes and shops near the lake flooded with a metre of muddy water. But the buildings had been left standing, and no one had been killed. The farms had been partly flooded, but automatic systems had minimised the damage.

The streets were empty except for cleanup teams here and there. She had worked on several of the teams over the last week, scrubbing walls and furniture with disinfectants, rigging up clotheslines to dry out garments and bedding and soggy computer screens. At least there weren't any fallen power lines to deal with – the power was broadcast from the plant in some way she didn't understand.

The colony had never faced anything worse than a bad thunderstorm: they had no disaster plans, no emergency services ready to cope with disaster on this scale. All they had on their side was the grim determination to get on with things and survive, she thought. The tigers had given them that. They were working like crazy to repair their city. The spirit of the Blitz, and all that, she supposed.

Anji hefted her backpack and followed the wet roads to the edge of the artificial lake. There was no grass any more, only mud, dotted with tree limbs and garbage, pieces of wood and sodden paper, mangled bicycles and broken furniture. People were wandering over the mud, their faces half covered with hankies or masks, plucking out chunks of debris and loading them into wheelbarrows. Others were shovelling up the mud itself and packing it into great sacks. Anji wondered whether they were going to use it for something, maybe the outlying farms to the south, or whether they were just trying to get all the slime out of the way.

There was a small group of tigers at the edge of the lake. They also had a little row of wheelbarrows. They were taking it in turns to dive into the water, returning with armfuls of detritus, or bowls full of mud. They were dredging the lake, Anji realised, doing almost the same work as the humans picking over the ruined lawns.

The two groups were keeping their distance, barely glancing at each other. It was the same throughout the city. Life was going on, nervous and silent, orderly and peaceful. The tigers weren't bullying anyone. They had what they want: control of the human population, and all the music teachers they could eat.

A frozen breeze cut across the lawns. Anji reached for the buttons of her leather jacket. The fact was, they still didn't know what had happened to the hostages taken out of the city. The tigers weren't saying much of anything; Big made a daily announcement, and the town council posted bulletins – literally posted them, pieces of paper on hastily constructed noticeboards, since the net wasn't coming back up any time soon. They were co-operating like crazy – the tigers had even let them out of house arrest, although the mayor was still a hostage. Essential services were being maintained, the farms were running, cafés were open.

No ships were coming to rescue the colony. Perhaps no ships were even due to visit them. And the Doctor had just walked away. She felt her mouth tighten with anger for the hundredth time. Without him, she and Fitz had no way to leave this planet. They were alone, a little town on a little island on a little planet at the edge of space, surrounded by tigers. And everyone was waiting for the next hurricane.

* * *

Fitz was at Quick's café. He was there most of the time, drinking coffee or beer in a quiet corner, chatting with anyone who happened to sit down at his table. At the end of each day he compiled everything he had learned into a report for the Movement.

Sometimes tigers came into the café. They hung around, just watching people, or used vocoders to order raw meat or sashimi. Some of them were developing a taste for coffee. They never paid for any of it.

When Anji arrived, there were just a handful of humans having lunch. She slid into the seat opposite Fitz. He gave her a grin from underneath the brim of his black hat. 'Much happening out there?'

She shook her head. 'Things are very quiet. How's the mitigation coming along?'

'Oh, fine,' said Fitz. He shuffled a sheaf of papers. 'Though with the net staying down, it's hard to keep everyone co-ordinated. If it wasn't for the Movement, we'd be in a much bigger mess – you've to give Quick his dues, he's a natural at organising people. Comes from spending all that time running a restaurant… Anyway, food and medicine are getting to anyone who needs them, and we've got tarps over all the broken windows and roofs. Things are under control for the moment.'

Anji nodded. 'Well. Is there any word?'

Fitz seemed to deflate slightly. He shook his head. 'No one's heard from the Doctor. You know what he's like –'

'You know what he's like –' said Anji at the same moment. Neither of them laughed. 'If he wanted to contact us, he'd find a way. But he doesn't want anything to do with us. Even *us*, Fitz.'

'I vant to be left alone,' said Fitz, in an accent Anji decided was a Greta Garbo impersonation. His voice dropped to a whisper. 'He must be so sick of trying to save people's arses, only to have them bugger everything up by losing their tempers.'

'I think he's looking for Karl,' said Anji.

They sat there for a few moments. Fitz glanced vaguely over his notes. Anji said, 'You know, this really suits you.'

'Why, thank you,' said Fitz, adjusting his hat.

'I mean, the whole part. Fearless agent for La Résistance, masquerading as concerned citizen.'

Fitz shifted to Bogey.'You're no shlouch yourself, shister,' he said. He tapped the table with a finger, and a small clock face appeared. 'It's time for the run. I was going to send Maria, but would you like to take care of it today?'

Anji looked around, instinctively. Even without the tigers themselves around, there was always the risk that some of the Movement's secrets would reach them from frightened or loud-mouthed humans. She nodded.

'Great.' Now he put on a Yogi Bear voice.'Quick is cooking up a pic-a-nic basket.'

'Fine – I'll tell the tigers I'm off to visit Grandma.'

Fitz touched her arm as he got up. 'Come back here afterwards. I want to make sure you're OK.'

'Here's looking at you, kid.'

Hitchemus University was barely ten years old, an afterthought of the Musical Academy. While the Academy's brushed-concrete buildings stayed locked and silent, its gardens untended and awash, students were still tiptoeing about the university on their way to lectures in science or economics or whatever.

In the tunnels that connected the campus's two libraries, used for shuttling books and librarians back and forth, a little group of music teachers lived on tinned food and artificial light. Even the students didn't know they were there. The Movement sent someone to see to their needs twice a day. The access point they used was a grungy door in a grungy workroom in the basement of one of the libraries.

The librarians pretended not to see Anji as she went in through the sliding doors. Even the woman in the lift, taking a trolleyload of electronic volumes to storage, stared straight ahead as they rode down to the basement.

Anji took a heavy torch out of her backpack. The tunnels had been used as a shelter during the hurricane, and then closed for 'repairs'. The circle of light picked out cabling and safety signs and crates.

She walked through the echoing concrete tube for half a kilometre until she saw the faint light coming from behind a door. By now they would have heard her approaching footsteps, and known that she was human. Still, she knocked gently on the door, flinching as the soft sound echoed up and down.

A dozen people were crowded into the narrow room. They barely bothered to look up at her from where they huddled on blankets and cushions. They took turns sitting on the floor or the counter. Lightsticks were scattered about, leaning on walls. The snack machines had long since been emptied of their pastries and drinks.

'Hello, hello,' said Anji brightly. 'We thought you might like a change from baked beans, so one of the cafés has packed a few things.' Eager hands took the backpack from her and started unloading its contents.

Besma Grieve gave her a dull smile. She was hunched in the corner, half wrapped in a dark blanket, reading one of the books the librarians had smuggled down. Its screen lit up her face with a grey glow. 'Pull up a piece of floor,' she said. Anji sat down with her back to a cola machine.

They spoke in whispers, their heads almost together. 'People are already talking about giving themselves up,' said Besma, glancing at the others, who were passing pastries around. She squeezed Anji's arm for emphasis. 'We can't stay down here for much longer. We're all so bloody *scared*.'

'We're looking for a place in the country to stow you,' murmured Anji. 'Probably on one or two of the farms. The real problem is working out how to smuggle you out of the city.'

'I'll run naked and screaming out of the city if I'm here for too long,' said Besma. 'Look, we have to find out what made the tigers turn smart. I can't do that from a dark room in a *basement*.'

'What do you want to do?' said Anji. 'The moment you show your face in town, the tigers are going to put you back in your house. Under proper guard, this time. You won't be much better off.'

Besma shook her head and hissed, 'Not in town. Out there. Out in the wilds. The secret's in the ruins. There's one called the Stela, way off the beaten track. The tigers visit it from time to time.'

'Why? What's there?'

Besma shook her head. 'No one has any real idea. Anji, we have to find out. The tigers' brainwave has to be something to do with the ruins. It must have, mustn't it? Something in them, maybe something from the colonists who were here before humanity.' She was all but bouncing up and down on the spot. 'We've got to get out there and find out.'

'All right,' said Anji dubiously. 'All right – I'll try to get the support we need.'

Besma's eyes glistened in the dim light. 'Sooner rather than later,' she said. 'The sooner the better.'

Besma Grieve, xenobiologist, says:

Did I ever get back to telling you about the Annihilists? They're one of the rationalist associations. More extreme than most – I belong to a couple myself. The Association for the Annihilation of Experience teaches that subjective experience is a myth. We don't have to wonder how animals or aliens experience pain, or happiness, or whatever, because *we* don't experience those things. Consciousness is just an illusion created by neurons firing and hormones flowing.

Larry joined the Annihilists in the second year of our marriage. He would bring up their ideas in the middle of conversations, leave their literature lying around for me to find. Some of it was perfectly sensible, warnings against projecting the human perspective on to other species, or on to the universe itself in the form of gods. But there was more. If you believe in experience, said the pamphlets, you believe in the soul, and if you believe in the soul, you believe in a divine plan, that the cosmos comes prepackaged with a meaning.

I know – I *know*, because it's my job – that evolution isn't trying to get anywhere. There's no masterplan pushing natural selection along. God didn't program this planet to make tigers, so we could ooh and aah and say how much they look like the ones back on Earth. That just happened to be one successful form for this particular ecosystem at this particular time. Not even the optimal form, some imaginary perfect form. Just one that happened to beat out the other forms that were available.

To the Annihilists, everything worked like that blind watchmaker. Let me give you Larry's favourite example. We only imagine we love people. It's really just evolution talking – bonding us to our mate, or to our children, with a rush of hormones. When we look at a cloud, he would say, we only think we see a bunny rabbit or a sailing ship; in the same way, when we look at our mate, we only imagine we *love* them. We don't love our sisters and brothers because we grew up with them: we love them because they carry half our genes. We're dupes of our DNA,

Larry said, corrupted by the superstitious belief that there's something more to us than whatever natural selection has spat out.

I would have liked there to be something more. I don't mean, I want to believe in God. I just wish Larry had loved me because he liked me, rather than because I stimulated his anterior cingulate cortex.

When Anji got back to the café, Quick was sitting with Fitz, going over the scribbled reports. 'Everything went well? Pull up a chair,' said the Movement's new leader.

Anji said, 'Dr Grieve has a theory about the tigers' intelligence. She wants to sneak out to the ruins to see if there are any clues there.'

'Think there's anything in it?' said Fitz.

Anji brushed her hair back. 'To tell the truth, I don't know how much of it is science and how much is Besma being stir-crazy. We've got to get them out of that hole.'

'All planned,' said Fitz. He flipped through the papers, pulled out a sheet, and pushed it across to her. 'One of the farms has agreed to take them on as a cleanup team.'

'Looks like it'll be at least a week before they can start,' said Anji. 'What a nightmare.'

'Better than being dragged off into the Bewilderness,' said Quick.

'True enough,' said Anji. 'Anyway, I'd like to round up a hovercar and some equipment and see if we can sneak out to the ruins.'

'Anji, we need you here,' said Quick. He put a hand on her shoulder, looking her in the eyes. 'We need you to handle risk analyses and strategy projection.'

Anji looked right back at him. 'Now that the worst of the hurricane recovery is past, what are we going to do about the tigers? More specifically, Mr Quick, what are *you* going to do?'

Quick gave a modest smile. 'I don't pretend to be some great general. All I know is how to get people moving. And that I won't let these creatures destroy everything I've spent my life building up. Who knows what they plan for us, in the end?'

'You know,' said Anji, 'sometimes I think they have no more idea of what's going to happen than we do. I don't think they have any plans at all.'

'Maybe we do need to be talking to them,' said Fitz quietly. 'The council are just taking orders. We need to find out what's going on in the tigers' heads.'

'Intelligence – if you'll pardon the pun – will be the basis of our whole operation,' said Quick. 'The more we know, the more control we'll have.'

'What about Grieve's idea?' said Anji. 'Imagine the advantage we'll have if we know the source of their brain power.'

'Perhaps later,' said Quick. 'Perhaps later.'

The rendezvous was in the quadrangle of the silent and empty Academy of Music. Anji led Grieve there through the dark, staying close to the buildings. No one saw them, no one stopped them.

Fitz landed the hovercar in the middle of the quad just as they hurried down the steps into the grassy rectangle. He slid out of the driver's seat. 'It's all loaded up with supplies. Anyone see you?'

'Not a soul.' Anji looked in the window. 'God, Besma, you'd better drive this thing.'

The xenobiologist slid into the pilot's seat. 'I'll give you lessons as we go.' There was a pile of stuff in the back, a mixture of camping equipment and things Besma had asked Fitz to bring from her house.

Anji said, 'Fitz, you will be all right getting back?'

'Got my cover story all worked out. There's a cleanup crew working by the creek. It's only ten minutes' walk.' He hefted a backpack. 'I've even brought them some extra lights.'

Anji pecked him on the cheek. 'Watch out for Quick. He hasn't got the first idea of what he's going to do. He could end up doing anything.'

'I'll try to keep him under control.' said Fitz. 'Hey, if you happen to bump into the Doctor, say hi for me.'

'If I find him, I'll drag him back here by the collar. He might not always know what he's going to do, but at least he knows what he's doing when he does it.'

Chapter Eight

The tiger whose human-name was Tiddles and whose like-name was Longbody arrived at the Gathering shortly before Big. She wanted to see how things stood before the boss got there. The last thing she expected to see was the leader of their enemies playing with a bunch of kittens.

The walk from the city had taken her most of the day, through a landscape rapidly drying out in the shimmering heat. She was still limping slightly, favouring the side where the pitchfork had gone in. The healing was going well.

Longbody's like-name described her elongated, slender torso. She was a lean eater, a good runner and a cunning hunter. And, after years in the city, she was an expert at feigning stupidity.

Bounce was waiting for her at the top of a rise, the edge of the Gathering. She made a couple of playful leaps, but Longbody wasn't up to a mock fight. 'You have to see the human we've got here,' said Bounce. 'He walked halfway here from the city. I brought him the rest of the way. He can speak our language, Longbody!'

'What's he want?'

'He wants to talk to Big, when he gets here. Come and see.'

Longbody followed Bounce into the Gathering. It was a wide, flat area, dotted with trees, beside the big inland lake. The terrain was wrong for nesting or hunting, so the tigers used it for meetings. Dozens of tigers were dotted about, talking or lazing.

A small crowd had formed around a hollow near the water. Longbody nosed through them until she saw what they were all staring at.

The man was jogging back and forth among a clutch of kittens, five – no, six – of them. He would let them catch hold of his legs for a moment; then he would dodge away again with a laugh. The infant tigers came up to the middle of his calves.

Longbody stared. The man was the Doctor, the leader of the Movement. She scratched irritably at the healing punctures in her side. Perhaps they had simply thrown him to the cubs to let them practise their hunting skills on him – he already had several tiny bites and scratches. But it looked uncomfortably like a father giving chasing lessons.

The Movement were the only enemies they had. The humans had rolled over at once, overwhelmed by the speed and power of the tigers' attack. Any fight they had left had been knocked out of them by the storm. Only the Movement were still trying to resist, acting like the small animals that lived in the undergrowth, harassing and stealing. The sooner they were eaten up, the better.

The man sat down, tickling two of the kittens' stomachs while a third tried to climb up his back. The other cubs chased one another round and round. Just wait till Big gets here, thought Longbody.

'What's this?' Big's voice boomed around the hollow. The other tigers moved aside to let him through. His whole body was twitching with the paternal instinct, the urge to rush in and kill the interloper.

The moment the Doctor saw Big, he flopped on to his back, arms folded on his chest. The kittens nosed and poked him, but he didn't move, his eyes fixed on the huge adult.

'See?' whispered Bounce. 'How does he know to do that?'

'Who belongs to these kittens?' roared Big. A couple of males came sheepishly forward. 'I don't want to see this happening again. Get them out of here.' The fathers herded the kittens out of the hollow. The Doctor glanced at them, but brought his gaze quickly back to Big.

The bulky male loomed over the Doctor, who said, 'The first thing you need to know is that I'm not human.'

'Oh,' said Big. His deep voice carried to everyone present. 'Are you disguised as one?' The crowd of tigers laughed.

'I lived among them for as long as I can remember,' said the Doctor. 'But I'm not one of them. Never will be.'

Big sat next to him, looking down. 'The humans choose someone to be leader all the time, don't they?'

'Not exactly,' said the Doctor. 'But I gather leadership is a situation-by-situation affair for tigers. You're in charge of this particular project, the takeover of the city.'

'That's right,' said Big, with a challenging glance around the crowd. 'And you're the leader of the troublemakers.'

'Not any more,' said the Doctor.

'Is the Movement surrendering, then?'

'No,' said the Doctor. He folded his arms behind his head. 'They can do whatever they like. I'm done with them.'

'So you're betraying them?' said Big.

Longbody grinned to herself. The Doctor closed his eyes and put a hand over his face, as though he had a headache. 'All I want,' he said, 'is to play in the premiere of Karl Sadeghi's Violin Concerto Number One in C minor. In order to do that, I need two things. One, I need to forge a peace between the tigers and the humans. And second, I need Karl Sadeghi.'

'Oh,' said someone. 'He means the violin teacher. Karrrl!'

The Doctor sat up and said, 'I want to see him.'

Big put a paw on the man's shoulder and pushed. The Doctor obligingly fell back on to the grass. 'If you came here,' he said, 'you're either a great big idiot and I'm going to gobble you up, or you have something we want – some reason why we shouldn't kill you. Which is it?'

The Doctor said, 'Oh, yes. I have something very important and precious. I've got the future.' The crowd murmured. 'Imagine this. Imagine humans teaching tigers all about music, not because they're frightened, but because they want to. No more dead tigers, no more dead humans, no more worrying about the Movement or the marines. Imagine an orchestra with humans and tigers playing side by side.'

Big, the great lunk, was taken in by this. Either that, or he was showing off his superior position by letting the Doctor say whatever he liked, because it didn't matter. 'How?' he asked.

'By talking,' said the Doctor. 'Just by talking. That's all I've brought with me, Big.'

Big turned to Longbody. 'Take him off to see the violin teacher,' he ordered.

* * *

A thick wood bordered the Gathering to the west. Longbody led the Doctor into it, keeping up a brisk pace. To her surprise, he didn't have any trouble following her through the undergrowth. Even more surprising, he didn't crash and bang around the way the humans did, but moved with quiet and ease. Perhaps there was some truth in what he had said about not being one of them.

The woods were thick with circles of feather-duster trees, leaning their vast orange heads together, and the mange trees that shed their bark in long, spiralling strips and whose stiff, angular branches locked together into shadowy canopies. There were no paths, the sort of thing the humans would have worn with their coming and going in shoes and boots. Soft tough tiger paws didn't disturb the undergrowth.

'Is this where you keep the teachers?' said the Doctor.

Longbody turned her head, eyeing him. 'Just the violin teacher. There's no way he'd find his way out of this tangle.'

'Have you been keeping all of them separately? All of this time?'

'Humans can be a lot of trouble in a group.'

'You've been injured,' said the Doctor.

Longbody stopped. He was staring at the neat row of circular wounds that disrupted the flow of the stripes on her flank. His eyes were the colour of the hot sky. She said, 'See if you can guess how that happened.'

'May I take a look?'

'We have our own doctors,' she said shortly. 'Oh look, it's Chew You.'

The shaggy old tiger was scratching his pale yellow back against the trunk of a tree, a little way up ahead. The colour of his fur had faded almost to white with age. Longbody ambled up to him. He glanced up at the Doctor, instantly losing interest when he couldn't categorise him as threat or food. 'What're you up to?' said Longbody.

'Taste runner taste me Chew You here,' he said.

Longbody sat down and opened her mouth.

'Fascinating,' said the Doctor. 'Do you have an analogue to the Jacobson's organ? Or is it more akin to the flehmen expression of a Terran tiger?'

'What are you talking about?' said Longbody. She turned back to Chew You. 'Right as always, granddad,' she said. 'There's one down the hill.'

'Here here Chew You runner taste eat good,' remarked the old tiger.

'Sure, but are you up to it?' said Longbody. 'I'll get it if you want. I'm not doing anything interesting right now.'

'Chew You!' The old tiger threw his head back. 'Chew You!'

'Off you go, then,' said Longbody indulgently. The old fellow was still in great shape – he wouldn't have much trouble bringing down a runner, so long as it wasn't a full-grown adult. She watched the yellow tiger as he trotted off through the trees.

Behind her, the Doctor said, 'Are all the grandparents like that?'

'Mostly,' said Longbody. 'They have a marvellous time out here – they only have the faintest idea of what's happening in the city. Still, they're brighter than our parents. Or cubs.'

The Doctor must have heard the bitterness in her voice. He said, 'Do you have cubs, Longbody?'

She shook her head. He frowned, indicating puzzlement, so she exaggerated the motion until he understood she was imitating the human gesture. 'No!' It came out as a bark. She lowered her voice. 'What would be the point? They'd be stupid as rocks.'

'But your grandchildren,' he said. 'They'd be just as bright as you. Wouldn't they? Or would they?' He was a bit too clever, thought Longbody. 'Clever, dull, clever, dull… The pattern goes on through the generations. That is sad. Not to be able to speak with your own child.'

'That's the way it is.' Longbody got up and started walking again.

The Doctor said, 'Perhaps it's a way of limiting the adverse side effects of intelligence,' he said. 'Stopping you from becoming too clever for your own good. Clever, dull… And then there's you, burning bright. Now, how did that happen?'

'Clever clever you me Longbody,' she said.

'You do have cubs, don't you?'

Definitely a bit too clever. 'Around here somewhere,' she said carelessly. 'I just laid the eggs. I really don't care what happened after that.'

'So it's just you,' said the Doctor. 'A flowering of intelligence, brief as spring…'

'It's just us,' Longbody told him. 'And after that, nothing. None of this is worth it. Not the city, and not you. We've got nothing to plan for. No future to worry about.' She gave an imitation shrug, feeling the sore muscles ripple along her flank. 'I knew that for certain when one of your little friends stuck the gardening tool into me. All we have is now. And not much of that.'

The Doctor closed his eyes, as though she had said aloud something he was thinking. 'You don't have a past, you don't know your future…' He looked at her. 'Then why on earth do you want to learn the violin?'

'If people want to waste their time,' said Longbody, 'let them.'

'But if you're not interested,' said the Doctor, 'then why spend so much time at Dr Grieve's house, pretending to be an idiot?'

'Because it's funny,' said Longbody. 'It's a joke. Because it beats chasing runners around when you're hungry.'

'Chew You's speech… small vocabulary, no grammar…' The Doctor had stopped in his tracks. 'Who taught you to speak?'

Longbody sat down, looking up at him. That was quite enough, she thought. 'Have you ever seen a runner?' she said.

'Just glimpses.'

'They're elusive. Very good at hiding. But we can always taste them on the wind. Come on, we'll take a peek at the one old Chew You is after.'

'I'd rather get on,' he said. 'I want to see Karl.'

'Karrrl isn't going anywhere. This will only take a moment. Come on, I want to explain something to you.'

He followed her reluctantly down a gentle slope. When she stopped suddenly, he crouched down behind her, still moving as silently as before.

A pair of runners were drinking from a creek, barely three metres away. They were immature ones, great lumps of dull fur, their long necks and legs sticking awkwardly out of their heavy bodies. Their tiny forelimbs waved about uselessly as they pushed their wedge-shaped heads into the water.

'Where's Chew You?' whispered the Doctor.

'He must be around here somewhere,' she said softly. 'Let's let him know where we are. *Hey!*' She reared up suddenly, balancing on her hindlegs, and shouted, 'Hey hey hey!'

The runners' heads snapped up, sharp beaks swivelling to point right at the Doctor. Longbody was already gone, loping off through the trees.

Runners mostly relied on their eyes; it was incredibly easy to hide from them, so long as you didn't make any noise. The Doctor wouldn't know about that. They also had foul tempers, but he'd probably already worked that part out.

One of the runners let out a hissing squawk and started stamping through the water, beady murderous eyes locked on the Doctor. He stood stock-still. Was he panicking? Or did he hope to fool the animal? Without stripes to break up his outline, he was clearly visible to the runner, whether he moved or not. Longbody had to stop herself from laughing. She didn't want to scare it off, not now.

The Doctor closed his eyes. The runner crashed up the slope towards him.

He reached above his head and wrapped his hands around a low mange tree limb. Longbody stared. With a sharp movement, he pulled himself up, swung to and fro gaining speed, and suddenly propelled himself upwards and backwards, grabbing for the branch above. He caught it with both hands, lost his grip with his right hand, kicked hard against the lower branch, and ended up awkwardly clinging to the trunk.

The runner arrived at the foot of the tree. It looked around in confusion, and then suddenly craned its neck to look up at the Doctor. Longbody knew how it felt – she had never seen anything that large climb a tree either. It shrieked furiously, hammering its heavy beak against the trunk, letting him know what it was going to do to him the moment he came down from there.

Chew You came out of nowhere, a sudden off-white flash. He

leapt on to the runner from behind, his whole weight crashing down on its back as its jaws sought the long neck. The runner screamed, the sound echoing up and down the creek bed. It kicked backwards, talons stabbing air. Locked together, the two animals crashed to the ground and tumbled down the slope, the creek exploding under their weight. Doused and astonished, the other runner hooted and vanished into the undergrowth.

Longbody came out of her hiding place. The Doctor was nimbly clambering down from the tree. He stood at the top of the slope, watching as the tiger and its prey thrashed in the creek, sending up sprays of water.

Then he turned to stare at Longbody. She recognised the look: it was the gaze of a tiger sizing up its prey.

'So now you know what a runner looks like,' she said. 'Come along.'

When they got to the place where the violin teacher was being kept, the Doctor left Longbody behind, clambering down the slope over rocks and bushes. Longbody settled on to a warm shelf of rock to keep an eye on them.

It was one of those natural clearings that happened when a ring of mange trees went rotten and fell down, leaving a wide circular space full of rich undergrowth. It smelled pleasingly of a mixture of damp decomposition and leaves drying to a crisp under the scorching sky.

Karrrl the teacher sat on a boulder at the edge of the grassy area, barely three metres away, with his back to them. His violin case sat next to him on the rock. Was he dozing? Longbody wondered idly. Or just sitting there, waiting to see what would happen next? She was pretty good at interpreting their voices and body movements, but this one wasn't giving out any signals.

The Doctor stopped a little distance away from him, as though he didn't want to startle him. Longbody swivelled her ears to pick up his soft voice. 'Honk honk,' he said.

Karl's back straightened a little, but he didn't turn around. To Longbody, he looked like a tiger about to spring or bolt, his body clenched tight against the sudden, violent motion. The Doctor walked around where Karl could see him and waited.

'Well,' said Karl. 'Well.' He sounded tense as a cramped muscle. 'Now you've gone and thrown things into confusion. I'd convinced myself that we'd never see each other again.'

'I'm sorry,' said the Doctor. 'I'm afraid I haven't come to take you away. Not yet.'

Karl nodded slightly. Longbody could see that he was staring at the ground, not looking up at the Doctor.

'Listen,' said the Doctor.

He picked up the violin case sitting on the boulder and took out the instrument. He thought for a moment, and then he began to play.

It was a sad tune, very sad, thought Longbody. It made her think of when her father had drowned in the rainstorm. It made her think of pulling the pitchfork out and dragging herself away, thinking she was going to die.

Karl did not move. But, after a few minutes, Longbody realised he was weeping silently. The Doctor didn't stop. The music began to swoop, like something flying around the clearing, curving higher and higher.

Karl started to sob. He wrapped his arms around his body, as though holding himself together. The Doctor stopped playing and crouched down in front of him.

'I wrote that when I was fresh out of the Academy in Nairobi,' said Karl. 'Before my Octagonal Serialist days.'

'Look at me,' said the Doctor. He took Karl's face between his hands and raised his head so that their eyes met at last. 'I have been a prisoner so many times that I can't – I literally can't – remember how many times. This will pass. It will pass.'

'The others,' said Karl hoarsely. He caught at the Doctor's sleeve. 'They're dead, aren't they? I'm the only one left.'

'No,' said the Doctor. 'They have no reason to kill any of you.'

Longbody wondered what would happen if she bounded into the clearing about now. She grinned, but stayed where she was. Let them have their chatter.

'Have you seen the others? Are they all right?'

'Not yet,' said the Doctor. He disentangled himself, and sat down on the rock beside Karl. 'The tigers want to keep their captives from conspiring together. I mean, you do look like a rather dangerous character…' Karl almost smiled. 'Tell me about the tigers. Are they good pupils?'

'Astonishingly. They're so keen. Some of them can already play simple pieces.' He made a small, dry laugh. 'I wish you could see them. Two tidy rows of pussycats practising their scales, sawing up and down in C major. They have enough instruments for a whole string section. They must have raided the Academy.' Now the Doctor laughed. 'How can they possibly understand music?' said Karl. 'How can it make sense to them? How can it have the same meaning to them?'

'They've grown up with it,' said the Doctor. 'Like a human child learning to speak by listening. This whole generation has grown up in and around the city.'

'I've been so cold,' whispered Karl. 'It's never warm here, not even in the middle of the day. Not even now. I wish I knew how to light a fire. The tigers know how to, but they wouldn't let me have one. When the storm came, I tried to shelter under a rock, but I got soaked through anyway.' He scratched at his face, which looked hairy. 'They've been feeding me flowers. Flowers! The kind that go in that fancy salad. It's the only thing I was sure I could safely eat. Sometimes they bring raw meat. I couldn't… I just couldn't.'

'I'll make them keep you together with the other musicians,' said the Doctor. 'If they won't let you go, at least they can take proper care of you.'

'How can you make them?'

'Oh, I'm very good at diplomacy,' said the Doctor. 'That's why I've come out here - to talk some sense into the tigers.'

'Careful,' breathed Karl. 'Oh, be careful. I think God's favourite colour must be orange.'

Longbody coughed. Karl started violently, nearly falling off the rock. She grinned at him as he whirled to face her.

'It's all right,' said the Doctor, putting a hand on Karl's shoulder. 'She's quite tame. Aren't you, Longbody?'

'Time for us to go,' she told him.

'I'll talk to them,' the Doctor told Karl. 'Remember. This will pass.'

'*Lo non mi period, dottor mio, di coraggio*,' whispered Karl.

They held on to each other for a moment. Then the Doctor followed Longbody out of the clearing and back to the Gathering.

The Doctor strode up to Big, who was scratching his ear with his hindleg, and shoved him with all of his strength. Big fell over with a 'Whoop!' of surprise.

Longbody, and a dozen other tigers hanging around the Gathering, all burst into gales of laughter. She could hardly wait to see what Big was going to do to him.

The Doctor crouched down next to the sprawling tiger and stared him in the face. 'It's completely unacceptable!' he shouted. 'You're killing your teachers. One by one they're going to lose their health and their minds. Is that what you want? Who's going to give you music lessons then?'

Big looked up at the helpless, unarmed man. He only needed to reach out a paw, and he could end the Doctor's life in an instant.

Big was right, thought Longbody. Either the Doctor was an idiot, or he had something they wanted. Or he knew something they didn't.

'What do we need to do to keep them alive?' said Big.

'Bring supplies from the city,' said the Doctor. 'Proper food, vitamin supplements, basic medicines. Blankets and warm clothing. Tents. You dragged them out here with nothing!' The Doctor shut his eyes for a moment, trying to calm himself. 'The humans will be only too happy to help you organise it. And keep the teachers together, not separately. They're not going anywhere – they'd only lose themselves in the Bewilderness. Out there they wouldn't last long enough to make it back to the city, and they know it.'

'How do you know they know it?' said Big.

'Have any of them tried to run for it?' said the Doctor. 'Even one?'

'Not even one,' threw in one of the tigers. They were all hovering around, waiting to find out what Big was going to do.

'You just haven't thought ahead at all, have you!' The Doctor started to pace. 'What are you going to do if the humans bring in reinforcements? You're right, aren't you, Longbody? The tigers are just living in the moment. It's all going to fall apart, Big. You can't sustain it. It's got to change.'

Big sprang on to the Doctor and brought him tumbling to the ground. There were cheers around the clearing. He pinned the man's forelimbs with the weight of his paws, and took his neck in his mouth. Longbody stood up, trying to get a better view.

Big held the Doctor there for several seconds, the tips of his teeth just pushing against the fragile skin of his throat. The Doctor stayed perfectly still.

Big let go and sat down on top of the man, half squeezing the breath out of him. He just sat there, while the crowd tittered and grinned at one another. Longbody combed her ears, hiding her disappointment.

When enough time had passed, Big got off the Doctor, who took a deep breath. 'Come with me,' said the leader. 'You still don't know our story. I want to show you the truth about us.'

Bounce the tiger says:

Have you ever heard the story of the tiger who lost his stripes? Well, he didn't *lose* them exactly: what actually happened was that when he was angry he turned all black, and when he was happy he turned all orange. And then one day something happened to him that made him happy all the time – or was it angry all the time? – sorry, I can't remember the story properly. Anyway, he turned all the same colour all the time, and of course all the runners and squawks and other animals could see him and run away from him. He wasn't much of a tiger after that.

I forget how it goes after that – what happened in the end?

Chapters Nine Ten Eleven Twelve

Anji's part

They left the hovercar four kilometres south of the ruins, on the far side of a ridge. It wasn't a hard walk, just a long one, letting them work the kinks out of their backs and limbs after the uncomfortable half-night's sleep in the little tin vehicle.

At the top of the ridge they stopped, and Besma pointed down into the valley. 'Can you see it? A sort of red-orange square. Close to the base of the next ridge, about ten o'clock.'

Anji squinted into the morning light. There – a straight-edged shape among the organic sprawl of the Bewilderness. It stood at the base of a great mass of rocks sticking up out of the valley floor. They looked as if they had all tumbled down from the high cliff behind.

'You're sure this area is tigerless?'

'Positive. Remember, I spent a year studying them in situ. Except for those rare visits here, they stay where the runners are, and the runners don't hang about in open, dry terrain like this.'

'Dry? What are we going to drink, then?'

Besma grinned. 'Can you see the sparkling on the side of the cliff?'

'Just about. I wish Fitz had been able to find us some binoculars.'

'Those are miniature waterfalls. Once we get across the plain, we'll have *all* the water we need.'

Anji looked back. There was no sign of the hovercar, lost somewhere in the endless tangled paper chains of feather-duster trees.

The plain was carpeted with thigh-high grass and fat vermilion flowers. Heat came up from the soil in waves. It made Anji think of wildlife documentaries – she'd always wanted a trip to Kenya. The terrain was flat and featureless. The plain just went on until it stopped at the rocks or the forest or some low hills. There were no trees, no animals that she could see.

She bent down for a closer look at one of the flowers, pushing aside the tall, dry grass stems. The 'flower' was a fleshy knob, spreading rounded leaves like petals, shedding pollen in a circle around its base. Thousands of them peppered the stiff yellow grass.

It would be easy for the tigers to hide in this stuff, she thought. They'd only need to stay close to the ground. Besma had better be right that they just didn't come here.

From time to time, their footsteps sent up a little group of flapping animals, a bit like dull grey chickens. Anji was sure Besma would insist they weren't birds, there were no real birds on Hitchemus, but they looked like chickens just the same.

After a while, Besma said, 'You know, I've never been to Earth. Tell me about it.'

'You first,' said Anji. 'Tell me about Hitchemus.'

Besma gave her a look, but said, 'There are a couple of competing theories about evolution on Hitchemus.' She hefted the dart gun slung across her arm, positioning it more comfortably as she strode through the grass. She was back in her element, thought Anji. 'It's hard to believe such well-developed flora and fauna could have sprung up on such a *tiny* landmass. We know the world ocean rose a few million years ago. So either this island was once a much larger continent, or there were many small continents with a lot of migration going on. In any case, there aren't many niches to go around: the tigers and the runners are the only really large animals.'

Anji said, 'When I visited the observatory, there was a lecture about the moon's rings. They said something collided with the moon, and the heat of the explosion melted the southern polar cap.'

'That's one theory,' said Besma. 'Oh, something hit the moon, all right, millions of years ago. But maybe it just knocked the moon into a further orbit. Most habitable planets have a big, close moon or two - they help keep the planet's tilt stable. A distant moon means a wobbling planet. That's more than enough to explain the ocean rise and any other climate weirdness. A shift of a single degree is enough to turn forests into deserts. Hitchemus's tilt varies from ten to twenty-five degrees.'

'So how did the planet get a reputation for great weather?'

Besma shrugged. 'The oceans tend to absorb a lot of the change. But the colonists were just lucky – they must have arrived during a good, moderate phase of the climate. We *must* be leaving that phase now. The next generation will look back at idyllic afternoons as a thing of the distant past.'

'I'm from the distant past,' Anji blurted.

'You're from where?' said Besma absently. Heat was shimmering above the grass. Instead of insect sounds there were tiny rustles and the whispering wind.

'The twentieth century,' said Anji. Why had she opened her mouth! 'No, the twenty-first, really. I can't tell you what Earth is like now, because I'm not from there now.'

'Oh,' said Besma.

Silence for a few minutes.

'I get it,' said Besma. 'You were frozen. There was a play about that. I didn't realise it happened in real life.'

'Well, no,' said Anji. 'The Doctor and Fitz and I travel around in time.'

Besma stopped and turned. Her face was shadowed by the wide brim of her hat. Anji braced herself for the angry dismissal, the amused disgust. Instead, Besma said, 'Why are you telling me this?'

'I don't want to keep any secrets from you,' said Anji. 'Not out here.'

Besma nodded. She turned away and started walking again.

'It's been driving me mad not being able to tell anyone,' said Anji, catching her up. 'I have to nod and smile my way through so many conversations, because I don't understand what anyone is talking about – bits of history, bits of culture. Fitz is used to faking it. And the Doctor seems to know it all anyway.'

'You know, the human race is pretty fragmented,' said Besma. 'Lots of colonies dotted all over space, barely talking to one another. People are used to allowing for foreigners who aren't up to speed with the latest news, or fashions or whatever. So why don't you just tell people? Admit it. "Sorry, but I'm from the twentieth century and I have no idea what you're talking about."'

Anji said, 'Come on, who'd believe me?'

Besma glanced at her, grinning. 'Well, you might be surprised.'

It was after midday when they reached the Stela. It wasn't until they were almost at the foot of the rocks that Anji could make out the shape. The waterfalls Besma had talked about were everywhere, a steady tinkling trickle like bells all around. Small plants, even some full-grown mange trees, emerged from the crevices. It was so rough they could probably climb to the top without equipment if they wanted to.

They had been aiming for the square red panel for the whole walk. After staring at it for hours, growing slowly larger as they marched over the plain, it was almost disappointing to see it this close. It was only a head taller than Anji.

Besma stepped up to it and wiped away some of the dust. There was detail there, a hint of bright colours hidden under the greyish powder.

Despite Besma's assurance, despite the empty plain, Anji still kept turning from side to side, aware of the weight of the dart gun in the crook of her arm.

'This is the only example of the former civilisation's writing that anyone's found,' said Besma. 'It was studied intensely when the colonists first arrived. Once they got bored with it, everyone just forgot about it for a century. Too busy playing their kazoos.' She was wiping away more dirt from the stone panel, using a handkerchief wetted in the waterfall. Anji could see complex characters emerging, carved circular symbols that ran in rows down the Stela. The edges of the carvings were sharp, the colours brilliant, reds and ochres and gold. 'You know, I sent off a recording of the Stela to the languages department at Lvan College, but they never got back to me about it. I should have followed that up.'

Something about the dust disappointed Anji. She explored her mind for the shape of the feeling. The Doctor... She had half expected the Doctor to have beaten them to the Stela, even to find him here, scribbling on the cuff of his sleeve as he deciphered the alien writing. But no one had been here for years.

Was that why she suddenly felt the need to tell Besma where she was from? If she lost the Doctor, she'd be stuck here. No chance of getting back to Earth, in this century or any other. Well, they could use a good economist or two. There was no way she was going to learn a bloody instrument.

She brought herself back to the present. 'How have the colours lasted this long? Look at it. This isn't a ruin. It's in perfect condition.'

'I'll tell you something else. This is metal, not stone.' Anji touched the surface, gingerly. The scientist was right. 'They maintain it,' said Besma. 'They must do. Give it a clean and a lick of paint every so often.'

'I'd pay to see that,' laughed Anji.

'I spent weeks on this spot, trying to work out why the tigers came here,' said Besma. 'But they wouldn't approach the Stela when humans were around. They even spotted a remote camera I left hovering among the rocks.'

'Why...?' Anji ran a finger over one of the glistening symbols. 'Maybe it's just a ritual. When they had a civilisation, tigers used to make a pilgrimage here, something like that. Or maybe they just have vague memories of this being important.'

'I think it's a machine,' said Besma. 'A machine for activating minds.'

Anji took a step back from the Stela.

'For activating them, and controlling them,' said Besma. 'I think that when the tigers last visited the Stela, they unwittingly set a new program in motion.'

'Like in *2001*,' said Anji. Besma looked at her, confused. 'Now I'm doing it in reverse. There was a movie in which an alien device made humans intelligent.' She was sweating in the high sun. Besma passed her a canteen, and she splashed water down her face and neck, kneading it out of her hair in quick, anxious fistfuls. This was not a movie. 'So maybe the Stela, or something else left behind by the ancient civilisation, is what causes the alternation of generations – smart, stupid, smart. But why would they set up something like that?'

Besma drained what was left in the canteen. 'Possibly it's supposed to make every generation "smart", but it works erratically. We have no idea how old it is.'

'What can the two of us find out about it?' said Anji.

'We'll have a good poke round the thing,' said Besma vaguely. 'Run the symbols through my computer and see if we can make any sense of them. Look for *more* writing. There are larger translators back at the university which can crack most codes, given enough text to work from.' She paused. She wasn't convincing either of them. 'Look, anything we can find out could be useful. This may be something even the tigers don't know about.'

They spent most of the afternoon scanning the Stela with Besma's slate, creating a computer model of it. Around dusk, Besma showed Anji a patch of plants growing at the base of the cliff, constantly watered by the trickling fall from the rock. 'You'll like these things,' said the biologist, as they tugged at the firmly embedded plants.

Anji stretched, rubbing her shoulders. 'They're a lot of work.'

Besma grinned, hauling violently at a stem. 'Better than being locked in that hole in the ground.' She stumbled backwards as the tuber tore loose from the soil, and tossed it into the pile. 'You know, we can stay out here for as long as we need. I ate all kinds of native foods when I was studying the tigers – standard rations get very *boring* very quickly.'

Anji watched Besma as she twisted and tugged another alien potato out of the muddy soil. How much could they really learn from the ruins? Neither of them was an archaeologist or linguist. Perhaps all Besma wanted was to run away, get as far from the tigers as she could. Hide herself in what she knew best: her work.

How would she react if a tiger popped up out of that long, concealing grass? Was she thinking straight?

Anji rubbed at her eyes, then blinked dirt out of them, cursing.

With the campfire lit, they didn't need the lightsticks. Anji was worried the tigers would see the smoke, but Besma was sure that the rough terrain would hide the escaping grey-black wisp. They wrapped the tubers in their own tough green leaves and pushed them into the embers. When they were done, Besma brought out a tiny bottle of peppery, salty sauce. 'This stuff can make anything taste good. I never bush it without some.'

Anji put her sleeping bag against a boulder and leaned back on it, holding a plate of tubers in her lap. 'The funny thing is, I don't feel lost,' she said. 'It's easy to get panicky, away from the Doctor.' She bit off a piece of tuber. It was soft, steaming hot, slightly bitter. 'When I was little I used to have this bizarre dream where I owned a spaceship shaped like a seashell. I would get into it and it would shrink down to a tiny size, small enough to enter this whole other universe. Most of the dreams were about being trapped there. It's been like that, sometimes. Feeling that I'm stuck in this other space. Sort of claustrophobia. But not now.'

'I've got used to this planet,' said Besma. 'It's – thinks – my *fifteenth* world. For the first few months it's so jarring. The light is wrong, everything smells wrong, you get incredible jetlag. But after three years… if I went to Earth now, I'd probably feel like an alien.'

'Me, too,' said Anji.

'Are you really a time traveller, then?' said Besma.

Anji grinned. 'Yeah. I'm the ultimate tourist. The Doctor and Fitz have been doing it for ever, but I'm only new at it.'

'So where have you been? Have you met Cleopatra, or Barbara McClintock or who?'

'God, no,' said Anji. 'Nothing like that. It's been one crisis after another. You turn up somewhere nice, start having a holiday, and then wham – you're hanging by your fingernails from the edge of a cliff.' Anji leaned back against the rock so she could see the burning sky. 'Right at this moment, I'm enjoying myself.' Out here it was easy to forget about everything happening in the city, everything that had happened to her since she had met the Doctor. 'God. It's so strange not to recognise any constellations. All right, now I feel lost.'

'Sorry,' said Besma. 'I'm not much help.'

'I wonder if the tigers have names for the stars.' Anji closed her eyes. 'God, I'm wrecked.'

'I'm writing a book about them, you know,' said the scientist. 'A popular science text on the tigers. I have some serious *revising* to do.'

'You can do interviews with them,' said Anji, half-jokingly.

'Yes,' said Besma. 'Oh yes. I have a lot of questions. How they were able to fool me all those years. How I could screw up so badly that I didn't even realise they were playing stupid. All those experiments they deliberately wrecked.'

'They fooled everyone. A whole planet.'

'But of all the people who should have seen through it! How can you examine your assumptions when you don't even realise they are assumptions? They have a *language* and I didn't even *know*.' She threw a twig into the flames, glowering. 'There's no way I can publish now. I'll look as much of an idiot as I feel.'

'Publish or not,' said Anji, 'you're still the best person to get inside the tigers' heads.'

'You know, they wouldn't talk to me when they were keeping me prisoner,' said Besma. 'Not even with vocoders. Just the occasional gruff word to keep me in line. They think I'm ridiculous.'

'No,' said Anji. 'They know how much you know about them. They were afraid you'd learn too much.'

'You might be right,' said Besma, tossing another twig into the fire. 'You might be right.'

In the morning they packed up the tent and camouflaged it and their other equipment under a pile of branches. Then they went back to the Stela, standing in its shadow, poking and prodding its surface. Looking for clues.

'I think these are controls,' said Besma, running her hand across a row of symbols. 'They feel loose. You're supposed to press them, or turn them…'

'They look like they represent numbers,' said Anji. 'My God, it's an ATM for tigers. I wonder who's got the PIN number.'

Besma said, 'Is that another twentieth-century thing?' Anji grinned. 'Maybe, once they get clever enough to start the machine, it takes them the rest of the way.'

'Do you hear thunder?' said Anji.

They both turned, scanning the horizon for the hundredth time that morning. This time, there was something to see.

A flock of the grey chickens was flapping up from the plain. A big flock, thought Anji. She had only ever seen two or three of the things at once, and now there must be hundreds of them wheeling low over the long grass.

'It's the runners,' said Besma. 'They're stampeding.'

Now Anji could make out the ostrich shapes of the big flightless birds, obscured by the clouds of panicked chickens. 'What's going on over there?' she said.

'Come on!' said Besma. She slung her dart gun over her back. 'Up into the rocks, right now!'

Anji ran to the rock face. Besma was already hauling herself up, finding easy handholds in the wide crevices. Anji struggled up after her.

'In here,' said Besma. There was a wide, shadowy crack in the rock. Anji wondered if it hid snakes or God knew what else, but Besma clambered in without hesitation. Anji followed her into the crack.

The crack wound away through the rock for a little distance. There was room for both of them to crouch down, facing the entrance, with a view of the plains below.

The runner stampede was a disorganised marathon. Little knots of the creatures ran at different angles, crossing one another's path. They were emerging on to the open plain from the thick forest to the west.

There was only one thing that would make those big, angry birds panic. Tigers, and lots of them.

They saw the tigers come out of the forest, minutes later. From a kilometre away, they shone out against the dull green of the plain.

'There's someone with them,' whispered Anji. 'I mean, a human.'

'I wish we had those binoculars!' Besma whispered back. 'Where are they all going?'

'Where do you think?' said Anji.

They watched the tigers parade across the plain to the Stela. It wasn't long before they could make out the solitary bipedal figure, standing in the centre of the streak of tigers. 'That's the Doctor,' whispered Anji.

He looked all right, although his clothes were worse for wear. He looked more than all right – he looked comfortable. as if he belonged with them. His hair was cut fur-short. He walked among them, easily, stooping to give a tiger a friendly cuff. Another reared up to rub its head against his shoulder while he scratched it behind the ear.

Anji rubbed at the tense spot between her eyes. How could she have forgotten that he wasn't human?

'Damn it!' murmured Besma. 'What are they doing down there?' The Stela was too close to the rock face; as the tigers came up to it, they went out of view. Anji and Besma inched forward, getting as close to the entrance as they dared.

They could hear the tigers crunching around in the long grass, and their growly voices. Anji could make out what she thought was the Doctor's voice, speaking the tigers' language.

Anji and Besma remained crouched in their hiding place, staying as quiet as they could, hoping the tigers couldn't smell them. After a while they realised that the voices and the sounds of movement had stopped.

Besma risked a glance, popping her head out of the crevice. Her face was astonished. 'For God's sake, where have they gone?'

They waited an hour. Then another. When it became obvious that the tigers weren't going to reappear out of thin air, they carefully climbed back down the rock face.

The Stela stood in the plain, alone and silent. Even the chickens had vanished back into the long grass.

'Maybe it transported them all off the planet,' said Anji. 'Beamed them up to the tigers' hidden mother ship. Or pussy cat heaven, or something. God, maybe it just zapped them all out of existence.'

'They went *somewhere*,' said Besma. 'Perhaps the symbols are a set of instructions on how to get there.'

'Of course!' said Anji. 'It's a doorway! The tigers and the Doctor went underground.' She looked down at the crushed grass surrounding the Stela. 'They're beneath our feet right now.'

'If there's a doorway,' said Besma, 'we'll find it.' She took out her slate and started scanning the earth, working her way outwards from the Stela in a slow spiral.

Anji had a simpler idea. She grabbed a shovel from their cache of equipment and started digging at the base of the metal slab. The loose, dry soil scraped away easily. The Stela continued down into the ground. How far down? she wondered.

The ground trembled.

They looked at each other. 'Oh, *now* what?' said Anji.

The shaking started in earnest. 'Quake!' shouted Besma. 'First one ever.'

'What?' Anji spun around on the spot, frantically looking about her. 'What do we do?'

'We're safer out in the open,' shouted Besma. 'Stay clear of the Stela in case it topples.'

Anji stumbled out of the artefact's shadow. The ground heaved underneath them, turning her stomach, sending them both sprawling in the grass.

Barely three metres from them, something big and dark thrust itself out of the ground. Dry soil poured down a dull metallic surface. It looked like a shark's fin.

'Jesus!' cried Besma. 'Did we do that?'

'Back up the rock!' shouted Anji.

They ran for the rock face, grabbing for each other, staggering and stumbling across the trembling earth. Another of the fins shot up out of the ground in front of them. They both yelled, throwing themselves to one side, running around the chunk of gunmetal grey.

The two women scrambled up the rock, holding on for dear life as the world shivered and hiccuped. As they tumbled into the crevice, Anji had a terrible vision of it slamming shut on them, but Besma was crawling into the back of the crack. Dirt and tiny stones were raining down on them.

She stared down into the plain. The fins were poking up everywhere, scattered through the long grass in a random pattern – forming little groups of two or three, separated by wide intervals.

'What are those things?' she shouted, but Besma was crouched at the back of the crevice, both arms covering her head.

The quaking subsided into bad-tempered rumbling and finally ear-ringing silence. Anji checked her watch. It had lasted just over three minutes.

The grey chickens were starting to call, their scraping voices filling the plain with the sound of leftover panic. In the back of the crevice, Besma was uncurling herself, dirt and tiny pebbles showering from her arms and hair. The dart gun was lying across her lap – even in the chaos she had kept hold of it. Anji's weapon was gone – she must have put it down when she picked up the shovel.

For the second time that day, they clambered down the rock face. There were sloping piles of rocks and dirt at the bottom, shaken free in the quake. Lines and groups of shark fins stuck up out of the plain in every direction. Hundreds of them, thought Anji.

'All right. Let's go and take a look at one.' Besma's voice was slightly hysterical.

There was a metallic sound, which made Anji think of a sword being unsheathed.

They both turned. A circle of ground was irising open at the base of the rock face, trickles of dirt from the quake falling into the black space below.

A single furry head popped out of the hole in the ground.

The tiger's eyes locked on Anji. Its lean body snaked out of the hole. She held the shovel in front of herself, trying to look dangerous.

It charged her.

In an instant it filled her field of vision. Anji batted at the tiger with the collapsible shovel, which promptly collapsed as the tiger crashed into her with its whole weight.

She was crushed into the soil and grass beneath the tiger's mass. Its fishy breath was right in her face. Any moment now Grieve would shoot it. Any moment now Grieve would shoot it.

Grieve shouted, 'Get off her!'

Instead of firing the gun right away, Grieve ran closer.

The tiger looked over its shoulder and twisted. It grabbed the dart gun in its feet. Anji had never realised how much like hands those back feet were.

For a moment, the animal's whole weight crushed down on to Anji, forcing the air out of her lungs. The tiger spun, suddenly, both legs arcing out as it swung the gun like a cricket bat. It connected with Grieve's head with a terrible crunching sound. Anji saw blood and something else spray into the air.

The tiger dropped the gun and turned back to Anji, baring row after row of tiny, tearing teeth.

She froze, trying to think what to do, which way to move, how to make it so this wasn't happening.

The Doctor roared. Literally roared, shouting out some word in the tiger's fierce language. The tiger held still.

Anji was aware of shapes moving around behind the looming tiger. 'Doctor!' she yelled. 'Doctor! Get it off me, get it off me!'

One of the other tigers said something. The tiger snapped its mouth shut, and backed off, crouching in the grass at her feet. Its hungry yellow eyes were fixed on her.

The Doctor stepped over Grieve's body, without even looking down, and walked towards her.

Anji sobbed, 'No,' and started trying to get to Besma, crawling across the grass. The Doctor picked her up and put her on her feet.

'There's nothing we can do,' he told her.

She looked at him. 'I don't believe you.' His long, pretty hair had been sawn back to a couple of inches, like a harvested field. His sleeves were ragged, his coat battered, his shoes nonexistent. He was dusted with orange pollen, bright stuff in his clothes and his hair. 'I don't believe you,' she cried. 'I know first aid, we could get an ambulance out here –'

'Why did you leave the city?' he sounded exasperated. 'I want you to go back there, now. Have you got a way to get home?'

Anji tried to tell him that, yes, there was a hovercar waiting for her, she had a rough idea of how to pilot it. The words scrambled as she tried to get them out of her mouth.

'I'm just a futures trader!' she shrieked. Her voice snapped back at her from the rock face. 'I'm a trader. What am I doing out here? I'm not supposed to do any of this!'

He glanced back at the wreckage of Grieve, as if noticing it at last. He put his hands on Anji's shoulders. 'I'm so sorry –'

'Don't give me that!' she yelled into his face. He was shocked backwards, letting go of her. 'It's not good enough.' Her throat was so tight her voice was coming out like the high-pitched buzz of an angry insect. 'You can't put on the sad face – oh-I'm-*so*-sorry after the fact. You had a moment to be human and you stepped right past it.'

'I *am* sorry…' he protested.

'Too little. Too late.' She gestured at him, wildly. '*Look* at you!' she shouted. 'You look ridiculous in those tatters. Why don't you put some fur on instead?'

'ANJI.' She jumped. He had never said her name that way before. His eyes locked on to hers. 'If you're not calm right this minute, they'll kill you.'

She was suddenly terribly aware of the orange circle around them. 'You'd let them?' she whispered.

The Doctor said simply, 'They're faster than I am.'

Anji just could not shout any more. She felt the weight of tears in her eyes. 'I was going to ask you to come back with me.'

He looked around. 'This matters too much.'

'To you?'

He was there in her face again, the way he always had to be in your personal space. 'They'll let you go,' he said urgently. 'I've given them my word. But the storehouse is too important – I've got to stay here –'

'Storehouse?'

'Yes, storehouse, it's got all the answers in it –'

'It teaches them,' she said.

'It teaches everything. I've learned so much already…'

'Besma was right.' Anji could see it, could see the intensity in his eyes. 'What it's done to them – it's done to you.'

He was reaching for her. 'Stay with me, Anji. You've got to see it for yourself –' She backed out of his grip, fast, stumbling as she tried not to back right into a tiger.

He held out his hand to her, his fingers gesturing, Come here, come here. 'Just trust me!' he pleaded.

They stood staring at each other.

Anji broke the silence. 'Don't be here,' she told him. 'Don't be here tomorrow.'

She turned away from him and started walking. She stepped through a gap in the circle of tigers, trying not to flinch as she passed them. But they let her go. She felt their eyes in her back as she waded into the long grass. His eyes.

He growled something to the other tigers.

At any moment, she thought, I'm going to hear the sound of someone following me.

But she didn't.

Karl Sadeghi, composer, says:

When something goes wrong in the rehearsal hall, and you don't know why, you just keep rehearsing that stretch, over and over. Trying to pick out who bent the note the wrong way, who rushed through a crucial phrase. What made the whole perfectly coloured passage suddenly turn into a, a train wreck.

You separate out the individual parts and pick through them, looking for who's to blame. And then it's… easy to fix, easy, just a few words in the right ear and then everyone's fine.

In the rehearsal hall, it is.

Fitz stood on the balcony of the Doctor's apartment, having a quiet smoke.

From here he could see the edge of the city, and beyond to the forest where the trees tossed their orange and pink heads in the breeze. Hard to believe that a couple of days ago you could hardly see the buildings right next to you for the pelting rain, that the sunny street below was full of rubble and rubbish floating around on scummy water. Today the sun was a hot little ball.

Not the sun, he thought, taking a deep relaxing drag. Beta Canum Venaticorum, the Doctor had said, also known as Chara, a G-type star in Earth's neighbourhood. Close enough that you could spot *the* sun, Earth's own G-type star, in the night sky. By now, Fitz knew to avoid the drowningly lonely experience of looking for it.

He squinted at Chara, so much like the real sun. Fake, he jeered.

In the street below, a few people scuttled, hidden under their wide-brimmed hats. Someone cringed along behind a wheelbarrow under the bored gaze of a loafing tiger. All the camaraderie that had followed the hurricane had worn off, replaced by gloom and nerves. The cleanup had become a chore, hauling away the last of the rubbish, disinfecting mouldy carpets. At least it was still giving everyone something to do.

Scared people would do anything you told them, thought Fitz. It was the uncertainty that chewed you up; every day was the same for years, and then wham, the flying saucers landed. Your brain was completely empty of ideas on what to do about it. So when a policeman or a doctor or anyone at all shouted at you to do something, you did it.

I never used to think this much.

Fitz took a final drag and flicked the butt off the balcony into the road. He went inside the Doctor's apartment.

It was cool in here, and very tidy. There was a great stack of scores on the desk; Fitz imagined some harassed cleaner plucking them up from the floor and the rug and the sofa. Around the room were some of the instruments the Doctor had bought since arriving on Hitchemus. A trombone stood on its stand, a collection of ocarinas in rainbow colours were scattered on a chair. Some alien thingamajig, all purple tubes and yellow keys, took up half the kitchen counter. Fitz struggled with it for a few minutes, but couldn't get a sound out of it.

Quick knew that the city's morale was crashing. He had to do something quickly, before everyone got too depressed, something that would rouse the rabble. Some grand gesture that would probably get a lot of people killed. And everyone would just go along with it.

Fitz slid open the desk drawer. It was mostly empty: there was a harmonica, half a dozen pieces of sheet music, a drum-tuning key, and what looked like a thick wallet. He just had to pick it up.

It was a wallet, an ordinary Earth one, the leather battered and faded. He found himself looking around, as though the Doctor could somehow detect him rifling through his funds. But the Doctor was miles away, out in the wilds – if he hadn't already made a nice second course at a tiger dinner. Fitz shuddered and starting going through the wallet.

About thirty-seven pounds in notes and coins. A mixed bag of other currencies, including some that couldn't be from Earth. A dozen credit cards with expiry dates in four different decades. Eighteen library cards. Lots of what looked like business cards in scripts he couldn't read. Receipts with doodles and obscure notes scribbled on the backs.

There were plastic sleeves for a dozen photos. They were all empty, except for one, a blonde girl in her teens – he didn't recognise her, but there was something about her eyes that made him think of the Doctor. He should ask about her later on. Or maybe he shouldn't.

He put down the wallet. He picked up a banjo from the chair and sat down.

How much longer could he stall Quick? How much longer *should* he stall? He was waiting for the Doctor to produce some miracle, something that meant they wouldn't have to fight the

140

tigers. But what if they had to solve this problem themselves? What if he had to solve it?

Shit, thought Fitz, that was my last cigarette.

His nervous fingers had begun to tap out a tune on the banjo. It had been a long time since he'd tried to play one, but the opening of 'Day Tripper' came back to him like riding a bike.

Suddenly he found himself smiling, imagining a little light bulb hovering over his head. Maybe this time he didn't have to play second fiddle.

The Movement members turned up one after the other, slowly, like people just wandering into a café in search of lunch. They passed Fitz as he lounged against the wall, giving him a nod or a look, or scrupulously pretending not to see him.

Once, a tiger strolled down the street, on its way to who knew where. They patrolled much of the time, but they seemed to be making the schedule up as they went. That actually made it tougher to elude them. This one looked around idly at the people it passed. Fitz slid into a seat at one of the tables on the pavement, fiddling with the sugar dispenser as though waiting for his coffee. The tiger didn't give him a second glance.

When the last people had arrived for the meeting, Fitz went inside. The Movement members were taking up a table for ten, leaving one chair for him. A few other Hitchemians were eating their lunch at the other end of the café, oblivious to the scheming going on in the same room.

Brock was already giving his report. 'We've been observing the tigers gathering up certain supplies,' said the skinny man, twisting the tip of his pigtail round and round his finger in an unconscious nervous gesture. 'They've been raiding markets for canned foods and pharmaceuticals. One was seen making off with a first-aid kit from the fire station. There have been other reports, too.'

'What are they doing with the stuff?' asked Ann.

'One tiger was seen leaving the city with a pair of baskets on its back – you know those saddlebag things they sometimes use? Full of blankets, apparently.'

'It's the music teachers,' said Ebtissam, a portly woman with dark startled eyes. 'Of course it is. They're taking the stuff out to them in the Bewilderness.'

'Then we know they're still alive,' said Quick. There was a shared exhalation of relief around the table.

'Why now, though?' said Maria. 'Why this sudden concern for the music teachers? The tigers have been ignoring requests to send care packages out there.'

'It's been a week,' said Brock. 'The teachers can't be in good shape. Maybe the tigers don't want to lose their hostages.'

'The council should repeat its offer of help,' said Quick. 'By co-operating we can get more and better supplies to them. Perhaps pass messages back and forth.' Murmurs of agreement.

'We should let their families know, right now,' said Ann. 'They –'

'No,' said Quick. 'We can't give away our intelligence operations.'

There were a few other reports, mostly the sorts of things that had become routine. Rebuilding, crop shipments from the south. An outbreak of tummy bugs in one street where the plumbing had been wrecked by the flood – nothing too serious. An angry confrontation between a panicked couple and a pair of curious tigers trying to make off with their accordion.

'All right.' Quick's voice dropped. 'The spaceport. By this time tomorrow, everything will be ready for the raid. We have enough weapons for a dozen people. Ebtissam has worked out how to bypass the computers and activate the comm systems directly. All we have to do is keep the tigers at bay for an hour, maybe two, and we'll be on the air and broadcasting to every ship in this volume of space. Once we've sent our message, the tigers will have no choice but to accede to our demands.'

'What are our demands?' said Brock.

'Return the hostages. Get out of the city. We'll worry about issues like reparations once we have the marines to back us up.'

Maria piped up. 'What about retaliation from the tigers?'

Quick said, 'We'll need to warn the population as best we can. Get people ready for what's going to happen.'

Fitz cleared his throat. Everyone looked up at him. 'Um, listen,' he said. 'I've got an idea.'

Quick was staring right at him, eyebrows slightly raised, waiting.

Fitz said smoothly, 'We're at a turning point. Morale has been dropping in recent days. And whatever happens, we're in for a rough time – a lot of casualties, especially if people panic. Before we go ahead with the raid, why don't we do something to rally everyone? Give them some energy and determination to cope with whatever comes next.'

'Go on,' said Quick.

'A concert,' said Fitz. 'We get together as many musicians as we can, and we give a concert from one of the rooftops, where everyone can hear it. Lots of noise and energy, lots of flash and sparkle. It'll show everyone, humans, tigers, that Port Any is still alive and kicking.'

Everyone hesitated, as though waiting for Quick's reaction before saying anything. Their leader's face was unreadable – he was waiting for *their* reaction. Come on, thought Fitz, somebody say something.

At last, Maria said, 'That's a bloody good idea.'

But Quick was shaking his head. 'I don't think we have the time to be putting on a show when our world is under siege.'

Fitz had expected that. 'We're not in any immediate danger – we don't have to rush our plans. Besides, it wouldn't take long to throw the concert together. It wouldn't mean more than a twenty-four-hour delay.' Any more, and someone was going to realise he was stalling for time. 'Plus it would be a great chance to get out the warning you were talking about – recruit people, spread the information while we have their attention.'

'You sound as though you've done this before,' said Brock.

'Oh, of course,' said Fitz casually. 'I was one of seven musicians who led the rebels on Cantonine 4 to the Momilogist's palace. On Telemahuka we gave a rock concert in the science compound to break the Caxtarids' mind control. All rebellions have their musical accompaniment.'

'Fitz,' said Quick, 'you always have good ideas. But how much of this has to do with public morale, and how much has to do with your own fear?'

'What?' said Fitz. This was an argument he hadn't anticipated.

'The last assault on the spaceport was a disaster,' said Quick. 'People died. They were eaten. That would be enough to frighten anyone into thinking, Let's put it off for a day. Then perhaps another day, and another.'

Shit, thought Fitz, I'm rumbled. The best option in such circumstances, he knew, was to keep your mouth shut. Let them do the talking while you thought fast.

Quick sat back, looking satisfied with himself. He didn't say another word.

Everyone was looking at Fitz.

'We're all afraid,' Fitz started. 'If any one of us wasn't scared out of our skull, they'd be out of their skull. We're not just popping down the road to the tobacconist's: we're going to be firing guns from behind a barricade while alien monsters try to eat our heads.' There were one or two smiles, but he knew he was saying exactly what they were all thinking. 'Everyone out there, on the street, is frightened. And they're going to be more frightened when, out of the blue, we start exchanging fire with the tigers. They need something to pep them up, give them some confidence. Remind them what it used to be like here, and what it's going to be like again when all this is over. Not just them, either. Us.' He looked around the table. 'All of us.'

The smiles had turned into grins. Quick was nodding, looking around the table, taking in everyone's approval.

Fitz avoided slumping in his seat. Actually playing in front of the whole city wasn't going to be as hard a performance as the one he'd just put on.

From the concrete rooftop, just four storeys high, you could see past the edges of the town to the horizon in every direction. The sky formed a brilliant dome, deep blue overhead, getting paler the closer it got to the hot ground. The roof was fenced in by a railing of crisscrossing metal poles, smooth and hot to the touch.

They had chosen the office tower because it was the tallest

building in Port Any – six whole storeys. A doorway in the middle of the roof led out from a dingy staircase into the open air. Two dozen musicians had followed Fitz up those stairs and out on to their improvised stage. Now they were tuning instruments, checking equipment. There was an electric string quartet, an old man carrying a didgeridoo and a palm-sized sampler, a flamenco guitarist, a Mbira ensemble, four gospel singers, a small taiko group, and all of Jam Tomorrow. A pair of muscular women were hauling Fitz's amplifier out on to the concrete and positioning it next to the deck. One of the great things about being in charge, he thought, is that you can get someone else to carry your amps for you.

Fitz leaned over the railing. There were a few people in the street, hurrying from one place to another without looking up. He still couldn't believe he'd pulled this off.

And he still hadn't quite got used to the speed and ease with which these twenty-second-century bands could set up their stuff. A lot of the equipment was simply invisible, literally made out of thin air. The mixing board was a plastic sheet as light as a feather, supported by a lightweight frame. The hardest equipment to get ready and hook up was his centuries-out-of-date rig, but by now Ewegbeni the pianist had got the hang of all the cables and pedals. He gave Fitz the thumbs up.

The microphone was a soft shimmer in the air, marking its position. He picked up his '53 Fender Telecaster – borrowed from the Doctor's private collection – set the level on the distortion pedal, and twiddled the knobs on his magic dingus box just for luck.

He looked around. Everyone had stopped moving.

Showtime.

Fitz took a deep, deep breath and kicked into the low, rhythmic grind of a single power chord, sliding up to it on the one beat, laying a groove that could lead anywhere from the Ventures to the Who.

Two bars in, the drummer and the bassist from Jam Tomorrow picked it up. Then the string quartet piled on to the chord, and the didgeridoo rumbled in key. One of the gospel singers started a rhythm on the lagerphone. One by one the others joined in, following him (following *him*!), building up the tension as the single pair of notes swelled larger and larger… until he leaned towards the floating blur, took a deep, deep breath, and opened his mouth.

'*Hello, Hitchemus!*' he shouted, and his voice ricocheted from the buildings all around. 'I'm Fitz Fortune, and these are the Fortunes of War, here to put a spring in your step and a twist in your tail, awwwright! Ja, ve are the first mit der hipsenschaken und der funkengrüven. So from our racks and stacks of tracks on wax, here's the man with the axe with a special tune for all you hepcats out there – TWO, THREE! –'

And the whole band stopped on a dime as he launched into a riff that had fallen off the back of Chuck Berry's lorry, and the drums blew like an H-bomb on the one beat, and they were off and galloping – the strings carving out chunky eighth-note chords like the fattest rhythm guitar ever, didgeridoo doing weird things under the other sounds' feet, and, up top, him, playing for his life, the notes ringing straight from his brain to the strings without any sign of his hands being in the way.

Fitz leaned into the microphone and started to sing.

> *Well if they use up all the ozone*
> *We'll say goodbye to LA*
> *'Cause we'll be surfing in the desert*
> *The global warming way!*

They'd had only about twenty minutes' rehearsal time, and they'd never played the whole song through together. Any minute now a fuse was gonna blow. Or the drummer would lose the beat, or the horns would screw up their entrance, or any one of a thousand things would send the moment crashing in a heap. But, from the edge of the roof, he could see people blocks away stopping and looking up, and if they weren't dancing in the streets they were at least staying in them, and he couldn't help feeling as if they could outrun all the problems, outrun everything, just as long as they could keep on playing.

> *And they'll be surfin' in Vegas*
> *Way down the Rio Grande,*
> *Salt Lake City and Reno*
> *And through the Indian lands,*
> *All over New Mexico*
> *And Arizon-I-A;*
> *Yeah, we'll be desert surfin'*
> *In the U-S-of-A.*

He launched into the guitar solo, cut-rate Dick Dale by way of the Yardbirds. From below there came a wave of cheering and applause. It stopped, surprised by itself, and then came back more strongly.

He leaned over the railing, stretching out as far as he dared, showing them the guitar. People were pouring into the street below. Dozens of faces were turned up to him. A couple of orange faces, too. But they seemed to be just watching, curious about the music.

He found himself thinking, I could stay here. I could be a hero. I could be a musician again. Even if the Doctor doesn't come back. Even if he does.

They made it to the end of the song, crashing to a halt among a long series of chords. So what if the drummers hadn't quite worked out when the song was finishing, or that the trumpeter had tried to turn the whole thing into jazz during his solo? So what if all those months ago Sam had told him that he'd mixed up everything she'd told him about global warming and the ozone hole was something totally different? Never mind the words, that was one hell of a sound.

'We're going to be doing more of these concerts,' he announced as the string quartet began the intro to their piece, his voice booming through the city. 'Auditions at the Albinoni Hall. If anyone wants to help bring the city back to life, just come and say hello...'

Fitz sat down in a corner of the rooftop, leaning against the railing, where he had a view of everything that was happening. The quartet were keeping the momentum going, furiously sawing their way through a deep, dark piece he didn't recognise. Now they'd played all together, each individual group would have its turn. The only style requirement that he'd made everyone agree to was that their music would energise people. The roof was thrumming with rhythm. He pressed his palms to the concrete, feeling the beat. This way there'd be time for him to think of something to do for the finale.

Blimey, he thought, I did this? I made this happen just by talking to people and getting them interested? I've come a long way from the garden centre in West Wycombe. Blimey.

Out of the corner of his eye he could see Ajamu Quick standing in the doorway that led to the rooftop, trying to get his attention. He can just wait, thought Fitz, wait until I get my breath back.

The roof shuddered underneath him, hard. The quartet must really be pumping it, he thought.

Then the concrete bucked. He fell forward, catching himself with both hands. The violinist staggered against the violist, her bow screeching across the strings. Quick was hanging on to the door frame, eyes and mouth wide with astonishment.

'Now what's happening!' shouted someone, as the music cut out all at once.

It's only an earthquake, thought Fitz. He opened his mouth to tell everyone what was happening, but nothing seemed to happen, as though the words were travelling from the horizon, and it would take them a while to get here.

He was trying to sit up when the next tremor threw him sideways against the railing, the metal thwacking painfully into his back. He clung to the metal poles, getting a giddying view of the edge of the roof as the building shook under him.

Things were coming out of the ground. It looked like one of those fast-motion films of plants growing. Or maybe metal fingertips, poking up through the pavements and the roads. Fitz had a sudden vision of a huge robot buried underneath the city, angrily woken by the blare from the rooftop.

People ran screaming between the stubby grey objects, stumbling and falling. 'What are they?' screamed one of the musicians. 'What are they?'

Fitz heard his voice say, 'It's only an earthquake.'

When the shaking stopped, it seemed like a long time before anything happened, anyone moved. He was on his knees, hanging on to the railing, the guitar a dead weight around his neck.

He pulled himself up, clinging to the metal poles. For a moment he thought the ground was shaking again, but it was him, feeling solid ground wobble the way you did after spending a day in a boat.

The street was a long way down. He pushed himself away from the railing, sharply, not sure of whether it would keep supporting his weight. For that matter, was the building going to stay standing up?

He pulled off the guitar, disentangling himself from its cords. He couldn't see any buildings that had actually fallen down. In the street, people were picking themselves up, clinging to one another, shocked into silence or babbling in frightened voices.

The street was full of the blank grey metal lumps, sticking up like shark fins from concrete and grass, pavement and paving, as far as Fitz could see. He turned slowly. Here was a row of the things, cutting diagonally across a street – one had tipped over a parked car as it forced its way out of the asphalt. There was one that had smashed through the corner of a building, pulverising part of the stairs that led up to the front door. There were great masses of them in the park, forming miniature curves and spirals.

The musicians were staring out at the city. 'There must be hundreds of those bloody things,' said Ann.

'Thousands,' said one of the drummers.

'Did the tigers do that?' said Quick, dazed. 'How? How did they do that?'

Someone clutching a guitar with a shattered neck said, 'Oh, God, what's going on?'

Right now, I'm the band leader, thought Fitz. He said, 'We don't know how much damage those things have done – or the quake. Let's get down to street level and clear of the building. No – leave the equipment. Let's just get ourselves out of here.'

They stumbled down the stairs, hands pressed against the wall as though they no longer trusted the floor to stay still.

One of the things was blocking the doorway. It had shattered the pavement outside, surrounding itself with a ring of concrete chunks and grey dust. The musicians stared at it, panicky, waiting for it to do something.

'Come on,' said Fitz loudly, 'let's get the emergency exit open.'

The taiko team helped him unlock the side door and hold it open while the musos spilled out on to the street.

There was no escaping the things. Three more had punched up through the asphalt, sending great cracks shooting across the road. A pair of tigers were sniffing at one of them, conversing in a low growl. They glanced up at the crowd of humans pouring out of the building, then went back to examining the object. It made Fitz think of a stunted, rounded Stonehenge.

'They don't know what they are, either,' he murmured to Quick.

'Never mind those for now,' said Quick. His confusion had worn off. 'We need to get teams out to help the injured and clear the roads. Where we can.'

'Right,' said Fitz. 'We'll worry about those things later.' That's if no more of them pop up in the meantime, he thought.

Fitz couldn't help wondering if the Doctor had somehow arranged the quake to delay the spaceport raid even further. It would be days before they finished picking up the city. The roads were the worst hit, fractured by the quake or punctured by the metal fins.

'Hurricane, flooding, quake,' he said to Maria as they hauled the last of the equipment out of the office tower and into the open air. With the side street blocked with metal lumps, they'd opened an emergency door at the front of the building, leading out into the courtyard interrupted by the single blunt monolith. 'All we need now is a fire, and we'll have the complete set.'

'Don't say things like that,' she said, carefully putting down the stand that held her mixing board. 'We don't need any more bad luck.'

'Oh, there's no such thing as luck,' said Fitz. He grunted, dragging his amps across the concrete. Ann stooped to help him lift the heavy chunk of electronics. 'Not around here, anyway,' he puffed.

Maria was setting up the deck. 'Give me a minute,' she said. 'I just want to make sure everything is still working.' Fitz sat down on the amp, wiping sweat from his face with his sleeve. Hitchemus's famous good weather was back with a vengeance.

Out of nowhere came a violent whine. The speakers, normally invisible, turned into shimmering, twisting patches of vibrating air.

Fitz said several choice twentieth-century words, grabbing for the deck. He stared at it in confusion. 'How do I switch off that racket?' he shouted.

Maria leaned past him and slid a control down to zero. The whine fell away to nothing as the speakers broke up.

'*Thank* you,' he sighed. 'What caused *that* little hiccup?'

Ann cracked open the toolkit. 'Give me a minute, Fitzie.' She took out a hand-held device and plugged it into the side of the deck.

Ewegbeni and Fitz went on loading stuff into the van while Ann fussed over the machine. After a few minutes she announced, 'There's nothing wrong with the deck. Something's interfering with its signal – disrupting the speakers. This used to happen a lot when we worked in a theatre that broadcast performances. They had a dirty transmitter. It leaked a lot of signal.'

'But the whole net is down,' said Maria. 'No media, no phones, nothing. Who's broadcasting?'

As one, they all turned to stare at the metal fin sitting in the middle of the pavement.

Fitz said, 'Whoah. Tiger FM is on the air.'

Ann unplugged her little device and, hesitantly, held it up to the machine. 'You're right – it is coming from this thing. Look at the meter.'

'Forget that,' said Fitz. 'You can hear it.' The thing was softly hissing to itself, like a wireless tuned just off the station.

He crouched down. There were symbols etched into the metal surface, right at the bottom. He reached out for them.

'I don't think we should touch anything,' said Ann. 'We should get someone to look at those symbols – see if we can decipher them.'

'The tigers. I'll bet they'd know.'

Ann said, 'Yeah, but do we really want them to know about this?'

'What if they already know?'

'They seemed as surprised as everyone else when those things came popping up like bread out of a toaster,' said Fitz. 'But, yeah, they might know what these symbols mean.'

'God,' said Maria. She was staying well clear of the metal curve. 'What if it's radioactive or something?'

'No,' said Ann, stalking around it with her meter. 'The interference pattern would be different. I think this is some kind of transmitter. Maybe the signal from the keyboard activated it.'

'Or maybe someone's trying to talk to us,' said Ewegbeni.

They all turned to look at the pianist. He was sitting in the back of the van, watching them with folded arms.

Ann crouched beside the metal fin, bringing her ear closer to its surface. 'Can you hear something?' she said. 'Crackling, or –'

'Can… hear me?' said the fin.

Ann nearly fell over. Maria and Fitz bounded to their feet. Ewegbeni just stayed where he was, watching with interest.

'Hello?' said the fin. The sound was mixed with hisses and crackles. 'Can you hear…?'

'Yes,' said Ann. 'We hear you.'

'Wait, wait,' said Fitz. 'Who *is* that?'

'If it's not anyone on the planet,' said Ann, 'it's got to be someone in space. Maybe there's a ship nearby.'

'Would that thing have the power to transmit out to space?' said Maria.

'It would if the fins form an array,' said Ann. 'Come in,' she told the fin. 'This is Hitchemus calling. Are you receiving us?'

'…hear you…' said the fin. '…out in space. Heading for

Hitchemus…'

'My God, we were right,' said Fitz. They crowded around the fin. Ewegbeni casually got up and walked around as though stretching his legs, keeping an eye out for tigers.

'…help?'

'Yes, we need help,' said Ann quickly. 'The colony has been invaded by indigenous life forms. Can you alert the military?'

Lots of whooshing and crackling. '…closer… wait?' Fitz wasn't sure if the voice was male or female.

'I think they want to wait until they're closer, and the signal is stronger,' said Maria.

'We can't wait!' said Ann. 'You've got to contact the marines. Get them here. The tigers have taken over. Do you understand?'

'…signal… stronger,' said the voice. Fitz found himself staring up at the sky. '…days… wait?'

'I think the signal's fading out,' said Ann.

'Well, get it back!' Fitz waved his hands at the fin.

'Oh, and how do you suggest I do that?' she said.

They tried powering up the keyboard again, but nothing happened. 'We don't know where they are, exactly,' said Maria. 'There might be a planet between us and them. We'll have to try again later.'

Ewegbeni started whistling. All three of them jumped back from the fin, grabbing their instruments and trying to look casual. A moment later, a tiger came around the corner. It sat down and watched them as they loaded the rest of their stuff into the van.

The van was parked outside Quick's café. They'd had to drive around several of the metal things to get here. Fitz and Ann carefully lowered one of the heavy amplifiers down to the asphalt.

Brilliant, Fitz was thinking, completely brilliant. If he could persuade Quick to use the fin things to call for help, the raid on the spaceport wouldn't have to happen at all. By stalling for time, he'd made the problem solve itself. All hail Fitz Kreiner, the unmover and the nonshaker!

Fitz squinted into the distance. There was a woman walking down the empty street towards them.

They hefted the amp into the café, depositing it in a corner under one of the tables, and went back out to the van. The woman was closer. She was a shabby, shambling figure, like a mirage in the hot sunlight.

'Anji,' said Fitz. 'Anji?'

She was limping slightly. One of her sleeves was torn, hanging loosely around her arm. Her eyes seemed to have retreated into her face, locked on him, staring at him as though from the other end of a tunnel.

'Fitz,' she said, stepping right up to him. He was expecting a hug, but instead, she grabbed hold of his shoulders. 'Fitz, listen. I know how the tigers got smart. I know how we can stop them.'

Fitz looked around, looked past her. Thank God, there were none of the stripy guys around to hear this. 'What happened to Dr Grieve?' he said.

'Listen to me!' Anji snapped. She looked a little crazy, looked as if she hadn't slept for a couple of days. 'I know how we can stop the tigers.'

'Come inside,' said Fitz. 'Come inside, right now.'

'The tigers have two hearts, you know,' she babbled. 'Besma told me. One in the chest and one in the abdomen.'

'We'll talk about it, all right? Quick is right in here. Come on.'

'All we have to do is blow it up.'

'Blow what up?'

'It's all we have to do. I'll tell you all about it.'

She was still holding on to his arm as he led her into the café, her finger pushing into his skin. He knew he didn't want to hear any of what was coming next.

As they emerged from the forest, the squawks started to panic. Longbody playfully leapt after a group of the fat grey animals as they flapped squealing up from the long grass. The runners were big shapes disappearing across the plain, some of them looping back to the safety of the forest, others just bolting in mindless panic. The tigers almost never travelled in such a large group. The runners must have thought the end of the world had come.

The tigers had taken turns carrying the Doctor on their backs, but it was too difficult to do it in the forest with its close trunks and low branches. He managed to keep up with them anyway. Now he stopped at the edge of the grassy plain, sniffing the air and eyeing the clouds.

'What do you think, Longbody?' he said. 'What's the weather forecast?'

'It should stay like this for a while,' said the tiger. 'Sunny and breezy.'

'Hmm.' He slowly turned on the spot, taking in the high waving grass, the gentle curve of the hills, the dramatic rise of the cliff with its skirt of mossy rubble. 'So much detail,' he said, taking a deep breath. 'So much life.'

The tigers sent up a wave of grey squawks ahead of them. The quasi-birds fluttered noisily overhead and landed behind them. One actually collided with the Doctor, bouncing off his chest and flapping off into the grass. It had probably assumed he was a tiger, and flown too low.

Longbody hadn't bothered to visit the Stela since she was a cub. It looked smaller than she remembered, and the trip across the plain hadn't taken as long. She remembered dozens of cubs bounding through the grass, chasing the squawks, being cuffed by impatient grandparents.

'Humans have been here,' she said. 'Look at the Stela – someone's cleaned it.'

'Are you sure it wasn't tigers?' said the Doctor.

'I can taste them,' grumbled Longbody. 'They've been here all right.'

'Well, they don't seem to have done it any harm.'

'These are words,' said Big. He pointed at the rows of symbols on the big red slab. 'You can move them by pulling them down and sliding them. Look.' He took one of the circular glyphs between his fingers and pulled. It came out on a little stem. He pushed it down, below the row, slid it along, and pushed it back into place in a new position.

'Of course!' said the Doctor. 'The smart tigers have language, but it's almost structureless. They can't order the symbols in a meaningful way. But you…'

'We can tell the Stela what to do by putting the words in the right order,' said Big. 'It doesn't take long to work it out. You have a try.'

'I'll need a little help with the symbols.' The Doctor stroked the stone. 'Your grandparents had to teach you their meanings, didn't they? And then they waited. Waited for their descendants to do what they couldn't do. To solve the puzzle for them.'

'Bounce,' said Big. The tiger who had brought the Doctor from the Bewilderness stepped up. 'You help him out. Longbody, you and I are going for a walk around the rocks.'

By the time they got back from their patrol, the Doctor was happily shifting symbols around on the face of the Stela.

'Got your tiger skin on?' sneered Longbody.

'If you like,' said the Doctor absently. 'I have a human skin to wear in the city. It's all a matter of perspective. Bounce – this is "open", right?'

'It's open.'

'There's a taste of humans about the place,' said Big, 'but we couldn't see anyone. Perhaps they came, examined the Stela, and left.'

'It must have been recently. I can't get them off my tongue,' said Longbody.

'You know,' said the Doctor, 'I don't think this is supposed to be a puzzle. It's not an intelligence test – it's just a control panel whose function has been partly forgotten.'

Big stood up. 'Do you think humans might have been able to operate it?'

'No,' said the Doctor quickly. 'Not without a knowledge of your language. To make it work, you need to think like a tiger. To wear a tiger skin, as Longbody so eloquently put it.'

Longbody stuck out her tongue, as though she'd eaten something bad-tasting.

'*Et voilà*,' said the Doctor. With a flourish, he plugged in the last of the symbols, and stood back from the Stela.

Nothing happened. He stared at it, then slowly walked around it.

'I'm sure I…' he said. 'Why are you all giggling?'

A sound rang out, like two knives being struck together. The tigers parted, staring back at the rock face.

Through them, the Doctor saw the entrance opening, a wide circle in the ground. The grass above it shimmered and vanished, like a mirage on a hot day. The doorway shrank back into itself, disappearing into the sides of the shaft.

The Doctor stared down into the cool darkness, hands on his knees. There was a sloping passageway, studded with rocks and handholds, going down into the earth.

Big said, 'We call this the storehouse.'

Big led the way, clambering easily down the slope. Little lights came on in the walls, following his movement. Longbody supposed they were something like the lights in the humans' houses.

The Doctor climbed down without difficulty, jumping the last metre or so into the wide, echoing space at the bottom. More lights came on, showing the distant walls. The chamber was huge, roughly oval, high enough for him to raise his arms over his head. Every surface was made of a coarse, dark-grey metal which seemed to eat sound, muffling the echoes of their movements. It was deliciously cool, like a deep cave. The wall opposite the entrance was a wide, flat rectangle.

'Where does the power come from?' asked the Doctor.

'We don't know,' said Big. 'Maybe something in the ground.'

More tigers were working their way down the slope, marching into the chamber.

'But there's nothing here,' said the Doctor. He crossed to one of the distant walls, and ran his hands down the smooth surface. He turned back to Big, looking worried. 'It's empty.'

The last of the tigers were crowding into the chamber. It had been spacious for a group of tumbling cubs, but it was only just large enough to comfortably hold them as adults.

'Wait,' said Big.

They waited. The chamber was full of the sound of tigers breathing, someone scratching behind their ear.

The wall at the far end of the chamber was starting to get lighter. It was barely noticeable at first. Longbody had a childhood memory of watching her own shadow darken on the grey floor.

The wall had everyone's attention now. Out of the rectangle of light a hazy image formed. It was a tiger, no different from any of the tigers sitting in the chamber. It looked out of the wall with a patient expression.

The flickering image on the screen held a single tiger's egg in its arms, a round, purple, gelatinous mass. 'Egg,' it said.

'Egg,' muttered all of the tigers, involuntarily.

The language lesson went on for half an hour. Longbody remembered spending days in front of that screen, excitedly gobbling more and more words and seeing at once how to put them together. By the end of their time at the storehouse, the cubs were all chatting away nonstop. Their grandparents watched them, pleased but puzzled, unable to follow what they were saying. Old Chew You had been there, Longbody remembered, doing as much talking as the cubs. It had been so strange for his familiar voice to seem like so much babble.

At the end of the first lesson, the screen faded into darkness. Longbody remembered there was a pattern of lessons and breaks.

The Doctor was sitting cross-legged at the front of the crowd of tigers. He had watched the lesson raptly. He seemed almost to be coming out of sleep as he turned to Big, blinking, and said, 'What else is there here?'

'Look around,' said the heavy tiger.

During the language lesson, doors had silently appeared in the walls all around them. The Doctor bounded to his feet, staring around. Some were open doorways, tall enough for a tiger to stroll through; others were closed doors, marked with the same word-symbols as the Stela, picked out in reds and golds. The Doctor went to one doorway, then the next, then another, unable to choose where to start.

Through one doorway, there came the sound of rushing water. Tigers were lining up to step through. The Doctor crouched down, peering past them into the dimly lit room beyond. 'A little door about fifteen inches high,' he muttered. Cold air leaked from the opening.

'There's an underground river in there,' said Longbody. 'To stop us from drying out while we're here.'

'Some of us have visited several times,' said Big, 'curious about what's in each of the rooms. We've learned so much. Now that we have control of the planet, we can begin to develop our own technology. We'll build, and invent. We'll get more of those doors open.'

Longbody gave a mew of disdain. Big ignored her. 'Come here,' he told the Doctor.

The Doctor followed him eagerly, stooping through the low doorway with surprising ease. Longbody followed behind.

The room was smaller than the main chamber – not meant to teach so many tigers all at once. Longbody had vague, cub's memories of the place.

There was another screen at the far end of the room, and objects all around the walls. Soft lights came on as they moved into the centre of the chamber. There was a wooden cart, a collection of spears, one of the harnesses with side bags, and several machines made of wood and metal, all different sizes. Longbody had no idea what most of the stuff was for.

'Different levels of technology,' said the Doctor. 'Another series of lessons? You're supposed to work your way up through fire and the wheel?'

Big said nothing. He turned towards the screen.

After a moment, it began to flicker with the image of a pair of tigers. In the background they could see some of the objects in the room.

One of the tigers was holding a small emerald-green flying animal. She had it by the feet. It kept flapping its wings and trying to escape. The smaller tiger standing next to her was fidgeting almost as much. 'Have a good look at this,' she told them. 'It's the last one of the green squawks. They used to live in the forest, but now there are more squawks on the plains. By the time you see this message, there probably won't be any more of the green ones.'

The smaller tiger pounced at the squawk, giggling. The speaker dropped it, swatting irritatedly at her companion. They started play-fighting while the metallic green bird flapped and panicked around the screen.

The image faded. Longbody was laughing. That message had been a favourite with the cubs.

The screen faded, then lit again with the image of an elderly tiger, her coat faded to a creamy yellow-white. 'There are only six of us left,' she said. 'We brought some of our grandchildren here, but it made no difference.' She shifted uncomfortably, as though her body ached.

'We've left so little for you,' she said. 'Some poetry, a few tools. There's a full record of the plague in the history room, starting with the earliest cases.

'No one bred while the plague was among us. We looked all through the storehouse for a cure. There are hints of medicine and methods that can cure anything. But we never found them.

'You find them. You might need them one day.'

She faded to nothing.

Big said, 'The storehouse's creators had high technology – better than the humans. And even they weren't the first – they found a deserted city and built on it. That was hundreds of thousands of years ago.'

'But you lost all that,' said the Doctor. 'How did you lose it?'

'No one is sure,' said Big. 'But there's a big gap in the record. We think that maybe there weren't any bright tigers for some centuries. No knowledge was passed on, and no one could enter the storehouse. The buildings fell down, the machines fell apart. It might have been eighteen or even twenty-four generations before intelligent tigers were born again.'

'Freaks of atavism...' said the Doctor. 'Throwbacks to that original, brilliant civilisation.'

'The storehouse creators realised that their children and their grandchildren couldn't sustain their civilisation, couldn't understand anything but the most basic language. So they built this place for anyone who came after them that could.'

'Isolated,' breathed the Doctor. 'Totally cut off from your past. An island in an ocean of time. Oh, yes.' He spread his arms, turning in a slow circle. 'But then there's this. This storehouse.' His hands dropped to his sides. 'It connects you with the other bright generations like a bridge across the river of time. Extraordinary. You're lucky. So lucky.'

'Our responsibility,' said Big, 'is to contribute something – if possible, something no previous generation has been able to provide.'

'Music,' said the Doctor. 'A piece of human culture.'

'Human music,' said Big. 'Past generations have developed technology, and science, and architecture. But we are the first generation to make contact with another culture. There are speculations about that in some of these archives.'

The Doctor began to hop from room to room, trying to take it all in at once. Longbody could barely keep up with his darting enthusiasm. In one chamber there was a model of Hitchemus itself, a small screen on which the planet rotated in fast motion, years passing in seconds. Clouds raced over the surface, the ringed moon swung around and around its parent.

'Is this a real picture?' said Big.

'Recording,' said the Doctor. 'Your ancestors launched satellites.' He sat cross-legged in front of the screen, head bowed under the low ceiling. He frowned, pushing his face closer to the screen. 'There's something…'

'What is it?' said Big.

The Doctor sat back, rubbing his chin thoughtfully. 'Let me think about it,' he said.

There were more doors, the closed doors, the ones they hadn't been able to open. Each had rows of symbols, more complicated than the Stela.

'These ones are tests,' said Big. 'Or locks. We don't understand why our ancestors would want us to have some of their knowledge, but not all of it.'

'It might be nothing more than practical reasons,' said the Doctor. He tapped a finger along the row of symbols. 'There's no point in teaching you to roast marshmallows if you haven't discovered fire. Or run a nuclear reactor before you know why the blinking red lights are bad…'

He trailed off.

'What is it?' said Big. The Doctor was ducking back into the room with the model of Hitchemus. Big and Longbody exchanged glances and followed him.

'Look at the axial tilt,' said the Doctor. 'The angle of the planet as it rotates. Your climate should be shifting wildly. Is this model accurate?'

'How would we know?' said Big.

The Doctor hugged himself. 'I've been so wrapped up in my own affairs, I never gave it any thought. Hitchemus, such a nice place to visit, with such marvellous weather, if you don't mind the hurricanes.'

'What are you talking about?' said Longbody.

'The climate on your world ought to be *wildly* changeable!' He flung his arms wide for emphasis. 'Catastrophic storms, all the time. I think your ancestors found a way to keep it under control. How else could you have survived so long?'

Longbody said, 'They didn't do a very good job, given the hurricane we just had to live through.'

Big was thoughtful. 'Perhaps it isn't working right. Or perhaps

162

it's not supposed to work all of the time. We must look for records.'

They all scrambled back out of the room. Bounce bounced up, dripping with water. 'Are we going to open another room?' she asked.

'I'll make you a deal, Big,' said the Doctor. 'I'll open a door for you – if you'll look for ways to co-operate with the humans.'

'Which door?' said Bounce excitedly.

The Doctor spun around on the spot, and stabbed out with a finger, apparently at random. 'This one!' he announced.

'Can you actually do that?' said Longbody.

'I've had lots of experience with alien languages,' said the Doctor. 'Puzzling out maths, scientific systems – you saw me work out the Stela! If anyone can bridge that gap for you, it's me.'

'It seems like cheating,' said Big. 'We're meant to make these discoveries for ourselves.'

Bounce said, 'But we are the first to meet people who aren't tigers. That changes everything.'

'I think you're just teasing us,' said Longbody.

'Oh, come on, come on,' said the Doctor. Longbody had seen the same excitement in a few of the tigers, the ones who wanted to know more and more. He wasn't interested in them half as much as he was interested in their storehouse of knowledge. 'Don't you want to know what's in there?'

'Not unless I can eat it,' she said.

'Go on,' said Bounce. 'Have a go at it. It's worth a try.'

The Doctor swivelled to face Big. 'Well? Do we have a deal?'

'You have to be more specific about what you're asking for,' said Big.

At once the Doctor said, 'The music teachers. Talk to them. Strike a bargain – return them to the city in return for continued lessons. Make sure they get the medical attention they need. A show of good faith.'

'We have to have the music, Doctor,' said Big.

'Yes yes yes,' he said. 'Explain to them why you want their help. I'll wager many of them will be fascinated – even flattered – if you treat them like friends instead of prisoners.'

'All right. If you can open any one of these doors, then I'll arrange it.'

The Doctor broke into a grin. 'I'll need Bounce's help again,' he said.

Bounce nodded vigorously, imitating the human gesture, spraying everything with water.

Longbody left the Doctor happily fiddling with the symbols on one of the doors. 'This looks a lot like Boyle's law,' he was muttering to himself. 'Base twelve, of course…'

She sank gratefully into the underground river, part of a miniature crowd of six tigers refreshing themselves in the frigid water. Her skin was dry and coarse after so long in the flavourless air of the storehouse. She floated for a while, just soaking it up.

A wave rippled through the river. She opened her sleepy eyes and looked around. The water was sloshing back and forth. Another wave, bigger this time, crashed over her head. 'What's going on?' she spluttered.

A couple of other tigers were bobbing around next to her. 'Feels like the ground is shaking,' said one.

Longbody exploded from the water. 'What's he done?' she roared.

She pushed past the crowd at the river-room entrance and bounded into the main chamber.

Tigers were hovering near the sloping exit, not sure what to do. 'Stay in the storehouse!' roared Big. 'We'll be safe down here.'

The new door was open. Light was streaming out of it. Bounce stood by it, uncertainly, her shadow stretching across the grey floor. 'Is he in there?' said Longbody.

'Yes.'

'He's trying to destroy us!' she yowled. 'He's trying to wreck the storehouse and kill us!'

'No,' said Bounce. 'The ground started shaking as soon as he opened the door. Whatever's happening, I think it was supposed to happen.'

'You're blinded.' Longbody shoved Bounce aside. 'I'm going to kill him.' She put her head through the doorway.

The room was full of light. She squinted into the bright patterns, trying to make out the shape of the Doctor so she could pull him out and bite off his head.

Someone hooked their claws into Longbody's arse. She yowled as she was hauled bodily out of the doorway.

It was Big. There was no way she was going to fight him. She rolled over, showing her belly.

Lying there, she realised the shaking had stopped.

Big bared his teeth at her. 'Go up and make sure the entrance is clear,' he ordered.

She got up and went to the sloping entrance. He was right – if the rock face had been damaged in the quake, there might be debris covering the entrance.

Longbody went up the slope. There was a simple control for the door. She pushed it, and jumped back as dirt and stones rained in through the opening entrance. But it seemed clear enough. She poked her head out to take a look.

The human that had stuck a pitchfork in her was standing not four metres away.

Hullow, thought Longbody, pulling herself up out of the hole. The human was clutching a different tool this time, but it looked flimsy and useless.

She launched herself into a charge. The tool broke and fell away as she slammed into her prey and pinned it easily to the ground. Longbody considered. From this angle, the easiest way to kill it would be to bite a big chunk out of it.

Grieve shouted, 'Get off her!'

Longbody turned her head. Grieve could fire her gun before Longbody could disengage from her prey and charge her.

But she didn't. She ran up, lifting the weapon, looking panicked. Longbody had no idea what she was planning to do – probably the human didn't, either. The instant Grieve was in range, Longbody kicked out and took the gun's barrel in her hind feet. She had no idea how to fire it, so instead she used it like a club, swatting at the human.

It connected with a bone-shattering crunch above the woman's shoulder. By the way she went down Longbody could see the blow had broken her neck and her skull.

She dropped the gun among the tall grass and turned back to her prey.

'Longbody!' yelled the Doctor. Another interruption. Her prey started wriggling and shouting for help. 'Stop!'

Big was there too. 'Let the human go, Longbody.'

There was nothing for it. Longbody slithered back off the human's body and crouched at her feet, watching her, ready to have another go.

The human tried to get up, and ended up crawling through the crushed grass. The Doctor picked her up. They started to argue.

Longbody glanced at Big. 'Told you I could taste humans.'

'I'm glad you didn't get more of a taste of that one,' said Big. 'Look – they must be friends.'

'You're right,' said Longbody bitterly. 'Friends.'

More tigers were coming up out of the storehouse. They smelled blood, and more of it to come, forming a loose circle around the Doctor and his raging friend. This was how the tigers picked off a panicked or injured runner, simply waiting for it to wear itself out, and then closing in on it from all sides.

The Doctor glanced around at the tigers. He knows, Longbody realised; he's trying to keep her alive by getting in our way – we can't kill her without killing him. With luck, both of them would go down under the hungry group. All the tigers were waiting for was a signal from Big.

But the signal never came. Big stayed still, and quiet, and the others couldn't act without at least a gesture from him.

Incredibly, the human was walking away – stepping through the circle of tigers! Longbody got up, but Big nosed her side, warning her to stay put. She sat down, grinding her teeth, watching that tantalising back disappearing into the haze of the plain.

The Doctor slumped a little, looking relieved. The circle began to disperse, disappointed. 'What are those things?' someone said.

Longbody turned to scan the plain. She had barely noticed the grey lumps sticking up everywhere, as though rocks had fallen from the sky.

Bounce tugged at the Doctor's ragged coat. 'Look what's happened.'

The Doctor turned slowly, staring at the big metal shapes sticking up out of the ground everywhere. 'What are they?' he whispered.

'I've never seen them before,' said Big.

'Good grief,' said the Doctor, holding on to his face as though he thought his head might burst. 'What have I done?'

Longbody was already at work on the human corpse, biting through the clothes to reach the soft flesh of a thigh. 'Get away from her!' snapped the Doctor. 'I won't have you eating people.'

'She's only dead,' she protested, but the Doctor looked ready to have a fight. Longbody backed off, crouching near the corpse, and went back to watching the departing human.

'She never even recognised me,' breathed Longbody.

Later, Longbody went a little distance from the storehouse, hoping for some privacy. It was pleasantly warm, and several tigers were taking a break from the dimness of the underground chambers, sunning themselves or chewing idly on squawks. Longbody stalked past them, the long grass brushing her flanks.

There were plenty of the things to choose from. They were scattered about the plain like the curved, mossy rocks that dotted the Gathering. But they were the wrong shape for sleeping on, or sitting on to get a view of your surroundings. They looked more like the crest on a runner's head, one side straight, the other curving up to a rounded peak. Longbody chose one and walked around it. It was about as thick as a tiger's body.

She sniffed at the metal, and ran her fingers over its surface. It was very slightly textured, like the concrete paths of the humans' city, and not at all shiny – even in the bright light, it looked dim and grey.

If this was some kind of machine, she thought, then it should have controls to make it work. But there was nothing, no break in the smooth grey stuff. The controls might not be here, she thought – after all, the Stela is a good distance from the door in the ground. And opening the door to what the Doctor had dubbed 'the weather room' was what had made these things come out of the ground in the first place.

She shied back from the lump of metal. If the Doctor did something else down there, who knew what might happen?

Longbody sat and thought. Everyone treated the ancients' stuff as though they were intelligence tests – like the tests that Grieve had always been giving them. She grinned to herself. The real test had been working out what you were supposed to do, and then completely failing to do it, as though you were an idiot.

But they weren't meant to be locks. There was no one beside the bright tigers who could get into the storehouse or any of its rooms. Not until now, anyway. And they weren't meant to be tests, either, not difficult ones. The ancients would have wanted it to be as easy as possible for their descendants to inherit their stuff. They just didn't expect so much to be lost between bright generations.

So these lumps had something to do with the weather. Maybe they could predict it, the way the humans' satellite could. Maybe they could protect an area against danger like a hurricane. Longbody leaned back, squinting up at the bright, cloudless sky. Had the hurricane itself triggered the things to rise from the ground, to fight it?

There were an awful lot of the metal things. Were they all the same? Longbody decided to tour around a few of them, despite her nervousness. She was a fast runner when she needed to be.

She looked at one after another of the things, frightening off a flock of curious squawks. They all seemed to be as identical as twin cubs – same curving shapes, same softly rough, featureless surface.

The twelfth one she looked at was different.

She found herself actually jumping back from the thing. She made herself sit still, a respectful distance from it, turning her head to scan the sky. It was calm and empty.

Longbody nosed up to the metal structure. She was right – there was a miniature row of symbols on its surface, close to the ground, following the curved edge.

She sat for a long time, reading the symbols. Then she reached out and carefully slid two of them into new positions.

She was sure the machine began to make a soft hum, perhaps a hiss, just at the edge of her hearing. Longbody grinned. It was more or less what she had expected.

She didn't expect what happened next. A voice said, 'You're right – it is coming from this thing. Look at the meter.'

There were other sounds. Longbody looked around, then walked around the machine. She couldn't see anything.

'Forget that,' said a different voice. 'You can hear it.'

The first voice said, 'I don't think we should touch anything. We should get someone to look at those symbols – see if we can decipher them.'

Longbody understood.

She looked around. No one had seen her, no one else was listening to the voices coming from the machine.

She made a careful mental note of the machine's position and slipped back to the storehouse. Big's vocoder was where the bulky tiger had left it, near the entrance. Casually, she picked it up and slung it around her neck. The sunbathing tigers either didn't notice or weren't interested.

A little distance away, she fiddled with the vocoder until it was working badly, making a lot of hissing and popping sounds and dropping words now and again. She went back to the machine. Voices and sounds were still coming out of it. She pressed her nose to the metal and said, 'Can you hear me?'

Karl Sadeghi, composer, polishes his glasses shakily and continues:

But then there are the times when each part sounds quite reasonable on its own. So you go back to the top, and run through it again, and it's still wrong. So you start looking further afield… You look at the other players, the ones you didn't think were at the centre of the problem. Over and over, searching for that flat note that brought it to, to ruin.

You wonder if the flaw lies with you. If you wrote the piece yourself, maybe you're the problem – your head just wasn't big enough to contain what you heard, you just couldn't squeeze those transcendent sound-shapes down into the right combination of dots on paper. You just couldn't hear the music that was happening around you. Or maybe you just can't understand it well enough to know what's going on.

So you go back to the top…

Karl's part

They were laughing. They were all laughing. Sour voices, hysterical voices; warm voices, relieved voices. Karl sat on a rock, looking out over them, and it was all he could do not to join in that murmuring, crazy sound.

The musicians formed a rough crescent, sitting on the damp grass in the new, hot sunshine. Many had taken off their sodden clothes and hung them from trees, or slung them over rocks. They were a muddy, half-dressed, ragged orchestra, instruments cradled in their laps. Two cellists sat on stones, pushing them into the soil first to make the improvised seats stable, giggling at their own ludicrousness. There were perhaps two dozen violins and violas, a handful of clarinets and oboes, a lone bassoon. The percussion section was represented by a pair of castanets and a triangle. A couple of synthesisers would have to fill in for everything else. The players held the translucent spheres in one hand, tapping at controls flickering across the surface.

The tigers had constantly been bringing instruments, sheet music and recordings from the city. They wore what looked like saddlebags, yokes of wood and runner leather that fitted over their backs, flanked with large baskets. Karl suspected the tigers were raiding the Academy, emptying it of everything they could find. But their last delivery had been different: blankets, boxes of food and medicine stamped with the emergency services' symbol, even a tent. They had gone through everything looking for messages, perhaps hidden from tiger eyes, but there was nothing. The musicians had murmured among themselves as they divided up the supplies, bandaged hands and feet, made the tent into a shelter for the ill. Had the tigers taken the things, or begged them, or been given them? And why now, why were the tigers caring for them now, why had they brought them together after keeping them alone for so long?

Karl knew. The Doctor was out there somewhere, with the tigers, speaking for them. Speaking in the tigers' own language. He was not afraid to put his head in the tigers' mouths and fight for them.

Karl felt as though the Doctor's visit had broken a spell he had been under. It was time for the musicians to speak in their own language, to fight for themselves.

He had appropriated a short, straight twig as a baton. Now he tapped the rock he was sitting on. To his surprise, the players quietened down just as though they were in a rehearsal hall rather than a meadow. He stepped up on to his podium.

'Well, ladies and gentlemen,' he said. 'I thought we should try something familiar. And something for which we happen to have the sheet music.' Another ripple of laughter. A violist wiped beads of sweat away with his shirt cuff. A cellist's eyes were full of tears. 'We've got rather a lot of gaps, so we'll just make a rough attack on it to begin with.'

They stood, or sat up straight, the flat white sheets laid on the grass in front of them or projected in the air at eye level. The pages would turn themselves, if the playing was clear enough for them to follow.

Karl raised his baton, and they lurched into the overture from *The Marriage of Figaro*. Stumbling, giggling, unable to hear themselves properly, held together solely by Karl's unwavering count of the beat. Even that wasn't enough to sustain them, phrases colliding halfway through the piece and clattering to a halt.

'Again,' said Karl. 'Let's try it much more slowly this time.'

He struck up the beat again, more gently this time. They still sounded like a school band, but they made it through to the end of the overture.

Karl glanced around the meadow. The tigers were leaking out between the trees, attracted by the music, itching with curiosity. Some of them carried instruments, as though hoping to join in. Karl was startled to recognise several of his students. When had he learned to tell one tiger from another?

'Once more,' said Karl. 'A little faster this time.'

The tigers closed in on the improvised orchestra as they made their third attempt at the overture. The sound of the music was terrible, but there was another sound emerging, a more important

172

sound. The musicians' backs were straight, their faces at once calm and taut with concentration. They ignored the tigers, eyes flicking from the score to his baton and back. They were playing together, energetically, angrily, well aware of their alien audience but stringently ignoring it.

Karl felt none of the music in his body. He felt something else, the power and rage of those with nothing to lose, he felt drunk with daring. No matter what happened next, he would be able to face it.

'All right,' he said. 'Just once more. At speed this time.'

This time the strings came in together, sharp and loud as they could. The tigers formed a ring around them, closing in.

The musicians belted out the last few notes (and, God, the timpani were conspicuous by their absence, but it didn't matter) and then stood there, panting a little, watching him, surrounded by orange.

Karl held up his baton in both hands and snapped it cleanly in half.

As one, without hesitation, the players lifted their instruments above their heads and smashed them against the ground. The cellists picked up the rocks they had been sitting on and used them to club the instruments.

There was a new music in the meadow, a music of splintering and snapping, of twanging strings and bending metal, of stamping and kicking. Karl stood and watched as the orchestra destroyed itself.

None of the tigers moved to intervene. It was possible they didn't understand what they were seeing.

'Right,' he said. His voice rang out in the silence after the massacre. 'We are not going to be teaching any more music here, with or without instruments.'

Now the tigers were beginning to understand. One reached out a paw and hooked up the mangled remains of a violin. It hung from a claw as the tiger looked over the remains. They began to talk among themselves in their rough tongue. Karl saw claws popping out, mouths opening to display teeth. Hungry eyes were turned on the musicians, helpless at the centre of the orange crowd.

There was a mighty roar from the edge of the forest. Everyone froze. The roar was repeated. Karl could not pick out the individual words.

There was a small group of tigers standing where the meadow met the trees. They ran across the grass, shouting their message. The orchestra's audience milled in confusion, turning away from their intended victims to these newcomers.

The tigers talked.

They talked, and talked, and talked. The new arrivals had a great deal to say, apparently, and, once they had heard it, so did their fellows.

Karl got the musicians' attention by raising his hand, just slightly, relying on their instinct for catching signals from the conductor. He lowered the hand, sitting down carefully on the rock. Each of the musicians followed suit, carefully moving bits of wood or metal out of their way.

Karl closed his eyes, enjoying the feel of the sun on his face after the long days of rain. Either the tigers were going to eat them now, or they weren't. Either way, there would be no more sleeping in wet leaves, no more raw meat, no more growled orders backed up by teeth and claws.

Is this what you would have wanted me to do, Doctor?

There was nothing to do now but wait. He had become very good at waiting.

Second Chorus

Chapter Thirteen

Longbody and the Doctor sat side by side in the newly opened room, staring into the wall.

The screen showed the city of tigers. It was an aerial view, a still taken from some kind of flying craft. 'I wish they'd thought to film the vehicle itself,' said the Doctor. He reached out to the row of controls under the screen, and slid the symbols into a new configuration. He was getting to know the storehouse much too well, thought Longbody.

Longbody had persuaded Big to let her keep an eye on the Doctor. It wasn't a difficult job. Instead of fiddling with more doors, he'd decided the best thing to do was to absorb as much information about past bright generations as he could.

Big, meanwhile, had sent half a dozen tigers back to the Gathering, with instructions to return the music teachers to the city. It was a terrible move, thought Longbody: without those hostages, the Gathering would be vulnerable to attack. What if the humans could remember the way back? Even if they only vaguely knew the Gathering's location, other humans could find it.

'Those things that came out of the ground,' said Longbody.

'Let's call them Nodes,' said the Doctor, 'since that's what they appear to be. Nodes in some kind of network.'

'You knew that was going to happen, didn't you?'

'No,' said the Doctor, without taking his eyes off the screen. 'But now they're there, we have to find out what they're for.'

'Perhaps it's a pretty sculpture,' said Longbody.

'I found a map here earlier that shows the locations of the Nodes. They're all over the continent. Perhaps all over the planet, if there are some under the water. That's a lot of trouble to go to just for art's sake.'

'Anything is a lot of trouble to go to just for art's sake,' said Longbody.

The Doctor rolled over, looking up into the tiger's face.

'Is this another joke to you?' he asked. 'Like fooling poor Dr Grieve? No no no, you're interested in the storehouse, despite yourself.'

Longbody showed her teeth. 'Big trusts you, but I don't. I don't trust you to leave things the way they are. You'll get everyone excited, but for what? For our brainless cubs? For some other bunch of tigers that might be born in a hundred years' time? We'll be so busy thinking about the future that we'll forget about danger that's here right now.'

The Doctor smiled. 'If other people want to waste their time, let them.'

'Anything tigers have, humans will want,' growled Longbody. 'They'll push us aside to get it. Nothing will be safe until we get them off our planet.' She put a paw on the Doctor's back, lightly, but so that he could feel her claws. 'These Node things. They have something to do with the weather, don't they?'

'I think so,' said the Doctor. 'The symbols on the door suggest it – that's why I picked this one.'

'I knew it,' said Longbody, but the Doctor went on.

'I think the storehouse builders found a way to regulate the climate. The remaining land had to be preserved, if the tigers were to have a future.'

'Maybe the Nodes are lightning rods,' said Longbody, 'like the humans put on their roofs…'

'You see? You're interested, despite yourself.' Longbody stuck out her tongue, but it only made the Doctor smile. 'Every intelligent being enjoys a puzzle. This is just larger in scale than most.'

They worked through the rest of the day and into the night. Sometimes Longbody left the Doctor to his own devices, muttering to himself as he watched the images dance across the screens. He manipulated the speed until the information was flashing by, almost too quickly to follow. During those times, she would find other tigers – out of earshot of Big, who was examining items left in some of the rooms – and talk to them.

'Big is ready to give up everything we've won,' she told them.

'We own this planet. We don't have to share it with the humans. We don't need any help to explore the storehouse. If we go along with what the Doctor wants, we'll be throwing away our advantage. Who's to say they won't just turn around and kill us all, the first chance they get?'

Some of them agreed. Some of them didn't. Mostly, they didn't seem all that interested. Longbody kept repeating her message to anyone who would listen. As easily distracted as the tigers were, she knew they would be thinking about her words.

Sometime in the middle of the night, she found the Doctor lying on his side in front of the screen, propping up his head with an elbow. He didn't seem tired in the slightest. Longbody slid in behind him.

He was watching the ancient city again, this time a street-level view, as though someone were just wandering around filming stuff. They had spotted one of the cameras in an earlier recording – they fitted into a shoulder harness, with a viewfinder that extended on an arm in front of the cameratiger's face.

The buildings were a mixture of brick huts, wooden halls and larger structures made of something that reminded Longbody of the concrete used in the human city. The shapes were rounded, low; probably a dozen tigers lived in each house, likely a father and cubs. Water flowed in geometric lines between the structures.

'The same pattern keeps repeating itself,' said the Doctor. 'Century after century. A bright generation is born. It finds the ruins of the city, and starts rebuilding them. It breeds – perhaps using the artificial lake, or the dam, as a safe and local breeding pond.' That was just what the screen was showing – a group of fathers splashing around in the lake, watching over their egg cases. It tugged at Longbody's memory. She had probably been shown it as a cub. 'And then their problems start. They can't pass on what they know – not to their children, not even to their grandchildren. As the intelligent tigers get older and begin to die out, their buildings and machines get less and less maintenance. The dam collapsed because there just weren't enough tigers around to repair the wear and tear it had accumulated.'

'And when the humans arrived,' said Longbody, 'they just built their own homes over what was left of ours. They built their streets over our canals.'

'To be fair,' said the Doctor, 'they've preserved areas of the city with obvious ancient ruins. But they certainly took advantage of the lake, and the cleared land. I've seen herds of runners in a lot of these recordings – the city dwellers bred and raised them for food, instead of hunting them.'

They didn't hunt? Longbody couldn't believe it. Without hunting, what were tigers? Humans, she supposed. Imagine if the Doctor and Big made them give up hunting.

The next footage was very different. The camera – or whatever device was being used – roamed a city that was falling apart. Storm-damaged buildings had collapsed into ruins. One had been destroyed in a fire, nothing left but a blackened rim of bricks. The canals were choked with junk and weeds. The lake's waters had shrunk, leaving just a scummy slick in the bottom of the artificial basin.

An ancient tiger, his fur snow-white, faded into existence on the screen.

'By now you've seen several recordings from chewed-up old beasts like me,' he said. 'Pitying ourselves because everything we've built is falling to pieces. Well, that's just the way it is. We can't sustain a civilisation like this.' Longbody nodded to herself. This recording was definitely familiar. 'Maybe, once upon a time, every generation of tigers was intelligent. Maybe that's how our ancestors got so advanced. What happened to us? Why are our cubs too stupid to build a fire, let alone a city?

'Or is it the other way around? Were all tigers once stupid?

'Are we supposed to live like our children – just running in the forest, hunting when we're hungry? Would that be so bad?

'All these questions. You're going to have to try to answer them, if you exist. I'm too worn out to care any more.

'Our children and grandchildren went back to the forest long ago. They're happy there. With the buildings falling down around our ears, it's time we followed them. We're about to seal up the storehouse one last time.

'Maybe you'll work out a way to make every generation of tigers a bright generation. That would be a real advance. Maybe it's the only one worth making.'

He faded away. The Doctor did something to the controls, stopping the show.

'That was two bright generations ago,' said the Doctor, 'if I'm understanding your numbering system correctly. There was something about the city they never discovered. The next lot did, though. Look.'

He started another of the recordings. It showed a big, rounded building at the northern edge of the lake. As they drew closer, they could see that the miniature dam was part of the building. 'It's a hydroelectric power station,' said the Doctor.

'What's that?'

'A way of making electricity. Your ancestors got their power the same way the humans do now. There's nothing at all left of that building now.'

The recording went on, turning back to the city. In its centre, there was a great, grey-black structure, its matt surface barely reflecting the light. Longbody glanced at the walls of the storehouse, wondering if it was the same stuff.

The camera followed the perimeter of the huge, featureless oval – the building must have been as large as a few city blocks, with long arms reaching out to extra buildings all around it. It looked a bit like a tree trunk with branches reaching out. Tigers stood around the huge structure, in small groups or small crowds. There was a single doorway, a long slit that went right up the side of the main part of the building. Tigers were going in and out, carrying things.

Longbody's back arched a little in surprise. She was certain she had never seen this before.

After a while, all of the tigers retreated from the grey oval building. It started to change. 'What's happening?' said Longbody. 'It's getting smaller.'

'It's sinking into the ground,' said the Doctor, fascinated. The view went closer, watching the great mass disappearing below the soil. At last it was gone, leaving a vast oval hole, tigers hovering at its edge as they looked into the pit.

The Doctor turned to Longbody. 'It's a second storehouse,' he said. 'A much larger one. Smack in the middle of the city.'

'How did you find that recording?'

'Oh, I know a little more than you do about science,' he said lightly. 'It's easier for me to decipher the ancients' records. Just like opening the doors. Bring Big here, would you? He's got to see this.'

Longbody hesitated in the doorway. What if she killed the Doctor, right here, right now? She could say they got into an argument, that he threatened her, even physically attacked her. Perhaps she could bring one of the weapons from the messages room and put it near him, to make it look as though he'd tried to kill her first.

No. Big's curiosity was too great. He would watch that recording, and know what Longbody had been trying to keep from him. And it wouldn't be enough just to kill the Doctor – the others should agree that he was wrong, dangerous, that he had to die. Ideally, Big should kill him.

'I'll get him,' she said, and went to find Big.

They went above ground for the meeting, blinking in the light of mid-morning. Big sent Bounce to gather up all of the remaining tigers. They sat in a circle on the dry grass, among the silent metal bulk of the Nodes.

The Doctor spoke. 'It's my belief that the Nodes – the metal objects that came out of the ground – are part of a weather-control system, built by your ancestors.

'If I'm right, then the hurricane and all the recent inclement weather means that the system isn't working properly. If we can learn enough to operate it ourselves, we can stop the storms. We need to go through all the records in the weather room to know for certain. In any case, there's a more important discovery. This is not the only storehouse.'

181

The tigers babbled. Big roared for silence.

'There's a second storehouse, under the city, much bigger than this one,' said the Doctor. 'But there's a problem. The recordings show the second storehouse rising up out of the ground, like the Nodes. If we activate it, it'll destroy a large chunk of the human city.'

Longbody said, 'The city is only a century old. This new storehouse is worth much much more!'

Big agreed, but he said, 'Maybe there's another way to get to it.'

Bounce said, 'Are there any more? There might be storehouses all over the place.'

'Oh, you're just full of ideas,' murmured Longbody.

'We'll keep going through those recordings, looking for them,' said Big. 'From now on, we'll be exploring the storehouse night and day, learning everything we can. We'll also be using the equipment in the storehouse to start making our own recordings.' He looked around at each of the tigers. 'Time is limited – only our lifetimes.'

The meeting dispersed in a flurry of excited babble. Tigers stretched, groomed one another, or bounded off through the grass in search of munchies. Bounce playfully jumped on the Doctor. Her weight knocked him backwards on to the ground. She nibbled on his shoulder as he flailed underneath her. The Doctor pushed his fingers into Bounce's belly fur and started to tickle her. She bounded off him with a whooping laugh. He gave her tail a tug as she ran around him, overexcited by the day's discoveries. One of the other young tigers jumped on her, giving the Doctor a chance to clamber to his feet and back off, looking winded.

Longbody had the urge to join in the game and knock him over a few times herself. She took a deep breath and shook her body, stretching. She must, must wait for the right moment.

That overexcited, overgrown cub Bounce was snuffling around a pile of branches. 'Come and look at this,' she called out.

Longbody jumped down and ambled over. She saw at once that there were things hidden underneath the leaves, human stuff. Bags and poles and things.

'No wonder I could taste them,' said Longbody. 'It was here all the time.'

'Those two humans must have left it behind,' said Bounce.

'Perhaps it's a trap for curious tigers,' suggested Longbody.

Bounce pulled her nose out of the pile. 'Do you think so?'

Longbody tilted her head, but said nothing. Bounce stuck out her tongue and went back to examining the cache of stuff.

'Here they come,' said Longbody.

A row of tigers were emerging from the forest. This time there was no stampede of runners. The big creatures must have retreated deep into the trees. Never mind – they would go and taste the air for them later on. In the meantime the squawks made a tasty mouthful.

There was a human perched on the back of one of the tigers, drooping forwards over its neck, one hand resting on its head. The tiger moved slowly, tolerantly, giving him a gentle ride.

Tigers were crawling up out of the ground to meet the new arrivals. The Doctor followed. His eyes went wide as he saw the human. 'Karl!'

The music teacher gave a small, tired smile. 'Good afternoon,' he called.

The Doctor was pushed up out of the hole by the next tiger. He jogged across to Karl, helping him down from the tiger. 'Thank you, Jeoffry,' said Karl.

The human looked as if he needed a good clean. His face was smudged with dirt and mud, pale beneath the grime. His clothes were battered and dirty, and the fur on his head was tangled.

The Doctor said, 'Why did they bring you here? What's happening?'

'All the others have gone home to the city,' said Karl. 'Some messengers arrived from Big just in time to, to save us all from my foolishness. They had to carry two people that couldn't walk. I hope they're going to be all right.'

'What are you doing here?' said the Doctor, taking him by the shoulders. 'Why aren't *you* in the city, where it's safe?'

'It was my idea,' said Karl. 'Another foolish idea. I wanted to see you.'

'You need proper food,' said the Doctor. 'You need medical attention. You need familiar surroundings.'

'It wasn't hard to find out what was going on here. The tigers are such chatterboxes.'

The Doctor looked at him. 'You're beginning to understand their language.'

'I've been having lessons,' said Karl. 'I can pick out a word here and there. And they like to talk to me. They try to speak like humans.'

The Doctor broke into a grin. 'It's already happening,' he said. 'The exchange.'

'They've been a lot more friendly since your visit.' Karl sank tiredly down into the grass, sitting cross-legged. 'I think I'd like to have a little sleep now.' His gaze was caught by a shape nearby in the grass. 'Oh. Oh, who's that?'

The Doctor turned to look at the neat pile of earth and stones. 'I'm very much afraid that's Besma Grieve,' he said.

Karl nodded. 'I want to know what happened,' he said quietly, 'later.'

Before Longbody could say anything, Bounce picked up one of the poles in her mouth and dragged it across the grass. She dropped it at the Doctor's feet. 'What's this?' she said.

The Doctor crouched. 'What have you found?' he said. He followed Bounce to where Longbody was sitting beside the pile. 'It must be Anji and Dr Grieve's camp. Karl, come here. No, stay where you are.' The music teacher was leaning on Jeoffry's flank.

The Doctor rummaged through the stack of stuff. 'Oh, this is excellent,' he said. 'Karl, I have something for you to eat.' He picked up a bottle and filled it at one of the waterfalls, and took what he'd gathered up over to the human. 'Here,' he said.

But Karl had closed his eyes in the drowsy sunshine. Jeoffry was dozing behind him. The human's narrow body shifted with the rhythm of the tiger's breathing.

'Later, then,' said the Doctor softly, leaving the goods beside his sleeping friend.

* * *

When the Doctor next came up for air, Big and Karl were sitting together. Longbody was eating a squawk, a little distance away, just keeping an eye on things.

Karl said carefully, 'I'm sure you've heard what happened at the Gathering. So I'm afraid I don't have an instrument with me.'

Big had his vocoder slung around his neck. 'That's all right,' said the box. 'I don't want to learn to play. I just want to understand more. I've heard a lot of music, but I don't know anything about it. How do you make it up?'

Karl's head tilted forward, so that his damp hair fell down across his eyes, and gave a small smile. He had taken off his muddy coat, and washed his face in the waterfalls that trickled all around. Longbody supposed he had eaten some of the food the Doctor had found.

The Doctor said, 'The tigers must have music of their own.'

'Of course,' said Big. 'But it's not much like yours. We sing. Haven't you heard us singing?'

'Good heavens,' said Karl. 'Yes, I think I, I have. So that's what that was.'

'And we stamp our feet on the ground, in big groups.'

'You'll have to give us a performance later,' said the Doctor. 'But for now, it's Karl's turn.'

'Wait a moment.' Karl reached into the pockets of his ragged coat and brought out a datacube. He held the glassy recording up to the light. 'Beethoven's complete works.' He glanced at the Doctor. 'Of course. You don't think it's too obvious?'

The Doctor shook his head.

'Big, I'm going to play you Beethoven's Symphony Number Five in C minor. It's one of the most famous pieces of music ever written. Most humans have heard it so many times that they don't see anything special about it. It's become a cliché, a joke. But, if you spend a little bit of time looking at it in detail, you can learn how to see what it is that made it so effective.'

Karl pressed his thumb against a control in the datacube. Two speakers formed themselves in the air nearby, just tiny ripples against the sky.

The opening notes of the music boomed out at them, startling enough to make Longbody's fur stand on end. She rolled on to her back and scratched her belly, stretching out, as the noise went on and on.

'Oh, I know this,' interrupted Big. Karl paused the recording. 'It goes mew mew mew MEW, mew mew mew MEW, mew mew mew MEW, mew mew mew MEW...'

A few other tigers drifted across to see what was going on. They turned to one another, repeating the familiar phrase in their coarse voices. 'Mew mew mew MEW, mew mew mew MEW...'

Karl and the Doctor exchanged glances. For some reason, they both put their hands over their mouths. 'Well,' said Karl, his voice sounding a little odd, 'I'm glad you're familiar with it, that's helpful. Let's listen the whole way through.'

When the movement had ended, Karl touched the device again. 'Now let's return to the beginning,' he said. He played the first bit of the music again. 'What does it make you think of?'

Big looked uncomfortable, rearranging himself in the dry grass. 'I don't know,' he said.

'Sounds a bit like thunder,' said Bounce, her words picked up by Big's vocoder. She cocked her head. 'Does it?'

'Good,' said Karl.

'It sounds like two people having an argument,' said Big. 'First someone angry. Then someone pleading with them.'

'Or maybe the same person,' said Bounce. 'Sometimes angry and frightening, sometimes happy and gentle.'

'Excellent,' said Karl. 'Let's go beyond your immediate response to look at some of the details.' He pushed his hair out of his face. 'The section you describe as pleading – that's the second theme.' He manipulated the device, and a screen appeared in the air, displaying a couple of sheets of paper covered in symbols.

Karl glanced at Big, who said, 'That's music, although I don't know how to read it.'

The teacher said, 'This is the score for the beginning of the second theme. Don't worry too much about the exact details for now. But look at this: do you see what the cellos and double basses are playing, here? These four dots.'

'All right.'

'Now, that's the same as the first theme.'

'Mew mew mew MEW.'

'Played very quietly, underneath the softer, sweeter second theme. Here – let's listen to it. See if you can pick it out.'

The music echoed from the rock face. Karl stopped it after a few seconds.

'I heard it!' Bounce was fidgeting with excitement.

Big said, 'That's very clever. I didn't notice it at all the first time.'

'It turns up everywhere, in different disguises. Listen.' Karl went back and forth through the piece, picking out the theme over and over, shortened or hidden or played by different instruments.

'The more you go beyond the surface,' said the Doctor, 'the more you look into the structure of the music, the more you'll hear. And, hopefully, the more you'll enjoy it.' He turned. 'How about you, Longbody?'

'What?' she rolled over. 'Sorry, I was watching a bug.'

Big put one of his large paws on Karl's knee. 'Show us more,' he boomed.

It was time to find out what the humans were up to. Longbody took another vocoder off one of the newly arrived tigers, and crept through the grass to the special Node near the Stela. Most of the tigers were underground now, helping to search through the records.

Big was becoming more and more drawn into the Doctor's plan. What would it take to persuade him to get rid of the humans, instead of getting lessons from them? If she couldn't get the tigers to act sensibly, maybe she could scare off the humans, or at least throw them into confusion. Time to see what they were up to.

It wasn't hard to remember the controls she had pressed yesterday. A soft hissing echoed from the Node. She turned up the volume, just a little.

'This is Hitchemus calling inbound craft,' it said. Longbody grinned. Oh, excellent! They were waiting for her. 'Hitchemus calling inbound craft. Ajamu Quick here. Are you receiving us?

Come in.'

Longbody pressed her fingers into the simple control on the side of the Node. 'Hello,' she said.

'Thank goodness,' said the Node. 'We thought we'd lost contact with you.'

'Don't worry,' said Longbody. 'We'll be there soon. What's happening there on Hitchemus?'

'Things are looking up,' said the voice at the other end. 'We've got the hostages back – all but one who elected to stay with the tigers. They're half starved and half frozen, but they haven't been deliberately harmed.'

'That's good. Anything else?'

'Some very good news. We've found out how the tigers became intelligent. There's some sort of alien device hidden under the ground to the north of the city. It's affected their minds.'

'What are your plans?' Longbody asked.

The human said, 'We're going to blow it up.'

Longbody took a swim in the underground river to digest that piece of information. She floated for a long time in the cool darkness. In some ways, she thought, it might be better to let the humans go ahead. No more storehouse, no more need for music, no more living for future generations that might never exist.

She still hadn't decided what to do when she came up above ground.

'He genuinely cares about you, doesn't he?'

Longbody looked around for the owner of the voice.

Karl was sitting alone, with his back to the rock face, half hidden by the long grass. 'He really wants you to succeed. It's not just an interesting intellectual puzzle for him, this storehouse thing and all its secrets. You're just as much people to him as we are. With your mysterious past and your uncertain future.'

Longbody coughed up a human phrase. 'Don't carrre,' she said.

'We're in agreement there,' said the human.

Longbody sat down, looking at him speculatively.

'I can play the notes for Big. For any of you. I can play the tune.

But without expression.' He shifted a little. 'The Doctor thinks we're all becoming friends. He wants that happy ending so much, he'll drag it out of us with his bare hands if he has to. He sees hints of it, hope for it, in everything. Even when you don't care and neither do I.'

For a moment, Longbody thought she saw loathing in the human's face. She wasn't expert enough at deciphering their expressions to be sure.

'I really believe you could tear him apart, and whatever was left would go on fighting for that happy ending. If you forced him to live terrified in a, a damp forest, he would go on looking for the path that led back to you, so he could persuade you to let him make peace.'

In her own language, Longbody said, 'He's a fool who's wasting his time.'

'A fool?' Karl raised the canteen to his lips and swallowed. 'Sometimes,' he said, 'I think he's more real than any of us. The alien genius who sees things the way they really are. The rest of the time, I think he's out of his mind. Playing at being a saint.'

Longbody barked, 'Like tigers?'

'Do I like tigers?' Longbody nodded. 'It looks so ridiculous when you do that,' said Karl. 'Do I like tigers…? Let me be honest with you. If every last one of you fell off the planet right now and went spinning off into space, like a lot of little orange dots disappearing into nothingness… I'd watch.'

Longbody exposed her teeth, giving him a hunting stare. 'Inna greement there,' she purred.

He had helped her make up her mind. She stalked through the grass until she found Big sunning himself on a rock. 'There's something you have to know about,' she told him.

The Doctor was in the weather room. Big pushed his shoulders and head through the low doorway. A moment later, he emerged backwards, dragging the Doctor out by the back of his coat.

Big dropped him on the floor of the main chamber, his feet still sticking through the doorway. The tigers crowded in around him.

The Doctor looked up at the circle of toothy faces, careful to stay on his back and remain still, waiting to see what would happen.

Big said, 'It's over. Your friend told the humans about the storehouse. Now they plan to destroy it. We are going to destroy them first.'

Longbody had expected alarm, even panic, from the Doctor. Instead he just lay there, frowning a little.

From across the big chamber, the human Karrrl called, 'Doctor, what are we going to do? We can't let them –' He stopped abruptly as someone sat on him.

The Doctor seemed to be thinking out loud. 'Why are you telling me this? You could have kept me in the dark until it was too late. Unless it's too late already?'

'I'm telling you,' said Big, 'because I want your help. You know the storehouse is everything to us, it *is* us, there are no tigers without the storehouse. I want you to help us protect it.'

'Let me talk to the humans,' said the Doctor. 'If they realise what they're doing, they may stop.'

'We should never have let your friend live,' mourned Big. 'We should never have let them find out about the storehouse. It can never be safe again.'

Longbody said, 'He knew that we'd kill her if she stayed here. That's why he insisted we let her go. Even if it meant she told all her little friends.'

Bounce said nervously, 'What if they find the second storehouse? Under the city?'

'Well, they're hardly going to blow that up, are they?' said the Doctor. 'Look, Big, at least let me try. Don't throw away tiger lives – the city will be ready for an attack.'

'We can't risk it!' cried Longbody. 'This isn't the only world with humans. But it is the only world with tigers!'

'She's right,' said Big. 'You chose to leave the humans behind and come here among us. You can't be in the city and in the Bewilderness at the same time.'

Longbody insisted, 'You have to choose whether you're one of us or one of them.'

The Doctor closed his eyes. For a long moment, he lay there.

'All right,' he said. 'I'll help you.'

A muffled sound came from under the tiger that was sitting on Karrrl.

'But there will be costs,' said the Doctor. 'Certain things I want. The first is that you don't harm Karl in any way. None of this is his fault.'

Big snorted. 'We can't have one of them hanging about here. We should have eaten that woman while we had the chance.'

The Doctor sat up. 'If you lay a paw on him,' he said fiercely, 'I'll destroy your blasted storehouse myself.'

Some of the tigers arched in surprise. Big drew back a little. 'All right,' he said after a moment. 'We'll keep him prisoner. But, if you do anything you shouldn't, we'll eat him up.'

He turned and gestured to the tiger atop Karrrl, who obligingly shifted, plucking the squashed musician out from under him with a paw. 'Doctor,' gasped the human, 'I can't believe you – you can't –'

'Karl,' said the Doctor sharply. 'Shut up.'

Big batted the Doctor with a paw, rolling him on to the floor. He reciprocated by catching hold of the tiger's tail and giving it a playful tug. Big roared a laugh.

Chapter Fourteen

Fitz was surprised at how easy it had been to make the explosives. The raw ingredients had come from the southern agricultural settlements, where dozens of music teachers were living new lives as farmhands: weeding and picking, fetching and carrying, giving lessons in dimly lit cellars. Tigers were rarely seen in the south. There had been a half-hearted inspection, once, a few days before the hurricane – tigers tramping over crops, poking around in sheds, with no real idea of what they were looking for.

A skinny man delivered the load of chemical fertiliser, hidden under a heap of hemp fibre in the back of a truck. 'I taught the kids piano,' he told Fitz, after they'd finished shifting the heavy bags. 'We moved it down to the cellar. We sheltered there during the big storm, too. Snug and safe. From the outside you'd never know anyone was down there.'

Anji said she had left the hovercar in a little valley north of the city, walking the last few kilometres home, dodging a couple of tigers on the way. She told Fitz that she had worked it all out during that long trudge. She had taken from the car's dashboard a device that let you fly it by remote control. It would give you a view through the windscreen, maps and co-ordinates, and you could set a flight path and wiggle a sort of joystick thing to steer. No more difficult than a video game, she said.

Quick and Anji had spent hours in the library working out how to make the bomb. The fertiliser had been made for them specially; it hadn't been used since settlement, to kick-start the least promising alien soil until the farmers could get more Terran organic matter into it. Fitz stayed well clear of the plotters, making his usual rounds, trying to work out the best thing to do. Trying to imagine what the Doctor would do.

Now he sat against the wall outside Anji's flat, combing his fingers through his hair, back to front, over and over. The Doctor

192

would just swoop in, change everyone's mind, disarm the bomb or whatever and save the day using a teaspoon and a couple of plastic bookends.

Nah. That was a cartoon of the Doctor. He could work miracles, sometimes, sure. Sometimes miracles just happened around him. But he wasn't the magic cure for everything – to save planet, just add water.

Fitz grinned. He did tend to win a lot, though.

But even the Doctor couldn't just make everyone act the way he wanted them to. He was always saying that people had to make their own decisions, make their own salvation, make their own mistakes. Which was fine unless you happened to get caught up in those mistakes.

Fitz chewed on the end of a pencil, wishing to God that some of those southern farms grew tobacco.

It was just real life, wasn't it? You couldn't choose where you were born. Even if you chose where you lived, other people weren't under your control. Go to another time or another planet and you just ended up with the same problem.

Fitz scrambled to his feet at the sound of approaching footsteps. Anji appeared at the end of the hall. She looked knackered – was she actually stooping a little?

'God, I'm glad you're here,' he said. 'I really need to talk to someone.'

'You'd better come in,' she said. She unlocked her door and leaned on it to open it.

Her flat was very similar to his – same dark wood panelling, same old-fashioned furniture. The place was pristine, as if no one lived there at all. He realised that Anji hadn't been home since getting back from the Bewilderness.

She fell across her bed, not seeming to care whether he was there or not. There were straws of dried grass in her hair, and fine particles of orange dust, on her boots and clothes as well.

'I'll go in a minute,' he said, sitting down on the floor. 'Look, the Doctor left me here to slow things down. And things have been pretty quiet, everyone's taking it easy. Not making any sudden moves, you know. Now you come storming back in with this plan to blow the tiger's thingamajig to kingdom come. And, before I know it, you've got Quick brewing up a ton of home-made dynamite.' Shit, he thought, imagine if the tigers find *that*. 'Somehow I don't think the Doctor would approve…'

'Balls,' enunciated Anji.

'Sorry?'

'Balls to the Doctor.' She turned her head so her voice wasn't muffled by the bedclothes. 'I wish you could have seen him. He thinks he's a tiger, now. He's living out there with them. Walking around in the jungle with his shoes off. For all I know he's eating raw meat.'

'Oh, come on,' said Fitz.

'When that animal killed Besma, the Doctor barely batted an eyelid.' She was utterly limp, only her mouth moving. 'He was too excited about the tigers' "storehouse". It explains everything, he said. He's found the source of their intelligence – just as Besma thought. That simplifies everything. Don't you see? All we have to do is wreck it, and it's all over. No more deaths. No more tiger problem.'

'What if,' said Fitz, 'the Doctor happens to be in the storehouse when you blow it up?'

'He's been warned,' she said sourly.

'Then he'll warn them!'

'So what? What can they do about it?'

'Are you sure you can even destroy it? You don't even know what's down there, exactly, do you?'

Anji shifted slightly. 'It doesn't matter what's down there if we blow away the entrance. Cover it in dirt and rock. Even if that doesn't work, the tigers will think twice about going anywhere near the place when we might drop another bomb at any time. You see, I've thought it all through.' She raised a limp arm and pressed her knuckles against her temple. 'I feel like my brain's been in a furnace.'

'You *can't* think it all through,' blurted Fitz. 'You can't know what's going to happen. We're on an alien planet, for God's sake!

Surprise after surprise after surprise.' He put his hands over his face. 'Anji. Are you *sure* you want to do this?'

She didn't answer. He looked up at her. She said, 'Of course I am.'

'Then why aren't you there?' he said. 'With Quick, getting ready to blow them away?'

'He's not coming back.' Fitz started. Anji said sleepily, 'Stop waiting for him to come back. Give up trying to stop things happening.'

Fitz shambled to his feet. He paused at the door. 'Hope you feel better in the morning,' he said. The Doctor's gone and Anji's flipped and I really need a cigarette. Augh!

The tigers sat in a circle on the dewy grass. The Doctor sat cross-legged with them at their round table, between Big and Longbody – as though he were a tiger, too, and they were all surrounding a problem, ready to pounce on it and kill it.

'All right,' said the Doctor. 'How did you find out about this plan to blow up the storehouse?'

'By using the Nodes,' boasted Longbody. 'I'll show you how. I speak into one here, and the humans speak into another one in the city. They think I'm another human!' There were growly laughs around the circle. 'They think I'm coming to Hitchemus from space. They are so stupid.'

Even the Doctor was smiling a little. He said, 'Just how much did they tell you?'

'Everything,' said Longbody. 'They're going to send a hovercar with a bomb in it, and crash it into the ground on top of the storehouse. They said tomorrow afternoon, when they've finished getting it ready.'

'Oh, Anji,' said the Doctor. He closed his eyes, rubbing at them. 'You must warn the tigers in the city – have them search for the hovercar.'

'Already done,' said Longbody quickly. 'I sent off a stripe an hour ago. They'll pick up some more tigers at the gathering. They should reach the city by morning.'

'All right. Does the storehouse itself have any defences? Can it bury itself deeper in the earth? Generate a force field?'

'We've never found anything like that,' said Big. 'I've got some tigers going through the records, just in case.'

'Perhaps we can disguise the entrance,' said the Doctor, not sounding convinced. 'Misdirect their bomb. No – Anji's not going to be fooled by such a simple trick.' He turned to Big. 'The best option is to persuade them not to send the bomb in the first place.'

'The tigers I sent will do that,' said Longbody.

The Doctor looked at her. She couldn't read his expression. 'If the humans are provoked, they're likely to panic and use the only weapon they have. You're going to *have* to let me talk to them.'

Big shifted, as though the grass were tickling his belly. 'I don't think so,' he said. 'The stripe sent to the city need surprise to do their work.'

The Doctor looked unhappy, but he nodded. 'Perhaps later,' he said.

Longbody knew better than to think the Doctor was completely on their side. He would still be trying to follow his own tastebuds. But she did believe he didn't want the storehouse destroyed. He could hardly take his eyes off the treasures inside.

In any case, if he gave them problems, she could always have Karrrl for lunch. They had put the music teacher into the memories room, where there were always a group of tigers to keep an eye on him. He might as well learn some more of their language. He was probably going to be staying with them for a very long time.

Anji dreamed of a winged Doctor flying over the city, naked as an eagle, feathers spreading out to the horizon as though to shield them from the rain.

She ran after him, over a field of grass, as though he were a lost kite. Dave was there, somehow. Her dead boyfriend held a bowl of microwave popcorn. 'Cool explosion, love,' he said. 'That was the greatest special effect in television history.' She couldn't stop. She ran past him, leaving him behind.

Darren, her bear of a boss, stood in the field. She swerved around him without stopping. 'A great piece of futures trading, Anj!' he called out. 'But what have you traded the future for?'

'Doctor!' she shouted, at the diminishing figure overhead. 'Come back! *What am I supposed to do?*'

But he didn't stay. He flew on for ever, leaving the sky empty. She woke up weeping.

The Doctor sat in the weather room with his knees drawn up to his chest, watching the image of the planet of Hitchemus, turning, turning. Longbody lounged in the doorway, keeping a lazy eye on him. Supposedly he was looking for a way to defend the storehouse, but all he seemed to do was watch a random show of images, flickering too fast for Longbody to follow, or sit there and watch the planet spin.

'Strange world...' the Doctor murmured, as if in a dream. 'Tiny world with strange children.' He reached out and brushed his fingertips across the screen. 'Life doesn't care how uncomfortable you make its home. Did you know, Longbody, there are living creatures inside stars? In the gulping emptiness of space, where only the leftover heat of the big bang warms their bodies above absolute zero? There's life in the Vortex itself, hungry, mathematical life.' His voice lilted, as though he were making music. 'The weeds shoot up through every crack in the universe.'

To Longbody's surprise, the Doctor reached out and began to stroke her on the back of the neck, just like one tiger grooming another. She was more surprised that she found herself relaxing under his hand.

'Life will find a way to inhabit every niche,' he murmured. 'That's what the humans are doing, though they may not realise it. Spreading out across the rim of the galaxy like seeds drifting on the wind, looking for new places to grow. They haven't yet worked out how to share those places with others, not on their own world, and not in the depths of space.'

'If they can't share,' purred Longbody, putting her head down on her paws. 'They have to go away. Go away and leave us alone.'

'There's something the matter with your world. Something you may need the humans' help to repair.'

'Why can't you just fix it?' snuffled Longbody. 'You're so clever.'

She watched the slow spin of her world on the screen, feeling him stroking, stroking her neck, until her eyelids became unbearably heavy. She felt she was seeing her home from space, from that great blackness out there, the deep black stomach of the universe. Her world was a tiny speck of food, swallowed up in all of that. There were so many specks. If this planet dissolved away into nothing, would it matter, with so many others to visit? Oh, yes, she thought, there were no other tigers. No other tigers anywhere, she thought, purring, as she slid into sleep.

The Doctor crawled through the long grass, careful to stay downwind of the storehouse. The orange flowers shed more of their pollen on to him. He hoped he didn't get a sudden attack of the sneezes.

As always, there were a few tigers lying about, soaking up the sunshine of a new morning, or stretching their legs after the long periods spent in their underground schoolhouse. The creatures stood out against the yellow of the plain and the grey of the rock face, bright flashes in the middle of nowhere.

It took him a few attempts to find a Node with the properties he needed. They looked very much the same until you examined the base for the discreet row of symbols, running downwards in a ribbon against the curving edge.

He grinned to himself. The tigers thought he had been wasting his time, just meandering through the weather room's records in the hope of stumbling across something useful.

There was a ridge of dirt around the base, forced up when the Node had pushed its way out of the soil. The ancients had had no choice but to build to last: despite having been buried for centuries, the Nodes were pristine. They must rest inside sheaths under the ground, he thought, popping out like claws when they were needed.

He slid the symbols carefully, arranging them into a command.

Immediately, the Node produced a soft hum. He glanced automatically at the sleepy tigers across the meadow, but there was no chance they would hear anything over the rustling grasses, not at this distance.

The Doctor put his face close to the Node and started to sing.

> *Sumer is icumen in,*
> *Lhude sing cuccu!*
> *Groweth sed, and bloweth med,*
> *And springeth the wude nu.*

He was cut off by an astonished voice. 'Hello! Hello, are you there?'

'Good morning,' said the Doctor. 'Could I speak to someone from the Movement, please?'

'Uh… sure, can you hang on a moment? Don't go anywhere.'

The Doctor heard footsteps, voices speaking, a general impression of panic. There was a rustling deep in the grass, somewhere behind him. Then a new voice said clearly, 'Hello? Are you receiving us?'

'Hello, Fitz,' said the Doctor. 'Not much time to talk. What's this nonsense I hear about blowing up the tigers' storehouse?'

'Doctor! What are you doing out in space?'

He had to stifle a laugh. 'I'm not. The Nodes form a communication system that blankets the continent.'

'The Nodes? These metal lumps?'

'Indeed. I'm afraid your astronaut is actually a very cheeky tiger.'

'Oh my God.'

'They know what you're planning. Expect a tiger attack on the city – watch for tigers coming from the Bewilderness, and get as many people safely into shelter as you can. Fitz, do anything you must to prevent that flying bomb being sent here. The storehouse must not be destroyed.'

'What *is* the storehouse? Anji thinks it made the tigers intelligent.'

'She's wrong. The storehouse is more like the Library of Alexandria.'

'You mean the one that burned down?'

'Taking a great part of human knowledge with it. The effect on the tigers would be even worse. I can't imagine how severe their revenge would be. Warn the city. And stop that bomb!'

'I'm on it, man,' said Fitz. 'You keep well clear. Just in case.'

'Don't worry. I've got something up my sleeve.'

Longbody's stripe came down from the hills in the north, appearing like blurs of hot colour in the yellow-green grass. She had chosen them carefully, after long conversations about the humans, and the future, and the neat row of raw-red scars in her side. They sniffed through the streets, mouths open, until they found a little knot of humans.

The fleshy aliens tried to run, but the tigers easily pinned them down, a dozen predators to a handful of people. 'Wherrrrrrre'z bomb?' they growled, pressing paws into chests, taking limbs in their teeth. One switched on a vocoder. 'Where's the flying bomb?'

The humans screamed, 'We don't know! Leave us alone!' But, after the tigers ate a few of them, their memories suddenly got much better.

Just as Longbody had told them, the tigers were sure to leave someone alive, a male who cowered against the wall of a building, the tips of his shoes in a river of blood. The tiger with a vocoder grinned at him. 'The Doctor told us to stop the bomb. He told us to do anything we had to do. When we get back to the wilds, we'll tell him all about it.'

Fitz ran through the streets of the city of tigers. The few people outdoors took one look at him and got the hell out of his way. He passed tigers, who glanced at him curiously, but thankfully none of them tried to stop him. They didn't know about the attack yet. But the big cats were all through the city. When that message arrived from the Bewilderness –

He ran right past the door of Quick's café, skidded to a halt, spun around, and jogged inside. 'Where is he?' he gasped at the nearest waiter.

'Quick?' She took a step back from him. 'He's not here.'

Fitz pushed past her and went through the kitchen door. Ann and Maria looked up as he banged into the kitchen, knocking over a stack of pans. He bent double, hands on his knees, trying to get his breath back. His legs were shaking underneath his palms.

'What's up?' Maria strode up to him, holding a glass.

'The tigers know,' Fitz wheezed. 'About the bomb.' He took a mouthful of water, not even able to hold the glass. 'We're in deep trouble… sending an attack force.'

'How?' said Maria. 'How do they know?

Fitz said, 'Not a ship… talked to a tiger. The Nodes connect up with one another.'

'Jesus Christ,' muttered Maria.

'Do they know where the bomb is right now?' said Ann.

Fitz shook his head. 'Don't think so. I think they're just going to attack the city. Everyone. We have to get everyone to safety. But we have to stop it, we have to stop the bomb.'

'What?'

'Anji's wrong about the storehouse. The Doctor says it's not what made the tigers smart after all. It's just a library.'

'Fitz,' said Maria, 'Quick has gone to launch the bomb.'

'What!' Fitz wheezed, 'Already! We've got to stop him. Where is he?'

'We don't know! Anji and he worked it all out between them.'

Fitz said, 'Where's Anji now?'

'I think she's resting.'

'At her flat?'

'I think so.'

Fitz ran.

Fitz limped the last quarter of a mile to the flats. Groaning, he staggered up the stairs and hammered on Anji's door.

The seconds ticked by. He leaned heavily against the door. What if she wasn't here?

He almost fell in when she opened the door. 'God, Anji, you have to stop him!' he wheezed.

'What's going on?' she said. She was wearing a bathrobe, her fine hair dangling down wet. Her eyes were red.

'You were wrong.' He sank down in the doorway. His lungs felt as if someone were trying to peel them.

'What?'

'The Doctor says... it's a library... stop them. Stop them from blowing it up.'

'What?' said Anji again. She put a hand on the wall, as if steadying herself.

'Told Quick. He's going to blow... blow it up right now.'

'Right now? But it's –'

'And maybe the... the Doctor with it.' He shifted, trying to relieve the stitch stabbing into his side. 'Stop them, Anji!'

Anji dashed into the bedroom, and emerged pulling on her hemp jeans. 'You spoke to the Doctor? How?'

'The metal things. He calls them Nodes. They're like phones or something.' Some part of Fitz's mind registered that Anji was topless. 'The tigers are going to attack the city. To stop us.'

She grabbed a shirt from the back of the door and dragged it on. 'Then *we'd* better stop us,' she said. 'We can still use the bomb as a negotiating point. Hide it somewhere in the south. I'll talk to Quick.'

She snatched up her shoes and sat down, shoving them on without undoing the laces first.

Fitz lay against the wall until it stopped hurting to breathe. His legs and chest had that funny, pleasant feeling you get when you stop exercising, and your muscles feel relaxed and calm.

He thought, Maybe I'll just stay here, sitting in Anji's apartment. She can handle this. It was her idea, after all. If they blow up the Doctor, we'll never get off this planet. We'll be stuck here with whoever's left.

He thought, Maybe I'll start running again. I can run right out of the city, right out of this mess. I won't have to be here when they all kill one another. I'll run south. I'll run for days, right past the farms, right into the empty grasslands by the sea where there's nothing at all and no one will ever find me.

'Come on,' said Anji. She hauled him to his feet, and they ran.

The Doctor stood in the centre of the meadow, in the middle of the Nodes. The long grass was waving furiously in the sweeping wind, sending his ragged coat flying.

The Nodes hummed. The sound came from all directions, making Longbody's ears prickle, the way her fur was prickling in the charged air. She twisted her neck to look at the sky. Clouds were rolling, so fast the movement was almost dizzying, pouring in from the horizon to form a thick sticky mass over the field.

It was as though they were at the centre of the world, she thought.

She had watched him talking to the Node, caught part of his conversation. Perhaps she should have killed him then and there: a single spring from the grass on to his back. But no, wait, wait, be sure the others know where his allegiance lies.

The Doctor reached out and touched the surface of one of the Nodes. He raised his other hand in a sharp gesture. Instantly, the dark blanket of cloud overhead was lit up by a flash that left her blinking as though she had grit in her eyes.

She growled, stumbling through the grass towards him, fighting the wind. Big was right behind her, and, further back, a handful of others. The rest would be clambering into the storehouse, terrified by the unnatural weather and the alien being at its centre.

The Doctor turned at their approach. His cropped hair was standing up from his head, and tiny fibres from his wool coat were standing out, haloing his body. He was grinning, teeth flashing in his shadowed face. Longbody couldn't see his eyes.

'This isn't for you!' roared Big into the gale. 'This is ours. Stop what you're doing.'

The heavy tiger lunged towards him. The Doctor raised both hands.

Longbody felt her fur lift up from her back.

A needle-thin line of light flashed in front of her. The wind stopped, suddenly. She blinked again, wildly, trying to get the hot black line out of her field of vision. Her legs were buzzing and prickling with a feeling like intense pins and needles. She shook her head back and forth.

The wind hadn't stopped: her hearing had stopped working. Muffled noises were starting to break through. She was panting in panic, but, when she tried to bolt, her legs shook and wobbled. She sank down on to the ground in a submissive crouch. Her mouth was full of the taste of smoke.

A little distance away, Big was sitting in a similar posture, eyes tightly shut and mouth open. The others had run for it.

The Doctor had turned back to the Node. He was touching its surface – Longbody couldn't see what he was doing. But he had called down the lightning. There was a smouldering black circle of grass between them, edged with tiny orange dots.

Big climbed to his feet, and staggered over to Longbody, shaking like a new-born cub. 'The grass,' he said. 'What if the grass catches alight?'

Lightning flashed again, accompanied by a rolling boom of thunder, making them both crouch and tremble. But this time it was high overhead. Instantly, the rain began to flood down, freezing cold, drenching them both.

The Nodes were dark shapes all around, visible only when the lightning cracked across the sky. Longbody couldn't even see the Doctor any more. She wished she could sink into the ground, away from the bitter cold and the terrible sounds.

'There!' shouted Big.

Longbody followed his stare. There was something up in the sky. Her back arched. It was a hovercar, it must be the humans' bomb. And the fools had run to the storehouse for safety, dozens of them.

Big was howling at the sky. 'No!' he caterwauled. 'Not yet! You mustn't do this!'

The lightning began to flash faster and faster, filaments of brilliance moving across the sky and gathering in one corner. The hovercar was lit up, standing out against the clouds. It was fighting the winds, coming closer and closer, lower and lower.

The Doctor turned to stare up at it. He reached out for it with both hands, as though he could snatch it out of the sky.

There was a single bolt of lightning, brighter than all the rest, the thunder so loud that Longbody was sure the ground shook.

The bruised blue of the clouds was illuminated by a vast ball of orange-red flame. Chunks of fire spiralled out of it, raining down to the soaked ground. Pieces showered down near Longbody, thumping into the wet soil. She watched, helpless.

The sky fire turned into a drifting, dirty patch of smoke, hard to pick out from the dark clouds. She could taste it, burning tastes mixed in with sharp, bitter, alien flavours she couldn't identify.

The rain went on and on, a steady thundering. But there were cracks in the clouds, now, the sky startling blue above them. Long curtains of light fell over the meadow, stretching away to the forest and the ridge, picking out the wet surface of the rockface.

A little distance away, the Doctor stared out at the slowly dissipating ball of smoke. He was as drenched as they were, his hair plastered to his head, his clothes hanging heavily from his slight body.

He let out a great peal of laughter. He spun around once, his hands over his head.

Longbody called out to him through the sheets of falling water. 'What have you done?'

'That was the bomb,' said the Doctor. He wasn't shouting, but his voice carried easily through the rain. 'A hovercar packed with explosives.'

'And now it's gone?' said Big.

'Now it's gone.' He laughed again. 'For once, I got to blow something up!'

'Will there be any more lightning?' Big asked.

The Doctor pushed his sodden hair out of his face. 'Oh, yes,' he said, suddenly sober. 'That's not the end of it, not at all. There's always more lightning.'

There was a sudden, steely sound all around.

Fitz walked. From time to time he gave a wheezing cough.

There was a great mass of black clouds in the north, lit with flashes of blue lightning that were brilliant even from here, too far away to hear the thunder. Hardly anyone was outdoors, but the handful of people he passed were all anxiously watching the distant storm.

Anji had left him behind, racing ahead as he started to limp and jog. 'The Academy!' she shouted over her shoulder. 'Main hall! Meet you there.'

Fitz sank down on a bench and struggled with one of his shoes. It hurt to bend down, so instead he leaned back and kicked the shoe off with his other foot. The stone that had been burrowing into his flesh rolled away. He was surprised at how small it was.

He was the only one out on the street, except for a solitary tiger sitting next to a defunct fountain a little distance away. The storm on the horizon seemed to be calming down; the clouds getting lighter. The city had fallen silent again, even the wind dropping away to nothing. Maybe they were the only ones left. Maybe everyone else had killed one another. That would make things a lot simpler, wouldn't it?

The empty street rang with a sound like someone sharpening a knife. Fitz found himself gripping the back of the bench, too weary to jump up with surprise. I'm all astonished out, he thought.

The Nodes were sinking back into the ground. All around him, they were retracting into the earth.

He watched one in the road as it pulled itself slowly back under the asphalt. The black stuff crackled and crumbled around it, giving off a hot roadwork smell and rolling away in clumps. Then just the tip was poking up out of the street, and then it was gone.

Fitz got up and went over to the hole in the ground. Little bits of road were raining down into it, forming a crust over the sunken Node. He looked around. Not all of them had disappeared – two were left in this street. How many through the city? And *why*?

Nearby, the solitary tiger had its nose in another of the pockmarks. It sat back, looking as puzzled as he felt.

The tiger caught him staring at it. They both looked away.

* * *

After a while Fitz picked up his shoes and walked the rest of the way to the Academy, favouring his bruised foot. The university was just six small buildings arranged around a central quad. He walked diagonally across the lawn, ignoring the KEEP OFF THE GRASS signs, his socks sinking deliciously into the cool grass.

The doors of the main hall were open. The Academy's lawn was spoiled where someone had driven a vehicle over it. He stepped over the tracks and went into the hall.

Inside, it was cool and dim and echoing. It reminded Fitz of a school hall: wooden stage at one end, plaques and banners arranged around the walls. Anji and Quick were sitting side by side on the steps of the stage, both holding on to the remote-control device for the hovercar.

Anji saw him. 'Thank God,' she said. 'I thought maybe they'd got you.'

'Were we too late?' he said mournfully, limping over to them. 'Who's they?'

'A gang of tigers,' said Quick, in a hollow voice. 'Roaming the streets, killing anyone they find. The precursor to an attack.'

Anji took the device out of Quick's hands and turned it around, passing it to Fitz.

He stared at it in panic before he realised he was only watching a recording. It showed a view through the front of the hovercar as it skimmed along just below the clouds. The Bewilderness unfolded beneath it, damp forests and dry plains. An icon showed that the playback was at triple speed.

The image darkened, suddenly. The sky was full of deep blue clouds. Lightning flashes were split-second patches of brilliance overhead.

The icon changed, the playback slowed. He saw a wide plain covered in long grass and peppered with Nodes, bordered by a forest on the right of the screen and rocky hills on the left. Even at normal speed, the clouds were moving incredibly fast, swelling and billowing.

The hovercar descended, clearing tufts of cloud-stuff, and turned. An icon lit up orange, showing what Fitz guessed was its target at the base of the rocks. The icon swelled as the flying bomb sped towards it.

Abruptly, the picture cut out. The screen went purple-white, then black, and then the recording began again.

'Oh, man,' said Fitz. 'Don't do this to me. What happened? Did it hit it, or what?'

'Wind it back,' said Anji. 'See the control on the left of the screen? That's it. Wind it back to just before the recording stops.'

The controls were pretty standard for Hitchemus. Fitz tapped the REWIND icon. It froze with the orange target filling up a quarter of the screen. He tapped it twice to make it disappear.

'Ye gods and little fishes,' he said.

Anji said, 'Zoom in.' He touched another icon.

There was the Doctor, frozen in a corner of the screen, the image crisp enough for you to make out his frown of concentration. He was standing in the middle of a group of Nodes, a couple of tigers nearby. Both fists were raised above his head.

'The next moment,' said Quick, 'lightning struck the hovercar. At least, that's what the diagnostics guess happened. We believe it was destroyed before it reached its target.'

Fitz stared at the image of the Doctor. 'You think he stopped it,' he said. 'You don't think a chunk of flying metal is a bit of a lightning rod all on its own? You think *he* made the lightning hit it?'

'Fitz,' said Anji wearily, 'do you really think he couldn't do that if he wanted to?'

'He's on their side,' said Quick. The man's eyes were haunted, as if he'd seen a demon on that screen, something the tigers had conjured from hell to protect them.

'He was just trying to save them from your stupid mistake,' said Fitz. He shoved the device back at Quick. 'To save us from your mistake. What do you think the tigers would have done to the city if that bomb had struck home?'

Quick just shook his head. He tapped an icon on the screen. The recording began to play again.

* * *

'He's on their side,' said Longbody.

Big nosed a piece of the charred wreckage. He drew his head back sharply at the stink. 'Perhaps you hadn't noticed,' he rumbled. 'He just saved our civilisation.'

'He contacted them! He warned them about the stripe I sent to stop them! We can't trust him for a moment. Who knows what he's going to do next?'

Big sat down and looked up. The clouds were still dispersing, boiling away at the edges of the sky. 'I don't think even he knows,' he said. 'But I do know he'll do anything to protect our storehouse. As long as that's true, he's one of us.'

'He stands on two legs! He has no tail! Where are his stripes?' Longbody snarled. 'He wants the storehouse for himself. If he's not one of them, he's certainly not one of us.'

'We'll watch him,' said Big, tilting his head to look at her.

'You'd better watch him,' said Longbody. 'The rest of us are guided by your orders. He does whatever he likes, he doesn't care what you tell him.'

'Longbody…' said Big, warningly.

Longbody shook her head, as though something bad-tasting were caught in her mouth. But she knew her words had struck home. She slunk off, keeping an eye on the clouds, waiting for more lightning to come.

Bridge

Break: 1962

Morning, and the man stands facing the temple, watching the sun bring colour to the sanctuary tower. His face is unchanged after more than twenty-five years – the hint of crow's feet no more pronounced than before, only his shaven head and saffron robes serving as a mark of time.

His dawn gaze still searches the detail of the tower: sandstone blocks and rows of guardians catch the eye like facets of a jewel. Sharp right angles and zigzags give the impression of curves, tapered tiers draw the viewer upwards. Beyond it the face of the cliff echoes the grey-brown-white of the temple stone; the sky above it still part of night.

Traditionally the temple should be at the peak, but evidently the tenth-century Khmer had decided that the jagged ridge above passed the bounds of practicality. So while on one side of the temple the jungle slopes sharply downward, revealing the world to them, on the other the cliff face overshadows all but the lotus bulb on the tower top.

Subhadradis likes this: he feels it keeps them all humble.

—You will be leaving us shortly, says Subhadradis.

The man nods, deflecting it with a smile. —I'm afraid I've never quite been able to get my head around the idea that being born again and again is something you should want to *stop* doing.

Subhadradis's face is curved and pliant, the lack of hair rendering him ageless. He has come up beside the man quietly, as is his habit. —I suppose I can see your attraction. To playing more roles than one can in a lifetime.

—He's said to have lived many lies in succession. Or was it lives? I never could remember what old Thomas was on about.

He'd finally found the dragon from the clipping, after a quarter of a century, mostly spent following other stories or no stories at all. Finally he'd walked alone through the wilds of China, Indochina, Siam, following new sightings across half a continent, till he'd come face to face with the truth behind the story. Since then he's stayed in the temple, recovering.

He'd entered the *Sangha* only on a short-term commitment, he'd said; while Subhadradis has seen many take vows to cover a period of months or years, this man had avoided the subject of whether his brief stay would mean days or decades. His original commitment had expired some time ago, at the end of *Khao Panasa*; since then he'd continued his studies more out of curiosity than devotion. And, Subhadradis admits, the curiosity flows both ways: they all wish to puzzle out this searching Westerner who speaks Thai as if he'd been born to it.

The dragon is gone now, and so are too many people.

They turn their backs on the sanctuary and descend to one of the ornamental ponds below. At its edge, Subhadradis supports the trunk of the dead tree while the man works his way around the base with a shovel, loosening the desiccated roots.

—Is it that you fear the war will be coming?

—There's always a war coming. (The man shifts his weight, leaning harder into the shovel.) —Sihanouk's just rattling his sabre again, and you won't have to deal with Laos for a while yet.

—But still…?

—Still. There's *always* a war coming.

Subhadradis looks: beyond the man's furrowed, intent face he can see the sanctuary above, the sculpted mountain of the *prang* overshadowing him. Perhaps that's what brought him here, thinks Subhadradis: a desire to be in a place that is older than guns. A place that knows what a thousand years feels like.

—I sometimes feel I could, you know, sweep it all away. Turn up, knock a few heads together, turn the whole world right side up again. All I'd need to do is do it…

He trails off, grins, suddenly shy and nervous. —That's an illusion, isn't it?

Subhadradis nods just a bit, tries to hide his sudden uncertainty.

The man turns. Pushes just a fraction harder. And Subhadradis leaps aside as the tree smashes into the pond – waves and ripples scattering in all directions, lotus flowers milling about on the surface in confusion.

He leans on his shovel; he hasn't even broken a sweat. When Subhadradis looks at him again, he sees a man spending a lifetime marshalling his energies, a tiger gathering itself to spring.

The man's smile is fleeting, then reflective. —I don't know my own strength.

He would never have stayed, thinks Subhadradis, not for long. Not with a monkey mind such as his, jumping from desire to bright shiny desire. For all his wish to understand, he's too much in love with being in this world to be able to view it from outside. For all his wish to be part of the vast whole, moving freely through the entirety of creation, he can't convince himself that he's insignificant in the face of it.

Or perhaps, Subhadradis thinks, perhaps he really is too big.

He sees the man one more time, later that day, as the storm moves in. Through the gates of the southern side, Subhadradis follows the familiar echoes of a soaring, bending, six-note melody, played on the man's battered Western violin.

The man's music has long been his favoured way of clearing his mind. He plays at a safe distance from the temple, supposedly not to disturb the others. Over the months Subhadradis has heard that familiar fragment of melody grow, vary, expand into hints of a sustained recognisable song, as the man feels his way through more and more of it – a song that the man always claims not to know, though he's sure that he can't claim credit for writing it.

Subhadradis has come to warn him of the oncoming storm. Instead he finds himself watching from the entrance to the temple galleries, reluctant to interrupt as the song wanders further afield. Gaining speed and confidence as the rainclouds close in.

He can just see the man from here: fingers dancing, whole body twisting with the music. He stands against the cliff face at the edge of the jungle, tucked beneath an overhang where some of the higher rock had collapsed. A dark-green dot set in the patch of grey stone, a tiny morsel in the great rock mouth. He's put on his old clothes, the ones he arrived in – silk and velvet clashing with the odd sharp shape of his shaven skull.

Subhadradis listens as the black clouds surge over the cliff face. Each rumble of the thunder is answered by a squall of notes from the man's violin. The wind pulls at him; he tosses back a jagged wail on the high strings. As the first huge drops hit, robbing the air of its heat, he sends a frantic run raining on to the sky. Louder, faster, more.

—Come on, says the man, as the first lightning spikes down. Muttering it over the body of the violin, his words picked up and echoed by the rockface. Repeating it, growing louder, throwing it out over the top of the maelstrom of notes. Shouting a challenge to the storm, to the jungle, to the mountain, daring it to be vast enough to swallow him up. —Come on. Come on. Come on! *Come on!*

He's gone by morning, with the rain.

Chapter Fifteen

Longbody went hunting later that day, hungry for something more substantial than a mouthful of squawk. She stalked smoothly through the long grass, heading for the forest. Her body was full of energy, energy she couldn't use, not yet.

Where the Nodes had retracted, there were flat oval mounds of crumbling soil, mixed with the roots and stems of the dry grass. Longbody sniffed around one of them, and dug a little way into the soil, but the Node was buried too deeply to get at. A handful of the big stones were still standing.

Strange to think they had always been there, deep beneath the soil, while tigers walked over them unknowing. Perhaps that was the way the humans felt about the bright tigers.

Longbody itched to be doing things. But there was nothing to do. She had wanted to travel with her stripe to the city, lead them herself. But she needed to stay here, where she could keep an eye on the Doctor. Oh, especially now he had brought down the lightning. There had to be someone near him who was ready to kill.

Longbody's long walk took her to the edge of the forest. She slipped into the shade, enjoying the change from dry grass to damp, cool undergrowth beneath her paws. She could taste runners, a little distance away. Shaken up by the tigers' arrival and by the storm and quake, they would have retreated deep into the trees.

She slipped through the forest, easily, following her tastebuds.

Longbody paused, her mouth opening wider. She turned her head, better to catch the puzzling sound.

The runners were coming towards her. She reared back, drawing in deep breaths. Yes – they were headed this way. But how many of them were on the move? A family group was more than a single tiger could manage. If she could get behind them, she could pick off a straggler.

Longbody moved to the side, keeping low, peering through the trees to catch that first glimpse of her prey. The taste was still strong, almost overpowering. She couldn't seem to get clear of it.

Then she saw them. Dozens of them. Moving fast, hampered by the thick growth of trees. It was another stampede.

Longbody reversed directions, quickly. She didn't know what had provoked them – other tigers, hunting in the forest? – but she didn't fancy finding herself on the business end of a mass of the big, angry birds.

But they seemed to be coming from everywhere. Another group shot out in front of her, only metres away. Longbody crouched, automatically, letting them pass – but that left her in the path of the first group.

She dashed in the only free direction, heading for the edge of the forest. She couldn't outrun them, but in the long grass it would be easier to see which way to go. Besides, they might be scared off by the proximity of so many tigers, visible in the distance against the rock face.

Longbody heard the sound as she broke into the open, but she didn't recognise it until the Nodes were pushing out of the ground in front of her, so close she was forced to skid to a belly-scraping halt in the stiff blades of grass. She turned hard, bolting in a new direction as the runners burst from the forest behind her.

Another Node began its fast rise from the ground, so close she tasted the dirt it was kicking up. She tried to clear it, her hindlegs slapping metal as she rolled awkwardly over it and tumbled into the grass, panting.

Tigers were not made for running. They were made for the sudden smash and grab, surprise and strength. Longbody was out of breath and out of power, her limbs stabbing with fatigue as she pulled herself up from the ground, fresh bruises and old injuries shouting for attention.

Another group of Nodes were unfolding themselves from the grass nearby. Longbody hurled herself at them, squeezed between two of them, and cowered in the shadow while the runners thundered past on the other side. The ground bumped and trembled underneath her as though the quaking had returned. The birds wheeled, leaving long tracks of crumpled grass. She watched them race across the plain, like a single grey-bodied beast with tens of heads.

And there –

There was the Doctor, emerging from the forest, looking right at her as though he'd watched the whole thing. As though he'd made it all happen. Had he learned to control the Nodes? How? How could he control the Nodes? He hadn't even touched them; he wasn't even a tiger!

He strode through the flattened grass towards her. She wanted to snarl at him, she wanted to hurl herself at him and crush him into the soil, but she just didn't have the breath. Later. It would be easy, the work of a moment. Later, she promised herself.

'So,' he said, shading his eyes with his hands as he watched the herd recede, 'now you know what a runner stampede looks like.'

Longbody showed him her teeth. 'You need killing,' she said. 'Lots and lots of killing.'

She turned to slink away. As she padded across the grass, panting hard, she heard thunder crackling at the distant edges of the sky.

The Doctor looked a bit depressed when he came back from studying the Nodes in the forest, so Bounce decided to cheer him up. A few of her friends came with her to the swirl of Nodes in the plain where he was working. Most of the big rocks had sunk bank down into the earth now, leaving just a few sticking up, like lost cubs.

He sat cross-legged at the base of one of the metal fins, hunched over, sliding the controls back and forth. His brow was furrowed with what Bounce had come to recognise as concentration.

The three young tigers chased each other's tails until the Doctor straightened up, leaning back on his hands. Bounce gave his shoulder a nudge, almost knocking him over. 'What is it you're trying to do?'

'There must be a way of controlling the weather on a larger

scale,' he said. 'It wouldn't do just to prevent the occasional local hurricane. If the Nodes keep your planet's climate stable, then there are controls for adjusting the entire system.' He stood up, stretching. 'If we can't find them, it will get worse and worse – probably until your miniature continent is swallowed by the world ocean.'

Bounce and Spotty and Zoom looked at one another, shivering. Spotty asked, 'Can you fix it?'

'It's not up to me to fix it,' he said. 'But I might be able to find how it's done.'

Bounce jumped up on the Doctor, putting her paws on his shoulders. He overbalanced, falling backwards, the long grass cushioning his fall. 'Oops, sorry,' she said.

He gave her a friendly cuff over the ear. 'You great daft pussycat,' he said. 'If only it was all playfighting. War without tears.'

Bounce got off him. He sat up, picking bits of straw out of his hair. Was that a flash of red on his arm, hidden by the sleeve of his shirt?

She said, 'Why was the recording about the other storehouse in the weather room, and not in the message room or the history room?'

The Doctor threw his arms wide. 'Of course!' he shouted. He pointed at Bounce. 'You're a genius. The global controls are hidden in the second storehouse – ready to be used by tigers who have mastered their first round of lessons here.'

'It's like following a runner's footprints,' said Zoom. 'They're leading us on a chase.'

Bounce, delighted, jumped on Zoom. They tangled in a mock fight, rolling around, mashing the grass. Spotty grabbed the Doctor's leg in his mouth, remembering at the last moment not to bite too hard.

Bounce stopped, her paw in Zoom's face. 'Wait,' she said. 'You said that activating the second storehouse would destroy the human city.'

The Doctor wriggled out of Spotty's grip. 'I can't believe the ancients raised the whole storehouse out of the ground every time they wanted to look something up,' he said. 'There must be another way in. A back door.'

'But what if there isn't?' asked Zoom muffledly.

'I'll burn that bridge when I come to it,' said the Doctor. 'In the end, the humans are in just as much danger from the weather as you are.'

'Hooray!' Spotty pounced on the Doctor and cuffed him. 'We're saved!'

The Doctor landed hard on the ground. He started to push himself up, then fell again with a gasp, lying face down in the grass.

Bounce came over and turned him over with a paw, gingerly. There was a great bruise on one side of his face, a trickle of blood escaping the broken skin.

Zoom started to caterwaul in distress. Spotty had hunched into a ball. 'Is he all right?' he whispered.

Bounce rasped the Doctor's face with her tongue, but he didn't respond. 'You shouldn't have biffed him so hard, Spotty. His skull isn't as thick as yours. Shut up, Zoom!'

Zoom got Spotty's tail in his mouth. 'Come on,' he said around it. The pair of them got up and started slinking off through the grass.

Bounce watched them go. She crouched down by the Doctor, waiting to see if he would wake up.

Longbody's stripe slithered through the streets, pouncing on anyone they found. They did not bother with the closed doors, even when they could taste dozens of humans cringing behind concrete walls. They loped after the ones that ran.

When they came to the hall that was supposed to contain the bomb, they growled and snarled, stalking around on the wooden floor. They drew in breath after breath, running it over their tongues. Something had been there, something that tasted alien, artificial. But it had been moved, hidden. Or already sent flying on its way.

The tigers chased back through the empty city until they found one of the Nodes Longbody had told them about. It took only a few moments to set the controls correctly. At once the Node began to hum and hiss. They barked her name until she spoke to them through the metal.

'The Doctor destroyed the bomb,' she said. 'Now I want you to tell the humans that we're going to bring the second storehouse to life, the one underneath their young city. When it rises up it will destroy all their buildings. Find anyone you can, and tell them. Shout it to them through the walls if you have to. And don't forget to tell them whose idea it was.'

'The Doctor,' they grinned.

Bounce was beginning to drift off to sleep in the heavy, warm sunshine when she heard the Doctor stirring. He moaned softly, throwing a limp arm over his eyes to shield them from the light.

She nuzzled him. 'Are you thirsty?' she said. 'Come and get a drink of water.'

She pushed her head under his body. He reached up and grabbed hold of her fur, hauling himself up on to her back as she slid under him. He ended up lying at an angle across her.

She carried him through the grass to the edge of the rocks. He slid down into the grass and cupped his hands under one of the waterfalls. When he had finished drinking, he splashed the water down his face and neck, flinching as he cleaned the cut over his left cheekbone and eye.

'Bounce,' he said, 'I'm going to go back to the city.'

'Spotty didn't mean to hurt you,' she said quickly.

'Of course he didn't. He was just playing. I'm not as tough as you are.' He raised his hands to his face, and she saw that his arms were covered in scratches and bruises. His sad, alien eyes seemed to be looking far into the distance. 'I'm not a tiger.'

'Can I come?'

He scratched her behind the ear with a damp hand. 'You'd better stay here in the Bewilderness. It's safer.'

'What will you do in the city?'

'Two things,' he said. 'I'm going to look for a way into the storehouse. And I'm going to take Karl home.'

Bounce's ears stood up with surprise. 'How?' she said.

He grinned at her. 'I have a lot of experience in freeing prisoners,' he said. 'Will you help me?'

Bounce jumped to her feet. She was about to jump on him, but then she remembered, and sat down instead. 'All right,' she said.

Third Verse

Chapter Sixteen

It took six hours to reach the city of tigers. The Doctor had to let Bounce come along; exhausted and malnourished, Karl knew he could never have made it on foot. The musician rode the sub-adult bareback, once again steadying himself with a hand placed on her head, fingertips pressing into her fur. By the time they came to the edge of Port Any, he was swaying, eyes closed, half asleep in the steady rhythm of her padding step.

The Doctor had been silent throughout the long walk. Karl had never known him to be so quiet. Only twice had he spoken, when Karl asked about the bad cut on his face. 'A lesson of my own,' he said ruefully, brushing his fingers over the bruised and broken skin. 'I don't belong in the Bewilderness any more than I belong in the city.' He smiled, but it didn't reach his eyes. 'I'm neither fish nor flesh nor good red herring, my dear Karl.'

The composer considered this as he dozed atop his steed. For long, terrible hours he had thought the Doctor had been lost to them entirely, that he had *become* a tiger, that the Bewilderness had become the home he was seeking. But belonging still eluded him. He was still, thought Karl, miscellaneous.

'Which side of a tiger has the more fur?' the Doctor asked Bounce, out of the blue, after they had forded a small stream. She couldn't guess. 'The outside,' he said, leaving her puzzled. 'The outside.'

They came into the city with the sunset behind them, through a cleared area full of stubble and weeds divided by freshly made roads, like a field ready to grow a new suburb. It segued into a street of shops, each of them closed and dark. Karl began to look around. 'It's like seeing it for the first time,' he whispered. 'Have they evacuated?'

The Doctor was scanning the windows above them as they passed. 'I don't think so.' He spoke in a normal voice, making Karl jump in the oppressive hush. Had he seen someone peeking out from behind a curtain? 'They're in hiding. I don't like to think what Longbody's stripe have got up to.'

When they reached the city centre and the block of flats, he helped Karl down from Bounce's back. The musician found himself swaying again, his stiff muscles melting to liquid as he tried to hold himself up. 'Wait,' said the Doctor, slipping a shoulder under his arm. Karl leaned heavily against the shorter man.

'Bounce,' said the Doctor, 'you should leave us now. It's dangerous for you here.'

She nudged his leg with her nose. Her mouth was still bloody from the bird she had pulled down during a pause in their long walk, and a little of the darkening liquid striped his ragged trousers. 'I want to protect you.'

He began to walk along, slowly, supporting Karl. 'The first person you see – human or tiger – will probably try to kill you. I want you to move back out into the Bewilderness, but stay near the city. Wait and watch for tigers you know are friendly.'

'Will Big be coming to the city?' asked Bounce.

'He'll have to. Otherwise he's letting Longbody call the shots. I think he knows he can't afford to let her do that. Now, go, please.'

Bounce flattened her ears, but crept away.

'You've got that one eating out of the palm of your hand,' murmured Karl. He blinked at the bitterness in his voice.

'She's got the optimism of the young,' said the Doctor lightly. 'She thinks I'm going to save her world.'

The Doctor half carried Karl up three flights of stairs. Almost at the top, they halted at the sound of footsteps. 'Coming this way,' whispered the Doctor. He gently disentangled himself from Karl, lowered the musician to the step below, and straightened up to face whoever was there.

Anji came through the door at the top of the stairwell, carrying a bag. She froze at the sight of them. For a moment, Karl thought she was going to run too.

She was looking at him, slumped against the wall behind the Doctor. 'Are you all right?' she asked.

Karl said weakly, 'I haven't become a decomposer yet.'

'The Movement's out for blood,' she said. 'If they spotted you two...' She shifted the bag in her arms. 'They might be coming for you.'

The Doctor gave a low laugh. 'They wouldn't dare.'

Anji started coming down the concrete stairs, keeping her distance from the Doctor. He held his ground, his eyes fixed on her, shifting his feet a little. Karl realised the Doctor was keeping himself between the two of them.

Anji saw the Doctor trying to get a glimpse of what was in the bag. 'It's just food,' she said, more loudly than was necessary. 'I've got to deliver this stuff...' She was past them, below them. 'Why don't the two of you just get some rest?' she muttered. 'I'll take care of everything for now.' She almost flinched as she said it, as though she expected the Doctor to lash out.

'Whoah!'

The Doctor whipped around. Fitz was at the top of the stairwell, agape, his sunglasses dangling from one ear. He coughed and straightened them up, leaning casually against the wall. 'Oh,' he said. 'There you are. 'Bout time you turned up.'

'Well,' said the Doctor, with equal offhandedness, 'it was a rather long walk.'

Fitz sat down on the top step. 'Anji's right, you know. The two of you ought to catch a few Zs. Nothing's going to blow up overnight.' He drummed his fingers on the stair between his knees. 'Can't stick around. I've got another concert to organise. But I've got a little something for you.' He started to rummage in his pockets. 'Been carrying this around in case we bumped into one another.'

Anji hovered at the bottom of the stairwell, arms wrapped around her heavy package. The Doctor turned, casually, to glance at her. Their eyes met for a moment. Neither of them said anything.

Anji turned her back on them and kept walking downwards.

'You're all right, Karl?' said Fitz, as he tugged something out of the inside pocket of his jacket.

'Yes…'

'Good. Thought so. Here, Doctor – catch.'

The Doctor's hand whipped out and snatched the little package out of the air as it arced towards them. He stared at it.

'Socks,' he said.

'Clean socks.'

'Why?'

'Well, what else would you need, after traipsing around in the jungle for all that time?' Fitz uncurled himself from the stairs and strolled down, giving the Doctor's arm a tap as he went past. He flashed them a smile, peering over the top of his sunglasses. 'See you round.'

Karl watched Fitz go. The Doctor stood there, staring at the neatly rolled socks clutched in one hand.

Without a word, he put them into his coat pocket, picked up Karl, and carried him upstairs.

The Doctor's apartment was pristine, smelling of cleaning and incense. The composer sank down on to the sofa. 'What are we going to do?' he said.

The Doctor stalked about, looking in cupboards. Karl realised the man's face and hands were as pale as ever; he had neither tanned nor burned while in the Bewilderness, while Karl's own skin was darkened and peeling. 'Take advantage of the amenities of civilisation. We need a shower. And you do need a good meal and a good sleep before you'll be ready to do anything.'

'Don't leave me behind,' said Karl. He took hold of the Doctor's sleeve. 'Don't leave me lying in bed while you face them.'

The Doctor sat down next to him. 'You've done enough,' he said. 'You've done that just by surviving. That's all that's required of you.'

Karl looked over the back of the worn sofa, through the big windows. With the lights out, the city seemed dead. Everyone he knew must be hiding inside those blank buildings, locked in cellars. 'No,' he said. 'It's not enough for me to be a, a casualty. I have to have a say in this.'

Something flared in the Doctor's eyes. 'You always want to come along,' he said. 'You won't stay where I tell you, where it's safe.'

'I know the tigers.'

'Do you?' said the Doctor.

'I taught them. Spoke with them. Ate with them –'

'You were brutalised by them!' The words burst out of the Doctor. 'Kidnapped by them, terrorised by them! You want to see them suffer as much as you suffered!'

Karl shivered. At the bottom of his mind, those images kept stirring around, images of empty forests, long rifles blazing, piles of skins and raw red meat.

The Doctor was insisting, 'Imagine an alien who fell into an ugly prison on Earth, full of torturers. Could they say they *knew* the human race?'

'Someone will hear,' murmured Karl.

The Doctor quietened. He gave Karl a look full of pleading: please, please don't die.

Karl laid his head down on the back of the sofa. 'I'm not letting you out of my sight again. We have a concerto to complete. I will not have you killed while I sleep between clean sheets.'

The Doctor opened his mouth again, but Karl pressed his weary fingers against his lips. 'I won't sleep while the future of my world is decided. I want to be there, beside you, while we make the future.'

'Whatever happens here, whatever world is created, it will grow out of the decisions made by tigers and humans. I can only try to stave off destruction long enough for one of those worlds to come to be.' The Doctor was staring off into nothing. He was seeing all those possible worlds.

And Karl saw them with him: worlds where tigers and humans sat side by side in symphony orchestras; worlds where every last tiger had been hunted down and shot; worlds where a high hard wall divided the continent; worlds where humans lived in the forest, hiding from tiger safaris; worlds ripped by hurricanes and constant war; worlds where the ocean had swallowed every last trace of their little island.

Karl brushed his hand over the Doctor's ragged head. 'Doctor, when this is all over…'

'Yes?'

'We have got to do something about your hair.'

Sometime in the night, the Doctor went to the trunk that doubled as an end table in the lounge. He put the terracotta pot of begonias on the floor, folded the embroidered cloth and put it aside, and opened the trunk.

Inside were the clothes he had been wearing when they first arrived on Hitchemus. He took each item out carefully and slipped it on. The soft white linen shirt with its generous collar, the buff flannel trousers, the double-breasted waistcoat with its Paisley silk brocade. The dark-brown frock coat, the velvet shining with metallic green highlights. The grey silk cravat with its amber and gold stickpin. There was a pair of low-heeled half-boots at the very bottom of the trunk. But no socks to be seen. Good old Fitz.

At last he stood in front of the full-length mirror in the corner. The outfit looked a little strange with the rough haircut, he thought. The short hair made his face look sharper, even harder. When he had washed it in the shower, a great mass of orange colour had run out, millions of particles of pollen.

His shirt sleeve hid the red armlet he had taken from the storehouse. 'That's our little secret,' he whispered to his reflection. The armlet had secrets of its own, he mused: the first storehouse had only hinted at the portable control's abilities to mould the weather.

In the end he decided to leave the coat and cravat behind in the trunk – he wouldn't need them in the heatwave that was gripping the island. His and Karl's Hitchemian clothes were a mass of tears and mud, beyond saving; they went into the garbage. In another cupboard there was a random assortment of apparel, left behind by the flat's various inhabitants over the years; some of them would surely fit Karl.

There was no hot water the next morning. There was no cold

water, either. The Doctor mournfully twiddled the taps in the kitchen sink. 'The next stage of escalation of this little war,' he said. 'I expect the tigers have got into the dam.'

'The hydroelectric plant,' said Karl. He was feeling more energetic than he had for… for however long he had been away. He wanted to be doing things. He wanted to be taking his planet back.

'I'm afraid we've eaten ourselves out of house and home,' said the Doctor, rummaging in cupboards under the sink. 'We'll have to go out in search of breakfast.'

'Never mind that!' said Karl, struggling into his new, mismatched clothes. 'If they've got the plant, they've got the city. What are we going to do?'

The Doctor straightened up. He put a thoughtful hand on his chin. 'Definitely breakfast,' he said.

Quick's café was dark and quiet, curtains drawn, big CLOSED sign in the door – firmly shut with an old-fashioned lock. The Doctor took an odd-looking tool out of his pocket and fiddled about with the keyhole for a moment, making a dreadful racket. Karl nervously looked up and down the street, but no curious tigers were attracted by the sound.

Nothing was happening. The Doctor put the tool carefully away and kicked the door open.

The café was empty and dark. 'They're not here,' said Karl.

'They'll be down in the cellar,' said the Doctor. He strode across the room and pushed through the door to the kitchen. Karl hurried to follow him through another door which led to a well-swept stone staircase leading down into the gloom.

'Don't shoot,' announced the Doctor loudly as he bounded down the steps. 'We're harmless.'

A whole flurry of gasps, sighs of relief and curses came from the cool, grey room below. As Karl's eyes adjusted to the dimness – the vast oval cellar was lit by a single lightstick held over what looked like a map – he could make out perhaps twenty skulking conspirators, sitting about on barrels or on the cold stone floor.

All of them were giving the Doctor resentful glances.

Fitz was there, and Anji too. She stood up, folding her arms, looking awkward. 'You almost look like yourself again,' she said quietly.

'What's all this, then?' said the Doctor, gesturing round the cellar. 'Gunpowder, treason and plot? I suppose you've cooked up a brilliant plan for taking back the hydroelectric plant. Frontal assault with tomato-sauce squirters? Nuke it from orbit?'

Ajamu Quick stood up from the map he'd been reading. 'We ought to lock you up somewhere,' he said.

'Oh, people are always saying I should be locked up,' retorted the Doctor.

'Now, children,' said Fitz nervously. 'The fact is, Doctor, we could use your help. The tigers have taken over the –'

'Yes, I had noticed,' said the Doctor. 'It's built over the tigers' own dam, isn't it?' Fitz nodded. 'The tigers are probably trying to get into the second storehouse. I'm sure the entrance is somewhere under the dam. Cutting off the city's utilities is just a way of making a nuisance of themselves.'

'Then it's true?' said Quick. 'The tigers warned us they were going to raise this storehouse of theirs. That it would smash the centre of Port Any to pieces.'

'Did they, indeed,' said the Doctor.

'So we're going to wreck it,' said Quick. 'We're going to get into it, any way we can, and we're going to make certain that it never rises from the ground again.'

There was a moment of extraordinary quietness in the cellar, as though even the dust motes were afraid to move.

The Doctor exploded. He grabbed Quick by the front of his jumper and bellowed, 'Are you some variety of pyromaniac? What is the problem with *Homo sapiens* that everything has to end like the *1812* overture? Was some ghastly mistake in DNA replication made in your early evolution? Or is it just that your tiny porridge-like brains have trouble grasping solutions more complex than smashing things with rocks?'

An almighty crack of thunder sounded overhead. Karl flinched along with everyone else. The sky had been clear when they arrived.

'There will never be another Port Any,' said Quick fiercely. He tore himself loose from the Doctor's clutches. 'There will never be another colony like Hitchemus! I was born here. I built up my business from nothing. I painted every wall of this café myself!' He gave the Doctor a shove for emphasis. 'I've watched this town grow from a handful of farmers and eccentrics to a prosperous city. We built it all ourselves. We *won't* let anyone destroy it.'

The Doctor blinked. He seemed utterly calm again. 'Hmm. Those should be my lines.'

'You're with us, then?' said Quick, breathing hard after his speech.

'Oh, no,' laughed the Doctor. 'I'm just going to get there before you do.'

Anji caught up with them in the empty café above. She got in the Doctor's way until he had to stop walking.

'Well!' said the Doctor.

'Listen...' she began, planting her hands on her hips.

They just stood there staring at one another. Fitz put a hand on Karl's arm and gently pulled him back, as though getting him out of shrapnel range.

At last, the Doctor waved a hand vaguely back at the cellar. 'Are you part of this – this vandalism?'

Anji looked past him, as though considering. After a moment, she said, 'No.'

He reached out and put his fingertips on her shoulders. 'Then come with me,' he said urgently.

She dropped her arms to her sides, staring up at him. She shook her head. 'I can't be sure. I'm going back to Besma's.' The name hovered in the air between them. 'To do a bit of research. To look for answers.'

'You still want it all to make sense, don't you? You think that, once you know, everything will be all right.' He snapped his fingers next to her ear. 'Just like that.'

'If you don't fully understand the situation,' she retorted, 'how can you know what's the right thing to do?'

'I want to know all about the tigers,' said the Doctor. 'Especially now that I've had a glimpse of their real potential. Of course I want to know all about them, but not because I don't know which way to jump.'

'What if you jump the wrong way? Face it, Doctor – you're not always right about everything.'

'There's an understatement,' drawled Fitz, sotto voce.

The Doctor said, 'You don't need to be an expert on the history and structure of Western music to know when a brass band is out of tune.'

'But how can you fix the band when you don't know how to tune a trumpet?' Anji grabbed her hair in frustration and pushed it back over her shoulders, almost locking arms with him. 'What are you trying to accomplish? What do *you* want?'

The Doctor took his hands from her. Very quietly, he said, 'Do you know, I've had a tune going round and round in my head for more than a hundred years. I don't have the slightest idea what it is. I want to know.'

Anji stared at him. 'What are you talking about?'

'Well, I can hardly work it out with all this fuss going on around me,' he said, with the hint of a smile. 'Once things are back to normal, I can get back to the music.'

It's the concerto, thought Karl. The Doctor wants to play first violin in my concerto. He wants it so much that he's going to save this planet just so he can do it. It is me, it is about me, after all.

The Doctor strode through the city streets, Karl and Fitz at his heels, trying to keep up. 'All right,' said Fitz. 'What now?'

'The power plant, of course,' said the Doctor. 'Think about it. Longbody's lackeys could destroy Port Any. Why haven't they?'

'Uh…' said Fitz. 'They want to keep the city intact, for themselves?'

'What use are our buildings to them?' said Karl. 'They can't even fit through most doorways.'

'Point,' said Fitz. 'Maybe they're planning to hold the city hostage.'

'Then why haven't they made any demands?' said the Doctor. 'All they've done is taunt the humans. But it's an empty threat.'

Fitz said, 'They can't raise the storehouse. They don't know how.'

The Doctor flashed him a grin. 'Better. They can't even get into it. If I'm right, they would have to have mastered the secrets of the first storehouse before they could hope to open the second. And Longbody and her friends scorn the schoolroom.'

The dam was in view, a long mound that rose from the northern end of the lake, topped by two buildings – a small cube, and a much larger one. A few clouds were wandering the sky, seeming to drift after them as they hurried through the city. 'So what are they doing up there, then?'

'Fiddling with the locks,' said the Doctor. 'And waiting for the rest of the tigers to arrive from the Bewilderness. If they put their heads together they may be able to puzzle out how to get that door open.'

'So we're facing a control room full of pissed-off tigers,' said Fitz. 'Er… what are we going to do when we get there?'

'Extemporise,' said the Doctor.

'You won't like this,' said Karl. His voice caught, and he coughed. 'But we should be armed.'

The Doctor turned sharply to look at him. 'That would only make things so much worse. Three guns against a horde of tigers?'

'We wouldn't stand a chance,' gulped Fitz. 'Of course, we don't stand a chance anyway.'

'Worse, worse,' said the Doctor. 'The very first image these creatures have of the human race is that of people with guns. Coming to slaughter them one by one, or to take them away for experimentation. We must never let them think that we are those people.' He laid a single finger on Karl's sleeve. 'We must not *be* those people.'

Karl touched the Doctor's hand. He found himself gripping it hard. 'I'm not sure,' he breathed. 'I'm not sure that I'm not one of those people.'

'I know,' murmured the Doctor. 'Please, Karl, just trust me.'

I trust *you*, thought Karl.

Tigers were splashing around in the creek, or sunning themselves on the bank, or crawling like insects all over the mound of the dam. A few swam on the lake.

The three of them hid behind a mound of branches and trunks, fallen trees that had been cleared up and piled for a bonfire. 'What are you going to do?' hissed Fitz. 'Walk out there and talk to them?'

'Of course,' said the Doctor.

'But they've been running amok,' said Fitz. 'Killing anyone they find.'

'Look at them, Fitz. There are dozens here – far more than Longbody's little squad of killers. The tigers are coming out of the Bewilderness, and not all of them are as unfriendly as her followers.'

Fitz didn't look convinced. The Doctor said, 'Listen. I want you two to –' Karl expelled a hard breath through his teeth. The Doctor softened. 'All right. But once you start to follow me, you'll have to follow through. There's no exit once they've seen us.'

Karl nodded hard. His pulse was thumping so powerfully that he could feel it in his throat. Fitz was trying to look cool behind his shades, but he was gnawing on his bottom lip as though he were trying to eat his own chin.

They all stood up together and started walking towards the tigers.

They had the creatures' attention, instantly – dozens of pairs of yellow eyes turning to watch their progress along the bank. Karl had a sudden, flinching urge to run back into cover, somehow to make it that those eyes had never seen him. He clenched his hands and his jaw and kept his gaze on the back of the Doctor's head. Beside him, Fitz was whistling tunelessly in a panicked pattern, his hands shoved hard into his pockets.

The Doctor broke into a jog as they neared the dam. The motion seemed to break the spell: suddenly tigers were pouring up out of the creek, swarming all around them. One roared angrily – no, he called out to them in the tigers' brutish language. Karl couldn't make out the words. 'Ahhh, jeez,' said Fitz.

They stopped, surrounded by an orange wall. The huge tiger that had spoken pushed his way easily through the crowd to confront the Doctor. They exchanged a rapid patter of snarls and growls and mews.

Whatever he was saying, it had an electric effect on the furry crowd: they all started talking at once. The big tiger roared over the top of them, as though shouting orders. Suddenly, tigers were climbing down from the dam wall, splashing away through the muck. Several of them emerged from the control room at the top of the dam wall, brandishing tools. They gathered in a crowd in the lake bed, a little distance away, faces turned upwards.

'What did you tell them?' whispered Karl.

'I told them about the bombs planted in the dam wall,' said the Doctor loudly. 'I just hope we're in time to disarm them before the entrance to the storehouse is destroyed.'

Fitz seemed to understand already what was going on. He took a deep breath and said, 'A lot of tigers could be killed if they're still near the dam when those bombs go off.'

'Come on,' said the Doctor. 'With your help, I'm sure I can defuse them in time.'

The three of them jogged through the mass of tigers and up on to the footpath that led across the top of the dam. The control room was a functional box, built next to the handful of stones that marked where the ancients had had their own power station. Oblong windows looked down over both sides of the dam, the glass freshly replaced after the hurricane. They ran inside, and the Doctor turned back to the door, locking it behind them.

The walls were covered in computer equipment, some of it quite old-fashioned – devices to measure the electricity, to monitor the weather, even a miniature seismograph. Chairs were scattered about, most of them knocked over. A door led to a corridor which cut across the dam to the power plant itself, a tall concrete box, its roof planted with grass and flowers.

In the centre of the control room floor there was a huge hole, smelling of freshly turned earth.

'Right!' the Doctor clapped his hands together. Karl startled as another crack of thunder split the bright sky. 'This place was never meant for a siege. I want the pair of you to barricade us in with anything that isn't bolted down. Then see if you can do anything about restoring water and power to the city.'

'What do we know about dams?' protested Fitz, jamming a chair under the doorknob.

'If the tigers could work out how to shut it all off, I'm sure you can work out how to switch it all back on,' said the Doctor patiently. 'Now let's see what they've got in this hole of theirs.'

The pit was surrounded by broken tiles and concrete. The control room had been built on a platform over the rounded hump of the ancient dam. The sides of that great mound had been skirted with concrete by the colonists who built Port Any, but the centre was still packed earth and stones, the building materials of the ancients.

The tigers had smashed their way through the floor, through the structures of the platform beneath, and dug their way into that mass of rock and soil. Partway down they had discovered part of the original entrance to the storehouse, a gently sloping tunnel. They had broken through it, making a hole large enough for a tiger to climb inside.

The Doctor retrieved a rope from an emergency cupboard. Fitz fastened it to a heavy pipe in the wall while the Doctor looped the other end around his body. Fitz heaved on the rope, slowly lowering him down into the tigers' rough hole. Karl watched, distracted from the control panels he was fiddling with, praying that the pit didn't simply collapse in on the Doctor.

'The original entrance must have been part of the tigers' own power plant,' the Doctor called, once his feet were planted on the muddy floor of the tunnel. He unlooped the rope from his body and left it dangling while he pulled out a torch. 'I can see the doorway from here. It's still firmly closed.'

'They're watching us,' said Karl. He was shifting the seismograph

237

in front of the door. 'There's a lot of talk going on down there.'

There was silence from the tunnel for long minutes. Fitz and Karl pored over the controls. 'Looks like it has an emergency power system, or something,' said Fitz. 'All the computers and things are still working.'

'Solar,' muttered Karl. 'It doesn't take much power to run all this, but without it you can't do a thing with the dam. I think this is what we want.'

He had found a console with what looked like simple diagrams of the river, the lake and the dam itself. By scrolling the diagram you could follow the course of the river, or the pipes that carried water into the city, each with its own miniature purification plant. Fitz reached out to trace the diagram with his finger, but Karl caught his hand. 'It's touch-sensitive,' he warned.

'Can you operate it?' said Fitz. Karl shook his head. 'I'll have a fiddle, then. Go and see what the tigers are doing.'

Karl went to the window. 'I think they're on to us!' he cried. He pressed his face to the glass, trying to see down into the creek. 'They're bringing their equipment to the wall down there. Shovels and things. They've got what looks like a battering ram.'

Fitz was next to him in a flash. 'Why don't they just attack the control room?' he gasped. 'Our excuse for a barricade won't keep them out for long, especially if they don't mind a bit of broken glass.'

'They don't know what we might do,' said Karl. 'We might be planting bombs of our own. All they care about is that storehouse of theirs.'

Fitz leaned over the hole. 'Doctor!' he shouted, his voice jumping up in pitch. 'The tigers are burrowing into the side of the dam.'

'What?' The Time Lord's voice echoed back up the shaft.

'They're digging into the dam. I think they're trying to reach the entrance.'

'Just a few more minutes,' called the Doctor.

'There's hardly enough room for you to move down there,' shouted Fitz. 'If they break through, you'll have nowhere to go.'

'You'll have to haul me up,' shouted the Doctor. Fitz grabbed the rope. 'Not yet!'

The sound of shattered concrete echoed from the wall of the dam. The tigers' ram, powered by at least a dozen of the animals, had smashed easily through the skirting. Immediately a team with shovels moved into the resulting hole, paws splashing through the creek. They stood on three legs, muscles rippling as they spooned out dirt one-handed.

'They're through the concrete!' yelled Karl.

'Yes, I heard it,' called the Doctor. 'Just a few more moments. I've nearly puzzled out these equations.'

Karl found himself turning back to the control panel. His mind suddenly felt out of sync with his body, as though he were floating, following its movements like a ghost.

His hands drifted to the controls. Once upon a time, he thought, he would have had to drag some stiff lever into a new position, or turn a heavy metal wheel. It might have taken more strength than he could muster, after a week spent slowly starving in a forest, surrounded by monsters who ate bloody chunks of meat. Every time they fed, he remembered the woman whose corpse they had butchered on the long march from the city, how her warm and breathing body had become so many joints and slabs and long, tough shreds. The word 'dismembered' surfaced in his mind again and again like a mental twitch until it took on a new meaning: no longer a *member* of the human race, any more than mutton was a sheep. He could not stop his spasming imagination substituting his own body in his image of their hungry dissection, the bodies of his sister, his lovers, the Doctor.

All he had to do was to slide his fingers along a flat panel. It lit up under his hand as it moved, indicating the level of pressure.

There was a grumbling noise that built immediately into a screaming roar. Fitz jumped and swore. From the bottom of the pit, the Doctor shouted something, but Karl couldn't hear it. He leaned back against the wall beside the panel and folded his arms.

Lightning flashed, followed instantly by thunder that murmured and then broke like a whip cracking. The sun was still shining brilliantly over the dam, the great flood that was hammering down into the bed of the creek, the orange bodies that struggled and spun in the gush.

Chapter Seventeen

Anji was alone in the library. She had broken the lock on a window to get in – a surprisingly easy thing to do, once you put your mind to it. It wasn't as dark as she'd expected – plenty of sunshine was filtering in through the high skylight.

She found a corner well away from the windows and settled down with her basket of computer slates. She had been afraid that Besma Grieve's house would be under some kind of watch, but there was nothing that organised in the city now, no guards or patrols. Twice she had seen gangs of tigers in the streets, twice groups of humans she recognised from the Movement. She avoided them both, taking off her shoes to run noiselessly along the pavement. Little Red Riding Hood tiptoeing through the city of tigers.

She had found the basket in Besma's empty kitchen, and stuffed it full of everything she could find in or on her desk. The lounge was still a wreck after their fight with the tigers. Now she huddled in her corner of the empty library, sitting on a cushion with her back to the wall, trying not to jump at the occasional growl or shout or shot from outside.

The slates had their own power source. Some kind of automatic indexing thing had organised the scientist's notes into something like an encyclopedia. She was surprised at how simple it was to find her way around in them.

There had to be something here that made it all make sense.

It felt like hours later when she stirred, stretching her legs out on the carpet. She put down the slate she had been reading and rested her forehead on her knees. Would it make any difference? Probably not. The Movement wouldn't be interested. The only person it would mean anything to would be the Doctor.

Then she would find the Doctor, and tell him. It didn't mean she had to go along with whatever he was going to do. It didn't put

241

her on his side. It was all that she could really do here. The future wasn't up to her.

She shelved Besma's slates at random in the fiction section of the library. They'd be safe there for now.

The noises outside had been getting louder and more frequent. Anji glanced at her watch, surprised to see that barely half an hour had passed since she had crawled in through the window. She paused there now, crouching down, peering over the sill.

A man was backing down the street, a long weapon raised to his shoulder. A flash of colour caught her eye: a pair of tigers, stalking him, using the parked cars for cover.

The man fired. The sound was like a thunderclap. She had a jarring moment of recognition: it was a rifle, streamlined in shape but otherwise indistinguishable from one from the twentieth century. How had that made its way to the planet – part of a treasured collection? Or left over from the colony's earliest days? How many more lethal weapons were out there now?

The man ran up a side street. The tigers loped after him, keeping low. His gun wasn't going to dissuade them.

When she was sure the street was clear, she climbed out of the window and started jogging towards the lake. The noises were coming from all around, making her change directions again and again to avoid them. Once, she had no choice but to run right across a road where half a dozen men and women were stabbing at a trio of tigers. Their lances were beheaded, sharpened brooms.

It was the uprising, she realised, the riot that Quick had been talking about. Not just the Movement with their little harassments, their little skirmishes: ordinary Hitchemians, coming out of hiding, exhausted by fear and spoiling for a fight that was soon going to fill the entire city. It was amateur mayhem, blundering violence; none of them had ever fought a war before. But, then, neither had the tigers.

She stopped for thirty seconds to pull her boots back on so that she could run faster. It didn't matter if they saw or heard her now. After all their efforts to hold its fabric together, the colony had finally come apart at the seams.

* * *

Karl stood against the wall, his arms folded, his eyes half closed. He felt restful, comfortable. Clean and warm and fed, and safe.

Fitz hauled and pulled until the Doctor appeared at the top of the hole. He grabbed at the broken concrete, trying to get a grip to pull himself up. Fitz grabbed hold of his arms and dragged him up the rest of the way.

Still tangled in the rope, the Doctor turned to stare out of the window at the flooded creek. He put his hands to his face. 'What have you done?' he whispered.

Fitz didn't say anything.

'We have to stop it.' The Doctor turned. It was only then he saw Karl, standing next to the control panel. A tremor seemed to travel through his whole body.

He stepped across and touched the controls. At once the roaring stopped. 'I've closed the floodgates,' he said. His voice was sticking in his throat. 'They may be damaged. They weren't meant to release such a large volume of water from the lake. Let's see.'

He touched the controls again. The sound of water began again, smoothly this time. Karl recognised it, after a moment: the sound of the dam operating at its normal capacity. One of the city's background sounds, taken for granted. 'I've restored the automatic correction systems,' the Doctor said. 'Power and water should return to the city within a few minutes.'

He looked up at Karl. All the tranquillity fled Karl's body. He gripped the Doctor's arms. 'I thought they were going to dig you out of that hole like a worm.' The Doctor's face remained impassive. His eyes looked through Karl as though he had turned to a sheet of paper, transparent and empty. 'We would have had to *listen* to it,' pleaded Karl. 'Please don't hate me. Please understand.'

With an abrupt movement, the Doctor snaked his arm around Karl's shoulders and grabbed the back of his neck. He dragged the startled composer across the room like a strayed kitten and made him look down at the creek side of the dam.

There were bodies everywhere, floating atop the scummy water or lying half buried in ooze on the banks. The water must have hit them like an avalanche.

'But I just wanted to stop them,' Karl said. 'I just wanted to save you.' He knew even as he said it that it wasn't quite true. His heart was beating fiercely at the sight of the destruction he had wreaked. And yet – and yet – 'God, please, say something.'

The Doctor turned away, speaking to Fitz. 'Get over to the power plant. You should be safe there for the moment.'

'And you?' murmured Fitz.

The Doctor's hands slid down on to the back of a chair. 'I mean to go and repair a little of the damage,' he said.

He hefted the chair. It moved in a smooth arc through the air. He let go of it at the last moment, letting it sail through the riverside window. The glass exploded outwards, showering down the muddy slope and plunking into the water.

The Doctor punched out the last fragments of glass, stepped up on to a darkened control unit, and sprang down outside the hut.

Karl was still standing with his back to the lake, feeling as though he would never, could never, move again.

'Come on,' said Fitz. The lad put a hand on his arm. 'Let's get over to the power plant.'

It took Anji half an hour to get across the last two streets before the creek. She had to wait for two women to shoot a lone tiger so full of tranquilliser darts that it stopped breathing, lying in the gutter like a badly parked car. The scene was lit up by fallen lightsticks, casting huge shadows on the wall of the theatre behind them. She had to hide in a doorway while a stripe of tigers loped down the street chasing a single screaming man. He was wearing bright-green running shoes. With a dull shock she recognised the man from the merry-go-round. Some part of her brain decided the tigers were really chasing the shoes, and, if he took them off, he'd be safe.

A bullet whizzed past her head as she sprinted across one street, like a breeze that ruffled her hair, an actual bullet. She stopped cold in the middle of the road and ran her hands through her hair again and again, terrified she would find spots of blood or bits of bone, but there was nothing. After a few seconds common sense kicked in and she started running again. The back of her neck tingled incessantly after that.

The Doctor was sitting on the muddy bank of the creek, next to the corpse of a tiger. His back was to her. Anji found her steps slowing as she approached him, found herself flashing back to a car crash when she was eleven, following her father to help the hurt people until she got too scared and ran back to their own car because there might be something too awful to see.

His hand was on the wet scaly fur of the animal's flank. The body was heavy and angular, stained with mud and tangled with stringy underwater plants. There was no blood; it must have drowned. The Doctor sat in the muck beside it, his head bowed as though he were searching for something in the water, waiting for it to appear.

Anji came up to him along the bank, her boots sticking in the ooze. She saw with a hard shock that tears were running down his cheeks, and she said, 'You're crying for it? But not for Besma?'

He didn't lift his head. 'For Besma,' he said. 'For Lorenzo Smitt, and for Felix Pink. And a lot of other names you wouldn't recognise. For little Bounce.' He stroked the tiger's stiffening body. 'For Karl.'

'Karl?' Something violent inside Anji was suddenly glad, glad that the Doctor had lost someone too. 'He's dead?'

'No,' said the Doctor.

She didn't know what to make of that. Instead of asking, she said, 'I think I've worked out how the tigers became so intelligent all of a sudden.'

He didn't answer. She went on, 'I thought they were possessed, or influenced or something. You and Besma thought they were throwbacks, that the genes were popping up at random. We were both wrong.'

She turned to look out over the lake shore, where small groups of tigers and small groups of humans were skirmishing. It was distant, like watching CNN, small bodies lying on the ground. Only here, as her foot bumped against the heavy sub-adult carcass, did the war seem real.

'Besma did a lot of work on the tigers' genetics. Apparently they've got a lot of mechanisms for shuffling their genes around. That's how the generations take turns – smart and dumb. But that's not all. According to her notes, a whole lot of different genes disappear and show up again in regular cycles. It's part of their adaptability to the planet's changeable climate.'

The Doctor was listening. Anji went on, 'So why not the genes for supersmart tigers? I think they show up regularly – maybe once every couple of centuries. The colonists arrived in between. This is the first bright generation since human beings arrived.'

She found herself scratching at the back of her neck again. 'There never was an ancient civilisation that fell. The tigers have *always* had to advance in fits and starts. Maybe that stops them from changing their environment too quickly, wrecking the tiny bit of land they've got to live on. Maybe being stupid is a good survival trait – at least, some of the time.

'I know it doesn't really make any difference. But at least I feel like I understand them now.'

'But that's it,' said the Doctor. 'Of course. As it emerges, each new bright generation is supposed to bring the weather system back under control. It couldn't remain stable by itself, not over such long periods of time.' He seemed to be talking to himself. 'We're just fulfilling their plan.'

The Doctor got up out of the mud, rummaging around in his pockets until he found a clean handkerchief. 'Well done, Anji,' he said, a little hoarsely. 'Now, I need to get inside the storehouse. Even if it's only for a moment.'

'If you –'

'Alone,' he said urgently. 'Do you understand?'

Anji looked up, following his gaze. A great wall of tigers were crossing the creek. They were swimming through the waist-high water, a bow wave spreading out in front of them. They were aiming for the Doctor.

It was like watching a tidal wave heading for the shore. Nowhere to run. So Anji stood beside him.

They splashed up from the water, all around, climbing up the muddy bank.

She found herself reaching for the Doctor's hand. She was about to snatch it away again, angry at acting like a child. Without looking, the Doctor reached out and laced his fingers with hers, holding her hand in a cool, firm grip.

A massive tiger pulled itself up and stopped less than a metre away, so big that when it sat its face was level with the Doctor's, so close that she could smell its fishy breath as it spoke. A second, smaller tiger sat next to it.

The Doctor spoke back. It startled her to hear those rough animal sounds coming out of his throat.

Anji jerked as the big tiger turned angry eyes to her, but the Doctor held fast to her. It spat out a series of what sounded like filthy words. The Doctor mewed back at it, softly.

They wouldn't hurt him, she thought. And, right now, she was part of him, attached.

The tigers started talking among themselves, a rumble of growly voices all around. The big tiger and the smaller, skinny one were spitting back and forth. Their yellow eyes were off her for the moment. 'What are you saying?' she whispered.

The Doctor glanced at her. 'Can't you understand it?' he said.

She shook her head. 'It's just a bunch of growling and mewing.'

'You've assumed that all along, haven't you?' said the Doctor. 'Listen. Let the words in.'

'This is no longer about discussing things and making deals,' said the big tiger, turning back to them. Anji jerked again, almost losing her grip on the Doctor. He squeezed her hand so tightly it started to hurt. 'This is about saving our civilisation. You're going to open the second storehouse for us, Doctor. The humans are going to surrender to us, right now, completely, and get off our world.'

'Or we're going to kill them all,' added the smaller tiger. 'How's that for negotiation?'

The Doctor looked at her with disgust. 'Oh, you tiny, tiny creature,' he said. 'All you can think about is revenge. All you can

247

imagine is getting your own back because a human bested you in a fight.' With another shock, Anji recognised the tiger she had stabbed, the tiger that had killed Besma. 'With all the potential locked up in the storehouses, that's all you can imagine? For your people? For your planet?' The Doctor sighed. 'All right, Big. Of course I'll open the storehouse for you. Go ahead and destroy the humans' colony. Once you're in control, let me contact the outside world, and I'll have the planet evacuated.'

'Yes,' said Big. 'You will.'

But, thought Anji.

She didn't say anything.

Chapter Eighteen

Karl found himself slumped against a dusty wall of the power station. The building was a large concrete cube, straddling the wall of the dam, its insides packed with a maze of old machinery and tubing and catwalks.

The corner where he crouched was cobwebbed. There was a spider making its way up the wall, no bigger than one of his fingernails. An illegal immigrant, he thought, another creature that should never have come to Hitchemus.

The power station gave the impression that it had been put together by a committee: none of the bits of machinery seemed to match, the catwalks seemed to have been joined together at random. Even so, the place had kept going for a century. Maybe it had got more patchwork over time as they replaced bits of the old-fashioned equipment with whatever they could get.

Repair work was still being done after the hurricane. Half a damp wall had crumbled in when the windows burst. Areas of the maze were marked off with fences of yellow tape, behind which the guts of frightening-looking machinery were spilled out on to the floor. Karl spotted a spilled toolbox lying on its side. The engineers must have had to flee when the tigers came to town.

He stood up to look through a window. 'Keep your head down,' advised Fitz, somewhere behind him in the gloom.

'I can't see much anyway,' whispered Karl. He turned to look up at Fitz. 'What do you suppose is going to happen?'

The young man just shrugged. 'Leave it to the Doctor now.'

Anji and the Doctor walked hand in hand to the control room at the top of the dam. She saw the chair lying in the mud halfway down the dam wall, the shards of glass around the base of the window. A lot had already happened here.

The tigers ushered them into the small room, shoving them with noses and paws. Then they were separated, Anji forced against the row of machines against the wall, the Doctor shepherded over to the broken hole in the floor.

As soon as she let go of the Doctor's hand, Anji felt lost. She hadn't realised how much his simple physical presence had anchored her. He was at home in this sort of situation. He seemed calm and confident as he faced the tigers, bending to pick up a loop of rope from the floor.

'I'll need your help to lower myself down,' he told Big, as he fastened the loop tightly beneath his arms.

The skinny, scowly tiger said, 'I'll send down a couple of tigers to help you.'

'But of course, Longbody.' The Doctor gave Anji a reassuring look as Big took hold of the rope, twisting it around his paws. 'Don't drop me, now.'

Moments later, he was disappearing into the hole. Anji couldn't see over the backs of the assembled tigers. Instead, she looked around at the banks of incomprehensible machinery. Computers had changed and changed and changed a thousand times since her time, and these ones weren't designed to be operated by anyone who just happened to pick them up. In any case, blinking red lights wouldn't be enough to distract the tigers. She needed to get their attention in a big way.

Letting her eyes roam around the room, trying not to look too much as if she was looking, she spotted an old-fashioned bit of equipment hanging in a neat cabinet on the wall. She inched towards it, covering the movement by pulling on her woollen jacket.

A claw caught in the jacket as she shrugged it on. She froze. The tiger on the other end of the claw gave her a meaningful look. She let her arms drop by her sides, and stood still, smiling weakly until it turned away again to watch the excitement.

She almost yelled. There was a face at the broken window. It was Fitz, just his eyes and hair appearing above the line of broken glass. He vanished again, and for a moment she thought she had dreamed him up.

An instant later, Fitz burst through the door, yelling like a dozen madmen. The tigers all arched their backs in astonishment. Before any of them could unfreeze, he had snatched the fire axe from the cabinet, swung it overarm into one of the computers, let go of it, and grabbed her by the wrist.

The machine exploded with a satisfying bang and spray of sparks. Fitz was dragging her across the room to the door. The computer began to smoke and crackle, a fire starting somewhere in its guts. Then they were out into the night, running for the power station.

Longbody was through the door seconds later. 'Eating you!' she announced, loping after them.

'Split up!' shouted Anji. She twisted free of Fitz.

'No, come on!' he yelled. But she had already run to the edge of the dam wall.

The concrete stopped suddenly, replaced by a great muddy slope. Anji's feet stuck in the stuff, sending her stumbling down the side of the dam instead of running across it for her life. She twisted, expecting to see Longbody's leering face.

But the tiger had followed Fitz. He was sprinting for the power station, the orange killer at his heels. There was nothing she could do.

Anji could hear the tigers arguing inside the control room. She inched closer, staying in the darkness of the wall, hoping no one would decide to help Longbody with her search.

'He's locked himself in!' a tiger was calling, from beneath the floor. 'We can't make the door open.'

'Well, try,' Big growled. 'You must have seen what he did.'

'Only some of it.'

'What does he think he's doing down there? I don't like this. He already learned much too much from the other storehouse.'

She grinned to herself, fiercely. You're knackered, mate, she thought. Once the Doctor gets into something, there's no stopping him.

Fitz slammed the power station door and turned to slap home its heavy locks. He heard the impact of Longbody's angry body on the other side. 'Bite me, hairball!' he shouted. 'Er. On the other hand, don't bite me!'

He looked around. 'Karl!' he hissed. 'Where the hell are you?' No answer. Had the composer panicked and bolted, like Anji?

He had found a cabinet marked EMERGENCIES. He went there now, hoping to find a tool or something to use as a weapon. Inside there was a jumble of equipment, wiring and stuff, and a bundle of lightsticks. He took one out, turned it down to its lowest setting, and held it out in front of him like a crucifix as he tiptoed around in the dark.

'Karl?' he stage-whispered. 'Goddamit, are you here somewhere?'

There was a breeze coming from somewhere. He had noticed it earlier, but had only really registered it now.

The banging and thumping at the door had stopped. Longbody had either given up, or she'd decided to sniff around for some other way into the building.

Instinctively, Fitz started heading upwards, away from the entrances. He climbed up a succession of sloping catwalks, his feet clattering on the metal mesh. From up here, the piping and wires looked like a cross between a modern art sculpture and an engine block. He was sure the breeze was stronger higher up.

Something below flashed in the soft glow of his lightstick, just for a moment. He stopped in his tracks, holding the odd lantern out over the rail at the side of the catwalk. No good – the feeble circle of light didn't even reach the floor, ten feet down. *There!* Something was moving down there. 'Karl?' he stage-whispered again. No reply.

Fitz twisted the dial on the lightstick, turning it into a spotlight. He swung it back and forth. Huge shadows stretched and moved on the walls.

He almost dropped the stick when a pair of yellow eyes flared in the shadows, throwing back the light.

He swung the stick, trying to catch the monster that was hiding down there. He took a few steps from side to side, trying to light up as much of the floor below as he could. There – the eyes again, just for a moment, and then gone. *Where was she?*

She stepped out from behind a chunky computer bank, long and sleek and scowling, eyes flashing red and gold where the light touched her face.

'How did you get in here?' gasped Fitz.

'Hullow,' snarled the tiger, opening her mouth wide to display her teeth. They glittered in the spotlight. She had her paws on the bottom rung of a ladder.

'Christ!' said Fitz.

Karl stayed where he was on the rooftop, his knees drawn up to his chest, leaning against the low wall at the edge. For now it was all he could think of to do. The Doctor had told them to stay in the power station. And so he would stay here, well hidden from the tigers, but with a view of everything that was happening.

There must be something else he could do. Something more.

He wanted to tell himself that he hadn't known what would happen when he opened the floodgates. That he had only imagined the water washing away the handful of tigers trying to get to the Doctor. But it wasn't true. He hadn't had any real image in his mind at all. He only wanted a weapon.

He would show the Doctor that they were still on the same side. He would find some action to take, some gesture to make that would make the Doctor realise he was still Karl, not some watery monster. When this was all over they would talk it through under the trees next to Emerson Creek.

He got up on his knees to look over the edge of the roof. A cold wind blew through his hair, and spots of freezing rain speckled his face and hands. The deep grey sky was smeared with a sickening yellow-green. Something was flickering down there, some light inside the control room. His heart leapt. Was it the Doctor, back from the storehouse?

The door of the control room opened. A deep electrical light burst out, forming a rectangle of glare in the dark wall of the building. The whole top of the dam was illuminated by it. Karl squinted into the purple-white blaze.

A group of panicked tigers ran out of the small building.

'Oh God,' he said. 'Oh my God.'

He fell to his knees, clutching at the wall.

The Doctor stepped out of the control room. He walked out to the centre of the dam and looked up at the sky. The rain began to hurtle down.

Karl was half blinded by the flash that cracked between the Doctor and the storm overhead. The fierce blue light surrounded the man for that instant, his body a silhouette inside the lightning at it shot up from the concrete to the clouds. When Karl could see again, the Doctor was still standing there, unburned by the bolt, laughing.

'Oh God,' he said again.

Neither of them had been made for this chase. Fitz could barely see what he was doing as he climbed up and down ladders and dashed along catwalks. Longbody was designed for short, hard sprints, not for this clambering pursuit through the pipes and wires.

Fitz took a deep breath and ran out across a pipe, arms thrown out for balance. He leapt across a gap on to another catwalk, slithering under the railing. Behind him, Longbody sniffed at the pipe, her mouth hanging open, and started looking around for another way to get at him. Fitz gave silent thanks for having been descended from tree-dwellers and legged it, looking for another ladder.

Was there somewhere to hide – a locked room, or even a cupboard? He hadn't seen anything except the blank concrete walls of the cube and the twisting machinery inside. Anyway, she would be able to use that taste sense of hers to find him. He needed to get back down to the door of the station, and outside. But then what? She'd just follow him.

While his mind was racing, his body was racing, too, running and clambering and climbing without benefit of his higher thought processes. It didn't need his help to obey the instinct of a cave dweller faced with a sabre-tooth. But one of them was going to run out of steam. And he needed to make only one mistake, give Longbody one chance, and the game would be over.

This was it, this was one of those *it* moments. Maybe the last moment of your life.

The hair on the back of Fitz's neck was standing up. He could detect an electrical smell, like something shorting out. He snatched his hands away from the metal rails of the catwalk.

The squares of windows close to floor level lit up. Lightning was flashing out there – that big storm was right on top of them. What would happen if a bolt hit the power station?

He ran right into something big and hard attached to the wall, a hose or a coil of wire or something, and let out a yell of surprise and pain, falling on to his arse on the cold metal mesh. Longbody was bounding towards him across the tops of a bunch of big machines. He scrambled for the ladder at the end of the catwalk, nearly going down it head first in his rush to get clear of the monster.

He found himself inside a cage of yellow tape, marking out a mangled rectangle of space around a looming chunk of misshapen machinery. His lightstick picked out a big yellow sign on the wall above: WARNING, HIGH VOLTAGE.

Fitz spun. The barrier was on all sides. He inched away from the machine and threw himself into a web of tape, trying to push and claw his way through it. It was tough and fibrous, stretching instead of tearing, grabbing hold of his clothes and hair.

The tiger appeared above, her head poking out above the ladder. His wildly flailing lightstick caught her face for a moment. Her eyes flared red and gold. Fitz found himself whimpering as he struggled in the tape, trying to drag himself through, another foot from her, just one more inch from her.

Longbody roared and leapt. Fitz screamed. The tiger landed elegantly on the floor and turned to make the kill.

Instantly she froze, staring at him with those huge headlight eyes.

Fitz flung himself backwards, uselessly, ripping down a great mass of tape as he went. The stuff fluttered down to cover him as he banged into the concrete wall.

Longbody was still standing there, trembling all over. Her mouth was hanging open. Smoke was coming out of it. Fitz flinched against the wall.

A moment later, he saw that, as she had turned, her tail had smacked into the machine behind her. Sparks were rippling up and down the length of her tail, disappearing into her back and flanks.

A moment later, there was a heavy thud as the tiger's body hit the ground.

Fitz realised he had thrown his arms up over his head, as though expecting an explosion. He lowered them, slowly, expecting the tiger to jump up at any minute and laugh at him before it ate him.

Longbody just lay there, smoking slightly. Fitz's nose wrinkled at the frying-fish smell. He stood up, keeping his back to the wall, well away from the creature's corpse. She might still be touching something live in there.

His legs were shaking badly, but he knew from long experience that he would still be able to walk away.

The tigers had never messed around with electricity, he thought. What was obvious danger to him was just some more human junk to her. She hadn't even guessed the meaning of the sign or the tape.

Death by culture shock.

There was another hurricane coming. It had to be. Anji watched the terrible sky as it turned the purple of a fresh bruise. The colour leaked in from the horizons, clouds merging into a single horizontal wall of heavy anger. The rain was thumping down like arrowheads.

The gods, she thought, are deeply pissed off.

She should find shelter. Lock herself in a basement, or curl against a wall in some strongly made building that had proved itself in the hurricane. Sitting here on the muddy wall of the dam, she was naked to the rising gale, easy prey for thunderbolts. Already her clothes were drenched.

But between her and the safety of the city was a barrier made of bodies. Dozens of tigers, springing and slashing. Dozens of humans, armed with absolutely anything at all. They slipped and splashed in the mud and the oozy water, stumbling over corpses.

The battlefield was strangely silent. There should be gunshots, she thought, cannon firing, clouds of smoke drifting across the tableau. There should be a constant blare of roars and screams. Instead there were soft, heavy sounds: blows landing, mud squelching, bodies colliding, the creek splashing, rain falling and falling.

There were screams, of course. From time to time, a torn body let out a shriek, as much panic as pain. Somewhere in the muck someone was screaming over and over. Anji couldn't pick out the trampled body from the others half buried in the churned and sticky mass.

What was the Doctor doing down in that pit? She imagined him at the controls of some ancient machine, struggling with rusted levers and arcane labels. Was he trying to avert the storm? Or had he made the clouds thicken like curdling milk, and was now fighting to control what he'd created, like the sorcerer's apprentice?

The day was dark as evening now, the sky a single shelf of cloud. Great patches glowed with lightning. Each spasm of thunder was no longer a throaty grumble, but a growl followed by a violent crack that echoed from the dam wall. Anji didn't know whether to go down, closer to the ground, or higher up, away from the water.

She didn't move. She felt as though she were watching a movie, loud and full of action, but on the other side of a screen. There was nothing she could do to change whatever was going to happen. She could only watch.

Lightning flashed again, this time a great tree that reached from earth to heaven, leaving brilliant lines on Anji's retinas. She yelled, but the wind and rain ate the sound. She blinked hard, trying to restore her vision.

The battle seemed to be losing momentum. Had the combatants stopped to look at the storm, wondering whether they were in

257

more danger from the sky than from each other? Or were the darkness and the rain starting to get in their way?

She suddenly realised she could see her shadow. It stretched out below her, almost as far as the water. The light behind her flickered, growing brighter. She twisted her head. Was something on fire up there? Where was it coming from?

It was the Doctor. He stood in the centre of the dam, looking up at the sky. He was outlined with hot purple light, sending out crackling fingers into the dark air around him. His short hair was standing out, rippling in the rushing wind, crackling with red sparks. His unbuttoned waistcoat flapped. One of his sleeves was rolled back, revealing something clasped around his left arm, like a fat bracelet. Anji recognised large tiger symbols on it, glowing orange-cherry.

He looked down over the battlefield. His face was a dark mask, obscured in the gloom. Only his eyes seemed to stand out, as though charged with the same fiery energy. He was laughing. She could hear it as clearly as though he were standing next to her.

Something was coming, something that made her hair stand up, literally standing out from her head and making her scalp tighten. Even the tiny hairs on her arms were taut.

Her chest convulsed, as though something heavy and sharp were lodged in it. She thought she was terrified. But, after a moment, she realised it was grief. What had the Doctor become? How would they ever get him back?

Karl clung to the edge of the roof, shaking, watching.

A couple of tigers started running up the dam wall, towards the Doctor, yowling in panic. He glanced at them, then up again. He raised a hand.

A cone of cloudstuff came down from the wall over their heads. Karl could see it slowly spinning in the light from the lightning. It stretched like candyfloss, a long line coming down to touch the wall of the dam.

It was a tornado. A baby tornado.

The Doctor gestured sharply. The whirlwind shot along the wall of the dam. The control room exploded when the tip of the cone touched it. The walls and windows burst outwards as though the little hut were a popping balloon. Fragments of glass and wood showered down both sides of the dam. There was a deep splash as a chunk of computer equipment hit the lake.

The tornado was moving down the dam and towards the city. Oh God, thought Karl, can he stop it, is he going to stop it? The survivors of the battle were shouting, scrambling away from the column of angry air. Was he going to kill them all?

The cone tore across the muddy grass and hit a greenhouse in the middle of the park. Instantly the tornado changed colour, becoming a roaring line of pink and green that connected earth to sky, the perfect mating of sound and colour and movement.

Karl was weeping. 'Oh Doctor,' he gasped. 'At last, *fortissimo*.'

When Anji dared look again – fragments of glass and wood showering from her hair – the tornado was widening, thinning out. Petals sailed down all over the ground as it wisped away to nothing. The Doctor was laughing madly. No. It was warm and genuine, his real laugh. There wasn't a hint of madness in it, just delight, elation.

He had gone native, thought Anji. He had become Hitchemus, hardwired into its atmosphere, into its air and water.

'That's enough,' he said. His voice was as clear as though he was standing next to her. 'No more. That's quite enough.'

The tornado hadn't been the thing that was coming. It was just an overture. The burning, tingling feeling in her hair and across her skin was intensifying.

The Doctor turned, his back to the city. The wind was being dragged across the dam, filling the air with specks of mud. They spattered against her face. She turned to get her back to the flying muck. Below, the shallow water was surging in weak waves. Everything was being drawn towards the east.

The sky darkened, the lightning dying down to nothing. Anji's hair flew in the wind being sucked into the horizon. She tried to breathe; the air whipped away from her face.

It all stopped, snapping off. The air sang with tension.

The Doctor stopped laughing. He raised his hands above his head and brought them sharply down.

Then it happened.

Anji broke the surface of the water, gulping at the air. She flailed around, grabbing out for anything to hold on to. Her hands slapped painfully against the concrete wall of the dam. She pressed them against it and pushed herself up out of the freezing water, sobbing.

She couldn't see a bloody thing, even when she held her hand up in front of her face. Was it pitch-black now? Had the clouds swollen until she was surrounded by dark mist? Or had her eyes been cooked solid by the flash? She couldn't even tell if she was really crying, water running down her face from her sodden hair.

When the sky had exploded, she had lost her grip on the dam, tumbling down the slope. The creek was no deeper than a bathtub, but she knew she could have drowned in those seconds when her stunned brain was trying to turn itself back on.

She was starting to see sparkles in the black. They swelled into an afterimage that filled up her whole field of vision, a floating rectangle edged in red. No amount of blinking and rubbing at her wet face would make the burning picture go away.

She had seen it for only an instant before she had begun her blind slide into the water. The entire eastern sky had burst like a flashbulb. It wasn't lightning, it couldn't have been lightning, not unless it was a bolt several kilometres wide. It couldn't have been a nuke – surely the flash would have been followed by a killing shock wave. It must have been some kind of futuristic weapon. That was it.

Whatever it was, it had hit the spaceport. She immediately imagined what must be left of the tarmac and its double arc of buildings. As if a god had pressed the tip of a cigarette to the planet's surface.

Some part of her mind was reeling off something about the power in a thunderstorm, how that much electricity could power an entire city for a year, or whatever it was. What if all that energy was concentrated in a single flash, instead of doled out in small doses?

Her face felt hot. She waved her hand in front of her eyes again, experimentally, and was surprised to realise she could make out the movement. Something glittered as she moved the hand back and forth. It was her watch, she thought. Light was shining off her watch.

The sun had come out.

The sky overhead was a blurry patch of blue, painful to look at, a hole in the middle of the clouds. It looked like an eye in reverse, blue pupil and black iris, staring down at the dam. Anji was shivering, soaked to the bone. Her clothes were steaming in the sudden hot sunshine. She tore off her sodden jacket, letting it fall in the muck, exposing her arms to the warmth.

'Do I have your full attention?' said the Doctor.

He was still there, at the top of the dam. He was speaking normally, even quietly, but the swirling winds picked up his voice and carried it across the dam. It was something like those invisible speakers they used here, thought Anji. She was certain that all of the combatants had heard it. Probably the whole city had heard it. Maybe the whole planet had heard it.

Now she could see the tigers and humans, cowering together at the edge of the creek. They stood stunned, or had sunk into the mud, sitting in astonishment, shaking their heads from side to side, rubbing their eyes. Faces were turned up to the widening circle of light above them, and the small figure beneath it.

'I've spent all this time encouraging you to find your own solution,' said the Doctor. 'I wanted you to work together to make peace. Well, now I'm going to *make* you make peace.'

Anji realised he wasn't quite touching the ground. The winds were holding him up, like a bird of prey hovering in place. 'Yes, I've destroyed the spaceport,' he said. 'I could destroy everything if I wanted to. All of it – the city, the storehouses, the Bewilderness. I could erase this last bit of land. Let the ocean swallow it up!

'But I'm not going to. Of course I'm not going to.

'I wish you could see yourselves. Tiny people. Miniature tigers.' He spread his arms wide. 'The tigers took this world and saved it, made it possible for life to go on here. They've reached incredible heights, again and again. The weather system they built stretches over the entire globe! I can – it can make cyclones, blizzards, the gentlest of sunshowers.

'And you're both arrogant enough to think that this planet is yours to control. Well, the planet is tired of your fumbling games.

'The human beings came here across the empty sky of the universe. Imagine it! You're both like sailors from different seas. Cast up together on the same little island. This tiny, precious island world.

'It's just you now. I could have destroyed anything, everything, but I've destroyed the spaceport. You're stuck here – with one another.

'This world is inherently unstable – like everything in life. The only way it can be made habitable is to correct the drift in the weather system. And I've done a little tinkering.' The band around his arm was glowing fiercely. 'I've just made that drift much, much worse. Your island will be ruined and gone within a decade unless you fix it. Neither of you have the skills to do that on your own, not before the hurricanes destroy you.

'The tigers understand how their ancestors thought. They can translate the archives, work the machines. The humans understand weather. They'll bring the scientific knowledge the tigers are lacking.

'It's up to you, now. I've finished here.' He laughed, brightly. 'Save your own world for a change.'

And Anji realised: he wasn't possessed, he wasn't transformed. He was, at last, absolutely himself.

His feet were back on the ground. He took a bow in the spotlight of sunshine and walked away.

Coda

The music stopped and I stood still,
And found myself outside the hill,
Left alone against my will,
To go now limping as before,
And never hear of that country more!
        – Robert Browning, *The Pied Piper of Hamelin*

Chapter Nineteen

Karl Sadeghi, composer, says:

And so the performance is over, just like that. The conductor's left the stage, met with massed silence, and you're sitting there wondering what went wrong in the music. Why in all the sound and fury of the climax of the piece, you still heard wrong notes, missing phrases, themes left unresolved.

So you want to go back to, to the top.

But you can't, really, because I've been struggling with the wrong metaphor. It's not really a concert, it's a - a jam session, every note improvised, the miracle of it not a perfectly crafted piece but a spontaneous one. One that came out of nowhere and disappears back there once it's finished.

I compose, I rehearse, I solve and craft. I want to go back and create the perfect piece, the perfect conclusion. But I missed my entrance at the end, I didn't play the part I needed to redeem myself, and now the music's gone.

Karl stood alone at the edge of an immense black circle, like the pupil of a green eye. In the mild sunshine, the melted black stuff glittered with fused soil and asphalt and metal. When he put his foot on it, it crunched and disintegrated. The circle was surrounded by a scorched ring of whitened soil and dead plants. Outside that, the trees and grass were growing normally, untouched by the mighty heat that had made this featureless monument.

He had spent the last week recovering from his time in the Bewilderness: three days in the hospital, another three at home, lounging in bed or on the sofa. He tried not to think about work, music, anything. But by the end of the week he found himself flipping back and forth through the concerto score, fiddling and annotating. It was time to get out and take stock of his changed world.

The Doctor hadn't visited. He'd heard that hardly anyone had seen the virtuoso since the night the war had ended. Rumour was divided as to whether he was hiding in a flat somewhere, or camping in the Bewilderness.

There was almost nothing left of the buildings that had once ringed the tarmac. They had become shapeless lumps at the edge of the cooked circle, metal and concrete supports sticking out like tangled bones. He could see a team of tigers and humans picking through those ruins, the same group he had caught a lift with this morning. The tigers optimistically wore baskets on their backs, in case anything could be saved. With the sea change in the economy over the next few years, they would need every bit of technology they could restore.

He wondered how many of those people, two-legged and four-legged, had taken part in that final, furious, tiny, muddy battle.

He had been horrified at the thought of anyone being caught in the impossibly strong blast of lightning, turned to ashes along with the buildings and ships. But the stories told in the hospital said one of the miniature tornadoes had menaced the handful of tiger guards, chasing them yowling into the forest. The singed survivors babbled about laughing winds and the sky falling.

267

Visitors could still land on Hitchemus, of course. The marines could send in thousands of fighters if they chose, peppering the island with troopers. Tourists from the refuelling ships could shuttle down and land in clearings. Universities all over local space had shown sudden interest in sending expeditions to follow up poor Dr Grieve's work. It was just more difficult, more trouble than it was worth – particularly for the overstretched military. The colony would be alone to sort out its problems.

Karl tilted his head back, looking up at the empty sky. Very much alone.

Another team, sweaty and sooty after their work, gave him a lift back to the city. Crammed into the back of an electric truck with a bunch of tigers, he knew he was the only one who still felt nervous. When the truck went over a bump and one of the tigers banged him with its soft shoulder, he shut his eyes and cringed against the wall. The other humans threw jokes around. Each tiger wore a vocoder, but already the humans were speaking a few words of the tiger tongue. Mostly rude ones, he guessed, judging by what he had learned in their company.

Images of raw meat would still loom before his eyes, sudden and unwanted. The doctors said it would take time for them to pass. But already he was recovered enough to manage the tigers' company, as long as plenty of other humans were around.

They drove into town past more teams working on buildings and streets. The Nodes had sunk into the ground again, for good this time – until they would be needed again for one last adjustment to Hitchemus's climate, one that should restore the planet's famous good weather for generations. In the meantime the broken roads and pavements needed repair, and the last of the hurricane damage was being fixed. He spotted two tigers standing on either side of a roof, holding a tarpaulin in their mouths and trying to argue.

When the truck stopped, the tigers leapt out and immediately doused themselves in the fountain, soaking their dry skins. There had been discussions of turning some of the damaged streets into canals to let the tigers get about more quickly.

So many tigers had lived in Port Any for so long, as silent spies or curious visitors, that it wouldn't take much adjustment for them to become a permanent part of the city. Others would be coming here for the first time, to mine the secrets of the storehouse, to teach and learn languages and science. Or just looking for more violin lessons.

The flow was going both ways. Karl passed a group of humans preparing for a long camp in the Bewilderness, packing food and tents and slates into hovercars. They were singing a work song, one he hadn't heard before.

Anji met him in the plaza. They bought chilled fruit juice from a stall and sat side by side on the sofa sculpture.

'I can't believe so much has changed so quickly, so easily,' he confessed. 'It's as though there was a war when I went to bed, and peace when I woke up.'

'Quick deserves a lot of the credit,' she said. 'Did you know he was in that little war by the lake? About five minutes after the Doctor gave his big speech, he was organising the survivors to haul one another out of the mud. He sent me and a couple of others running for ambulances. By the time I got back, he and Big were working side by side. You know, I think they actually like one another.'

'You have to give them credit,' mused Karl. 'They know when a fight is over.' He took a long drag on his straw.

'He also gave us one week to get off Hitchemus,' said Anji wryly.

Karl closed his eyes. Someone in hospital had mentioned it, that the aliens would be leaving. It had struck him at the time that the tigers weren't 'aliens' any more. The Doctor was. 'You're going with him, then?'

'Yeah…' said Anji. 'I did consider going to Earth, actually. I want to see what it's like now, and Quick said he could arrange passage with one of the university teams.' She hooked her hair back over her ear with a finger. 'But when I thought about it, it felt like leaving my family behind. Like a pair of brothers who drive you crazy but you love to see.' She grinned at Karl. 'Silly. We've hardly got any DNA in common.'

Karl gave one of his small smiles. They sat quietly for a few minutes and finished their drinks.

'I wish you could have seen the official ceremony,' Anji said. 'The mayor sat down on the steps of the town hall. I thought the whole crowd was going to panic when Big started climbing those steps. The mayor's eyes just about left her head. But Big walked right up to her and put his head down in her lap. Like a unicorn meeting a virgin,' she laughed. 'At first I thought it was surrender, it really took me by surprise. But when I talked to a few of the tigers, I realised it was a gesture of trust between equals.'

'What did the mayor do?'

'Put a lei around Big's neck,' said Anji. 'Once the net's running at full strength, you've *got* to see the footage.'

He couldn't laugh. 'Why aren't they at one another's throats?'

'They have been, quite a few times. Quick and Big have been coming down hard on anyone who stirs up trouble.'

'How long will it take them to, to work out how to get into the storehouse?'

'No one's sure. There's a joint team working on the puzzle lock, night and day. The Doctor wouldn't say a word about it. I think they'd like to shake the secret out of him, if they could lay their hands and paws on him – or on that device he was using. Thank God it's safely back in the storehouse. Until they open it up, anyway.'

Karl shook his head. 'He's put us all in danger.'

'He's made you safe,' insisted Anji. 'Neither side can risk a fight. There'll be petty outbreaks of violence, there'll be hate, there's been a lot of talk about blame and reparations and calling the marines – once a new transmitter gets built, anyway. But the war is over.'

Karl sighed. 'At least the weather satellite is working again. So we'll get a bit of warning, next time…'

'Oh, it was working the entire time – we just couldn't receive signals from it. It confirms everything the Doctor said. Hitchemus's climate is spinning out of control. There'll be quite a few storms to weather before we learn enough about the Nodes to fix it.' Her mouth twitched in a smile. 'I mean, before *you* learn.'

Anji pointed Karl in the general direction of Fitz. On his way, Karl passed a group of about a dozen tigers. They were making music, tiger music, stamping the grass of a small park with their paws in a complicated rhythm. He watched for a few minutes, fascinated, trying to pick out the different strands of the beat.

The tigers all sat down, suddenly, and began their wailing singing. It rose and fell, a shrill polyharmony that wove in his mind like coloured ribbons, green and gold and red. He could not tell if they were improvising it, or if it followed a musical system too new and strange for him to grasp.

A handful of humans were watching, recording the performance on their slates. There would be time, thought Karl, to analyse the music of tigers. He walked on.

Fitz was sitting on a grassy slope just outside the city, with a view of the sparkling lake, playing his guitar.

When Karl was close enough to make out the melody, he stopped to listen. Fitz nodded at him, but didn't stop playing. Six notes that rose and fell in a pulsing curve.

> *Sail on, sailor, sail on,*
> *Still listening for your siren song;*
> *Tomorrow is your only home…*

The voice trailed off, the hands kept playing for a few more bars, rounding out the chorus. 'I never could come up with a last line for that bit… I suppose it's kind of fitting, in a way. That it's not finished.'

'Why is that?' said Karl softly.

'It's about him. I wrote it about him a long time back now, before… before we met Anji. Maybe one of these days I'll play it for him again.' Fitz gently laid the guitar down on the grass. 'You know, I wish we could stay.'

Karl came closer, squatting down beside him. 'Not everyone thinks you should leave, you know,' he said. 'Quick's order has more to do with getting control back over the situation.'

'Oh, yeah,' said Fitz. 'Got to keep rolling on, that's us.' He turned the guitar pick around and around in his spidery fingers. 'The Doctor sometimes tells me, "Fitz, we're fated to find no resting place." I guess that's what he means.'

'Most people don't spend their lives hopping from planet to planet.'

'That's why we have to.' Fitz grinned. 'This has just been another ride in the greatest amusement park ever. You know? Some rides are a lot more scary and dangerous than others. But there's always another one to try.'

'Is that how the Doctor thinks of us, then?' said Karl sadly. 'Just another ride?'

'Oh, no. He takes it much more seriously than I do. Why don't you ask him yourself?'

'Where is he?'

Fitz jerked his head at the slope of the hill. 'Go higher,' he said.

Karl spotted the Doctor from a distance. He was lying at the top of the hill, sprawled on the sward, half vanished into the long, waving grass. Little orange flowers were coming up everywhere, encouraged by the recent rains. For a moment he was absurdly afraid that if he looked away, if he even blinked, the Doctor would vanish like a summertime vision.

The composer was struck by a strange mixture of feelings. While the Doctor was in this world, everything would be all right, nothing could be all right. He would always be surrounded by storms. But look around. Even Hitchemus, with its infection of hurricanes, was calm and bright today.

Karl's heart sank to his boots as he trudged up the hill. The Doctor didn't seem to have noticed him. Or was he simply ignoring him? He fought down the urge to turn around and head back to the city. The Doctor would be gone in a day or so. Life would go on.

He sank down into the grass, at arm's reach. The numen had left the Doctor: he was no longer a god of thunder, but only a beautiful man lying in the grass.

The Doctor opened an eye. 'It's you,' he said.

Karl had no idea how to take that. He took a deep breath and said, 'I still want you to play in my concerto. I can work something out with Quick. Please. Forgive me. Forgive me, and stay.'

The Doctor rolled on to his side, resting his chin in his hand, and twirled a strand of grass around his finger. He didn't say a word.

'Then take me with you,' said Karl desperately. 'I'll forget all about Hitchemus. I'll have adventures with you. As silly as you like.'

The Doctor still said nothing, but tilted his head forward, looking down at the grass. Karl suddenly recognised the gesture: he was trying to hide his face with his long hair. It was already growing back, startlingly fast, like spring flowers. But it didn't quite hide his eyes.

'I can't, can I?' said Karl. 'I have to stay and clear up the mess I helped to make. Like everyone else.'

'You must help yourselves,' said the Doctor softly.

There was a few minutes' silence. Karl felt himself relaxing, just a little, now that it was all decided. So easily, after the week of waiting and worrying, so easily.

'I've had three tigers try to join the orchestra already,' he said eventually. 'I've had to explain that a handful of lessons does not a professional musician make. But they're so keen to learn. Jeoffry is something of a prodigy. Within a few years, there won't be anything out of the ordinary about tiger musicians.'

'Tigers with tablas,' said the Doctor.

Karl's mouth twitched. 'Moggies with mandolins.'

'Furry flautists.'

'Catrabasoons.'

'Honk honk.'

They stopped, smiling at each other. Karl was struck how those blue eyes could burn with rage or glitter with laughter, equal parts frightening and attractive. Like lightning, of course.

'I can't play your music any more, Karl,' murmured the Doctor. 'I don't forgive you, I understand you. I know the ferocity it took to throw open those floodgates and drown your enemies. But my passion is for something different. Not for vengeance.' He ran his fingers through the grass, through the soil and flowers and ants. 'For life. Inexorable, relentless, dogged life.'

He threw his head back and looked at the sky, at the clouds sailing the high breezes above the city of tigers. 'I've already played my concerto.'

Acknowledgements

'Hullow.'

The Year of Intelligent Tigers began as a conversation with my husband and co-author, Jonathan Blum, while picnicking on the shores of Lake Burleigh Griffin in Canberra. We co-wrote the outline for the novel. Jon also wrote a breakdown of each chapter, wrote the two historical interludes and various other bits and pieces, and provided an enormous amount of feedback, support and large chunks of dialogue.

I'm indebted to Lance Parkin and Lloyd Rose for their invaluable comments during the writing, and to the eagle eyes of the read-through crew: David Carroll and Kyla Ward, Alryssa and Tom Kelly, Neil Marsh, Rupert Booth and Trina MacGregor.

Thanks are due to the denizens of bionet.mycology; to Jennifer Tifft for her expert analysis of the Doctor's costume; and to Phyllis and Sam Blum for the chocolate martini recipe!

Lastly, a quick plug for our email newsletter, *The Butterfly Room*, with the latest news about our writing efforts. Visit http://groups.yahoo.com/group/butterflyroom to join the mailing list.

'Hooroo.'

About the Authors

Kate Orman was born in Sydney, Australia, where she currently lives with her husband and co-author Jonathan Blum. She has written or co-written ten Doctor Who-related novels. Her short fiction has appeared in *Interzone* and *Realms of Fantasy* and in anthologies.

Jonathan Blum was born in Maryland, USA, and works as a software engineer and occasional filmmaker. Besides co-writing three Doctor Who novels with Kate, he has written *Fearmonger*, a seventh-Doctor Big Finish audio story, and the upcoming *The I Job* for BBV (featuring the I from *Seeing I*). His short fiction has made it as far as the *Short Trips* and *Missing Pieces* anthologies. He doesn't play his guitar nearly often enough.

BBC DOCTOR WHO BOOKS
FEATURING THE EIGHTH DOCTOR

DOCTOR WHO: THE NOVEL OF THE FILM by Gary Russell
ISBN 0 563 38000 4
THE EIGHT DOCTORS by Terrance Dicks ISBN 0 563 40563 5
VAMPIRE SCIENCE by Jonathan Blum and Kate Orman
ISBN 0 563 40566 X
THE BODYSNATCHERS by Mark Morris ISBN 0 563 40568 6
GENOCIDE by Paul Leonard ISBN 0 563 40572 4
WAR OF THE DALEKS by John Peel ISBN 0 563 40573 2
ALIEN BODIES by Lawrence Miles ISBN 0 563 40577 5
KURSAAL by Peter Anghelides ISBN 0 563 40578 3
OPTION LOCK by Justin Richards ISBN 0 563 40583 X
LONGEST DAY by Michael Collier ISBN 0 563 40581 3
LEGACY OF THE DALEKS by John Peel ISBN 0 563 40574 0
DREAMSTONE MOON by Paul Leonard ISBN 0 563 40585 6
SEEING I by Jonathan Blum and Kate Orman ISBN 0 563 40586 4
PLACEBO EFFECT by Gary Russell ISBN 0 563 40587 2
VANDERDEKEN'S CHILDREN by Christopher Bulis
ISBN 0 563 40590 2
THE SCARLET EMPRESS by Paul Magrs ISBN 0 563 40595 3
THE JANUS CONJUNCTION by Trevor Baxendale
ISBN 0 563 40599 6
BELTEMPEST by Jim Mortimore ISBN 0 563 40593 7
THE FACE EATER by Simon Messingham ISBN 0 563 55569 6
THE TAINT by Michael Collier ISBN 0 563 55568 8
DEMONTAGE by Justin Richards ISBN 0 563 55572 6
REVOLUTION MAN by Paul Leonard ISBN 0 563 55570 X
DOMINION by Nick Walters ISBN 0 563 55574 2
UNNATURAL HISTORY by Jonathan Blum and Kate Orman
ISBN 0 563 55576 9
AUTUMN MIST by David A. McIntee ISBN 0 563 55583 1
INTERFERENCE: BOOK ONE by Lawrence Miles
ISBN 0 563 55580 7

INTERFERENCE: BOOK TWO by Lawrence Miles
ISBN 0 563 55582 3
THE BLUE ANGEL by Paul Magrs and Jeremy Hoad
ISBN 0 563 55581 5
THE TAKING OF PLANET 5 by Simon Bucher-Jones and
Mark Clapham ISBN 0 563 55585 8
FRONTIER WORLDS by Peter Anghelides ISBN 0 563 55589 0
PARALLEL 59 by Natalie Dallaire and Stephen Cole
ISBN 0 563 555904
THE SHADOWS OF AVALON by Paul Cornell ISBN 0 563 555882
THE FALL OF YQUATINE by Nick Walters ISBN 0 563 55594 7
COLDHEART by Trevor Baxendale ISBN 0 563 55595 5
THE SPACE AGE by Steve Lyons ISBN 0 563 53800 7
THE BANQUO LEGACY by Andy Lane and Justin Richards
ISBN 0 563 53808 2
THE ANCESTOR CELL by Peter Anghelides and Stephen Cole
ISBN 0 563 53809 0
THE BURNING by Justin Richards ISBN 0 563 53812 0
CASUALTIES OF WAR by Steve Emmerson ISBN 0 563 53805 8
THE TURING TEST by Paul Leonard ISBN 0 563 53806 6
ENDGAME by Terrance Dicks ISBN 0 563 53802 3
FATHER TIME by Lance Parkin ISBN 0 563 53810 4
ESCAPE VELOCITY by Colin Brake ISBN 0 563 53825 2
EARTHWORLD by Jacqueline Rayner ISBN 0 563 53827 9
VANISHING POINT by Stephen Cole ISBN 0 563 53829 5
EATER OF WASPS by Trevor Baxendale ISBN 0 563 53832 5

COMING SOON:

THE SLOW EMPIRE by Dave Stone ISBN 0 563 53835 X
(July '01)
DARK PROGENY by Steve Emmerson ISBN 0 563 53837 6
(Aug '01)
THE CITY OF THE DEAD by Lloyd Rose ISBN 0 563 53839 2
(Sept '01)
GRIMM REALITY by Simon Bucher-Jones and Kelly Hale
ISBN 0 563 53841 4 (Oct '01)

THE MONTHLY TELEPRESS
The official BBC Doctor Who Books e-newsletter

News – competitions – interviews – and more!

Subscribe today at
http://groups.yahoo.com/group/Telepress

PRESENTING

DOCTOR WHO

AN ALL-NEW AUDIO DRAMA

Big Finish Productions is proud to present brand-new
Doctor Who adventures on double CD!

Available from May 2001
LOUPS-GAROUX

A four-part story by Marc Platt.
Starring **Peter Davison** as the Doctor
and **Mark Strickson** as Turlough.

*Germany, 1589: the townspeople of Cologne pronounce the death sentence on a mass-murderer
who has stalked the countryside in the guise of a ferocious wolf.*

*Russia, 1812: retreating from Napoleon's invading forces, a merchant's daughter is rescued from
bandits by a handsome partisan with a ravenous appetite.*

*Brazil, 2080: the Doctor and Turlough arrive for the Rio de Janeiro carnival. Wealthy heiress Ileana
de Santos is not all she seems - and what sinister ailment afflicts her invalid son, tended by the
mysterious Dr Hayashi? And who exactly is Rosa, engaged on a secret quest to fulfil the destiny of
her extinct tribe?*

*Time is running out for Rosa, Ileana and the Doctor, as the fearsome shadow of an ancient
werewolf moves ever closer...*

If you wish to order this, please photocopy this form or provide all the details on paper.
Delivery within 28 days of release.
Send to: PO Box 1127, Maidenhead, Berkshire. SL6 3LN.
Big Finish Hotline 01628 828283.

Please send me [ ] copies of *Loups-Garoux*
each @ £13.99 (£15.50 non-UK orders) Prices inclusive of postage and packing. Payment
can be accepted by credit card or by personal cheques, payable to Big Finish Productions
Ltd.
Name...
Address..
....
Postcode...
VISA/Mastercard number..
Expiry date..

Signature...

Other stories featuring the Fifth Doctor still available include:

THE MUTANT PHASE   WINTER FOR THE ADEPT

For more details visit our website at
http://www.doctorwho.co.uk